Lost Lyrics of a Forgotten Song

W.G. Sharp

Acknowledgements

It turns out it's a bit harder than you'd think, this writing malarky, and without the support of some exceptional people, I would never have been able to complete this book.

In truth, I might never even have started. As a fourteen-year-old at Larbert High School, an English teacher called Ron Livingstone suggested to me that I should 'have a go at writing something'. He's the only teacher that I can recall encouraging me to do anything, and it stuck with me. Forty-five years later, I decided to have a go. Thank you, Mr Livingstone.

Writing, as well as being a bit hard, is a solitary and self-indulgent pastime. I am forever indebted to my wife, Fiona, for her unfailing, enthusiastic support. She willingly gave me the freedom and space I needed to squeeze the words out onto the page, and then to rearrange them into the correct order. And, as my first reader, she gave me the confidence that the text was good enough to share with others.

One of the most precious gifts that you can give someone is your time. Dozens of people willingly gave me theirs to read previous drafts of this book. I listened to everything all of you said. Your advice helped me to sharpen the text, and your generous feedback spurred me on to publication. A special thanks also goes to Sue Irving for the amazing cover design.

Finally, none of this would have happened had it not been for one other person, who pushed me on to do the best I could, taught me to stick at things even when they got difficult, and told me never to believe anyone who said I wasn't good enough. You were right… thanks, mum.

Prologue

17th July 2018.

If my name had not been Robert Baker, my book would already be published. I don't mean this book, the one that you are about to read. I mean mine, the one that describes my career as a court reporter, a chronicle of the most striking criminal cases I have covered over the last thirty years. The negotiations with the publisher were all but complete. They said the subject appealed to them. It fits into a popular contemporary genre, where professionals - judges, doctors, barristers, and the like – break ranks to candidly recount the secrets of their worlds. They liked the title - "*Baker's Dozen: The Life and Crimes of a Court Reporter.*" The reader, they said, will understand what is on offer. They even said they liked my style of writing, which was a relief, as I've been using it for thirty years and I'll be buggered if I'm about to learn another one now.

Then, at the final meeting, I am advised they have identified 'an issuette' with my manuscript.

"There are only twelve cases," says the young lady.

"Yes, that's true," I reply, nodding.

"It's called Baker's Dozen. There needs to be thirteen. A baker's dozen. Thirteen. That's what a baker's dozen is."

"Does it matter that much?" Sensing horror, I attempt to retreat. "I mean do you think anyone will actually count the chapters?"

"Yes. I do think it matters actually – rather a lot. How can we expect our audience to accept the accuracy of the detail contained within the work, if it is structured around a fundamentally false premise? It puts into jeopardy the sacred bond of trust between reader and writer." I try to look composed. I clearly fail.

"It needn't be a showstopper," she says. "Why don't you go back through the pudding of your archives and pluck another plum to add in?" Then she clarifies, "but of course, it must be a fresh plum, not rotten fruit, buried within to make up the weight. It has to be interesting, and different from any of the other twelve. Preferably unique. That would be my suggested course of action." She smiles a watery smile. I thank her for her judicious advice and leave for the railway station.

Baker. Of all of the bloody occupations to be named after. If I'd been Robert Butcher I would never have stumbled into this trap. Or Robert Candlestick-Maker, though that would have been a tough ask for any boy at the school I'd attended. On the train back to Liverpool two alternative courses of action suggest themselves to me.

1. Find another publisher, one whose mastery of arithmetic is restricted to the fingers of their two hands, putting this particular issuette beyond their range. Dismissed. I've endured enough pain in finding this one, and we are so close to getting it over the line.

2. Change the title. Again, no. They are bought into it, so I don't fancy the idea of renegotiating at this delicate stage. Anyway, what about me? I like the title.

Later, at home, consoling myself with a generous malt, I sift through my records of the cases I'd covered down the years, looking for anything that might pass for a fresh plum. Nothing. Picking up the tumbler again, I survey my notebooks. The answer has got to be here, somewhere on this coffee table. I'm right… but it's not anywhere within those decades of scribblings. My mobile phone sets off vibrating on the glass surface. It's an old contact from the police, with something that he is sure will interest me. I listen, my breathing shallow, as he outlines a case that has progressed from being rather unusual to frankly astonishing. This has to be it. Number 13. I'd already heard of the DJ fella, even before this incident. I enjoy his show, tried to catch it if I wasn't in court. He played a mix of old stuff I liked and new stuff I didn't know I liked. And he was smart, always trying something different. The trial is due to start soon. I will be there.

* * *

Although he was never to know it, Robert Baker would only ever witness the part of this story that lay on the surface; to understand all of it, we must journey deeper.

Part One: FAME

"I think fame itself is not a rewarding thing. The most you can say is that it gets you a seat in restaurants."

David Bowie

Chapter 1

Three months before that phone call Charlie Munro, the DJ fella in question, walked onto Williamson Square in Liverpool. He was on his way to Studio Two at the top of the Radio City Tower to present the breakfast show. For the final time. Radio City hadn't retired him, or reshuffled him to the coveted Tuesday at midnight slot, or sacked him for saying something indiscreet on air (though there had been a couple of narrow squeaks). No, Charlie had been headhunted. By the British Broadcasting Corporation. In one week he would be swapping central Liverpool for MediaCity in Manchester, breakfast time for drivetime, moderate regional recognition for national fame.

The April sun was rising, sending shafts of light through gaps between buildings. Charlie was early, over an hour too early but, unable to sleep, he had got up and got going. His head was buzzing. He needed some time to think, to address the question that had kept him awake.

How the hell did I get here?

All of the benches surrounding the square were empty, take your pick. Obvious. Charlie selected one facing the tower. His thoughts turned to that nagging question, then to the C.V. he had created five years ago, immediately before joining Radio City. He'd never looked at it since, not even when he'd printed it off that morning and stuffed it into his bag. It had never been his idea to create one in the first place. It was his dad's.

Charlie had casually mentioned to him that his career felt stuck, so his dad had gone online and found a template for him to complete, something to send to prospective employers. When they met a week later it was the first question he asked.

"You haven't finished it? Have you even started?"

"I've tried, dad, but the layout doesn't work for me. The way the sections are split out, work in one bit, personal stuff in another, my life isn't like that. They're tangled together. One makes no sense without the other." His dad looked unconvinced. "And the form is too… what's the word… too linear. It might work if your career is on a precise course, carefully calculated in advance, like a NASA space launch. That's not me. My career path is more like those dodgy rockets you used to set off from a milk bottle in our back garden on bonfire night. Roughly upwards, but with a load of haphazard weaving from side to side thrown in, whether you want it or not." Charlie knew his parents worried about him, and could see his dad was disappointed that his suggestion had not helped.

"Think about it, dad. Where on that form could I record the really important moments? Like say…", he cast around his mind, "… my tenth birthday? Twelfth of March 1993. My milk-bottle-rocket moment. When you lit the blue touchpaper and retired."

Charlie's dad looked at his son, a man now, thirty. He smiled, recalling that day. For his birthday they had given Charlie four CDs and a raspy little music system on which to play them. His first four albums. The boy had been beside himself with excitement.

"Dad, is this a record collection?" Charlie senior thought before he answered. He was not aware of any international standards governing the minimum number of thingies of a specific type you needed to own in order to declare A Collection. Possibly three? Before he was married, he had considered the three ancient, undrivable rusting vehicle shells on the driveway to be his Classic Car Collection. But hold on. What about Ian, his work colleague? Ian was an impassioned collector of postage stamps. Pretty sure if I wandered into the Post Office, bought a book of ten, and claimed I too was now a philatelist, Ian wouldn't have it. Not even if they were the Christmassy ones with individual festive designs. It must depend on the thingy he concluded. And the owner. He looked at the four CDs, then at his son's beaming face.

"Charlie," he replied, "that is a record collection, for sure."

Whether four albums were sufficient to constitute a collection or not soon became a moot point. Charlie had played them all by lunchtime. Three times each by that evening. The next day he played them all again. And again. He did this in enthusiastic innocence, oblivious to the harvest this fervour would soon yield. After a fortnight of unrelenting repetition, his parents began to feel that, fabulous though these songs had once seemed, they were starting to lose some of their sparkle. Being of modest means, they were not in a position to afford the expense involved in having their lad's room professionally soundproofed, so opted instead to buy him an additional four albums from the second-hand stall on Chorley Market, an outlet where grime was a condition of sale rather than a yet to be discovered music genre. The playlist had doubled overnight. The respite period was further extended when they lent him a few of their own albums, ones that they guessed he might like. They guessed right. And, with his newspaper delivery round funding one further album per week, by his eleventh birthday, Charlie had a Record Collection that saw him established as the go-to music guru of the school playground, even amongst the cool kids in the year groups above him.

It's a hefty responsibility to be a go-to guru in any subject at such an early age, but Charlie was already showing himself to be a boy who thrived on such challenge. As the library of music flourished, he turned his attention to his library of books. Comic annuals and football journals were banished to the 'things I have grown out of box' beneath his bed, their places on his shelves now occupied by volumes on the music industry. He acquired publications that focussed on specific music categories, that told the story of a particular era, general histories, reviews, and biographies. As Charlie had always been a reluctant reader, his parents were delighted to see him spend hours poring over them, filling his young, developing mind with facts and background information. There were certain passages (particularly in some of the more candid hard rock musician biographies) that he didn't fully understand, but he was already smart enough to know that he'd best not ask his parents what they meant, lest they started to pay keener attention to the exact contents of his reading list.

His obsession meant that by the time he was in his second year of high school Charlie, uniquely amongst his peers, already knew what he wanted to do in life. This was to his great good fortune, as he and the rest of the year cohort were about to be passed through the muscular, manipulative hands of the school's Careers Advisor, Mr Brown, formerly Corporal Brown of the British Army. Loyal and passionate, Brown used every opportunity afforded by having a child before him to extol the virtues of a life in the Forces, a vision utterly at odds with Charlie's blueprint. The boy was determined to make a career by sharing his passion for music, unaware of how obstacle-strewn such a route would be. First such obstacle, his half-hour interview with Mr Brown. Years of military training and field manoeuvres had made him a wily, worthy adversary.

"Music?" he barked in disbelief. Then, with a combatant's eye for an enemy weakness, Brown struck. "Excellent choice. A sure-fire route to getting into one of the platoon bands. Comradeship aplenty, splendid uniforms, and, who knows, maybe one day the opportunity to Troop The Colour? How many men can say they have done that, young Munro? I shall make enquiries on your behalf." In unenlightened innocence, Charlie countered with a ploy that resulted in him leaving the room without having taken the King's Shilling (or whatever equivalent post-decimalisation coin of the realm the monarch was offering up at the time).

"No," he said, polite but firm, "please don't do that." Stunned, Brown folded. Though the corporal was crestfallen in defeat, he should not have been. That day he had taught Charlie the greatest lesson of his school years. If he could vanquish the formidable Mr Brown, Charlie believed he could take on the world. At home that evening, with a politician's flair for spin and omission, he told his parents that Mr Brown had said a music career was an 'excellent choice'. The blue touch paper was well and truly alight.

How the hell did I get here?

Thirty minutes had drifted off since Charlie had first sat down. Williamson Square was stirring, stretching, readying itself for the day ahead. Drooping night shifters had begun heading home, sluggish early shifters were heading out. A scraggy pigeon strutted around Charlie's feet. Relieved to have made it through the barren winter months, he was pecking at a chunk of yesterday's pastry with gusto, each beak thrust firing his meal across the pavement, so that it had to be pursued with haste to ensure ownership was retained. Charlie pulled the C.V. from his bag and unfolded it. Curriculum Vitae. The course of your life, that's what his dad had told him it meant. He must have recorded something about those crucial school years. He scanned the first page. His efforts were more threadbare than he remembered. He flicked to page two. What had he recorded about 2008, the pivotal year? What had he said about that, the year that his professional and personal lives became fused with an unbreakable bond?

2008. Charlie was eighteen, and as well as a diverse music collection, he had developed an eclectic taste in clothing that made him stand out in any room, clad in outfits that his peers would be mimicking in a year's time. He had negotiated the exam scoring system with sufficient guile to allow him to enrol onto a Media Production course at Liverpool University. It began promisingly. On his first day he met Jonathan Jacobson who Charlie, with a penchant for brevity, instantly dubbed J.J. Within a fortnight the foundations of a lifelong friendship were laid, though within a term it was obvious to both that their career paths were destined to diverge. J.J. was eager to learn about the technical and business aspects of the industry, to build a holistic picture of the profession he had chosen. Charlie, meantime, wanted to get stuck in. He spent an increasing proportion of his time in the makeshift studios of college and hospital radio, or out crisscrossing the city to provide music in pubs or at weddings and parties. It could be dire - occasionally dangerous - work. Some of it he did once and vowed never again, but it was all experience. When he wasn't working, he was listening. He tuned into a broad mix of radio stations from around the world, awesome to awful, analysing, learning all the while. Success, he figured, was not guaranteed just by playing some decent records - of course they mattered - but what turned a great playlist into a standout show was what happened during the gaps in between.

Then in the winter of his first college term, he had the luckiest of breaks.

Charlie was darting along a hospital corridor to host his evening show on their radio channel, on time, but barely. The sensation of having something other than linoleum under his foot, and the crunching sound that it made, were simultaneous. No chance to react. Looking down, he saw an NHS staff name badge, its clear plastic holder shattered into several pieces. With no time to drop it back at Reception, he gathered the fragments and stuffed them into his pocket. Only after he had played the first few songs did he call it back to mind. Charlie used the next break between records to say that if Nurse Jessica Howarth wanted to collect her badge, he had found it. When no one came to claim it, he presumed Nurse Howarth must have finished her shift and gone home. He was tidying around the little studio, preparing to leave, when the door opened.

"Hiya, I'm Jess. Howarth. I think you've got my badge?" Charlie studied her face, looked down at the badge on the desk, then back to the real Nurse Howarth. Petite, with brown wavy hair resting on her shoulders, eyes radiant, she looked nothing like the po-faced mugshot on her hospital I.D. He realised he was now staring, borderline creepy gawking, and stopped.

"Sorry," he said, picking it up. "I found it. With my foot. The case is a bit broken, well, extremely broken." He held out the fragments to Nurse Howarth. She smiled.

"Don't worry," she said, "the pin on the back wasn't closing properly, I've caught the thing hanging off a couple of times already this week, but managed to grab it. I'll get a new one."

Do not dither, Charlie. Ask. Now.

"Do you fancy going out for a drink sometime, let me make up for the damage?" Nurse Haworth's hesitation was a fraction too long. He followed up fast. "When are next you off?"

"Thursday and Friday," she replied. A wispy cloud of caution drifted over her shining eyes. He could not risk leaving it in her hands to arrange.

"Great. Can I be cheeky and ask for your number?"

"Mum, I've met someone who works at the hospital. Charlie. We've been out together twice. I'm meeting him again next Tuesday. I wonder if you want me to bring him round here first?" Works in the hospital… terrible choice of words. Too late. Jess knew what was coming.

"And may I ask," said her mother, "what colour of uniform does this Charlie wear?", smiling and raising her eyebrows. Inside her head, she was willing only one reply. Purple-Consultant-Purple-Consultant. Jess considered her response. She wanted to land it well.

"He doesn't wear a uniform, mum. Actually, he doesn't work at the hospital as such. He's a volunteer." Her response had landed alright. Like a cowpat. Diane's raised eyebrows descended, hot in pursuit of the rest of her falling face.

"Oh," she managed, with some effort.

"On the hospital radio station."

"Oh. I see. What does he do in real life?"

"He's at college." There's hope. A profession, an accountant, like Jess's dad had started out as. "He's studying to become a radio presenter." Jess watched as the final

14

glimmer of joy disappeared from her mum's face, like the glint of a jilted lover's ring down a kerbside drain.

"Oh, only I thought you might have met someone more like…"

"A doctor?" Jess suggested.

"Well, not necessarily," said Diane, "I didn't expect a disc jockey."

"He's training to be a radio presenter mum, not a D.J. Charlie says D.J. makes you sound like someone who spends their time swapping over CDs as if they're flipping burgers."

"Sounds as if he knows a lot about flipping burgers. That might come in handy before too long." Jess's sigh was weary.

"So do you want me to bring him round or not?" Diane composed herself.

"Yes. Of course I do. If you like him, I'm sure he will be… nice."

The next week Jess did bring Charlie over, then twice the week after that. Despite mounting a stirring defence, Diane warmed to him, but thought (more hoped) that he might be part of a phase for her daughter. Surely Jess must know that realistically he wasn't ever going to have a proper livelihood?

This was no phase. Charlie and Jess got together as often as their workloads allowed. In Charlie's case, the workload now featured very little college, and the less time he spent there the more irrelevant it became. When the exam results were revealed at the end of the first year, Jonathan Jacobson had achieved a distinction. Charlie was involved in a dead heat for last place with a bloke they'd rarely seen, the dishevelled guy with the ethnic alpaca hat, that they'd speculated must be pursuing a combined honours qualification: Media Production and Pot Smoking.

Charlie was counselled by his tutor, who outlined two

options. Though he didn't position them in such stark terms, they were: One: resit your exams, or Two: scuttle off home to a job in the local supermarket. Charlie opted for Three. He would continue with his current approach. He had already built a decent network of contacts across Liverpool, and with the unwanted distraction of college behind him, he drove forward with renewed vigour, pushing at doors to see if they would open, oiling those that required persuasion, kicking down others that were more stubborn. He and J.J. became flatmates, and when J.J. graduated and began picking up work in the city, their paths began to cross professionally.

By now, Charlie had managed to secure a slot on a local commercial station. Jess had graduated as a psychiatric nurse and was studying for a music therapy qualification. Charlie, never having heard of it, was fascinated to hear her case studies, moved by her descriptions of how music could change lives in ways he had never imagined. As they talked, so they increased the overlap in the Venn diagram circles of their worlds. Charlie knew that many of his young listeners experienced mental health issues, and Jess told him that talking openly about them could be hugely beneficial. However, at the time the topic was firmly in the dirty laundry bundle; not to be aired in public. When he suggested his latest idea to his boss, Big Steve, he anticipated he might encounter an element of pushback.

"Charlie, I like you mate, you know that, but I have no idea what planet you hail from. Welcome to Earth. I am your leader. None of that is happening. I know you're knocking off that nurse, but we're not having a bunch of mentalists banging on about their problems on air. What's next, eh? Irritable Bowels? The Clap? We've got sponsors and advertisers and listener numbers to think of. No. Forget it." Charlie took this as a tentative yes and put a slot in that day's show anyway.

It went better than he dared hope. Big Steve had never had a response like it on any of the shows he had worked on, and told the Big Boss that it had all been his idea. Charlie gave not one flying flamingo. He pushed on, finessing the way he approached this and other difficult subjects, moving left then right, show to show, gaining audience share. The rocket had left the milk bottle. We have lift-off. Then, after a period, it all seemed to slow, as if an unnoticed, favourable tailwind had turned, stalling his progress. This was when his dad, always uneasy about his son's career, led him into the land of the curriculum vitae. Charlie senior need not have acted. His son may not have known it, but he was being noticed. Within days, oblivious to the existence of his flimsy resume, Radio City made an approach.

How the hell did I get here?

Charlie lifted his gaze to the circular crow's nest on top of the Radio City tower. The light from the rising sun now glinted off its windows, the graceful concrete shaft supporting it was lit up orange. When Radio City offered him the job, Charlie not only persuaded J.J. to come with him, but also to move from the production to the presentation side. It was inspired. Their friendship, their warm closeness, was unmistakable to listeners. In less than a year they were hosting the big one, the breakfast slot. And after six months that rocket, whistling at speed through the sky, finally went bang.

Charlie arrived at work to see his co-host pacing around at the entrance to the building, waiting to greet him.

"We've got Bowie," J.J. said. "Next Friday morning." Charlie looked at him in disbelief.

"David Bowie?"

"No, Frank Bowie, of 'Frank Bowie - Merseyside Skip Hire'. Of course David Bowie." Charlie looked stunned.

"David Bowie? Jeez, how did you swing that?"

"I found out he was going to be up here for a few days," J.J. replied, "so I got my people to contact his people…"

"J.J. stop. You don't have people. You've got two mangy cats. And you can't get them to do anything. Most of the time they won't even use the litter tray properly."

"Fair enough, I got in touch with his people. He's got loads of them it turns out. I was trying to jazz it up for you."

"You don't have to." Charlie stopped speaking and shook his head. "A superstar. Biggest guest Radio City has ever had. Amazing. You're a bloody genius." They made their way to the building, already mapping out the show.

"Are you going to ask him about the different coloured eye thing?" said J.J.

"Nope."

"Why not? Too personal?"

"No. It's complete bollocks. The reality is when he was a teenager he had a fight with his best pal over a girl and got a biff in the left eye for his trouble. It made his pupils two different sizes – permanently - so it looks like they're different colours. It's called anisocoria. Him and his pal made up by the way, stayed friends for life." J.J. called the lift.

"So what are you going to ask him?"

"Obviously we'll talk about his music, plans for the future. But he's had mental health issues, so I might see if he's okay to discuss those."

"Has he? Are you sure?" said J.J.

"Well, back in the seventies he used to keep bottles of his piss in the fridge because he thought witches might steal it and put a curse on him. Now I'm not a qualified psychiatrist but…"

"Seriously?"

"Seriously. I'd never mention it without his say-so, but it would be great for our listeners if they could hear someone of his stature talking about the times when he has struggled."

J.J. shrugged. "God. If you would have told me that Bowie kept his piss in the fridge I'd have assumed you were talking about the skip-hire geezer."

Based on her mum's initial reaction, Jess had kept discussion of Charlie's career to a minimum, focussing instead on the social side of their lives. One passing reference to the upcoming show turned that upside down.

"David Bowie? Theeeee David Bowie is going to be on… Charlie's radio program?" said Diane.

"Yes," said Jess, surprised at the strength of the reaction. "I didn't think you would be interested."

"Of course I am. David Bowie! When I was a girl I had a major crush on him. Aladdin Sane."

"What? A lad insane?"

"Exactly. The first album I bought. Oh, I loved everything about him. The music, his hair, his clothes. He had a huge lightning bolt down one side of his face." Jess masked a smirk.

"I never knew this, mum." Diane's visage, as visibly charged with electricity as Bowie's, turned wistful.

"I was a lot different when I was younger," she said, then clarifying what younger meant, "before I met your dad." She examined the fingernails of her left hand. "He was a good man, your dad, definitely, but quite set in his ways. Don't get me wrong, we got on fine, right up until he died. But thinking back now, somehow over the years, Diane the David Bowie fan... slipped away." Jess had never heard her mum express this before. Regret.

"You should listen to the interview," she suggested.

"I don't even know what station Charlie works at."

"Radio City, it's one of the biggest ones round here."

"Oh. Right. I think I will listen. When is it on? Will you show me how to tune in to Charlie's wavelength?"

The Bowie interview could not have gone better. Before it began, he told them that he was happy to talk about anything. Charlie and J.J. were on form and the star himself was a true gent, self-effacing and charming. And did not take himself too seriously.

"Your number ones," said Charlie.

"I've had a few," David replied.

"I know. And I believe for a while you used to keep them in bottles in the fridge so the witches didn't get them?" David grinned, then went on to talk candidly about those dark days and his recovery. The rest of the show went well too. The other guest, Bowie's unusual support act, was a local baker, who had invented a new flavour of pie (Cheese and Marmalade if you are wondering, never really took off in the way its creator had hoped). Charlie's interview with him was a joy. As well as being astute enough to know he was no rock superstar, Simon the Pie-Man, as Charlie named him, was eloquent and funny and told a string of pastry-based anecdotes that were just about believable. Following his appearance, Simon sat around in Radio City's reception for over two hours to get a quick photo with Bowie as he exited the building. It now hangs proudly behind the counter in his shop. He is, unfortunately, unable to confirm if The Thin White Duke ate the cheese and marmalade delicacy he gave him.

Charlie's audience numbers grew. Now included amongst them was Diane Haworth who, after her inaugural experience, told her daughter Jess that Charlie 'is very good, isn't he', though she expressed surprise that he hadn't ask David about his different coloured eyes. Oh, and vowed she would never eat a cheese and marmalade pie. Charlie got better and better, and so did the show, aided by the unsolicited, but invaluable, advice he was receiving from the woman who was now his mother-in-law. He and J.J. were coming to the attention of those involved in national radio. The BBC was the first to make an approach, and when the news broke others followed, with more lucrative offers. These he rejected. Charlie had made a commitment and intended to stick to it.

"What are you doing sitting here?" Charlie squirmed around on the bench to look behind him. It was J.J. He spotted the paper in Charlie's hand. "What's that?" he asked. Charlie passed it to him. J.J. scanned the sheets. He burst out laughing. "Is that it? Your C.V.? Four words. Name - *Charlie Munro*. Current Job Title - *Radio Presenter*. Thank god you didn't have to rely on this for work. C'mon, we've got a show to do." Charlie rose and he and his friend walked across the square to the tower.

Three hours later, Charlie's Radio City career spanning four and a half years now had four and a half minutes left to run. He felt a thudding heartbeat in his stomach. Nerves? At leaving, or at what was to come? He flicked his microphone on for the final time. Big moment. Keeping his voice as solid as he could manage, he thanked all of his listeners and colleagues who had made his spell at this desk fly by. He invited his co-host to say a few words, then cued up the last song. As the opening bars of The Beatles 'Hello, Goodbye' began and the microphones shut off once more, he slumped back in his chair. On the other side of the desk, Sally, the producer, smiled at him and gave him a thumbs up.

"Went well that," said J.J.

"Yep, thought it was good," Charlie replied. "The timing went a bit off at the end of the quiz when I asked Maureen from the Wirral if she wanted to say Hi to any family and friends, and she took Friends in the social media sense."

"Yeah. Read out the Liverpool phone book then had the nerve to finish off with 'and anyone else that knows me'." Charlie put his laptop and notebook into his leather bag and walked towards the door. "Don't forget, seven tonight at Central Station" said J.J. Charlie gave a backward wave and left the studio. Once in the car he took his notes for the show out of the satchel, replaced them with the ones that he needed for his meeting with the BBC, and set off towards Manchester.

*   *   *

"Can't believe we're having to queue," said Jess, "with you guys being so famous."

"No bookings here," said Charlie, "even David Bowie would have to wait for a table."

When the four were finally shown to their seats in the small Asian street food restaurant, they squeezed into their places, trying not to disturb those already there. Charlie surveyed his fellow diners. A woman at a nearby table caught his eye and gave a smile of recognition. J.J.'s wife, Alice, spotted it.

"We've only been in town an hour, and four strangers have come up to you and wished you luck," said Alice. "And I've seen a good few others staring like that lady just did. I know we've joked about it, but this is going to go off the scale. There's a big difference between regional and national radio. I was looking at my dad's Radio Times. They put little pictures of the presenters in there."

Charlie grinned. "I can't see big gangs of screaming Radio Times readers hanging about outside your house hoping for a glimpse of J.J. in his undercrackers through a gap in the curtains."

"I suppose not," said Alice "I think I'm just worried because of my dad."

"I didn't know your dad was famous," said Charlie.

"Well, he's not really. It's because he looks like that Doctor Harold Shipman, you know, the one that murdered loads of his elderly patients. Teenagers used to shout some terrible things at him in the street. He had to change to a different style of glasses." The other three burst out laughing.

"It's not funny," she said. "He shaved his beard off in the end."

"Sorry, Alice, it must've been terrible," said Charlie. "Hey, it could make a good phone-in for the show." J.J. picked it up.

"Are you often mistaken for someone famous?" he said. The two were on it. Alice made J.J. swap seats to make it easier to talk to Jess.

"Go on then," she said, settling down, "the new house. J.J said you used to live there before?"

"Yes, when I was younger. It's a cottage at the far end of Stanford. After I'd left for college, my parents decided to sell it and moved into a bungalow in the next village. By chance, a few months ago, I spotted a For Sale sign at the front of the old house and persuaded Charlie to go and have a look. I'd talked about it a lot, but he'd never been inside."

"Must've been strange going back."

"A bit, but other than a new kitchen and modernised bathrooms, it was almost the same as I remembered. Honestly, I only went to look for old time's sake, and before you know it we'd put an offer in that day, last month we moved in."

"Buying your childhood home… does it feel like a new house?"

"I lived there from when I was born until I was seventeen, so it's not new to me. And it has 1784 written in black letters above the front door, so no way could you say it's new." Alice quizzed Jess room by room, building up a picture in her head of their new home.

"I thought you said it was a cottage? It sounds massive."

"It's a big step up for us," Jess replied. "That's why my parents sold, it became too much when dad started to become ill. You and J.J. need to come for a look round."

"Oh, we'd love to. And he says you're busy at work too?"

"Manic. You know how a bit ago I qualified as a music therapist?"

"Yes, but I don't really get what it is. I mean, who are your patients?"

" All sorts. Tomorrow I'm going in to see a guy who lost movement in one arm after a motorbike accident. Playing drums is helping to bring it back. Then I'm seeing a little autistic girl, she struggles to communicate with words but can through music. It also works for patients with all sorts of mental health issues."

"Really? My brother has had depression for years, all the doctor seems to do is up the pills."

"It could help him. I'm not saying that he won't still need meds, but music can lift your mood, it releases all those feel-good chemicals."

"I'll mention it to him, it sounds brilliant." Jess nodded.

"The reason I've been so busy is that I'm going solo, setting up on my own." Alice looked non-plussed. "I found it hard to get it established in the NHS, there's so little money around," Jess explained. "I kept coming home to Charlie and complaining about it. You know what he's like, nothing is impossible, so one day he said to me why don't you break away and set up a service yourself? At first, I thought he had lost it, but he started to come up with all these ideas for how it could work, and every time I pointed out a problem he came up with a way around it. I've got all of the funding there, set up my own charity to manage it and the builders have almost finished refurbishing the property we'll use. It's going to be fantastic. It's so powerful, it can change people's lives."

"That's brilliant. All I change is people's tax codes," said Alice, finishing the last little bit of wine in her glass. "We could do with another bottle," she said, looking around for a waiter. "I think what you're doing is bloody amazing. Honestly." Jess looked down.

"Thanks, but it wasn't just me. I've been lucky to be put into contact with some brilliant people along the way. And," she said, lowering her voice, "don't tell him for God's sake, but no way would any of this have happened without Charlie. Honestly, he just won't take no for an answer, and won't be intimidated by rules and people saying that's how it's always been done."

Once the bill was settled they headed off to catch a couple more drinks before home, Charlie nipping to the Gents on the way out. When he emerged through the door onto the darkened street, he was blinded by bright white lights. Bang. Bang. Bang. His eyes adjusted to see Jess, Alice, and J.J., phones in hand, adopting paparazzi poses. He pulled his arms over his face and let them fire off another round. Then, glancing behind him and seeing the iconic Radio City Tower, he raised his left hand over his shoulder to point at it and smiled as Jess took the final shot.

*　　*　　*

When he awoke the next morning Charlie could hear that Jess was already up and busy. He joined her in the kitchen.

"It feels odd having a free week, no show tomorrow," he said, as they moved around the kitchen, preparing a late breakfast.

"Free week? Can I remind you of all the things you've put off doing because they would be better done in this free week?" Charlie smiled.

"I know, I'll start tomorrow, with a massive garage clear-out."

"What are your plans for today?"

"I've promised the BBC that I'll send over an outline of the first show, then do the hospital slot." For others in the industry, hospital radio had been a stepping stone to further their career, but Charlie still volunteered there. It was a place where he had fallen in love with his trade, the place where he had fallen in love with his wife. The guys at the BBC had no issue with him continuing, but had queried why he wanted to. Charlie told them it was special, and it kept him grounded.

"I should have a couple of hours free in the afternoon. I'll maybe go out on the bike."

Jess puffed out her chest and, in a pretty passible impression of Charlie's mum's voice said "Well, if you do Charles, you must remember your puncture repair kit. Have I ever told you about the time he went cycling without it, Jess? He had to walk miles home in the pouring rain. He was bedraggled."

"Aye, very funny," said Charlie, wearily. "I take it everywhere with me now. Mum." Whenever they drove down to Norfolk to visit his parents, Jess and Charlie played Anecdote Sweepstake, each predicting which of his parents' standard tales would be first to be told that weekend. Anecdote Sweepstake has one rule. It is forbidden to try to steer the conversation towards them telling the one you have nominated.

Once Jess had set off for work Charlie settled down in the smallest spare bedroom, the one he had requisitioned as his office. The BBC did not want him to change the format of the show, so it was just a matter of pulling together some ideas for each section. He wrote up a broad outline, and emailed it across. Only when he'd done that did he force himself to do a few other bits of paperwork that Jess had been pushing him to complete, before heading out on his bike.

Much of the area around where they lived was reclaimed land, as flat as it was fertile. It was a great place to cycle. Charlie set off south following his favourite circuit, thirty miles in length, passing along the quiet lanes that weaved among fields of vegetables, huge cauliflowers, leeks, and lettuces, purple and bright green. After a winter off the road, he could feel the power returning to his legs. Spring. A new start. It was exhilarating.

Sunday at Southport General is almost as busy as a weekday. The place never stops, a myriad of activities underway simultaneously. At two-thirty, Jess said goodbye to the little autistic girl and began to put away the equipment they had used. At the same moment across in the main building a teenager was being attached to a dialysis machine, a boil on an old man's leg was being lanced and bandaged, a baby girl was being born, a young man was being wheeled out of an ambulance into Bay Six in A&E, a stroke victim was being discharged to his relieved family, and a woman who had fallen from a horse weeks ago was taking her first shaky steps in rehab.

In Bay Six, the A&E team crowded around the bed. On the consultant's cue, the paramedic began the handover.

"Unknown male in his thirties, he was found at the roadside, suspect Triple A. His blood pressure is currently…." For one of the nurses, his words became a background hum. She looked on in disbelief. When the handover was complete and treatment was about to commence she spoke.

"His name is Charlie Munro. He does the hospital radio sometimes. I know his wife, she works here. I've seen her here today. Please can I try to contact her?" Mr Davenport, the consultant in charge, nodded and she sprinted through the doors. She took out her mobile phone and called Jess, praying she wasn't with a patient. Thank God she answered immediately.

Before that day, if you would have asked Charlie what a Triple-A was, he'd have told you it was one of the little thin batteries in the remote control for the TV. Nurse Jessica Munro would have given a different answer. Triple-A is medical shorthand for an Abdominal Aortic Aneurysm. This is the fancy medical name for a bulge that forms in your aorta, which is the fancy medical name for the massive, critical blood vessel that runs from the heart down through the chest and abdomen. There are a couple of issues with the non-battery sort of Triple-A. Firstly, you can be carrying it about inside of you for years and not have a clue that it's there. Secondly - and here's the worrying bit – they're prone to rupturing at the most inconvenient of moments, though it's hard to envisage when would be a marvellous time to have umpteen pints of your blood leave the well-worn tracks of your circulatory system to go sloshing uncontrollably around your insides.

That afternoon Charlie had travelled barely two miles from home when he knew something was not right. It started with that thumping, pulsing feeling in his stomach he'd had in the studio the day before, the one he had put down to last show nerves. A twinge in his belly turned rapidly into excruciating pain, he felt dizzy and unsteady on the bike. Then nothing. Even if he had remained conscious, it is unlikely that he could have deployed his Halford's Bicycle Puncture Repair Kit to successfully treat this particular burst. And he was now in the middle of nowhere on a seldom-used, single-track country lane.

Then Lady Luck stepped in. As Charlie's bike went from underneath him onto the road, the clatter and scrape of metal on tarmac caused the sole person within miles to turn towards the sound. The dog-walker started towards the cyclist, slowly at first, with more purpose as it became pretty obvious the guy wasn't getting up. His overweight Saint Bernard lolloped along behind, enjoying the game, trying to keep up with his master. As he looked down at the man lying prostrate on the road, he dropped his shit or, to be more accurate, he dropped the lukewarm, weighty bag of Samson's shit that he had been carting around with him for the last half hour.

Samson's owner pulled out his phone. Again Lady Luck was by Charlie's side. One tiny little bar of a signal. He called 999, doing his best to describe where he was, whilst following the advice that the call handler gave him to try to stabilise Charlie. For a third time, Lady Luck turned to face Charlie and smiled upon him. An ambulance, heading to a patient who phoned on a daily basis requesting assistance with various spurious ailments, was no more than a mile from where he lay. It was immediately diverted to his aid. Charlie was blue-lighted to hospital, sirens scattering nervous Sunday drivers.

Mr Davenport delivered the list of actions with clarity and speed. If he was to have any hope, Charlie needed to be operated on, and quickly. The theatre was prepped, the team assembled and Charlie was wheeled there at pace. Theatre Two, like Studio Two, was crammed full of equipment, only these machines don't make music, they make your lungs go and your heart go when you're not able to do it yourself. Under Mr Davenport, Charlie was in the sure hands of one of the most talented cardiovascular specialists in the country. He could not have a better chance of recovery.

Sadly, this was the point at which Lady Luck decided she had some more important matter to deal with, and exited the building. A quarter of an hour into the operation, the machines started going crazy as they struggled to compensate for Charlie's failing organs, their loud and regular bleeping not sufficient to drown out Mr Davenport's expletives. As the blood first wept, spurted, then fountained all around them, experts in each of the medical specialisms worked frantically to stabilize the patient.

Waiting in the corridor, as close as she could get to the theatre, Jess saw Mr Davenport emerge, peeling off his blue latex gloves. She stood up and began to pace toward him. In a cruel trick, time had stood still for Jess, or she would have realised that the twenty minutes that Charlie had been in theatre was nowhere near long enough for the procedure to have been completed successfully. Mr Davenport removed his mask and watched the young woman advancing toward him. She did not need to ask. The look of utter dejection on his face broke the worst news she would ever receive, without a word being spoken.

Two minutes earlier, at 15.18, Charlie Munro had been pronounced dead.

Chapter 2

Jess lowered her gaze once more to the island counter in her kitchen, specifically to the tiny moleskin notebook that she had found in Charlie's office. How could such an insignificant item appear so daunting? She jerked it towards her, flicked the cover over, and looked at the first page. It returned a defiant stare, a blank, yawning acre of space no bigger than a postcard, awaiting unspeakable words. Nibbling on her upper lip, she picked up her pen.

Dear Journal,

I've decided that's what I'm going to call you. Journal — not Grief Journal. It's more friendly, less intimidating. Who knows, maybe I will still keep talking to you if I ever stop grieving.

You are not my idea - Sam at work suggested it. She says she has a friend that was helped by keeping one. I have no plan as to what I am going to write in you, whatever comes into my head I suppose. I doubt I will ever share these words with anyone else, it will remain between you and me. I promise one thing — this will be no bragging social media 'look how great my life is' deal - the marks I make on your pages will be a true account of how I feel.

I'm not ready to start doing this, but I will force myself. I'd try anything to feel better than how I feel today. So there you go, these few sentences might not be much, but I've started.

Without rereading her words, she closed the book and shoved it back across the counter.

Two days had dissolved away since she had risen from the chair outside the operating theatre, the moment when she had taken her first unwilling steps on a hellish journey to an unknown destination. Jess had been distraught when she had lost her dad ten years previously but, given his declining health, there had been an inevitability about it. Then she had been heartbroken when Grandad Joe had died in 2015. This was on a different plane. She was crushed.

Two days previously, on Sunday evening, after it had all happened, she'd sat in her living room. She was alone, not sure how long she had been there, drinking a coffee that she could not remember making. She looked along the couch. It now seemed excessively, pointlessly long. She knew that she had to tell other people what had happened, but also knew that to do so would make it real. What bloody right did she think she had to go upsetting other people by telling them something that she refused to tell herself? That's an excuse, Jess. She picked up her phone.

She began with her mum, doing her unconvincing best to stop her from worrying, telling her that she was fine. Diane knew she wasn't. That call was a run-through for the toughest one, Charlie's parents. No crying, no fuss, their distress was marked by endless, wordless chasms. Though she had done nothing wrong, when she finished the call Jess felt as if she had slain their son and, in doing so, had slaughtered their entire futures. Lastly, she rang J.J., who listened in disbelief. When she completed this third call, the flimsy silver lining that she had was an agreement from both sets of parents that they would break the news to their respective sides of the family, and from J.J that he would tell everyone else he could think of who knew Charlie.

She drifted into two days of daze, lost, trying to make sense of it. But how? In her soul-searching, she recalled when, as a student nurse, she had been taught the theory of the Seven Stages of Grief. She could still remember them now.

Shock and Denial. Pain and Guilt. Anger and Bargaining. Depression. Upward Turn. Reconstruction and Work Through. Acceptance and Hope.

Fine words, a fine theory. Jess recalled the lecturer emphasising that they do not necessarily all occur, or have to follow on, one after another. At the time she'd thought it was the most wicked To-Do List anyone had ever created. Now she knew different. Real life, real death, was markedly more cruel. Several of the named stages had been severely underplayed, and others were entirely missing. In those two days alone Jess's itinerary read: Despair. Fury. Crash. Ache. Despair. Rage. Collapse. Hysteria. Utter Despair. Delusion. Ache. Rage. Amnesia. Fury. Stupor. Anguish. Fury. Crash. Delusion. Collapse.

A journalist from the Liverpool Echo had somehow obtained her number and made contact. He wanted to write an article about Charlie. Would she mind talking briefly to him? It was his good fortune that he chanced to ring during a Collapse phase rather than Rage or Fury. In helpless resignation, she agreed. They spoke for half an hour or so and, as a result, he penned a touching piece about Charlie - who he was, where he was going in life, and how The Great Conductor in The Sky had laid down the baton when Charlie was only just finishing the first verse of his life's song. On publication, the paper's web page was immediately filled with condolences, memories, and thoughts. She revisited it several times that day to read them, watching their number grow. Charlie was more popular than even she realised.

Maybe they soothed her, maybe it was exhaustion, but Jess slept better that night. She awoke with new energy and threw herself into the practical things that she recognised needed to be done. Though she did not admit it out loud, or even internally, she harboured a faint hope that if she completed that list of tasks then everything would be all right again, back to how it was. Her mum and Charlie's parents offered to come over to help her, but Jess politely declined. To witness their pain first-hand would only add to her anguish. All similar offers were rejected, until J.J managed to breach her stone-wall defence. On hearing what had happened, Radio City asked him if he would like to come back to work for them as a producer. With Charlie gone, he knew the BBC job was never going to develop as intended, so he agreed immediately. It would offer a safe place where he could try to get his head around what comes next. Fortuitously, it also gave him an excuse to call round to visit Jess. Cards and letters for Charlie were pouring into the station, and J.J. happily agreed to deliver them.

J.J. had never visited Charlie's new home. Turning onto the gravel driveway, he took in the cream-coloured building before him. This was not what he had imagined. It was a good-looking house, but set over two floors and stretching a long way back into the large garden, it pushed the definition of cottage to its limits. He rapped the iron knocker, and stepped back when he heard footsteps from within.

"Hi Jess," he said, "Postman." He held out a large carrier bag, trying to sound upbeat, but dismayed at how drawn and tired she looked.

"God, there's loads," she replied. "Come on in."

"How are you doing?" he asked, as Jess made them both a mug of coffee.

"Right now, not bad," she replied, "Ask me again in ten

minutes and I could say bloody awful. My mood is all over the place. Sometimes, when I get on with things, I feel okay. At other times, I'm on the floor. And the strangest thing, my brain won't always work properly, it's as if I'm in some kind of trance. You won't believe what I did earlier. I went to the supermarket, filled my basket, and carried it out of the shop without paying."

"Oh no."

"A security guy came up to me as I passed through the doors… 'Excuse me, madam, are you intending to purchase these goods?' I was mortified, so humiliating."

"Did you have to go back in and pay?" Jess shook her head.

"Do you know what I did? I laid the basket down on the floor, burst into tears, ran back to my car, and drove straight home. The guy must have thought I had flipped."

"Oh Jess, that's awful."

"I know. I felt stupid. Had to pick up milk from the corner shop so I could have a brew. I can't seem to focus, keep forgetting things." J.J. squeezed her hand.

"No wonder. We're all in shock. There must be something I can do, Jess. Anything. Do some shopping for you. I'll even pay for it." Jess hit him on the arm.

"Actually, there is something. I've collected Charlie's death certificate, and tomorrow I want to start to plan his funeral. You could come round and help me, if you've got time. I'd like to have a rough outline before I speak to his folks about it."

"Of course, I'd love to."

After he had left, Jess emptied the cards and letters into a mound on the living room floor. Too much. She turned and left the room. In the kitchen, she drank another cheerless coffee, then shook herself, and returned to the pile. She slumped onto the floor beside it, exhaled, and started. The fourth one, she opened made her smile. Then cry.

"Dear Mrs Munro, I was lucky enough to be on your husband's show three times. He was so kind and enthusiastic. I even changed the name of my shop because of the nickname he gave me. Without him playing on the radio, mornings in that shop will never be quite so cheerful. Thank you for lending him to the people of Merseyside for the last few years. We will all miss him. Sincere condolences, Simon The Pie-Man."

Many cards were from people who lived on their own and regarded Charlie as a friend. A good number came from listeners who had been helped by a specific item that they'd heard. With each envelope opened her pride rose. Jess set herself a goal to read them all that day, and did it. It was as well. The following morning when she answered the door, J.J. presented her with another similar-sized bag.

"More?" J.J. nodded. "Thanks. It took me till after tea-time to open the ones from yesterday, but it was worth it. They were so kind. Lots of them made me cry, though to be honest, I cried this morning when I emptied the pockets in a pair of Charlie's jeans and found the receipt from our meal last week. I mean, a receipt?" When she had made them both a drink, Jess laid a brown envelope on the kitchen counter.

"Right, let's find out what he wanted," she said.

"What's this?"

"Remember we went to his auntie's funeral last year? Driving home, he said to me that though it was sad, it had been a good day. I told him that was because she had planned it all out before she died. Thought about what she wanted to be included, and wrote it all down, like the planning he did for his radio show. I suggested he should do it for his - told him I'd

37

do it too. And so we did." Jess slit the sealed envelope open with a kitchen knife.

"He never mentioned it," said J.J. "I'm surprised you got him to do it."

"You know Charlie. I had to print off a form and hand it to him. Along with a pen. And a glass of wine. We did it that Sunday afternoon, with the fire on and a few more glasses. He did look like he was filling it in but he wouldn't show me."

"Don't want to trash your hopes, Jess, before he died I saw his effort at a C.V. Jeez."

"Oh, I know. It wouldn't surprise me if he's done a load of dubious doodles, shoved it in here, and sealed it. He'd know that if I'm opening the envelope it'll be too late for me to kill him because something - or someone - else must've beaten me to it." Jess pulled out the piece of paper and unfolded it. "I take it back," she said, "he's done it. Though there's not much." As she laid the form down on the table, J.J. could see a series of typed questions, the large space beneath each containing a tiny amount of his friend's familiar scratchy writing in blue ballpoint. He moved closer to Jess so that they could both read it.

"He was writing for over three hours," she said, "what was he doing?" J.J. studied the form a little more closely.

"In his defence, Jess, his school teachers would be proud of him - he's attempted to answer every question. Don't leave any blanks, you never know where you might pick up an extra mark or two. Let's see."

1. Do you want to be buried or cremated?
Cremation? With all that global warming? Buried it is. In one of those biodegradable wicker coffins, that looks like a big laundry basket.

2. Do you have any wishes about how your body should be prepared? E.g. any special clothes you would like to wear?

Jess to choose my clothes. (If Jess has tragically died at the same time as me, please pass this responsibility to anyone except my mother).

3. If you want to be buried, who would you like to carry your coffin?

Six individuals of similar height – no desire to make a grand entrance to my own memorial service looking like a badly hung shelf.

4. Where would you like to have your funeral?

Our local church, St Jude's. He's the Patron Saint of Hopeless Causes. By this point, I might be too far gone, even for Jude's holy powers, but it's worth a shot.

5. Who should be invited?

All welcome. Oh, except for Mad Mac, maths teacher and educational dinosaur, who told me as a 12 year old boy that I was "destined to be one of life's rejects." Tosser.

6. What music would you like played?

I've already selected enough records for several lifetimes. Jess to choose from the attached shortlist.

7. Who would you like to do readings or make speeches?

I know you'd hate to do this Jess (so I'm tempted to insist). Dad and J.J.? J.J. can get some presenting tips from dad.

8. What would you like your family and friends to wear?
Nothing. Let me clarify, by that I mean nothing in particular. But definitely something. (That thought made me queasy).

9. Would you want people to send flowers or donate to a charity of your choice?
Donations, to my amazing wife's amazing new charity, The Stables Institute.

10. Would you like family and friends to have a wake, gathering, or party afterward? If so, where?
As if I could stop them. The Bell. The best pint for miles.

"There's nothing we can't manage there," said J.J. "No twenty-one gun salute. No flypast by The Red Arrows." Jess shook the manilla envelope and two further items fell onto the counter, a smaller sealed envelope and some folded sheets of paper. The little envelope was marked 'For Jess – to be opened when you feel ready'. On the sheets, in capital letters, it said 'MUSIC'. She placed the little envelope back inside the large one, then passed the sheets to J.J.

"Will you take a first look at the music?" she asked. "I'd already thought about his clothes. I'd like to remember him looking just like he did when I last saw him. Not absolutely the last time – when I left for work on Sunday he was wearing an old T-shirt and a pair of boxers. I mean when the four of us were out in Liverpool. I'm going to have him dressed exactly like he was that night."

"I like that, it's a nice touch."

"Also, I want to put some things in there with him, that he might, well you know…"

"Need?" J.J. suggested. Jess smiled.

"I know, it's daft, he's going into St. Jude's, not the Valley Of The Kings. I've got a metal biscuit box, the one we brought back from the trip to Bruges when he proposed to me. I've been putting little things in there as I come across them. I know they're going to be no good to him, but it's a gesture."

"It's a great idea."

"And he's right about the speech thing, you know. I dread public speaking at the best of times. There's no way I stand up and talk at his funeral."

"If you want to pull together a few words, maybe I could read it for you?"

"Would you? That would be such a relief if you did." That momentary flash of light in her eyes, it was as close as he had seen to the woman he remembered.

"I'm not just saying this, Jess. It'd be an honour to do it," said J.J., who had now unfolded the paper, not one, but five sheets, covered in lists of songs and artists. He fanned them out before her. "I think may have found what he spent his time doing on your planning day."

"Oh my God. There must be well over a hundred songs there," said Jess. She looked more closely. "Oh, we both liked that one," she said, pointing to the first sheet.

"Yes. Might need to take some care here," he cautioned. "I've already spotted 'Going Underground' by The Jam."

Dear Journal,

J.J. came round again today. I am glad he did. I willed myself to be cheerful and 'normal' while he was here, but as soon as he'd left I caved in. I did nothing for the remainder of the day, except lie on the couch, crying. I hate myself for wasting time like this, I've got a lot of things I must sort out.

I can't be bothered to analyse what I feel like any more. I'm done with this for today. Sorry.

*   *   *

As a village Stanford is small, but enough people live there - or more precisely die there - to sustain two funeral companies. Jess had no idea which to pick but, based on a recommendation from her mum, she rang A & L Knight. L(ee) answered and said that A(lex) would call round to Jess's house tomorrow morning. When she opened the door evidently Jess's face betrayed her surprise.

"Hi, I'm Alex." With straight blonde hair and a reassuring smile, the lady looked to be in her late twenties. "Don't worry," she said, "I'm used to being a shock. It's short for Alexandra." Jess invited her in.

"If you don't mind me saying, you don't look like a funeral director. You don't look…."

"Miserable enough?" Jess smiled. "We're a family business, set up by my dad. Over the last few years he's taken a back seat, my brother Lee and I more or less run it now."

"Let me get you a drink," said Jess. Once Alex had a mug of tea, Jess passed her Charlie's wish list. Alex scanned the form, nodding at each section, and smiling at some of the entries.

"I wish more people did this," she said, "your husband must have been very organised."

"I'm not so sure about that," Jess replied. "When hounded, perhaps."

"It will make a lovely service," she said, laying the sheets down on the counter. As she looked up she could not miss Jess biting her bottom lip in an effort to keep it steady it. Alex saw heartache every day and had learned to cope with it. Now and then though, a customer's story would come along that beat her. She trapped her own tears before they flowed. "Jess. I'm a funeral director. I can't promise to make all your sadness go away," she said, "but I promise we can support you through this part. We will make the service happen in the way that Charlie wanted."

"Thank you so much."

"Come on, let's make a list of all of the things we each need to do between now and then."

*   *   *

Two days later Jess went to the dry cleaners to collect the jacket that Charlie had been wearing on the night out in Liverpool. Although it was going to be encased in a laundry-basket wicker-coffin, then buried for all time under six feet of Stanford's rich black soil, she felt better knowing that she had tried to make Charlie look his best. Next, she headed to Knight's Funeral Directors, situated just off the village square, or the village triangle as Charlie called it, since it was one side shy of the full quota required to pass muster as quadrilateral. Jess had walked past Knight's office on countless occasions, but had never paid it too much heed; Knight's, after all, was not the sort of emporium that attracted window shoppers or impulse purchases. Jess entered the small, scrupulously tidy office, its walls painted bright white. Two desks, a filing cabinet, and half a dozen grey chairs were strategically placed to make practical use of the limited space, yet still offer grieving customers a degree of privacy. A few healthy houseplants and a couple of innocuous watercolours completed the restrained decoration.

Sitting at her desk, Alex looked up and smiled at Jess. At the only other desk, a man in a smart suit, whom Jess assumed must be Alex's brother, was seated. He spoke in a low voice to a tall man wearing blue workman's dungarees, standing to his side.

"Hi," said Alex as Jess approached her. "Please take a seat. How are you? Coping?"

"Just about," said Jess. "It's been hard." Alex listened with care as Jess described the turmoil she had gone through since Charlie's death. "Anyway," she concluded, "I think I've managed to do all of the things that you asked." She passed across a bag containing Charlie's shirt and jeans, washed and ironed. Next, she produced her biscuit box. The contents broke the quiet, rattling against the sides as she laid it on the desk.

"These are the things that I was hoping could go into the coffin too."

"No problem," said Alex "Lots of people do this. Can I take a little look? We need to make sure there's nothing dangerous in there."

"A bit like boarding a plane," said Jess. Alex opened the box and saw a dozen or so small items.

"Goodness me," she said, "you've been busy."

"I kept adding things in as I came across them." Jess watched on as she sifted through them.

"That's a ticket stub," she said, pointing at a tatty square of cardboard. "First concert he ever went to." Alex picked up a small silver pendant with a jagged black etch line across its face.

"That's unusual," said Alex "what is it?"

"It's a little soundwave from a song we had at our wedding, etched onto a pendant. We had matching ones made."

"It's lovely. Would you like him to be wearing it?"

"Yes please. And the watch. It used to belong to my grandad. And his wedding ring too." Alex nodded. She picked up a small oblong tin box.

"And this?"

"It's a puncture repair kit for a bike, a bit of a family joke," said Jess. She related an abridged version for Alex. "I don't think it'll be much use on this journey, but it was the one thing his mum asked to be included."

"These are all fine," Alex said, "and they're by no means the strangest things that I've been asked to place in a casket."

"Oh, one more thing. You asked me about a photo for the Order of Service. I got a great photo of him just last week in Liverpool, in front of the Radio City Tower. I want him to be remembered the way he looked that night so can we use that? It's on this memory stick," she said, laying it on the desk with all of the other things.

"Great. To be honest, Lee is more of a technical whizz than me." Lee came across to join them.

"Hi, Mrs Munro," he said, "I spoke to you on the phone the other day. So sorry for your loss."

"Thank you."

"This is Tom, by the way," he added. The thin, pasty man in the blue overalls crossed the room. "Tom will be digging and infilling the grave. He will make sure it's all done correctly." Jess looked at them. Office-based Lee was a golden brown but Tom, outside all day in a graveyard, had the pallor of underdone shortbread. "Now," said Lee, "about this photo?"

"Yes," said Jess. "Some of the people attending might not have seen Charlie for months, maybe years. I'd like them to see him as he was. Would be possible to blow it up, you know to, say, poster size, and make a couple of copies to put outside the church?" Lee surveyed the items on the desk and picked out the little memory stick.

"I'll have a look at it," he said. "If the resolution is good enough we'll get it enlarged for you." Jess thanked them and left. Next, she was going to the supermarket, determined to walk in with her head held high, and to leave having paid for her goods.

*   *   *

Dear Journal,

Last night I phoned Charlie's parents again — I was too exhausted afterwards to write about it. His dad still has no idea what to say, his mum talks and talks. I think it helps her, but it's hard to hear. It reminds me of what we have all lost.

Today when I woke up I was wearing an old checked shirt belonging to Charlie. Can't remember putting it on. It was massive and baggy on me. I looked ridiculous but it felt comfortable. It's a worrying sign. I've asked J.J. to come over and help sort through all of the clothes and to go through the stuff in his office. It will be tough, but if I don't I'm scared the house will end up like a shrine to Charlie, and I will never move on.

J.J. followed Jess into the small office and looked right then left, across the various shelves, the desktop, and the floor. Every available flat surface was stacked high with paper.

"If you look under the desk you'll see loads of folders that are marked 'Work'," said Jess, directing him to an area of the stash he hadn't yet spotted. "There are some more on the third shelf of the bookcase. Can you go through them, check if there's anything worth keeping? I wouldn't have a clue what I'm looking for. Anything that's never going to be useful goes into one of the black bags in the hall for shredding. I'll start on these bundles on the bottom shelf, they look more like personal papers."

"I'm on it," J.J replied, taking the top folder. As he did so he spotted a radio on the desk. "Fancy a bit of music?" he asked, stretching to turn it on. Jess shook her head, mute.

"I'm scared to." J.J. withdrew his arm. "I'm afraid they might play some song that hits home and sets me off." He nodded an okay. The pair settled onto the floor and into the task. J.J. tried to keep the conversation going with encouraging remarks about the headway they were making, progress he measured by how quickly they were filling bin bags. He felt good to be doing something positive. "These blue folders are crammed full of the notes for each show," he said. "it looks like he's kept every single one. It's like reliving them, I can remember so much. A bit sad really."

"Are you okay doing this?" Jess asked.

"Yeah, fine. Have to say they're pretty well organised, in date order. To be honest, they're pretty well worthless now. I might keep the odd one or two if that's okay?"

"Yes, take whatever you want." Jess dropped another bundle down on the floor beside her. "I wish I could say this lot was well organised. I have no idea what kind of filing system he thought he was operating. He's kept every piece of paper that's passed through his hands in twenty years - old bank statements, fuel receipts, utility bills, dental appointment cards, you name it." She had six bundles of paper on the floor, each one a category of document that was worth keeping, and for the remainder of the morning she grew each pile with items from the shelves. J.J. didn't like to ask, but then found he didn't need to. His stomach emitted a thunderous rumble.

"Sorry," said Jess, "let's have some lunch." They prepared a couple of sandwiches, eating them in the kitchen.

"Oh, I almost forgot, wait till you hear this," she said. She held up a card with a pastel print of a lily on the front. "This came in the bag you brought round the other day. Here goes. 'Sorry to hear of your sad loss. My thoughts are with you at this difficult time. I used to go to school with Charlie. He was a great character who will be sadly missed. Regards, Ronald Snow'.

"Nice," said J.J., through a mouthful of ham and cheese.

"Ah yes, but then Ronald has added a P.S." J.J. stopped eating. "'P.S. Did he ever mention a CD called Power Ballads 2? I know it's a long while ago but I lent it to someone in our class and I wondered if it was him. It's sort of purple with lightning bolts over a city at night'." J.J. gasped in a huge breath.

"No!"

"Yes. Bloody cheek. So if you happen to come across 'Power Ballads 2' let me know. I would love to reunite Ronald with his CD. I even know some A&E staff that could help him get it back out of there if I haven't shoved it too far up." For the first time since he had been round to help J.J. laughed. "Not that I think you'll find it," Jess continued, "I'm sure Charlie had replaced all of his CDs. He only had the digital stuff and his vinyl collection. Oh, and if you find a little key with the red plastic fob let me know. It's for the storage unit where he put his records when we moved house. I'll have to work out what to do with them." J.J. did not reply, but you can say a lot in a look.

"J.J., what is it?"

"I'm guessing he hasn't said anything to you." Jess's expression said both no he hasn't, but yes, carry on. "Charlie said that when the two of you came to view this house, he did it because he thought you fancied looking round the place. But then he saw what happened when you got in, he said you… lit up. And you know what he was like, so impulsive, he said he told you that if you liked it you could afford it."

"Ye-es, that's right. The BBC job was better paid, and he said he had inherited some money when his auntie died."

"Not exactly. There was no inheritance. He saw you loved the house, knew the chance would be gone if he didn't get an offer in straight away, and so…"

Jess looked stunned. "He's sold some of his records?"

"Again, not exactly…"

"What? He's been collecting them for years, they're his pride and joy." She shook her head. "Don't say he sold all of them?" J.J. nodded.

"As a job lot, to raise the deposit. To a dealer in London. He told me he got forty grand, there were some real rarities in there. I found the receipt earlier but didn't like to mention it. Look." He quickly laid his hands on a small slip of paper and passed it for Jess to read. "I tried to encourage him to tell you but it looks like…"

"He didn't." Jess shook her head and sighed.

"Sorry," said J.J.

"No. Don't be daft, you've nothing to apologise for. Neither has he I suppose. I can't blame Charlie for being… Charlie." She read the receipt again. "C'mon, let's get back to work."

J.J. could see that the news had affected Jess. She was distracted, but as the afternoon wore on she settled down. She looked at the bulging bags of discarded paperwork. This was taking her in the right direction. She had moved onto the drawers of the desk and was finding more recent items. Any that required immediate action were placed together. Towards the end of the afternoon, J.J. became aware that she had gone quiet. He looked up to see her staring at yet another sheet.

"Are you okay?" he asked.

"Not really," she replied.

"What's up? Bad news?"

"Ever since I found out this morning that he had sold his records I've been worrying, thinking what else I might find. This is one I was dreading. You know how Charlie has always been self-employed, Radio City pays him to provide the show but he's not an employee?" J.J. nodded. It was a common practice in the business. "I've just found this." J.J. moved across and looked at the paper she was holding. It was an application form to join a private pension scheme, completed, signed and dated. 22nd April 2018. The day that Charlie died.

"I have been nagging him to do this for so long," she said. "He told me weeks ago it was all in hand. He must have filled it in on Sunday afternoon. This is Charlie through and through, does the things which interest him, anything else is left till last." J.J. thought he knew, but he thought he better ask anyway.

"So what does that mean?"

"Obviously the application is worthless here. It means no pension, no lump sum, nothing." J.J. watched as Jess picked up the notepad she was using to keep a list of actions.

"What are you going to do?" he asked. Jess sighed.

"We – sorry, I mean I - have got a scary mortgage on this place. I can't afford to pay it on my salary." She picked up her pen and began to write. "I'm adding the estate agent to the list of people I need to contact."

*   *   *

The last three funerals that Jess had been to were those of her dad, Grandad Joe, and, most recently, Charlie's aunt. Each was upsetting, but all three leading players were advanced in years and so the attendees, Jess included, consoled each other with the stock phrases of funeral participation. In each case, it was agreed over thick tea and thin sandwiches that they'd 'had a good innings'. Whilst Jess's dad was the youngest of them, the commonly held view was that towards the end his quality of life was so poor that 'it was a blessing'. She had harboured a vague hope that the cumulative experience of these three events might prepare her for Charlie's funeral. She was sorely mistaken.

St. Jude's church is by no means grand in scale but it is an altogether splendid building. Its walls are constructed from hand-cut stones, of varying sizes and shades. This irregular fashioning gives them a natural feel, allowing the church to blend in seamlessly with its rural surroundings. It has a squat, square spire, watching over a small knave. The plain white plaster walls create a bright, airy space. When it was built in the seventeenth century, St. Jude's was - and remains – of a scale perfectly suited for a regular Sunday morning service in a small village. Its modest dimensions were never conceived to cope with an occasion such as Charlie's funeral, and the feat of accommodating all who attended was yet another undertaking for Saint Jude to add to his program of hopeless works. The two banks of twenty short pews either side of the aisle were fully occupied long before eleven o'clock when the service commenced. Charlie's young friends gave up their places in favour of older family members, so that both side passages and the entry porch quickly filled with mourners, and all subsequent arrivals had to congregate in haphazard groups in the area before the main entrance. They were joined by a small film crew from the local news channel.

Arriving as the service was about to start (as is the form on these occasions), Jess saw nothing of this lead-up. She walked through the crowd, a vast patchwork of faces, impossible to absorb. This was all wrong she thought. There were so many here, and so many of them so young. These people did not look funereal, not sad or sombre. They were shocked and bewildered, mystified as to why they were there, why they had been invited to this event that should never have been arranged in the first place. So wrong she thought, so wrong. They should be out there ripping into all that life has to offer, not staring at each other with wide, red-rimmed eyes, trying to figure out what in the name of God is going on. Jess walked steadily up the steps, smiling as she did, a weak, dilute shadow of her normal smile. As she proceeded down the central aisle, the sun, streaming through the simple stained glass windows, created incongruous kaleidoscope splashes of vivid colour on the floor before her. When Jess had taken her place on the pew at the front, Charlie's mum rubbed her arm in a gesture of affection made altogether too vigorous by the depth of her feelings.

The day passed in accordance with Charlie's sketchy plan. The six coffin bearers, all fully clad and of approximately equal height, were Charlie's dad, an uncle, three cousins, and J.J. Aside from the brief period when they ascended the steps, his coffin remained horizontal throughout. Alex Knight led them in. Dressed in a black suit and white blouse, with her long blonde hair neatly arranged in a plait, she looked radiant. Predicting that the church was likely to overflow, J.J. had borrowed a small public address system from Radio City so that those unable to get inside could follow the service. They heard the music, favourite songs of Charlie and Jess. Charlie's dad delivered the first of two eulogies, speaking lovingly and movingly about his son, his love of music and life.

Next J.J. stood up and, occasionally fighting to control his radio voice, delivered the tender words that Jess had written. "I hope I've said everything you wanted, Jess," he said, as he concluded, folding up his notes. From her pew, Jess nodded in approval, mouthing thanks. "I'd just like to add one thing. I recently found out that Charlie had a teacher at school who told him that he was destined to become one of life's rejects. That teacher could not have been more wrong. Life may have rejected Charlie far too soon, but not one of us did. To us he was no reject, he was our shining star, a man who lit up the lives of everyone who met him and I am proud to have been able to call him my best friend."

Outside the entrance to the church, standing between two huge prints of the photo that Jess had taken on the celebratory night out in Liverpool, the funeral party shook hands and hugged each of the mourners. The majority then headed off for the wake at The Bell, while a small number of close family and friends attended the graveside. Charlie's plot was in the corner furthest from the church, a pretty, quiet spot. They watched as the coffin was borne down, then lowered into its resting place.

Jess took a handful of soil and threw it onto the coffin lid. Two pebbles bounced around on the uneven wicker surface and then settled together. Through tears, she blew Charlie a kiss goodbye, before walking over to a nearby bench and sitting down. Intuitively the others understood that she wanted a moment alone, and began to move steadily back up the graveyard. When they had gone a sufficient distance, Jess produced a small envelope from her handbag.

"I'm ready now," she said. Using her longest fingernail, she slit along the top and pulled out a folded notelet. She opened it.

'*Dear Jess,*

The day before my aunt's funeral, I interviewed a lady who was visiting the remote islands around Scotland. She was meeting the oldest residents, and recording them as they sung their traditional folk songs, ones that told the stories of their lives. The words and tunes are dying out and she knows that there is a real danger that they will soon be lost forever. I hope she captured them all.

Since you're reading this I know that I must have gone. Can I ask one thing? Please don't allow the song of your life to die out. Keep on writing it. No one knows better that you how it should go, what the next line should be, when it should speed up, when it needs to slow down. Let it tell the story of the most astonishing person I ever met, and sing it every day. Never let it fade away, the lost lyrics of a forgotten song, let it be celebrated forevermore.

Charlie x'

Jess refolded the note and returned it to the envelope, placing it in her bag, before heading up the graveyard to where the others were waiting. As she did so she passed a tall man, walking stooped and with a slight limp. Beside him was a young girl. The man smiled kindly at Jess. Meanwhile, the young gravedigger she had met in the funeral director's office had already made his way across, ready to complete the final act in Charlie's interment.

By the time their party arrived at The Bell, the mood had already begun to lighten, in no small part due to its being a Premises Licenced For The Sale Of All Intoxicating Liquor.

Small groups had formed, jackets and ties were shed, and drinks were being downed, in an effort to wash away the stress and heartache of the day. After the wake, Jess was given a lift home by Charlie's parents. They sat around, quietly reminiscing in a way that would have been lovely, had the circumstances been different. Every recollection was tinged with the sad knowledge that there would be no new stories, that the fund of anecdotes was full as it would ever be.

Chapter 3

It was dark. Not a wishy-washy half-dark, this was black, as black as the scorched cover of Satan's burned bible. All around was a dense, impenetrable, enveloping oppressiveness, accompanied by an empty, deep space silence. There were no stimuli for the senses to capture, to transmit to the brain, nothing that could be analysed to garner some understanding as to what was going on. Minutes passed. Maybe they were hours. And then slowly, stealthily, Charlie began to be able to pick out an odd brooding shadow, the subtlest variations in hue. There was nothing he could identify and give a name to, they were no more than amorphous shapes, silhouettes of ghostly ships drifting in a fogbound sea of gloom, emerging then disappearing. He lay still, and several more of the minutes or hours or whatever they were ticked by.

As some flickering sense of the surroundings came to him, so too did his sense of self. He felt distinctly odd, hazy, like the morning after a hugely miscalculated night out. Groggy. Piece by piece, what had happened was coming back to him. No wonder he felt odd; he should not have been feeling anything. Charlie remembered that he was dead. The last thing he could definitively recollect was being flat out in a dazzlingly bright operating theatre, surrounded by medical staff, uniforms of every colour, the full spectrum of specialists, including one in his mother-in-law's beloved Consultant Purple. They were jostling for position around him, attaching wires, inserting tubes and needles, filling him full of medicines and bags of other people's blood, all the while shouting about the little thin batteries that go in the TV remote control. Next came dizziness, a weakness, then a trance, a dream. Then nothing. Utter blankness, the duration of which he had absolutely no measure. He lay a little longer, his senses sharpening. He could smell something now, the air around him. It was moist, though not at all musty. More earthy, like mushrooms. Then, from somewhere deep within the void, there came a voice.

"Hello."

Charlie had interviewed numerous psychiatrists on his show. They were talented individuals, all devoted to trying to understand and patch up the most complicated thing on this planet (maybe this universe), the human brain. Working as they did at the boundaries of Man's knowledge, Charlie was unsurprised that their theories varied, but on certain matters they were consentient. This was such an instance. They had unanimously confirmed to Charlie that when it comes to the number of voices in your head, if all's going well up there, there will be just one. Yours. That single voice on the inside of your coconut, the one that you use to run through thoughts and silently talk to yourself, sometimes saying the things you wouldn't dare say aloud. One. This is not an approximation, it is exact. Any more than one voice in your head and you will be receiving additional messages that are most unlikely to be helpful. Any less than one – zero - chances are you're dead.

"Hello." The voice was heavily muffled but Charlie sensed it was female. He lay there a few moments more. It had stopped. Nope, it hadn't.

"Hello-o. Hello-o-o."

"Hang on a minute," Charlie said to himself, using the voice in his head that he knew well and could typically trust. "That voice is coming in through my ears. I can hear! And voices in your head don't come in through your ears, they're inside already, they don't need to. To respond or not? Someone more timid might have delayed. Charlie engaged.

"Hello," he replied, pitching his tone as confident but not bullish.

"Ah, you're there. Please, there's no need to be alarmed," said the lady. Her speech was becoming clearer to Charlie, as his ears grew accustomed to the bizarre, leaden acoustics. "I'm your neighbour." Neighbour? I've got a neighbour?

"And I too am your neighbour." This voice was male. Okay, there are two of them. Before he gave this circumstance any credence, there were some fundamentals to establish.

"How do I know that you are real?" he asked.

"Pardon?" said the man.

"Not a hallucination, a trick of my mind." The female voice replied, her tone soothing.

"We understand your concerns," she said. "This must seem strange, but please trust us. We have gone through the same thing as you, awaking confused and unsettled."

Charlie's brain was quickening. Bit by bit, functions were returning, yet she was correct. He was confused. He recognised now that his surroundings were no longer uniformly black. Through the darkness, vague shapes loomed, no longer melting away. Where on earth am I? Stop, rewind. Who says I am even on Earth? This man and woman were his best and only hope of coming to an understanding. Let's suppose I'm not on Earth, where might I be? Start with the two most obvious alternative candidates. Although the surroundings he found himself in were utterly bleak and dismal, Charlie had always been an optimist and, on balance, he reckoned he had lived a good(ish) life.

"Is this Heaven?" he asked.

"Good Lord, no," said the man. Then, appearing anxious

in case his dismissive delivery had frightened the newcomer, he followed up, "but it's not Hell either. You are in Stanford. Saint Jude's churchyard to be precise." Positive news thought Charlie. A plausible answer, what this man is saying has a ring of truth. Double positive news, it appeared that he had not been damned to the fires of Hell for all eternity.

"How long have I been here?"

"Not long. Your funeral finished perhaps three hours ago," said the man.

"Is that all? It feels like months." Charlie tried to peep round in the direction of the speaker, who was behind him and to his right. All he could see was what looked like the end of a large box. He tried to see behind his head, where the woman's voice had come from. There was another similar shape. More perplexing, it seemed he was looking through the two shapes, and could pick out… soles of feet. He could think of no way to phrase this delicately.

"Are you two in… coffins?" he asked.

"We are," said the lady. "My name is Rita. What's yours?"

"Charlie. Charlie Munro."

"Hi Charlie, welcome," said Rita. "Please try not to be scared by what I'm about to tell you, but I am dead. And - there is no easy way to say this, son - so are you. I'm really sorry." Charlie scanned his surroundings once more. His eyes were tuning in by the minute, and based on what the lady said, he could now more clearly discern the outlines of the ends of two caskets. These people or zombies or whatever they were, they were telling the truth. Intuitively, with no experience or formal training in how to address the deceased, Charlie elected to do what he knew best. He slipped into interview mode, using the techniques that had served him well to date. Stay calm, be friendly, ask clear concise questions, and listen. He drew another breath, or at least it felt to him that he did.

"It's all right, Rita," he said. "In the last seconds that I can remember I was in the hospital and things were going quite badly. Now I appear to be under the ground in St. Jude's graveyard, so hearing that I'm dead doesn't come as a complete shock to me."

"I am relieved," said the man. "I would hate for you to have suffered the terrors that I did."

"Sorry sir, can I ask who you are?"

"I'm Doctor Dennis Dean. I am, well I was, a GP," he said. A proud, confident voice Charlie thought, slightly pompous. "Let me introduce our other resident," the Doctor continued. "Isabel, would you like to welcome our new friend."

"Hi," said a female voice, younger than the other two.

"Hi, lovely to meet you," Charlie replied, before realising it sounded a bit weird. Three of them now. "Are there any more of you?" he asked, "only I'm starting to lose track."

"No more, just we three - and now you," said Rita. "There are half a dozen plots in our little corner. Think of us as if you were looking down into an egg box, two rows of three. On the top row, from the left, there's Doctor Dean, myself then an empty space. On the row beneath is Isabel, you, then there is an empty plot beside you."

"Thanks, I think I've got my bearings now. Sorry, can we just go back? Terrors you said, Doctor. Did you have a bad experience?"

"Indeed I did," he said. "I died seven years ago, 2011, I was seventy-two at the time. Fell victim to a dreadful chest infection that turned into pneumonia. When I arrived here and came round, I was convinced that I had been buried alive."

"Oh my God," said Charlie "that thought hadn't crossed my mind. So if we're not buried alive… what are we?" The doctor cleared his throat with a rattle that made Charlie doubt that his pneumonia had fully cleared up.

"What we are is a very interesting question, one that I have been attempting to understand and describe ever since I arrived here. I have to report that, despite my extensive medical training and almost forty years of conspicuous success in General Practice, I have yet to fully resolve the matter." The doctor tailed off, dispirited, though only for a moment. "But all is not lost. We have part of the solution in that we believe we can answer the question *why* we are. As Rita is the custodian of the key information in this regard, I think it is only right that she should relate the most remarkable story you will have heard in your life. Although," he added, being a stickler for accuracy, "strictly speaking, it's come a little too late for you to have heard it within that timeframe." Rita butted in with a speed that hinted to Charlie that when the doctor paused for breath, you should grab the microphone.

"My full name is Rita Jackson," she began. "I've lived around here all of my life. Are you from Stanford, Charlie?"

"No, but my wife is. I'm fairly new to the place."

"Well, my family have been farming the land round here for hundreds of years. Generation after generation has cleared and ploughed and drained and fenced and planted and harvested. It's us and the likes of us who've shaped what you see today."

"So were you a farmer, Rita?"

"No, though I've lived on farms all my life. I married a farmer, and when my dad became too old to manage his farm, we took it on. I've always helped at weekends, but I had a full-time job. When I was sixteen I began working at the local council, a junior in the Archivist section."

"Archivists?"

"It's a little department that looks after local records. It covers all sorts - births, deaths and marriages, histories of local trades, churches, estates. I loved history at school so it wasn't like working at all. I learned so much about this place, particularly about the Stanford family. The village is named after them. They had bequeathed bundles of old documents to the council's collection, covering their past. No one had ever had the chance to properly look at them so I volunteered to do it in my spare time."

"Interesting?" Charlie asked.

"Fascinating, son. I loved it. I could tell you such stories. They were a good family down the years, particularly Albert, the 12th Lord Stanford. He lived in the 18th Century but was far ahead of his time, improving conditions for the people who worked on the estate. Then his grandson, Edwin, came along and ruined everything. He was a waster, a real Champagne Charlie. Ooh, sorry, no offence, Charlie."

"That's all right," Charlie replied.

"He was a gambler. It's a bad choice of hobby when you drink brandy for breakfast - I found the bills that he ran up with the wine merchants. Unbelievable. In the space of a decade, he had frittered away all of the money and was the downfall of the family. Their grand home is a ruin now. Anyway, when I was looking for a plot to get buried in, this little corner of the churchyard closest to Stanford Hall, was the obvious choice."

"What has all that got to do with us though, Rita?" Charlie asked.

"Some of the documents mentioned a well with health-giving properties in the estate grounds. People who drank or washed in the water drawn from it seemingly recovered from illnesses and afflictions."

"Really?"

"So they said - and they had some horrendous skin diseases and such-like back in those days. Now, let's stop talking for a minute and you listen." Silence fell. As Charlie concentrated, he picked up a sound.

"Is that running water?" he asked.

"Exactly!" said Rita. "There's an underground stream linked to the well, running a few feet below us."

"And you think that it's the stream that means we're kind of only half-dead or whatever we are?" asked Charlie. "What do you make of that as a doctor, Doctor?" Denis Dean gave another throaty ahem.

"My specialism, Charles, is medicine. It is a discipline founded upon science. My approach to all decision-making is based on evidence and fact. Let us consider. There are six burial plots in our little corner, directly above the stream. Two of them are empty, we occupy the other four. We are the only individuals within the boundaries of St. Jude's to show any signs of 'life', everyone in the other three hundred or so plots scattered around this graveyard is thoroughly and completely dead. Implausible as it seems, it appears that those waters beneath us are conferring some sort of extension to our existence." Charlie's mind had already jumped ahead. He had to ask.

"So is there any hope that maybe it could make us better, that somehow we could go back to our former lives?" The response from Doctor Dean was firm and unambiguous.

"No, Charles, absolutely not. I think it's only fair that I set your expectations. You have embarked upon a one-way pilgrimage, bound for a destination I know not where. What we are experiencing is but a hiatus, a short respite, before the guard blows the whistle and our onward journey continues. You are dead. Only not quite."

"Jeez," said Charlie. "I hadn't thought much about what it would be like to be dead, but if I had, I would not have come up with this."

"Quite. We do not fully understand our situation, but there are some things we do know. Would you like me to elaborate further?"

"Please do," said Charlie.

"Very well," said the doctor. "Here are some of the basics that we believe to be true regarding a condition I have named Dean's Syndrome." Charlie stifled a snigger.

"After yourself?"

"Indeed, yes. I hope you won't think me presumptuous for calling it that, but as I am the only qualified person so far to have identified and researched it, I feel it is justified and in keeping with the long traditions of exploratory medicine."

"Absolutely, Doctor Dean. Can I ask, do you mind if I call you Denis? Or maybe Doc?" Doctor Denis Dean hesitated. No one had ever been quite so forward with him.

"If I am to be abbreviated, Charles, I think I rather like Doc."

"Okay, Doc it is," said Charlie, pleased with this choice.

"I have identified three key characteristics of Dean's Syndrome. Characteristic One. As we have demonstrated, you can see that we are able to speak to each other. It's almost instinctive, you have already done it yourself by replying to us.

How would you describe the way in which you did this?" Charlie thought.

"I'm not sure. I didn't move my mouth or anything, I ran the words through my head in the way that I've always put together sentences."

"Precisely. That's what I am doing now and you can hear me. Now to Characteristic Two. Can you describe what you have seen so far in the time since you joined us?" Charlie went through the events of the last half hour in his mind.

"Nothing at first," he said. "It was just black. Then gradually I began to pick some shapes up. It was like when you are sleeping in an unfamiliar room and you wake up in the night. You're disorientated at first, then you start to pick out a few objects."

"And now?"

"Not a lot. Some gravestones and grass, but from a peculiar angle."

"When I arrived, there was only Rita in situ. We found that we could talk, which was a boon... though Rita did rather monopolise the dialogue, something I felt inclined to tolerate on account of her having been here alone for eight years. We were frustrated that we could not see each other. And in seeking to rectify this I made my first ground-breaking discovery. It was obvious to me, as a cadaver, that I could not move to see Rita from a different angle, but I considered the way that our ability to speak functioned. Perhaps if I thought about looking at her from above, so we were face to face, it would occur. I knew that I must try but it was an experiment I embarked upon with no little trepidation."

"In case it didn't work?"

"No, Charles, in case it did. I was fearful that Rita would be in an advanced state of decomposition. I have seen some horrific things over my time in practice and they can haunt you. This, however, was no time to be squeamish. I pushed the thought of changing position through my brain and, lo and behold, I found myself looking down on a lady of advanced years who, despite a somewhat waxy complexion, was not at all decayed."

"Really?"

"I didn't believe him," said Rita, "so to prove it I asked him to describe me. And what did you say?" The Doc blustered.

"With the passage of time, I can't recall my precise words."

"I can. You said I had a considerable face, and that my hairstyle was grey and frizzy, like Albert Einstein's."

"I meant only that your face was comely. And any comparison to Einstein is a compliment. He was a genius."

"Not with a hairbrush, he wasn't," Rita replied.

"The point is, Charles, that Rita tried and found that she could do it too. We all can. It makes for a much more sociable experience in our limited little world."

"Do you think I should try?" Charlie asked.

"I don't want to rush you, but there is nothing to fear." Charlie took a moment to steady himself, before putting the idea into his brain. It happened in an instant, his whole perspective changed, like turning his head in his previous life. There were now three people before him. The man was clearly The Doc, and Isabel and Rita could easily be told apart. The Doc's description of Rita, whilst unfortunate, was entirely accurate, aside from his omitting to mention also that her eyes bulged out of her skull. Charlie considered asking if she had met her end by pushing her fingers into a live plug socket, but held off. It was early days in their friendship.

He looked at the others. Isabel was around fifty and had a thin, pinched face. The Doc wore a dark, old-fashioned three-piece suit, his jowls overhanging the collar of his thick white shirt. The extra layer of his waistcoat made him appear rounder than his actual physique, no mean feat. Charlie was sure that had he and J.J.'s proposed mistaken identity item ever gone ahead, The Doc would surely have been regularly confused with Toad Hall's prime resident.

"This is amazing," he said, looking on his new neighbours for the first time.

"Yes. My discovery," said the Doc. "Are you okay? I understand that this is a lot to take in, particularly when you must still be getting used to the idea that you are recently… deceased."

"I'm fine," said Charlie, "all of this is better than the alternative." He studied the three coffins. Those occupied by Rita and Isabel were simple and unfussy; The Doc's was an altogether grander affair. "Nice coffin, Doc," he said.

"Thank you," he replied, "English oak, solid brass fittings. I was pleased with Mrs Dean's selection. She knew me to be something of a traditionalist in such matters."

"Charlie, are you ready for Characteristic Three?" Rita asked.

"I think so."

"Okay," Rita continued. "This is something that we agreed we would do when the next person arrived. Ready? One. Two. Three",

"Hello-o-o" came the inharmonious chorus. Charlie looked on, stunned.

"You all waved. How did you do that?"

"Same principle," said The Doc. "Of course, we don't actually move but if you think about that, or any other gesture, the others can see it." Charlie nodded. "There," said The Doc, "we just saw you nod your head."

"Incredible," said Charlie. He studied the three smiling individuals before him. And then he pulled himself back. "There is something I need to ask you. He took their silence as approval. "It's about how you feel. None of you seem to feel very, I don't know, guilty for having died or anything, you're not…what's the word… griefy."

"Griefy? I wouldn't try playing it in Scrabble," said Rita, "but I know what you mean."

"The reason I'm asking," said Charlie, "is that I feel the same. I'm sure the people I've left behind up there, at least a few of them, will be sad right now."

"Indeed," The Doc agreed. "We know that for the living it may take months, years, to get over a loss. Some never do. But your case confirms what we have already observed; for the dead, the grief we knew does not appear to exist." Questions were flying into Charlie's head at a furious rate, but the others insisted that he tell them more about himself. He summarised where he was from, his family, and growing up. The Doc interrupted his flow.

"If it's not an impertinent question, Charles, how old are you now?"

"I was thirty-five on my last birthday."

"Ah, I must tell you about a nomenclature that I have devised for our ages. It puts together our age at death, followed by the number of years we have been here. So, for instance, I am Seventy-two-Seven. Rita is Eighty-Fourteen. And you Isabel?"

"Forty-eight-Two."

"I see," said Charlie, "so I reckon I am Thirty-five-Zero."

"Correct," said The Doc. "Now, you were telling us about college I think?" Charlie resumed his story, going through his career, ending with the BBC job.

"That is a tragedy, Charlie," said Rita, "so close to your big break after all your hard work. It can't get much worse than that."

"It can," he said, "I haven't told you about my pension. Or lack of." He then went on to describe the financial mess that he had left behind and the implications for his young widow.

"She will be more concerned about losing you than any money, son," said Rita which, whilst he believed it was probably true, was little solace to Charlie. Rita and The Doc then branched off into a detailed discussion about the relative merits of the pension provision they had left behind. Charlie took the opportunity to talk to Isabel, who had said the least since he had arrived.

"Were you on in the morning at Radio City?" she asked.

"Yes."

"I thought so. I've heard you, I recognised your voice." Charlie encouraged her to open out about herself, to tell a hard story, one of cancer, remission, recurrence, and early death, leaving her twelve-year-old daughter behind. It made his abrupt demise seem breezy by comparison.

"Sorry if I droned on about dying earlier," he said, "it seemed a big deal to me until I've heard your background. I hope your little girl is okay."

"She's doing well," Isabel said. "My brother looks after her now. You'll see her, they come to visit sometimes."

"I'll look forward to it," said Charlie. Isabel smiled warmly, knowing he meant it. As Rita and The Doc seemed to have resolved their personal finance matters, Charlie jumped in to ask him some more about Dean's Syndrome. Two hours later, punch drunk, he concluded one of the least enlightening interviews of his career. Not because The Doc was reticent to speak; quite the opposite. Charlie had never met a man who had such a range of longwinded and convoluted ways of expressing the three words 'I don't know'. He looked up and saw that it was growing dark above them.

"I can't see so clearly out there, now that night is falling."

"No," The Doc agreed, "although we are able to see each other all of the time in this subterranean environment, we cannot see the world of the living when the sun sets. The reason for this I have yet to fathom." Charlie felt exhausted.

"One final question," he asked, "do we sleep"?

"Yes, son," Rita replied, "we sleep."

Chapter 4

The five, five and nine on Jess's digital alarm reconfigured their little semaphore limbs and became six zero zero. This was her target time. Jess had been lying awake in bed since four two two, and had told herself that six o'clock was the moment to give up the pretence that she could fall back asleep. From the small table at her side, she picked up the book and pen.

Dear Journal,

That's it, the funeral is over. After three weeks of preparing, it was gone in a heartbeat. Like Charlie. I did my best to smile my way through the agony. A milestone supposedly. I don't feel it. No closure. No 'let's move on'. Just emptiness.

Jess laid her book down and rose. She stood in front of the full-length mirror in their bedroom. Her bedroom. She barely recognised what she saw. Hollow. Her eyes, her cheeks, shoulders, and stance, all hollow. She climbed back into bed.

Dear Journal,

I look a wreck. Worse, I look like the photo on my hospital pass that Charlie constantly took the piss out of. I do not know where I will end up, but this can't be it. If I achieve one thing today, no matter how low I feel inside, I will walk out of my front door looking human. I promise this to me.

Jess laid down the book and pen once more, swung back up out of bed, and went downstairs. She began by tidying up the living room, judging that it would be a good warm-up for the altogether more challenging exercise of tidying up herself. She washed the crockery from the previous evening, the uneaten biscuits, gone soft overnight, went into the bin. The house looked okay. Me now. Showered and dressed she felt better, well enough to make toast, well enough to eat part of one slice. Before nine the doorbell had rung twice, yet more flowers, despite having suggested charity donations instead. In a way she was pleased. She had already used all available vases, (plus the two odd urn-shaped things that she and Charlie had received as a gift from his now-deceased aunt, but had never managed to divine their intended purpose). These latest bouquets lent weight to a decision that she had already taken. She would return to St. Jude's today and place these and a few others on Charlie's grave.

On arriving, as soon as she opened the car door, she heard a blackbird pipe a lilting tune from the yew tree that overhung the church's car park. Was he playing those cheerful notes yesterday? Surely she would have noticed. It would have sounded so inappropriate, not that he could be blamed. She walked into the churchyard. Compared to yesterday, she was struck by the lack of sound, not peaceful, but eerie. She looked at the tombstones, most straight but others tilted, as if those they honoured had disturbed them in an effort to exit the cold beds in which they lay. The powerful drystone wall snaked, around them, tightly following the rolling contours of the land, an unbreachable barrier, ensuring that all those deposited within its bounds, stayed within.

Jess looked left, downhill to the far corner where her husband now lay. She saw two figures whom she recognised, the tall, heavy-set man she had seen yesterday with the young girl, standing by the plot just to the left of Charlie's. Between the church and the wall, a broadly elliptical gravel path wound through the heart of the graveyard. If that path was the face of a clock, she'd joined it through the gate at around one o'clock, with Charlie now residing somewhere around five. Not wishing to encroach, Jess took the longer route, setting off against the clock through twelve, eleven, ten. As she descended the hill, approaching seven, the man motioned to the girl, and the pair walked towards the slatted wooden bench that Jess had sat on yesterday. She noticed again that the man moved with a slight limp, so she further slowed her pace, giving them time to become settled.

As he had done the previous day, the man looked at her and smiled. Jess placed the flowers onto the freshly dug soil and stepped back slightly. She turned towards the couple. Sufficient eye contact passed between them to make conversation a less awkward option than silence.

"Hi," she said, "I saw you here yesterday." The man nodded.

"Yes, we'd come to visit my sister but didn't want to intrude on your, eh, ceremony, so we've come back today. My sister is buried here, next to your…"

"Husband. Charlie."

"I'm Mick," he said, gesturing to the headstone in front of him. "Isabel was my sister. This is her daughter Mia, my niece."

"Hi, Mia, my name's Jess." She smiled at the girl, who was in her early teens with short-cropped hair, wearing a black tracksuit. Jess stole a glance at the headstone to work out how long Mia had been without her mum. Mick spotted the eye movement and read her intention.

"Two years ago now since we lost her," he said.

"I'm sorry to hear that," Jess replied, surprised that he had read her purpose with such ease.

"How are you doing?" Mick asked. "I remember what it was like for us at first when Isabel died. Tough. So raw, the slightest little thing can set you off." Jess nodded, thinking back to the restaurant receipt.

"You must still miss your mum," she said to Mia.

"I do," she replied, "but it does get a little easier. I'm just as sad about it, but I think I'm better at coping with it." Jess's nodded. "You have to try to keep moving on," the girl continued, "because everybody else around you soon does. You can't freeze time, and if you could why would you choose such a sad moment to live in?"

"That's true," said Jess, wondering if the early loss of her mother had accelerated growing up for the young girl. For a moment the three fell silent.

"Shhhh! Shhhh-shhh!" Charlie whispered, entirely without purpose as he was the only one on the below-ground level in St. Jude's making a sound. "It's Jess, my wife. I can hear her!" The others held their silence, giving him the space to become immersed in her voice, more magical than any music he had ever played. He could see her now. She looked amazing, exactly as he remembered. Then she turned and the sunlight struck her face. She looked drained. Eventually Isabel spoke, in a loudish whisper.

"That's my brother Mick I told you about, and my daughter, Mia." She fell silent once more, as the conversation from above recommenced. It seemed hauntingly distant to Charlie, yet clear enough that he could make out every word. Mia explained to Jess how her emotions had changed over time. Charlie fixed on every word she spoke. The depth of feeling from someone so young was striking. Even if he had wanted to, he would not have been able to interrupt, to break this spell.

"You're sure they can't hear us?" he asked.

"Charles, I was a leading player in the local amateur dramatics company," said The Doc. "Within those circles, my vocal projection was the stuff of legend. I have tried on several occasions but have never yet managed to make myself heard to anyone up there. I am minded to declare it a Defining Characteristic of Dean's Syndrome."

"That's a shame. I'd love to tell her that she needs to get some rest. Your daughter and your brother seem lovely Isabel, really kind."

"Yes, they are. He's a good man, Mick. I owe him so much," she replied. "Everything really." Once again, there were voices from above.

"Come and sit with us if you'd like," said Mia, shuffling across to her left. "There's plenty of room on Rita's bench." Jess stepped over and read the small brass plaque between uncle and niece.

"In memory of Rita Jackson, who dearly loved Stanford." Jess sat down beside them.

"Do you live in Stanford?" asked Mia.

"Yes, in a cottage just on the other side of the village. Although I'm thinking about moving."

"Oh." She wanted to ask why but thought it might be deemed rude by her uncle. "What job do you do?" she asked instead. Jess told her about nursing and music therapy. Mia had never heard of it, and as Jess described the patients she treated, she peppered her with questions.

"I go out to the community too," she said, "to places, like care homes…"

"Mr Wilson next door to us, his wife has had to go into a care home," said Mia. "She gets upset and angry because she can't remember things, unless they happened ages ago. She's got Alzheimer's. Is it good for people with that?"

"It's great for people like Mrs Wilson," said Jess. "They love the music and singing - you can see their faces light up. And that means a lot to Mr Wilson too. In those moments he has his wife back. I'll have my own place soon," Jess added, explaining about her charity, and the new unit she was setting up. "What about you?" she asked.

"I'm still at school," Mia replied, "but if I pass my exams I'll go to university. I want to study criminology. Uncle Mick is a policeman, you know."

"Was a policeman," said Mick. "I'm retired now." Jess acknowledged the correction with a nod.

"Criminology? Sounds very exciting," she said. "I'm sure you will pass your exams. Your mum would be proud of you." Mia gave her a shy smile.

"I hope so, she was very sick so I always did my best at school so she didn't worry. Since she died I've lived with Uncle Mick. I never knew my dad, they split up when I was little." She smiled. "So Uncle Mick is my guardian. If I start bunking off school to smoke cigarettes and shoplift mascara and lipsticks, it's all his fault."

"You better hadn't," Mick replied. "Come on young lady, I'm sure Jess has better things to do than answer your questions." He gave her a nudge, and all three of them stood up and took the few steps required to stand before the graves again.

"It was lovely to meet you both," said Jess. "Maybe we'll see each other again."

"When do you think you'll be back?" asked Mia.

"Well, I think I will be busy this week, back at work, but these flowers will soon look scruffy. I'll probably come back next Saturday and tidy them away."

"Oh, we will see you then," Mia replied. "We come every Saturday about this time before I go to my judo lesson. Then we go to Angelo's café. Maybe Jess could come there too?" she said, looking at her uncle. He left Jess to respond.

"I'd like that," she said. "It'll give me something to look forward to." She noticed a movement on her left. It was the young gravedigger from Charlie's funeral the previous day. She studied him more closely. His hair was lank, the colour of filthy straw and he had an angular, bony physique, moving like a cheetah going through a long, lean period of hunting on the grasslands. His eyes darted towards them from beneath their hooded brows, before returning to the tools in the barrow he was pushing. When he was close enough, Mick spoke to him.

"Are we in the way?" he asked. The young man replied but didn't look up.

"I need to dig out that one there," he said, pointing with his long-handled shovel at the space to the right of Charlie. As he glanced up he saw Mick looking at his shovel.

"I have to do it by hand," he said, "you can't get a mechanical digger down into this corner." Mick considered the access route.

"No, I don't suppose you could."

"Well," said Jess, "We're finished here, so we'll let you get on with it." As they moved away, they heard the rhythmic clicking of blade into soil, loud at first, then fading as they approached the gate. When they reached the car park, Mick turned to Jess. He looked awkward.

"I don't want to interfere," he said, "but earlier you mentioned that you were thinking of moving house. It might be an idea to take time to think before you do anything. You must already have a lot on, having just lost your husband. Sorry, I know it's none of my business."

"No, thanks for your advice," Jess replied. "Only I'm in a tricky position." She could tell he had not been comfortable making the suggestion but had pushed himself to do it. "I'll tell you about it if I see you both next week." They said their goodbyes and Mick waited for Jess to pull away. As she disappeared from view he turned to Mia.

"Why did you say that we come here every Saturday? We did at first when your mum had died, but it's more like once a month now."

"I know, but I can remember how I felt. She seemed sad, I thought it might help. And I liked her." Mick nodded, put the car into gear, and moved off.

Charlie willed himself to isolate the voices from the sounds of the digging, desperate to hear Jess's voice for as long as possible, but with each step the three took their words slipped to a faint mumble, then nothing.

"Well, Charlie, how was that?" asked Rita.

"It was great to see her," he said. "But hard. It forced me to face up to the mess I've left behind. She's going to sell the house. Her cottage. I was supposed to get that pension set up, in case anything like this happened. Too busy doing other things that were more important than my wife's future. I feel selfish, bloody awful." Rita could hear the anguish in his tone.

"Charlie, stop. We all come here with regrets son, things we wished we'd done, things we wished we said, things we wished we hadn't. You can't stew on them." Charlie was unconvinced.

"But this mistake, it's not a tiny slip. For Jess, it's a disaster."

"I listened to your wife," said Rita. "She will find a way through this."

"Do you think so?"

"I do." The sound of the digging was getting louder, as the hole deepened, reaching the level where they all lay. "Anyhow, you need to cheer yourself up. You'll be welcoming a new neighbour soon."

By the evening, it was quiet. There were no visitors, the digging was finished, and the others settled in their thoughts. Charlie took the opportunity to absorb what had gone on. Two days ago he'd been somewhere up there, presumably in the funeral director's office, oblivious. Dead to the world. Now here he was, under the ground, over a stream, surrounded by these... souls. Is this real? Is it really real? He flipped his viewpoint so that he could see their gravestones and, in the failing light, read the inscriptions, Rita's, Doc's, Isabel's. They're real all right. Hold on. His eyes went back to The Doc's. He could not contain himself.

"Doc, do you remember yesterday we were talking about birthdays? Seventy-two-seven?" The Doc nodded. "I've just noticed the date of birth on your headstone. Would it have been your eightieth birthday tomorrow?" Creases appeared on The Doc's forehead as he carried out a mental calculation.

"I hadn't thought of that. Yes, I suppose it would have been."

"We should have a birthday party." Doc's expression, initially disbelief, morphed into one of pity.

"Charles," he said, "you are clearly a bundle of energy, and

I'd be the last person to dampen your natural ebullience, but I simply don't believe that will be achievable. Consider the items one would traditionally preface with the word 'birthday'. Card. Cake. Presents. I don't think we are in a position to furnish ourselves with any of those."

"Maybe not. But we should do something to celebrate. You must mark your birthdays somehow." Rita and Isabel had now tuned in.

"No," said The Doc, "we've never thought to."

"Well, how about we start tomorrow? Doc's eightieth. Be here for ten a.m. Come as you are," he said, then remained awake a little longer than the others, lining up the next day's events.

At ten o'clock, celebrations commenced with a chorus of Happy Birthday To You. True, it was a little discordant, and there was some confusion at line three as to whether they were wishing it to dear Doc, dear Dennis, or dear Doctor Dean, but given that the choir members had not sung it (or anything else) for some considerable time, Charlie considered it a success.

"Let's start with Dead or Alive," he said. "No, not a discussion about us… it's a quiz. I'll read out some famous names. Some of them sadly passed away last year, others are still with us - well, with everyone up there. All each of you has to do is to say who is Dead and who is still Alive."

The event was tackled more competitively than Charlie had envisaged, particularly by The Doc, who seemed to believe his medical background empowered him to predict the longevity of luminaries whom he had never examined in person and had last laid eyes on eight years since. Rita was in high spirits and gave a resounding cheer at the news that the (presumed dead) David Attenborough and Mick Jagger were still going strong.

The passing of Bruce Forsyth came as a blow, but she and The Doc were mollified on hearing that he had been deservedly elevated to Sir Bruce in 2011.

"Next," said Charlie 'a question for each of you to answer. What clothes do you wish you'd been buried in and why?" The Birthday Boy insisted that he got to go first.

"You know, Charles, I was buried in a suit, the one that I used to wear when I worked in the surgery. I do like it, and it does confer a certain gravitas. However, I look at you in your modern 'man about town' styling and I am a little envious. I was in my twenties during the Flower Power era and so, as you can imagine, I had an extensive collection of bohemian shirts. I never threw them away, but Mrs Dean disbarred me from ever wearing them. The difficulty with my current attire is that I feel that I am working - which I am in a sense with my research into Dean's Syndrome - but I'd like to be a little less formal now and then." Once the others had given their responses, Charlie moved on, not wishing to lose any of the momentum he had created.

"Game Three," he said. "We've got two vacant plots, one beside Rita, and the one beside me which has been dug out. Someone is on the way. Who would you like it to be?" Isabel came straight in.

"My ex, Mia's dad." Charlie, recalling his first conversation with Isabel, was surprised but his face remained neutral.

"Do you miss him?" he asked.

"God no, it's just so I could be certain that the bastard is dead." She paused, "but then I'd have to put up with him down here, I can't think of anything worse, so forget that."

"Okay," said The Doc. "I'll go with the TV chat show host Michael Parkinson. Down to earth, a skilful interviewer of a wide range of celebrities and politicians. He would have many entertaining anecdotes for us I'm sure."

"Right. I'll go for one of his most famous guests," said Rita. "Billy Connolly, the comedian. I'd love to hear what he'd make of our world."

"Okay, a question again, this time about yourselves," said Charlie. "What is the most satisfying accomplishment of your career?" The Doc butted in.

"Why don't you go first on this occasion, Charles?" Happy to keep it flowing, Charlie agreed.

"I'd say the features that I've done on my shows about mental health. I'm not a great campaigner or an expert, but I did start to highlight it when it was considered off-limits. I had bosses who told me that it would be too depressing to talk about depression. But I persisted and I know it helped people. What about you, Rita?

"Mine is easy too," she said, "though it's a bit of a story."

"It's all right," said Charlie, "we've got time, I don't think any of us has somewhere we need to be."

"I was a couple of years off retirement, 1982 it was, when I heard that the council's Planning Department had approved a proposal to build a ring road around Stanford. I never trusted Planning. Grey men, grey suits, grey shoes. No sense of the history of this place. Sure enough, I found out that the route ran right through the Stanford Estate. It would separate the original manor house from here, St Jude's, the church built by the family for the community all those years ago. I was furious. I tried everything I could to stop it, but the decision had been made."

"So what happened?" asked Charlie.

"They'd been working from the most recent map of the estate but, because of all the research I'd done, I knew there were three earlier versions that had been created over the years. Those early ones were all drawn by hand. So," she hesitated momentarily and drew breath, "what I did was I changed the three previous estate maps. There was already an area on them that belonged to the church, marked as consecrated grounds. I extended it out a bit to cover where we are today."

"I don't understand. Why?" said Charlie.

"Two reasons. Firstly they had to re-route their road round the south side of the church, meaning it didn't split the estate anymore." Doctor Dean stepped in.

"Now hold on, Rita, I presume that you must have had to follow some sort of formal process to affect the changes."

"Oh yes. I formally asked my boss for access to the documents. I formally waited until everyone else had gone home. I formally took my rubber and rubbed out the existing boundary. I formally took a fancy draftsman's pencil belonging to my friend who worked in Architects and I formally drew the new line. Then I formally gave them back to my boss." The Doc's response was a stunned silence.

"You said it meant two things," said Charlie "What's the second?"

"It created this tiny corner in the churchyard with the stream running directly beneath it. I was thinking ahead, I thought it would be nice to be buried here."

"It does seem to me," said Doctor Dean, "that the actions you took were highly irregular. "I'm not saying necessarily that I disapprove, I am sure that we all agree that a good outcome has been achieved but…" Isabel, who had been listening in silence throughout, interjected.

"Do we all agree? How do you know that? Have you ever asked?" The Doc looked flustered.

"No, not specifically but I thought…" Isabel did not allow him to complete his sentence.

"Okay, since we've been asking quiz questions today, here's one for you and Rita. I've been here nearly three years, how much do either of you know about how my illness affected me?" Rita said nothing, leaving it to The Doc.

"Eh, well, you had cancer, which initially appeared to have been successfully treated, but then you had a recurrence and…" Isabel interrupted.

"I didn't ask for my medical history," she said, "I wanted to know if you understood how it affected me." She received no reply. "Let me fill you in. My first cancer treatment was bloody awful. I was so sick, in hospital for months. They didn't think I would survive, and that's a frightening message to hear in your twenties. But I did. I was fine for a few years, then it came back again. You'd maybe think it would be easier to deal with second time, but it was worse. I knew what to expect and how hard it was going to be. And I had a tiny child by then, so I was frantic with worry about her. Somehow I pulled through again, then two years later my cancer returned for the final time. It was right through me, everywhere. There was to be no recovery. Day after day my little girl came to visit, and watched as my life trickled away. It had beat me."

"I'm sorry," said The Doc, "I didn't fully consider how arduous your journey has been."

"You've never asked me. Not properly. For years before I came here I have had my life hanging by a thread, not knowing if I would live or die. I've had my hopes raised and then had them smashed to pieces. Again and again. So sometimes I see things differently. Some days, this thing we have feels like a burden, it's me stuck in limbo again, not alive, not dead, no hope of recovery. Death's waiting room. At those times, I don't think it's such a great thing as you seem to."

Charlie scanned the three faces. He was pretty sure his arrival had been the catalyst for these home truths but, as the new boy, he thought he should stay clear.

"I used to pride myself on my bedside manner," said The Doc, "but it is obvious that I have let my standards slip. For that I sincerely apologise, Isabel. I now appreciate how your experience has given you a different perspective on our situation." Rita, normally combative, was subdued.

"I'm sorry too," she said, "but please don't blame me for what's happened." Her tone bordered on pleading. "How was I to know? I wasn't expecting all this. I just thought it might give me some kind of peace once I'd gone."

"I don't suppose you did," said Isabel, "just bear in mind that everyone might not see things the same way." She paused. "Anyway, I don't know where all of that came from. Some days it gets me down, others I'm fine. I know that we've been thrown in here together, and we need to get along. So, sorry from me too, I didn't mean to spoil your birthday party, Doctor. I've enjoyed today, it's been entertaining, pretty exciting. Come on, Charlie, another game."

"Right," said Charlie. "Have any of you ever been mistaken for someone famous?" The Doc piped up immediately.

"Does anyone mind if I go first?" he asked. "I think you can probably identify that handsome Hollywood leading man that I bear an uncanny resemblance to?" Silence.

"It might help if you give us a small clue, Doc?"

For a further two hours the games continued, until eventually The Doc said he was exhausted.

"I hope you enjoyed it," said Charlie, "sorry there were no presents."

"Actually I did receive a gift today," he replied. "I was given some honest feedback from Isabel."

"I didn't mean to spoil your birthday," Isabel said.

"No, no. You haven't. What you said was both well-intentioned and truthful, and I intend to act upon it accordingly. I have something else that I must say, to you, Charles. I retract my comments of yesterday, when I cast doubt on your plan for today," he said, in a tone more humble than Charlie had heard him use. "We could have a party. We did have a party, and it was the most splendid day I can remember in the Eight of my Seventy-two-Eight. Thank you."

"Ah, no problem, Doc, it's the sort of stuff I did for a living. Trying to bring a little glint of sunshine to proceedings."

"You succeeded. I fully understand why the BBC came calling for you. You are a remarkable chap. Within forty-eight hours of arriving here, with few resources, you organised a successful event that delighted some people that you barely knew. I am convinced that had you lived longer, your stardom would have been assured. I think we would all agree that we are fortunate to have you amongst us. And if I may be so forward, can I suggest we hold a similar event on each one of our birthdays?"

"Of course."

"Mine is next," said Rita, "in June. I'll be ninety-five."

"And," continued The Doc, "if the others are agreeable Charles, I will take up the role of Master of Ceremonies when it's your first birthday with us."

"Oooh, I'd look forward to that, Doc," said Charlie, his mind boggling at the prospect of what might ensue. "When is yours, Isabel?"

"November. The fifth."

"Wow, Bonfire Night – with a bit of luck I might even be able to arrange a few fireworks to go off for you up there."

A quiet calm descended. It was getting close to the time when typically they drifted off into sleep.

"Rita? Are you still awake?" Charlie asked.

"Yes son."

"The Hall you're talking about, the one where that family lived, is it the one on the edge of Stanford, set back in the trees?"

"That's right, just before the bridge."

"I've got some good news for you. About ten years ago the council bought it for a tiny amount, a pound I think, because it was falling apart and they were worried that it would be lost forever. All they've done is shore it up, while they looked for someone to redevelop it."

"And have they found someone?"

"Yes and no. Not for the Hall itself, but do you know the large stable block to the right as you go in?"

"Yes."

"That's the building that Jess is having renovated as a base for her music therapy charity."

"No!"

"Yes. Honestly. At the time I died, it had been completely gutted, and was being repaired and kitted out. It's going to look amazing. The hope is that when it's occupied, there will be interest in the rest of the Hall."

"Oh, Charlie, that's fantastic news."

"Would I be right in thinking," asked The Doc, "that this is one of the best presents you have ever received – and it's not even your birthday?"

"Absolutely. And it'll be a big day for you tomorrow,

Charlie. You'll be getting your new neighbour. Who do you think it might be?"

"I don't know. Parky? Or The Big Yin? As long as it's not Isabel's ex I'll be happy."

*　　*　　*

Dear Journal,

Yesterday I went back up to Charlie's grave. I thought if I don't go now I maybe never will, and I can't live my life pretending that St Jude's does not exist. It seemed quiet after the hubbub of the funeral, but I can't say that I felt at peace.

I met a man and his niece there – his sister, her mum, is in the plot next to Charlie. They were so kind to me. Mia is about fourteen I'd say and is insightful for a young girl. She says they go up there every week, and I've arranged to meet them next Saturday. I enjoyed talking to them. This is going to sound bad. I'm contacting family and friends regularly, but I have to push myself to do it. I get the same feeling from them when they call me. Mick and Mia are like the strangers on a train. It's easier to open up to them about how impossibly hard I'm finding this.

Jess broke off as her phone rang. She looked at the screen. Ray the builder. She picked it up and tapped the green circle.

"Hi, Ray," she said, determined to sound as positive as possible.

"Hiya love," he replied. "How are you doing? I hope the funeral was okay."

"Yes, it was… good, thanks. Everyone who came was very thoughtful. I'm glad you've rung, I'm conscious that I haven't spoken to you for a couple of weeks."

"Don't worry," Ray replied "we've been getting on with the work. We've been trying not to pester you with questions, but we're at the point now where we could do with a few decisions… if that's all right with you. We can wait if you're not ready?"

"No, that's fine. I want to keep things moving forward. Life can't stop for Charlie Munro. Is it best if I come up to The Stables?"

"If you don't mind. I'm here till six."

"I won't be long."

As she turned off the main road and onto the driveway leading to the Hall, Jess got her first surprise.

"Cobbles," she thought. "The drive has been paved with old-fashioned cobbles." She wound her way up and pulled up on the area in front of The Stables.

"Where did those come from?" she said to Ray, pointing at the drive.

"They didn't come from anywhere," he replied. "They were there all along. We found them buried beneath the layer of tarmac and tidied them up. Are they okay? If not we can remove them."

"No, they look great."

"Thought you might say that," he said. "We're following your instructions, retain and repair as many original features as possible." Jess surveyed the exterior of The Stables building.

"God, you've made loads of progress," she said.

"Wait till you see the inside," said Ray, glad to be able to provide Jess with some good news. They entered the first room. "Plastering all done and dry. Joiners in tomorrow for skirtings and doors. These guys will have all of the electric sockets installed this week. Just a few questions for you though."

Ray and Jess moved through the building, pausing long enough in each room for Ray to ask for any information he needed. After an hour, they emerged from the far end of the building into the courtyard. Ray double-checked all of the decisions she'd made, then described where they intended to plant trees and shrubs, where car park spaces would be painted, how the old well was to be restored, confirmed where outdoor seating would be placed, and where the security lighting would be installed. Jess thanked him again, then headed back home.

Dear Journal,

Me again. I have just visited The Stables. While I was there I felt like it gave me a lift. Ray and the guys have done an amazing job. But now that I'm home I feel numb. It's as if I was a visitor, looking at something that wasn't ever my project. I feel like Life is hurtling along, I'm a spectator looking in on it - and nothing looks the same any more. J.J. and Alice came round again last night. I didn't mention this to them. I perked up and smiled for a couple of hours, for their sakes if nothing else.

Chapter 5

The spirit below ground had changed. Charlie knew it within hours of The Doc's birthday party finishing. It had awoken something in the dead. They seemed more… what's the word, he thought… lively? Is that possible? That evening, he listened in as the others babbled about the events of the day, the threads of conversation burning quick and sparky like the cord on a stick of dynamite. Although this was only his third day here, Charlie sensed a new closeness existed between the others. He had no idea where this life-death-life thing was going, but at least for now, he felt okay. From above he heard the distinct loud, long hoot of an owl. Rita broke out from the conversation.

"That's Casper," she said.

"Casper?" Charlie asked. Another hoot echoed through the silence.

"Yes. When Doctor Dean arrived the first thing I had to do was explain to him he hadn't been buried alive. The second was to tell him that the sound he was petrified of wasn't a cemetery ghost come to haunt him." Charlie chuckled.

"I see. Casper, The Friendly Owl."

"Correct."

"It was an understandable mistake to have made," said The Doc. "I had only just arrived and, even for a graveyard owl, he has an uncommonly plaintive call."

"He has, Doc," Charlie agreed. The sun slipped down to hide below the horizon as day began to lose its battle with night. Charlie felt tired. He had slept solidly the previous two nights, better than when alive, but then he had never slept anywhere as dark and quiet as St. Jude's. His eyes were heavy. He felt sure he would sleep right through once again.

When Charlie did awake, it took him a moment to realise why. Blackness everywhere, it certainly was not morning. He thought he might have heard a bang. He listened. It was raining, not a light shower, it was lashing, pummelling the hardwood boards that had been placed over the newly dug grave to his left. Perhaps he'd heard a clap of thunder? He lay awake, listening to the incessant drumming. It sounded familiar. It clicked, he was back there, childhood summers spent in the family's caravan in the Lake District. And then it changed. Though the rain continued to pound down, the drumming sound faded slightly, replaced by a scraping noise, then a dull whoosh. One of the boards had been removed and placed to the side. The sound of rain on board ceased altogether as the second was shifted. There was a distinct thud close to his left. Someone had dropped down into the hole.

Charlie had once asked Radio City listeners what place they would least like to find themselves alone at night. He'd warmed them up with his own choice.

"A multi-story car park," he suggested to Merseyside. "Scary. Those low ceilings, that dim lighting, they're cramped, shady places. If you're watching a T.V. drama or a film and they cut to a night scene in a multi-storey car park, you know that something ugly is about to happen to the good guy." (Following J.J's advice he elected not to mention that, in addition, their stairwells carry the caustic stench of drunkard's piss, biting enough to make your eyes smart and singe the hair out of your nostrils. J.J. could be an excellent filter). The most common answer they received that day, far exceeding any other? A graveyard. In the end, Charlie could only agree. You need a world-class reason to go skulking around a graveyard in the hours of darkness.

It was black out there, blacker than crows' eyes. Charlie didn't know what time it was. Maybe two a.m.? He could not see a thing but he was aware of movement taking place to his left, at his level. Then it began, the rhythmic sound that he had heard yesterday, Tom's spade digging into the soil. Tchick, tchick, tchick. As he lay there in the darkness he could hear the volume increasing, marginally, but surely. Rita was next to stir.

"What's going on?" she whispered to Charlie.

"No idea," Charlie whispered back, without querying the need for secrecy. "He must have come back to finish digging it or something. But in the middle of the night? In this weather?"

Tchick. Tchick. Tchick. Isabel, then The Doc followed in quick succession, the same question, same answer. The sound was getting louder, stronger, with each stroke, particularly for Charlie.

"He's not going deeper," he said. "I think he's coming sideways, towards me. What the hell is this all about?" Before anyone had an opportunity to reply there was a different sound, a thud, and Charlie felt a judder on his left-hand side, as Tom's spade came into contact with his coffin.

"Jesus," he shouted.

"Do you think so?" said Rita. "Come to whisk you off to Heaven? I doubt it's him, son. I think it's more likely that it's the gravedigger." The noise had changed. It was scrabbling, the sound of smaller, more precise movements of the shovel, expanding the channel in the soil. Then it stopped. All four held their breath, held their silence. It was shattered by a thump. Charlie felt an enormous smash onto the side of his wicker casket. Thump, another. His coffin shuddered along its entire length. Thump. Again. And again. Charlie looked down at the point of attack. He could see that the wall of his coffin was now damaged, caved in, a few inches below his waistline. Another smash, and another. The indentation was now a hole. Charlie could sense a movement of damp air and, as he continued to focus on the spot, he saw that torchlight had begun to leak in. Any lingering hopes that this could be a legitimate enterprise were eradicated with another crash. This time, in the light, Charlie caught sight of steely grey metal.

"He's smashing his way into my coffin with a lump hammer!" he shouted to the others.

"Oh my God," said Rita, horrified, aware that Charlie was powerless to halt the onslaught. There was now a distinct, fist-sized hole. The battering around its edges continued, increasing the diameter with every blow. Now the fist could have been inside a boxing glove and still passed through unimpeded. Alongside the crash of the hammer, Charlie picked up something else. It was a voice, spitting out words in a hoarse whisper, one word for every thump. Faint, masked by the blows, he struggled to pick it up. Finally, he got it.

"Dead! Men! Tell! No! Tales!… Dead! Men! Tell! No! Tales!"

Then it stopped. Charlie lay still, fearing for his life in a way he never had when it had still been his to lose. There was an influx of dancing light as a torch shone directly through the jagged entry. And then the light faded once more, its passage interrupted by the dim silhouette of an invading arm. He looked on as the hand fumbled around, feeling for the desired area of his body, like a clumsy adolescent at the back of a cinema. It recognised his elbow, then inched downwards, progressing over his forearm until it arrived at his wrist. Once there, he felt the fingers move round to the inside of his wrist, the place where, up until a few weeks ago, his pulse had resided. They found the clasp on his watch strap, flicked it open, then with a deft pull, stretched it down over his cold, stiff hand. The arm retreated and disappeared through the hole in the coffin wall that it had created.

"He's got my watch," Charlie told the others. "Unclipped it from my wrist and taken it out."

"Foul play!" shouted the Doc, as if he had been pickpocketed on the streets of Victorian London and was seeking to attract the attention of the neighbourhood bobby. "Outrageous. Theft, pure and simple."

Tchick. Tchick. Tchick. The soil that had been dug away to form an access route between the neighbouring plot and Charlie's grave was now being replaced.

"He's covering up everything he's done," said Charlie. "No one will ever be able to tell that this has happened." The sounds became more distant with each passing minute, as the casing of earth around Charlie's coffin became complete once more. The boards were dropped back into place, and the drumming of the rain resumed, but there was no other sound. He had gone, seeped away into the dank night.

There was a stunned silence amongst the four.

"I do not yet understand why it is that we have to sleep," said The Doc, "but on this of all nights, I think it is wise that we do. Let's try to get our heads down and assess these events in the morning."

Part Two : TRUTH

"Truth is like the sun. You can shut it out for a time, but it ain't goin' away."

Elvis Presley

Chapter 6

Of one thing Charlie was certain. The Law had been broken the previous night. Precisely *which* law had been pulverised into smithereens with a lump hammer, well, here he was less sure. On his radio show, he had once interviewed a chirpy young Q.C. called Carson Bryce. Carson's knowledge of The Law was exhaustive. Charlie had done his best to keep up as he'd explained the differences between Theft, Robbery, and Burglary. The Law, it became apparent, is Complex. And Packed Full Of Capital Letters. What's more, it's all-encompassing. To illustrate its span, Carson went on to inform Charlie and his audience that it is illegal to gamble in a public library, to cause a nuclear explosion, or to allow your pet to mate with a pet from the royal household.

"Well," Charlie told Merseyside, 'if this means you have to revise your plans for the coming weekend… I suggest you seek help, urgently.'' The Law, it appeared, was Quite Old and Quite Mad in places.

Although Carson had not specifically mentioned the act of taking stuff from a dead person, Charlie was certain it must have violated some clause of some act or other. As he lay in his battered coffin the following morning, his best guess was that he had probably been the victim of a Domestic Burglary. This occurs, Carson had explained, when an offender enters any building where people live (including caravans and boats) intending to steal. But hold on… suppose you are already dead, can you be considered to be living anywhere? In the absence of his expert legal advisor, Charlie owned up to himself that he did not know. The Law is Perplexing and can be Terribly Specific on such matters.

Despite The Doc's exhortations to sleep, no one (The Doc included) had managed as much as to ease down from furious boil to gentle simmer, far less shut the gas off. By six o'clock it was daylight once more, and the debriefing was underway. Charlie remained on the fringes, listening as the others expressed unanimous outrage at this shocking intrusion into their hitherto peaceful world. Isabel was first to note Charlie's limited contribution.

"Charlie, you're quiet. How are you feeling?"

"Mixed up. Stunned. Upset. Furious. But most of all, I feel helpless. That watch belonged to Jess's Grandad Joe. He had it most of his life. When he died and I found out he'd chosen to leave it to me, I… well, honestly, I melted. It's not right that anyone should go against his wishes and take it away."

"It's terrible," Isabel agreed. "I do sort of get how you must feel. Do you remember the first day you came here, when you asked me about Mia's dad?"

"Oh yeah, him. The waster. Didn't want to know when you got pregnant. Mick warned you about him but you didn't listen. Eventually he cleared off and never came back."

"What I actually said was that I never saw him again. He did come back, worse luck. When I was taken into hospital the second time he got wind of it. Mick was looking after Mia at his place, so my house was empty. He still had a key, came back and cleaned me out."

"What? You mean he sneaked in and stole your valuables?"

"Valuables? I'd none of those. Essentials, more like. Microwave, clothes, every stick of furniture. Took the lot and sold it. I came out of hospital to a house that was an empty shell."

"What a despicable thing to do," said The Doc. "I am so sorry, Isabel."

"Mick was so good. He helped me get back onto my feet - and never once did he say I told you so."

"God, it puts my problem into perspective," said Charlie. "I've only lost Grandad Joe's old watch. I don't get why he would have gone to all that effort to get it. In all honesty, I'd have thought the puncture repair kit was worth more."

"Makes me glad they only buried me with a jumbo crossword puzzle book," said Rita. "He's welcome to take that, I don't even like them. Hey, Charlie, maybe it was valuable. Do you know where Jess's grandad got it?"

"Not exactly. Only that he'd come by it during the Second World War from somebody he fought beside. That was all he said when I asked. Grandad Joe would talk forever, especially if I got him onto music. But when it came to his time as a soldier, there was always some diversion tactic - he'd change the subject, hear an imaginary doorbell, make an urgent toilet visit, any excuse. I know he was stationed all over the place. I've always thought he might have got it from somebody in the Indian Army because I know that he fought alongside them. And because of the maker - it was Patel I think. I can't believe it was worth much."

The Doc gave one of his ahems. Since arriving, Charlie had been observing these and, like a naturalist studying primate vocalisations, he could now decipher individual calls. This was a warning ahem.

"I am not sure about that, Charles," he said. "I hope you do not think me intrusive, but I did notice your watch before it was so rudely - and unlawfully - removed from your person."

"Did you?" asked Charlie, surprised.

"Yes. I always believed that part of my success in General Practice stemmed from the holistic approach that I took to the examination of my patients. Most were overly hasty to display whatever was troubling them, a boil or bunion, or on one ghastly occasion, an unsolicited stool, conveyed to the surgery in a plastic lunchbox. I augmented their narrative with my personal observations of how they presented in my consultation room. Poverty and poor health are, unfortunately, common bedfellows. A down-at-heel shoe or frayed collar can often be more instructive as to a patient's well-being than any suppurating sore. Old habits die hard, and although I am no horologist, when I spotted your watch I thought it to be a handsome timepiece. One of some quality… and ergo… value."

"So it might have been worth serious money, Doc?" The Doc considered before answering.

"I did not want to intrude into your personal circumstances, Charles, but when I saw it, I assumed that your fame had occasioned an associated fortune. For that, I believe, is what would be required to purchase such a piece." Charlie felt sick.

"It's a disaster. I could have left it for Jess - I did I suppose, but we all thought that the only value it had was sentimental. If you're right it could have solved the missing pension problem…" The sound of footsteps from above halted the discussion. Someone was approaching the plot. It was the young gravedigger again.

"The old adage," said Rita, her large face heavy with indignation, "criminals always return to the scene of the crime." Once more the two boards were laid to the side. Then, wielding his shovel, he began to fill in the grave next to Charlie, the one which he had spent hours digging the day before, but into which no body had been interred.

"Oh my God," Rita continued, "do you see what he's doing? He is completely covering his tracks. No one will know what happened last night."

"This is flagrant," said The Doc. "I expected that there would at least be an associated funeral, an attempt to confer some legitimacy to this skullduggery. The whole enterprise has been a complete charade." They watched as Bennett carried on, the pile of soil shrinking in height, the base of the hole rising towards it, until finally they met and that patch of St. Jude's consecrated ground was level once more. Placing his tools in the wheelbarrow, he moved off back in the direction of his shed. It was as if it had never happened. Charlie spoke, his voice a stunned monotone.

"Gone. Grandad Joe's watch, gone without a trace. I have to say he may well have committed the perfect crime. And I'm stuck down here. Can't dial 999. How the hell would anybody ever know it had happened?" All fell silent, feeling Charlie's frustration and pain. Only Isabel spoke, and then with hesitation.

"I might know something you could try," she said. She sighed, then continued in reticent fragments. "I've never mentioned this before… I was sure you'd think I'd cracked… I'm reluctant to say, but when I see what's happened to you, Charlie…"

"Come on," said Rita "If you think you can help, you should do. You said it yourself yesterday, we've been thrown together here, we must do our best to look after each other."

"Okay," said Isabel, steeling herself. "Think back to when I first came down here. Mick would bring Mia along to the graveside, my little girl, so lost and so upset. She couldn't understand what had happened and just wanted her mum." Isabel's voice quavered. "I'm sorry, but it brings it back. The third time Mia visited, she was sobbing so hard she was shaking, Mick couldn't calm her down and I couldn't stand it anymore. I needed to get to her somehow, to soothe her." Isabel paused, and assessed the three faces before her, then took the final step. "I wished, harder than I'd ever wished for anything and… I swear I left this grave and found myself somehow up inside my little girl's head." She stopped, waiting for a reaction, adverse or otherwise.

The Doc cleared his throat. Supportive ahem, thought Charlie. "Can you describe in a little more detail what happened?" he asked. Isabel replied at a pace that showed she had unburdened a weighty secret.

"I can try, Doctor, but it's not like any feeling I ever had when I was alive. It was like I was in her mind, right at the heart of what she is. And I just tried to hush her and tell her everything would be alright. I can't say for sure how long it lasted, I would guess half an hour. Then I was back here, exhausted." She slumped momentarily, reliving the sensation. "But ever since that day I've thought Mia was so much calmer, better able to cope."

"Do you know, I did notice a change in her," said Rita, "but thought something must just have clicked inside her head."

"It did, but it was me that clicked it," said Isabel, now speaking in the enthusiastic tone of someone being believed. "Here's another thing. I've tried to do it again, get back to her… I couldn't make it happen. It's as if I was able to do it once and that's it."

"Well," said The Doc, "this is a remarkable moment in our understanding of Dean's Syndrome. We have considered communication with those we left behind to be a one-way street, from them to us. If this is confirmed to be the case, it opens up a whole new set of possibilities. With your permission, I would like to have a more thorough debrief in good time, but that is for another day. Now we must focus on how this might assist Charles in his predicament."

"I thought that maybe Charlie could do the same thing with Jess," said Isabel, "you know, try to tell her about the robbery and the watch. It might not work but I thought maybe you could have a go?" Doctor Dean shook his head slowly.

"I must say, instinctively, as a clinician, I am dubious. This business of entering the head of another, it seems like an option that carries much risk. The human mind is both complex and fragile. Of course, I am as disgusted as any of us at this despicable crime but..." Isabel interrupted.

"Yes, but being disgusted won't get Charlie his watch back, Doctor. Have you got any better ideas? Any other ideas at all?" The Doc was stilled.

"I have to confess," he eventually admitted, "I have not. It is a matter for Charles to decide if he wishes to try this unproven procedure." Charlie had listened agog.

"Try? Try stopping me. Five days until Saturday, Jess told Mick that she would meet them then. That's when I'll give it a go. I can't thank you enough, Isabel."

Charlie had another troubled night. Not due to any unwanted visitors - there were no thieves in the night, no smash and grab. His turmoil came from within. When Isabel had introduced the possibility yesterday he'd jumped at it, certain it was the right thing to do, but having slept on it, or rather having stayed awake and stewed over it, he was wavering. As soon as Isabel was awake he spoke to her.

"Isabel, can I ask you something?"

"About Jess?"

"Yes. That thing with Mia you described, it was spontaneous. It happened before you knew it."

"Yes."

"It's different for me. I'm consciously deciding to do it... and I don't know if it's right."

"How do you mean?"

"I know she is - was – my wife but, you know, to go poking around in someone's head, is that an okay thing to do? Find out their deepest secrets, their darkest thoughts, their past indiscretions... even if I was only to find out why she never wore that jumper I bought her last Christmas. It's her private stuff. Shouldn't she be allowed to keep it that way? I mean, would you like to have someone roaming around in your mind?"

"Charlie, it wasn't like that. I didn't see any of those things. It was more as if we were close for a moment, like in the old days, when I was alive. We were with one another. You need to weigh it up, but I think it's your only chance to do something that might make a difference." Charlie nodded.

"I didn't want to do something that's wrong. Thanks, I feel better about it now. And you are right, it's all I've got."

* * *

Dear Journal,

I feel embarrassed writing this down, but I promised I would be honest with you. Yesterday evening at bedtime, I contemplated taking some blankets and going to sleep on Charlie's grave at St. Jude's - like some kind of human version of Greyfriars Bobby. I miss him so much. I wanted to be with him, feel what he was feeling. Thank god I stopped myself. As a compromise, I've decided that from now on I'll walk down to the cemetery to see Charlie, whatever the weather. It only takes half an hour and the exercise and fresh air will do me good. Charlie is out there in all conditions, so it'll make me more closely tuned in to whatever he's experiencing.

As she approached the church the next day, Jess saw Mick pulling onto the car park. She watched as the two got out. Mia spotted her and waved. Seeing that they were waiting for her, she speeded up slightly.

"Hi," said Mia, "Are you okay today?"

"I'm fine," Jess replied. "Thanks for coming to meet me." Mia smiled. The three stood by the car ostensibly catching up on the events of the week. In reality, Jess could tell that they were trying to establish how well she was coping. She detected that their inquiries were pre-planned, and although their questioning was clumsy at times, she was touched to think that they cared for her, someone that they barely knew.

At the far end of the graveyard, oblivious to this conversation, Charlie was more nervous than he had been for years.

"It's like going on my first date with her all over again," he said. "Suppose she doesn't show up?"

"She will," said Rita. The group tried to occupy him with small talk. To no avail. He may no longer have had a timepiece, but Charlie knew she was late.

"She's always on time," he said, shaking his head. "Always. Suppose she's forgotten me already?" Mercifully, Mick and Mia's car park clinic had drawn to a close.

"Shall we go in?" said Mick. He pulled the large iron gate open and stepped to the side, allowing Jess and Mia to enter. As they walked down the hill, their conversation continued until all three were stationed on the bench. True to her promise of the previous week, Jess gave them an outline of her financial predicament, and how it had led to her decision to move house.

"I've thought about the advice you gave me," Jess said to Mick. "I think you're right, I've not put the house up for sale just yet. I think I could do with some stability rather than more upheaval." Mick nodded, then thinking it best not to dwell on the subject, he moved the conversation along.

"I see your husband's new neighbour has arrived," he said, indicating towards the plot beside Charlie. Jess had already noticed the mound of raised earth to the right of Charlie's grave.

"Yes, it's filling up around here, must be the latest up-and-coming area in Stanford." All three surveyed the scene before them.

"Have you noticed anything strange about it though?" asked Mia. Jess and Mick looked again.

"No, what?" said Mick.

"I know we couldn't put mum's gravestone up straight away because you have to leave the ground to settle for a few months, but look, there is nothing at all here. No flowers, no sympathy cards or messages. Nothing." They looked again.

"Oh yes, you're right," said Jess.

"I've seen lots of new graves since I've been coming here to be with mum. All of them have had something on them. But this person doesn't."

"No mementos. That is odd" Mick agreed.

"Do you think it could be a pauper's grave?" asked Mia. "We got told about them at school. They were common in the olden days but they can still happen. It's where a person has no family or they have no money at all and so they're buried in the ground without any proper marker. I think it's tragic.

No one should be forgotten like that, just because they have no money. It made me sad for them." Mick and Jess stared at the empty space in a way that led Mia to surmise that it made them feel sad too.

"Uncle Mick, if that is what has happened, do you think I could do some sponsored events to raise some money? Not for a big headstone, I know they are expensive. Maybe a little cross made of wood, something with their name on it, so that they will be remembered. Jess squeezed Mia's arm.

"That's so kind," she said. She stopped and thought. "Have you ever heard of something called match funding?" she asked. Mia shook her head.

"It's an important part of how I set my charity up. I agreed to raise money and the government said whatever I managed to collect they would add the same amount in. The council too. It's a way of sharing the costs around. It could be that a wooden cross with a little plaque on it is still quite expensive so I think that if you were to raise, say fifty pounds, I could chip in the same." Given the conversation they'd just had, Mick stepped in quickly.

"I'll go halves with you on that, Jess. Between the three of us I'm sure we could get something." Then he held his hand up, in an old-fashioned policeman's 'Halt!' gesture. "But before we get ahead of ourselves, first let me speak to the church. We would need to get agreement from the person's next of kin. Meanwhile, let's go for that coffee and hot chocolate. Come on, Mia, let's give Jess a little time on her own, we'll wait for her by the car." Jess looked at Mick and smiled thank you, as he and Mia headed back up the slope. Charlie's moment had arrived.

"Any last-minute things I can do to prepare?" he asked Isabel.

"No. It just happened. Like I said to you, Charlie, it was sort of unconscious. I don't think you could do it by brute force."

Jess was now looking down at Charlie's grave. A small card from a bouquet had found its way there, blown from a nearby plot. Charlie tensed his frame, concentrated as hard as he could on the figure before him, closed his eyes, then held his breath.

Nothing. He held his rigid posture for another five seconds. Then five more. He opened his eyes. Jess bent down and picked up the card. She read the message, then walked over to replaced it beside the flowers, before returning to the bench. Charlie cursed. It hadn't worked, it hadn't even nearly worked. Worry flooded through his mind; Charlie upgraded it to panic. Maybe Isabel was wrong, maybe she had seen Mia's mood improve and assumed she must have influenced her daughter. Worse. Maybe Isabel was right, that this was possible, but that he, Charlie, simply wasn't up to the task.

"Isabel."

"Yes?"

"Nothing happened. I'm still here. It's gone wrong. I didn't go anywhere." Isabel could hear the anguish in his voice. Jess picked up her bag from the bench and set off to the left, taking the long way round to the cemetery gate.

* * *

The Secretary of State for Health sat at his stout wooden desk in his stout wooden office in Whitehall. He looked at the message before him, titled 'Essential Departmental Budgetary Realignment'. He never thought the day would come, but he wished he could swap places with Hector Carmichael. Easy for Carmichael over in Defence. All he had to do is tear up that foolish multi-million-pound contract he'd signed for those revolutionary new helicopters, the ones that it was bloody obvious to everyone were destined never to fly. Cancel the contract, make the savings, bury the cock up. Win-Win-Win. Before you know it he'd be Lord Hector Carmichael, snoozing away lazy afternoons in the other place. He opened his laptop and began to type.

In less than ten minutes he had drafted the email. He reread it. Rather good, he surmised. Not the most positive message obviously, but I've managed to suitably contextualise the situation, to sympathise and, most importantly, to emphasise the non-negotiable imperative of meeting the challenge. He clicked Send, closed the lid on his laptop, and headed off to his home in the Hampshire countryside for a well-deserved long weekend. It was Wednesday after all, and it had been a difficult and demanding week.

His well-crafted words were greeted with indignant fury in offices up and down Whitehall. How the bloody hell are we going to save that amount? So what that Culture and the Arts have got much bigger cuts to make in percentage terms? How the hell does that help us? The Heads of Departments who received the message knew the correct approach to adopt in such circumstances. The email was duly forwarded on to those managers whom they managed, so bequeathing the headache to those further down the ladder. After several iterations of this tried and tested process, a proportion of the problem ended up on the considerably less wooden, rather more vinyl-coated plyboard, desk of Colin Stones, down on the bottom rung.

Colin's eyes scanned down the top page of the bundle he had collected from the printer, a list of all of the charitable health projects in North West England to which the government was providing direct support. It would require a skilled balancing act to make reductions on this scale whilst minimising the impact on the public, but his boss had instilled one guiding principle to be followed in such situations. He must be ruthless. Colin knew this was the case. He had been promoted into his current role because the chap who was his predecessor was so lacking in this quality that he had earned the nickname Ruth. Poor old Ruth, leaving the organisation today by mutual agreement, to allow him to explore alternative career opportunities. Opportunities currently on display on small hand-written cards in the Job Centre window.

The fact that neither Colin, his extended family, or indeed anyone that he had met, had ever required to seek support from the types of organisations on the list could have been construed as a disadvantage. In his mind, it meant that he could address the task without prejudice. The first pass was simple and surprisingly fruitful. Anything that referred to Drugs or Alcohol was gone, the responsibility thereby shifting from the nanny state to the individual. Stop getting pissed and stoned. On the next run-through, he targeted anything to do with diet or obesity. Similar principle, up to those chubsters to make healthier lifestyle choices. He tallied up the pointless spending now avoided and worked it out as a percentage of the overall budget. He was close but hadn't quite achieved the required figure. He would have to be a little more ruthless. In practice, this meant scanning down the list and picking off anything that he didn't much like the look of, anything that sounded a bit airy-fairy. He gave his watch an anxious glance. This was a time-bound project.

Music Therapy. What sort of bull was that then? The accompanying descriptive phrase said something about it being used to help people's mental health. Isn't that what all those anti-depressants are for? They've got to be cheaper than guitars and trumpets.

"Col, are you coming?" His colleague, Tony, had appeared through the door. "C'mon, Ruth's leaving do in The Greyhound. He's getting them in." Time was almost up. Colin looked down at the list. He picked up his pen, and scored through the row, before thrusting the bundle of paper into the top drawer of his desk and striding out in pursuit of Tony and several pints of piss-poor lager. So it was that without reference to the one hundred and thirty-page business case, or to the two-page executive summary, or the current status of the project, or to anything else at all, the crucial central government element of the funding for Jess's project was gone. One casual stroke of a ten pence biro pen and Jess's dreams hung in tatters; rags and polythene on a barbed-wire fence of faceless government targets.

*   *   *

"Jess, it's James, from the council."

"Hi, James." James had spoken to Jess only once since Charlie had died, to pass on his condolences. And now he had to do this to her.

"I've got some really bad news," he said. There was no response. "The Department for Health is backing out of The Stables project." Jess had no idea what to say.

"You're kidding," she replied eventually, knowing that no one, not even the persistent guy from open-mic comedy night at The Bell, had a sense of humour this grim. "How much have they withdrawn?" she asked.

"All of their share. Everything."

"But we're so close to finishing. It doesn't make any sense. Have they said why?"

"Essential Departmental Budget Realignment it says. It's complete madness."

"This can't be right, there must be a way to challenge the decision."

"Sorry, there isn't. I wanted to speak to you first, but I'll forward the message to you now. It says 'There is no appeal process. Please do not reply to this email'."

"Oh my god. What does it mean?" They both knew that they both knew.

"I've already asked around the council, begged people, right up to the Chief Exec, but there is no way that the authority will be able to plug a gap of this size, not until the next financial year. Probably not then either. We have to stop spending immediately. I'm really sorry."

"What about Ray?"

"Well, that's my next call. It's a mess. He's been working at risk throughout this because we've told him that the government money will be coming any day. He is going to be massively out of pocket. I need to stop him right away. I'm dreading speaking to him."

Jess was dreading it too, but she did not have long to wait. Within five minutes her phone rang. She could tell from his voice he was upset.

"I'm at the Hall now," he said, "can you meet me here?"

"I'll be there as soon as I can."

The scene on arriving was devastating. Instead of Ray's team working to convert the old buildings for their new lease of life, they were loading materials, plant, and equipment onto wagons and trailers, salvaging what they could for his business.

"I'm so sorry," Ray said to her, aware of how painful this was for Jess. "I just can't finish it, not without the money."

"I understand," she replied "It's not your fault, none of it.

114

You've been fantastic throughout. I've loved working with you." Ray gave a smile of appreciation.

"Look," he said, "we'll leave the site as organised as we possibly can. If there's a change of heart, get in touch with me immediately. I promise I'll drop everything to get this finished."

"Thanks so much," she replied, "but I don't think there will be a change of heart. For a heart to change you need to have one there in the first place."

Downcast, Ray made his way into The Stables building where the painter was busy navigating his small brush precisely around the frame of a door.

"I'm sorry," he said, "when you finish this room you're going to have to stop."

"Eh?" As Ray explained the situation, the painter became visibly upset.

"Jeez. What a shame for the lady," he said. "She used to do a session in the hospice my dad was in at the end. It was the highlight of his week, gave him something normal to talk about. It was a good thing that she was trying to set up here."

"I know. I'm gutted." Ray carried on through the remainder of the rooms, giving a similar message to each of the tradesmen working there, before heading back outside. "At least we haven't tarmacked the car park," he thought. "That would be twenty grand I'd never see again."

"Brian, could you just help Dave put the last few blocks up so that we've finished restoring that stretch of wall, then call it a day."

"Will do." Brian picked up his trowel and bucket and walked across the courtyard, shocked and disappointed.

"Okay," he said to Dave, "what do you want me to do?" With his head thrown by this sudden change, he completely forgot that he had blocked off the stream at the base of the old well to allow him to replace some of the bricks that had become dislodged from the bottom section of its circular wall.

*   *   *

If any of the small army of men so busy stopping work at The Stables had looked west, beyond the two fields to the left, they would have seen a lone individual labouring harder than any man should. The farmer sploshed and squelched across his waterlogged terrain, hauling behind him a heavy-duty hose of the weight and girth used for refuelling ocean-going tankers. His feet slipped occasionally under the load as he progressed towards a deep drainage ditch at the far side. Exhausted, he summoned a final effort and threw the end into the trench, before turning and retracing his sodden steps. There was a belch of smoke and a stench of diesel as he fired up the rusting yellow generator and it shuddered into life. The hose inflated from flat to circular, turgid with muddy water that it was there to remove.

Alan looked back across the field. He was no King Canute. Given the scale of the problem this intervention was bordering on useless, but it was all he had. And the rain came on again. He climbed back into the cab of his tractor and headed towards the farmhouse. Entering the porch, he kicked off his boots and hung up his coat and hat. Water ran from them onto the stone floor as he made his way through to the kitchen. At the stove, Ann was heating soup for lunch.

"Any better?" she asked. He could not lie.

"No, worse," he said. As she turned towards him, pan in hand, he noticed the bulge of her belly. It had definitely grown since last week. He took his place at the scarred wooden table. What a world to bring a child into.

Dear Journal,

I can hardly bring myself to pick up my pen today. But if I can't find the courage to write about this then there is no point in writing about anything. Today I found out that my dream of setting up my music therapy unit in The Stables has been wiped out. It wasn't just my dream. Charlie shared it with me. And he has been taken from me too. They say these things come in threes. Well if so, take me next, because I don't know how much more of this I can stand.

Chapter 7

The small weathered notice, attached by rusting pins to the side door of St Jude's Church, has been there for over twenty years. It announces in rain-smudged, hand-written block capitals that on Tuesday and Thursday mornings, between the hours of nine and twelve, Mrs Edith Harkness will be present in the vestry to answer any queries you might have regarding the church (including churchyard). At nine-fifteen on Tuesday, Mick - being a man with such a query - entered the church, and made his way to the vestry at the far end of the building. As he neared the door, which was slightly ajar, a female voice barked from within.

"Who's that?" Convinced that it would be easier to introduce himself whilst in the same room, Mick carried on a few more steps and entered.

"Hello," he said, "my name is Michael Williams. He was addressing an elderly lady in a matching skirt and jacket, tailored from a fearsomely jagged fabric. She was sitting on a rickety wooden chair behind a sturdy wooden desk. She did not speak. She stared.

"Is it Mrs Harkness?" Mick asked. Silent as the bare stone walls, the lady declined to divulge any of her Personal Data to a stranger with such abandon. Instead, she continued to monitor his oscillating stance, as he shifted his weight awkwardly between his good leg and bad. Finally, she eased her grip on the drawstring that held tight her pursed lips.

"How can I help you?" she snapped.

"I'd like to ask about one of the grave plots," said Mick. Mrs Harkness softened a little. She liked graves and accordingly, liked grave-related conversations. She opened the lower drawer of her desk and pulled forth a thick, bottle-green notebook. As she did so Mick, having never visited a vestry before, scrutinised the room. Dusty and dismal, there was nothing within it that looked or smelled as if it could have been introduced in this century. His roving gaze stopped on an extraordinary painting on the left-hand wall. Having laid the ledger on her desk, Mrs Harkness traced his stare.

"I painted that," she said.

"Really," said Mick. He studied the small picture of Jesus more closely. An arc of small yellow lightning bolts danced haphazardly around his oddly-shaped head. He was presumably meant to be giving a blessing, but the fingers on both of his hands were contorted in the manner of a New York street gang member, perhaps giving the symbol for a handgun, a warning that he intended to pop a cap in yo ass. Notoriously difficult, are hands.

"It's very good," said Mick.

"I'm not a professional," said Edith, "I did one year of an art course for retired people. Then the council stopped providing it for free, so I gave it up."

"How frustrating, when it was going so well," said Mick. "Mrs Harkness, I don't want to take up too much of your time, I just wondered if you could tell me who was buried in the plot in the bottom left corner of the graveyard last week?"

Edith scowled, backsliding to her original brusque tone. "No one," she replied. Not being a deeply religious man, Mick feared he may have breached a little-known eleventh commandment; Thou Shalt Not Begat False Information About Graves. "No one was buried there or anywhere else in

St Jude's last week."

"Are you sure?" said Mick before, not without some trepidation, going on to describe the timing and location of what had happened.

"Utter rubbish. Of course I'm sure," she said, opening her timeworn book immediately at the correct page. "You are mistaken. Plot E76 is unoccupied." Mick tilted his head, as if attempting to comprehend the bewildering columns of information, recorded in a spidery, old-fashioned hand. He did his best to feign surprise that the official records may be flawed.

"Well, I'm sure it was dug out and filled back in. I wonder why? Perhaps the intended occupant improved?" Today's next lesson was that burial was not a subject to be treated with any levity.

"What? Like Lazarus of Bethany? Don't be absurd. No such thing will be possible until the Second Coming of Our Lord," said Mrs Harkness, pointing at her wall-mounted likeness of The Saviour for emphasis. "I monitor this graveyard precisely. I have to, it's filling up. In case you hadn't noticed, the dead, they don't go anywhere. Those plots are the next ones that will be used. Tom Bennett, that's the gravedigger, he knows that, but he will not dig them without my say-so, unless he's a bigger fool than I think he is."

"Honestly," said Mick, "If you would like to walk down with me I'll show you what I mean."

"I beg your pardon? Me, walk all the way down to that far corner? Don't be ridiculous. I'll never get down that slope. And if I did I could never get back up it. You'll have me in Plot E76." She folded her arms. "There have been no interments at all in St Jude's last week and that is that. If there had been I would know about it. I maintain the records on behalf of the diocese. Any such activities can only be undertaken with my prior authorisation. All parties are well aware of that." I bet they are, thought Mick. This line of inquiry was going nowhere.

"You're right, I must have been mistaken. So sorry to have troubled you." At his outright capitulation, Edith softened her tone.

"Yes, well, if you have any other queries, you can contact me. I have all of the information at my fingertips," she added, with an arthritic flourish of her gnarled digits across the pages of her notebook.

As he emerged into the sunlit churchyard, Mick heard the squeak of the cemetery gate and watched as the young gravedigger entered. Seeing Mick, he stopped and stepped to the side to allow him to pass.

"Thanks," said Mick, before halting beside him. "I wonder if you can help me… it's Tom, isn't it? Tom Bennett?" He looked at Mick, confounded that this stranger knew his name.

"Yes," he replied.

"I've just been speaking to a lady from the church, Mrs Harkness, about the plot down in the corner." Bennett's blink rate went wild, as if Mick had launched a handful of coarse-grained sand into his face.

"What about it?" Drawbridge up, portcullis down. To an old cop, that defensive edge in his voice spoke unambiguously. You are hiding something, my young friend. Mick followed up, no change to his affable tone.

"I noticed it had been dug and refilled last week, but she thought it was unused." Tom looked down at his muddy gravedigger's boots and, addressing them rather than Mick, he replied in a low, lame murmur.

"It's not used. It was a mistake. I dug it out by mistake, so then I had to fill it back in. As Tom's head remained bowed, Mick carried on, addressing the shapeless tangle of murky blond hair.

"Oh, I see. I wondered if the person had any family. If not then we thought maybe we could have helped to tend the plot." Tom raised his head. Edgy eyes met Mick's.

"There's nobody in there. There's nothing down there. Just the soil that's all. It was a mistake, that's all." Mick nodded.

"Right, I see," he said. "I'd best get going. I expect you've plenty to do, looking after all of this," he said, indicating towards the various boundaries. He carried on and exited into the car park, certain that the young man's gaze would be tracking his uneven gait until he disappeared from view.

* * *

Charlie was not himself. Although the others had only recently come to know him, they could sense it. Their assessment was correct. Following his unsuccessful attempt to commune with Jess, he had been subdued, steeped in thought, rattled by his failure. Why had it not worked for him? Had it really worked for Isabel? She believed she was only allowed one go at it – had he blown his single chance? By the following Saturday, a week of brooding took him precisely back to where he had been seven days before.

"Isabel, when Jess comes later this morning, I've decided I'm going to try again. I've nothing to lose." Isabel nodded, but it was The Doc who responded.

"Charles, do you think it would be beneficial if I were to deliver a tutorial on how I might approach penetrating the human brain?" Isabel rolled her eyes, knowing this would end only one way. Waffle, failure, and Charlie moping for another week. She answered on his behalf.

122

"No, I don't, Doctor," said Isabel. "Charlie, I can tell you have been fretting about this all week. I think you're going about it the wrong way. To be able to make this journey…" She stopped, thinking how best to explain. "It's not like you need to learn to drive to get there, learn about steering wheels and clutches, mirrors and gears and signs and stopping distances. You'll never do it that way. You need to sense it, in here," she said, pressing her small clenched fist to her heart. As she spoke, Isabel studied Charlie's face, watched as it eased, his jaw unclench, his brow unfurrow. "That's it," she said. "No one needs to say anymore, least of all you. Calm down, shut up and think what you'd like to say to your wife. And feel it in here." Charlie heard her passion. He was convinced. She had done this before, it was plain. And she wanted him to do it too.

"Thank you, Isabel. Calm down, shut up, think what to say. That is exactly what I'm going to do."

The bearer of bad news. It's not a tag anyone wants to have attached to them thought Jess, as she walked through the graveyard towards the bench where Mick and Mia were sitting. So, should she mention her funding issue to them? Husband dead, personal finances trashed, now this… but then, they had been interested in her work. If it crops up I will tell them she decided.

"Hi. Had a good week?" asked Mick. "Back into the swing of things at work?" It's cropped up.

"It's not been great," Jess replied. "Right out of the blue, the government has pulled their part of the funding for my charity." She outlined events and the implications for The Stables, keeping her language and tone as cheerful as she could manage. The disconnect between the content of the message and its buoyant delivery puzzled Mia. She needed to understand.

"Does this mean you haven't got a job anymore?" she asked, her eyes filling, shining like swollen raindrops on glass.

"No, don't worry, I've still got a job. I'll carry on working through the health service. It just puts the charity on hold temporarily." Mia looked a little relieved.

"Will the boy whose hand got caught in the car door still get to learn to play the recorder?"

"Absolutely!" said Jess. "All of the patients I've told you about will still be treated. I'll make sure they are." Mick had spotted his niece's unease, He thought he understood Jess's response but wanted to be sure.

"Jess, Mia has made you some biscuits." He held his car keys out towards his niece. "I know you were going to give them to Jess to take home but why don't we all have one now?"

"Okay," she said, taking the keys and heading off up the path. He watched her progress and when he was happy she was out of earshot he spoke to Jess in a low tone.

"It sounds bad," he said.

"It's dire," she replied. "I didn't want to upset Mia. There are a few avenues I can explore to make up the shortfall, but realistically the institute is done for. What I said at the end was true though - at least I do still have a job."

"What a shame, you were so close," he said. "Speaking of close." He nodded towards the gate, where Mia had reappeared, carrying a small plastic container.

As she heard the story unfold above, Isabel was sure that the inner calm she had managed to foster in Charlie would disappear. She looked on as he listened, as he took in the gravity of the situation, yet remained composed. The worse the news, the higher the stakes, the more serene he became. Charlie steadied himself. He allowed chocolate chip cookies to be consumed and conversations to finish.

"Come on," said Mick to his niece. "You know the drill, let's give Jess five minutes on her own."

"I hope she won't be on her own for long," thought Charlie. He slowed his breathing. Above him, Jess was standing still, head bowed at the foot of his grave. He looked at her and thought about the times when they had sat at home alone, the two of them, sometimes not exchanging a word for hours, just being together, as one. He closed his eyes once more, this time much more gently.

Whoosh.

One of many things that Charlie loved about working in the Radio City Tower was the final leg of his journey to work. The lift. Four hundred and fifty feet skyward in less than thirty seconds. He had no idea what that meant in miles per hour, maybe not much, but in those initial seconds, when you felt your stomach and testicles bungee down to somewhere round about knee height, you were a fighter pilot. What he had just experienced was like the Radio City lift on rocket fuel. For a fleeting moment he was soaring, feeling the changes in air pressure around him, before decelerating at a frightening rate, all of his internal organs and the two small semi-external ones jolting back into their normal locations. He came to a shuddering standstill and unscrunched his eyes. He was looking at his own burial plot.

"God. I've done it," he thought. Charlie tried his best to stay collected, but after several weeks of being dead, this was sensory overload. He was no longer seeing through his own eyes. Instead, everything he observed was coming right through Jess's. He had no control over it. Whenever she made any head movement or took the merest glance in a different direction, the image changed. And the colours, they were so vibrant. He had become accustomed to the sepia tones of the grave layer. Now everything was wild, like a world created by the fabric designers of the psychedelic beatnik shirts that Mrs Dean had barred The Doc from wearing.

The sounds were supercharged too. Although it was possible to hear bird song from the grave, it was much sharper up here, beautiful, musical. Then there was the smell of cut grass in the newly mowed section of the cemetery over by the church. It was heady, dizzying. Charlie had barely begun to drink it all in when he pulled himself out of it. He had no idea how long this would last. He had decided that if he got here, there were two things he needed to try to achieve. Firstly, he had to let Jess know that he was really-really-really-really sorry about the life insurance. Secondly, he had to try somehow to get the message to her that he had been the victim of a Domestic Burglary (or similar).

Charlie appraised the situation. Fortunately, it didn't appear to be as daunting as he had anticipated. For a start, a knowledge of the complex anatomy of the human brain did not appear to be necessary. In addition, all of those fears he'd had, that he would be thrust into a storeroom crammed with private thoughts and feelings, were unfounded. As he settled into it, he appeared only to be experiencing what Jess was experiencing right now.

There is no manual available to explain to a dead person how to speak to the living. If and when someone gets round to writing one (it will, of course, have a Forward by Doctor Dennis Dean, leading authority on Dean's Syndrome) it is unlikely to suggest that you set off rattling out detail with the pace and ferocity of an assault rifle. In the ensuing moments, Jess got no sense of unsubmitted insurance paperwork in his office, of gravediggers appearing in dead of night, sideways excavations, lump hammers, watches, and refilling of graves. None of it. Charlie sensed that he was floundering. He thought back to what Isabel had last said to him.

"Feel it in here." He stopped jabbering and listened. He could kind of sense what she was thinking about. The Stables. The Stables. Then it moved to her mum, then to worrying about the cottage. There was a blank as she looked down. Through her eyes, against her skin, Charlie caught sight of the pendant with the etched soundwave from their wedding song. Without thinking, Charlie began to hum the tune. A stillness fell. His moment. Focussing his mind, he thought about how proud he was of her, and how much he wanted her to move on. She must look after herself. He thought about how sorry he felt about the mess he had left her in. He thought about the theft of Grandad Joe's watch, hoping she would pick up some sense of his distress. He thought about how it might have helped with the cottage, and now with the charity. And he thought about that final note he had left for her, exhorting her to continue to write her life's song.

Jess felt a little unsteady. She sat back down on the bench. She stopped thinking about all of her problems and thought only of Charlie. God, he seemed so close. What would he have said? She knew, it would be the same things he always did. Never give up, go with your instincts, forge ahead till you find a way. But right now she sensed he was trying to tell her something else. Something is wrong - with Charlie – and yet… that should give her hope.

Without warning, as abruptly as it had begun, their spell was broken. Jess did not delay. She picked up her handbag and headed for home.

Dear Journal,

Charlie came home once and said he'd had a professor on the show who had written a book about the brain. He told Charlie that humans have around 6,200 thoughts every day. Over the last few days I've spent 6,000 of mine flicking between Charlie and The Stables, the spare 200 have just kept everything else ticking over. Today was the same, until I went to the graveyard. Something happened and I got a feeling so intense that it jolted me out of that rhythm. St. Jude, the patron saint of hopeless causes – could it be his influence?

The first thing I did when I got back was to dig out the handbag I took to the funeral. I reread the little note Charlie had left for me. I felt better in a way, the best I've felt since losing Charlie. Then at the same time, I got a nagging feeling that something is not right with him. I won't leave it like this. I am uneasy. I don't know what I will do yet, but I know I will do something.

Jess closed the book and picked up her phone. Pouring a glass of wine, she flicked through the music playlists. There it is. 'Charlie's Funeral Songs'. She clicked play, then turned up the volume.

"I loved these songs," she said aloud, "we both did, and tonight I am claiming them back."

Chapter 8

Sotheby's Auction House is old. In the year 2044, when it reaches its next big birthday, a whopper of a celebratory cake will be required, big enough to accommodate three hundred candles. It is a company that is proud of its heritage, proud of its lofty reputation, proud that it has been entrusted with the sale of some of the most exquisite items ever fashioned by the hands of Man.

But tradition alone could not have guaranteed such longevity. Over the centuries, Sotheby's has continued to adapt and evolve in a world changing around it. Nowadays if you wish to know the value of some family heirloom uncovered in the attic, there is no need to journey by stagecoach to their London offices with your prized artefact held secure in a wooden tea chest. Sotheby's has embraced the digital age. A quick email, attach a few photos of the item, and their experts will soon tell you if it's a winner or a binner. Any fool can do it. Many do.

On Monday 28th May 2018, Giles Sanders was sifting through an in-box full of such emails. He had already dealt with and dismissed most of what had appeared over the weekend, including another from the ageing duchess, who regularly sent images of herself wearing items of her jewellery, but very little else. Bare buff, wrinkly, pearl-necklace nakedness. The next message caught Giles's attention. He was a junior within the organisation, and watches were not his strong suit, but this one looked like it was worth forwarding on for a second opinion. He drafted a succinct, polite covering note, reread it, then with a little hesitation clicked one more icon on the screen before hitting the SEND key.

In his office, surrounded by dusty encyclopaedias, directories, and almanacs, Ralph Chapman tutted out loud. The only pity was that he did not share his workspace with anyone else, someone who could have appreciated a tut of such power and purpose. Whilst Sotheby's had embraced twenty-first century technology, the introduction of hi-tech must never be at the expense of high standards. Ralph believed that, when sending an email to a colleague within the company, the use of the red exclamation mark to indicate that what you have sent is of High Importance was thoroughly bad form. It is as if one is pushing one's way to the head of the queue, without regard for others who were there before you, waiting patiently. He looked at the name of the sender. Giles Sanders, a young man, been with the company less than a year, rather headstrong no doubt. He would have a discreet, but firm, word. Then he read the Subject line, and the irritation that occupied his mind was forcibly evicted by intrigue. 'Unusual Patek Philippe? 1518?' This email had stuck out its pointed elbows and barged its way to the front.

Chapman browsed the message at speed, before hastening to the attached photographs. Opening the first, his eyes crisscrossed the image, darting top to bottom, side to side. He gave the second and third attachments the same treatment and immediately picked up the phone.

"Giles. Thank you for your email drawing my attention to this item. It does indeed look worthy of follow-up. Can you please contact the vendor, Mr Glen, post-haste? Impress upon him our credentials and our interest in this piece. Until we establish precisely what we are dealing with, we should keep the prospect of any potential sale with Sotheby's."

*   *   *

Charlie awoke following his visit to Jess feeling drained, as if he had done a hilly fifty miler on the bike the day before. Exhausting as the experience had been, the debrief with The Doc was more taxing.

"Could you identify the constituent parts of the brain, Charles, the frontal lobe, cerebellum, brain stem, and such like?"

"It wasn't like looking at a diagram in an anatomy textbook, Doc. Isabel's right, it's hard to describe. You're inside them, in their brain but not in the way that you're imagining. I was joined with her, seeing what she saw, getting a gist of what she was thinking. I was in amongst what your brain does not what it looks like."

"Extraordinary."

"And what about you, Charlie," asked Isabel, "how did it make you feel?" Charlie cast his weary mind back.

" At first, I was steady. And hopeful. I believed it might work. When I knew that I'd done it, I got anxious, it was like nothing I'd experienced before so I had no idea how to react. I think I got a bit agitated. Then I remembered what you had said, Isabel. I paused, and when I went with the natural flow I started to get somewhere. I thought what I would have said if I was just talking to her, and I had this powerful sensation that I was getting through."

"That's so similar to what happened to me with Mia," said Isabel.

"Once I'd settled down, it felt warm and comfortable. And now, lying here? I feel contented, like I've done my best to make up for the mistakes I made when I was alive." Charlie noticed that Rita, who generally had an opinion about everything, hadn't chipped in.

"Sorry, Rita," he said, "I think we've gone on enough about it. Let's talk about something else."

"No, son. I am listening, it's interesting. I'm washed out today, and I haven't been on a journey anywhere. I'm pleased you think you've made things better."

A metallic scrape from above brought the discussion to an end.

"Stow the family silver," said The Doc, "here he is once more." Tom Bennett had emerged from his shed, carrying a variety of the tools of his earth-shifting trade. He threw them into the tray of his wheelbarrow, and trundled it down in their direction, coming to a halt in the space to Rita's left. From the armoury before him, he selected his pick. With a mighty swing from his slender frame, he crashed it into the soil, sending a huge turf flying behind him.

"Here we go again," said Charlie. "He's digging out the one next to you this time, Rita. He'll be after your compendium of crosswords." The owner of the puzzle book did not reply, nor did anyone else speak, as Bennett continued with the excavation. Since the robbery there had been an unspoken shift in the atmosphere, everyone on edge, like the curtain-twitching residents of a suburban cul-de-sac which had experienced its first-ever burglary. Lee Knight's arrival, around forty minutes later, was greeted with relief. He surveyed the plot.

"Looks good," he said. "Great job, Tom."

"He hasn't said anything about the one that was dug beside me," said Charlie. "Bennett must have done a perfect cover-up job."

"Can you get the artificial grass matting laid around the edge now? It starts at one-thirty." The two then separated, Tom heading for his shed whilst Lee walked off up the graveyard.

"Thank god, looks like it's for real this time," said Charlie.

* * *

Two weeks on from Charlie's funeral, Radio City was still receiving a trickle of sympathy cards and letters. J.J. continued to carry out the delivery duties.

"Thanks," Jess said, as J.J handed her the latest batch. "I read them all you know. That bundle over there are ones that I'm keeping, at least for now. I don't want to cling onto the past, but each of them said something that persuaded me to hold onto them."

"The response has been incredible," said J.J.

"I didn't know quite how well-liked he was. But then I'm wondering if there are other things about Charlie that I never knew." Jess spoke in a way that would not allow J.J. to ignore it and pass on.

"What do you mean?"

"I don't know. I have just had this uneasy feeling the last few days, since Saturday when I went to St. Jude's. It's as if there is something about him that I don't know. Do you think Charlie kept any secrets from me?" J.J. looked at her quizzically, as Jess continued. "I don't mean little things, like whether he was planning to get me another hideous jumper for Christmas. I mean more serious stuff."

"What sort of thing? Sorry, Jess, why do you ask?"

"Well, he sold his record collection to raise money to buy the house without letting on. It's this nagging doubt I've got that he's got mixed up with someone that's not good for him.

Could he have been up to something he shouldn't have been? Drugs or something? Could he be in trouble with a dealer?" J.J. burst out laughing.

"Drugs? Yeah, aspirin after a night on the ale. There is a fair bit of that goes on in our industry but it didn't interest Charlie. Despite that name of his."

"I didn't think so. What about other people? Did he have a possessive fan, you know, a stalker, that he was maybe scared to tell me about? I've looked for tell-tale signs in the letters but can't see anything." Again J.J. shook his head.

"None that he ever mentioned. I'm sure he'd probably have told me - and definitely would have told you. What's this all about?"

"It's this feeling I've got that everything isn't right, something unresolved that needs to be dealt with." She briefly told him about her experience in the graveyard.

"Maybe it's something to do with grieving, getting used to the new way of things?" J.J. suggested.

"Maybe. But I don't think so. Something is wrong. I can't rest till I sort it out."

*   *   *

At around two, after a short ceremony, a group of mourners walked down the graveyard, following the coffin. Without the need for words Lee Knight, who was bearing the front right-hand corner, steered the others to a spot alongside the grave and had them lay it down. The mourners shuffled around the hole, spreading themselves evenly.

"They're an unusual mix," said Isabel.

"What do you mean?" asked The Doc.

"I can't tell who the main group is, you know, the person's closest relatives." Charlie looked at those above. He did not

134

have a massive amount of funeral experience to draw upon, (despite being front and centre, he had picked up nothing from the last one he attended), but he saw what she meant. There was a group of three older ladies, then two gents of a similar age. Next to them was another lady, perhaps in her thirties, holding the hand of a young boy. Finally, there were another three men, standing beside each other, more for comfort and support rather than through any familial ties.

"I can't work out who is who," said Isabel.

"Patience," said The Doc, "instead of indulging ourselves in unfounded speculation, let's ask the person themselves once they join us."

"I can't see who's in there," said Charlie.

"One never can, Charles," said The Doc, "not until they arrive down here." They did not have long to wait. The ceremonials over, a nod from Lee Knight let the other five know that they should each pick up their tapes, to complete the final stage of the journey. The six men moved the coffin directly over the grave, then fed the tape steadily through their hands, until it landed lightly on the soil. Charlie could now see that they had been joined by a woman, probably mid-seventies, wearing a thick overcoat and a rumpled grey hat that gave the appearance of her brain having popped out through the top of her head. From above, some of the mourners threw small handfuls of earth onto the coffin lid. Lee Knight withdrew with his head bowed. As he did so he placed a hand on Tom's arm and indicated to him he should also move further back.

"Give them a little more time and space," he whispered, as the last of the three young men threw his soil into the hole. Gradually they all moved off up the graveyard until only Tom was left. From below they watched as he waited until the last of the mourners was out of sight, paused momentarily, then began shovelling the pile of soil. Once his work was done he replaced his tools into the wheelbarrow and moved toward his shed.

"Who is going to speak to her?" Charlie whispered.

"I usually do," Rita replied. "but why don't you do it this time, Doctor? I don't feel up to it today." The Doc's already replete chest puffed out further.

"When will you say something, Doc?" Charlie asked. "Now?"

"I'll give it around two hours," he said. "We should give her time to settle in."

"Of course." When the time had passed, Charlie prompted him.

"Hello," said The Doc. That one whispered word transported Charlie back to the moment three weeks ago when he realised that he wasn't quite as dead as he had imagined.

"Hello," The Doc repeated, this time fractionally louder. There was no response.

"Let's leave her for a little longer," he said. "She'll come round soon." While Rita slept, the others talked in hushed tones, keeping it light, in case the old lady came to unexpectedly and got the fright of her life. The Doc broke off occasionally to try to attract her attention, and when after six hours there had been no response, Charlie felt bold enough to ask.

"Is this unusual?"

"Very. You and Isabel were more immediate."

"Maybe this lady was so ill that she can't recover," Charlie suggested.

"Charles, in case it has escaped your attention, we were all as ill as it is possible to be when we arrived here," The Doc replied.

"Perhaps the goodness of the stream can't penetrate that big coat and hat she's wearing," Charlie suggested. "Or maybe she is deaf, can't hear you speaking."

"That's possible," said the Doc. "but it can't be the full story. She is showing no signs of life. Perhaps the restorative qualities of our stream are not as ubiquitous as we had hitherto believed them to be. This is yet another fascinating characteristic of this syndrome that I have discovered, surely one of the most intriguing conditions that mankind will ever know."

Chapter 9

At first, Jess thought she must have miscounted, skipped over one or two. It must be this brain-fog. She was walking through Stanford, en route to St. Jude's, totting up her visits to Charlie's grave. Even including today's uncompleted sojourn, the unstable five-bar gate in her head had only the four shaky uprights, with no diagonal cross-spar to hold them firm. Unbelievable, way less than she had imagined. She was apprehensive. The events of last Saturday had profoundly affected her. What if it happened again? She was not sure she was ready for a repeat.

Arriving at the churchyard she hesitated in the gateway before moving within. The previous day she had flipped the kitchen calendar over, May to June. The morning air was still, but heavy with damp warmth. She looked left and right. Aside from the insects, buzzing as they slalomed their way between the uprights of the stones, she was on her own. She took the long way round, down to Rita's bench, and sat there, awaiting the others. No strange sensations. Jess was relieved. She tipped her head back and closed her eyes, letting the soothing sun warm the lids, allowing her thoughts to float through. Less than ten minutes had passed when she heard the growl of the ancient diesel engine of Mick's car, the clunk of two doors, then peace again. She kept her eyes shut, savouring the tranquility. Only as she felt them near did she pull herself upright.

"Hi," said Mick. "You looked deep in thought."

"Hi. Yes, I was." Mick sat down on the bench beside her. They waited to see if she would volunteer any more.

"Your charity? Or Charlie?" asked Mia.

"Charlie. He's been in my mind all week." Jess paused. She intended to tell them what had happened, but she needed to find the right words to broach it. "I've got something I want to talk to you about," she said, "but I need to make something clear before I do. I am not a believer in supernatural mumbo-jumbo. Some of the girls at work are, but it's not for me." Their bemused expressions told her she needed to explain. "Once a year they used to invite this guy round to one of their houses - he said he could contact spirits and see into the future. You'd think he would be out buying winning lottery tickets, but no, he was scraping up a tenner a head to tell them what was coming their way. They said it was only a bit of fun but I knew they believed. Some of them made huge decisions because of it - got married, looked for a new job, tried for a baby. Ridiculous. They often asked me to come. I politely declined. Psychic Cedric he was called." Mick laughed.

"I know him!" said Mick. "Cedric, A.K.A. Norman Berry. When he wasn't contacting the spirit world, he was labouring in a timber yard in Preston. I locked him up. He latched onto an old lady who loved cats, told her was receiving messages from the other side, saying that she should give money to a particular cat charity. Her son got suspicious and contacted us. When I investigated, the charity was non-existent, apart from a bank account in the name of Norman Berry. He got four years." Jess clapped her hands.

"Sorry, I should be more respectful in a graveyard," she said, "but well done, Mick. I knew he was a conman." She took a deep breath. "So when I tell you this, bear in mind I'm a sceptic. I had a strange experience last week. While I was here

I felt like Charlie was with me. I mean I think about him all the time but this was different. It was as if he wasn't, you know…", she gestured to his plot, "under there. It was not even as if he was beside me." She touched her heart, then her temple. "It was like he was right in here. It was so powerful." Realising this might sound frightening to a child, she broke into a smile. "I do sound like a crazy psychic lady, don't I?"

Mia shook her head. "No, I don't think you're crazy. Ever since mum died I've thought that this is a special place. What was it like?"

"It was a strange feeling. It was peaceful at first, as if we were together like before. But then it changed. You know sometimes you get a sense that someone you are with is troubled, without them saying anything? I got that feeling. I felt that someone had done Charlie some harm."

"Was it upsetting?" Mick asked.

"That's the funny thing. No, it wasn't, because at the same time I felt like, as usual, he could see a positive side, and that he was pushing me to look into it so that I could see it too. I'm convinced something has happened but I don't know what."

Mick raised his eyebrows. "Maybe you were tired, you've had a lot to think about, that business with your charity and so on."

"I don't think so." She paused again, searching for the words to help them to understand. "I feel bad for even saying this, but I was so struck by it that I asked his best friend about Charlie, wondering if he might know if he'd kept any secrets from me." Jess gauged their reactions. Mia looked surprised. Mick's face was one of dread at what might be coming next. "Turns out he didn't," she added, "at least none that J.J. knows about, so it's a mystery." Not wishing to make them uncomfortable, she decided to change the subject. "Anyhow, I see the last plot in our little corner has now been taken. And what about the other, the one next to Charlie? Did you manage to find out about the family?" It was Mick's turn to measure his words.

"Yes, I found something out, but I've got a mystery too," he said.

"There's no family?" asked Jess.

"Correct. And more than that… there's no body."

"What?"

"No body. Nobody in there. No deceased. The lady from the church who keeps the records told me that the plot is unused." He could see that Jess looked perplexed.

"But we saw it being dug," she said.

"I know, but here's where it gets interesting. I bumped into the gravedigger and asked about it. What did he do? Immediately buttoned up, would not talk about it. It smells funny."

"To your copper's nose?" asked Mia. Mick nodded.

"Your what?" said Jess, lost.

"It's a police thing," said Mick "we used to talk about developing a copper's nose. You instinctively pick up when something isn't right. You'd be out on patrol and see people hanging around for no reason, or a car being driven aimlessly. Nine times out of ten if you had a chat with them they'd react like he did, give you some half-baked story. The gravedigger told me that it had been dug by mistake and refilled. He was lying."

"Are you sure?" Jess asked.

"Certain. I have been told thousands of lies by hundreds of better liars than him. He was not telling me the full story. So uncomfortable, evasive. I don't know why, but he was

141

spinning me a line."

"In my job you get suspicious of coincidences," said Mia.

"Sorry?" said Jess. Mia continued.

"I never get away with anything, and that's one of Uncle Mick's phrases when he catches me out." Mick laughed. "It seems strange that you got that funny feeling, Jess, and then Uncle Mick finds out the gravedigger is lying. Could be to do with Charlie?"

"I don't know," Mick replied. "I can't see how. I suppose we'll never know."

"Never know, Uncle Mick? Are you going to ignore your copper's nose? Suppose he's carried out a serious crime? He might do another one if you don't do anything. You could investigate. I could help." Mick sighed.

"Mia, I'm not a policeman anymore." He sounds flat, Jess thought. Maybe Mick was one of these retired people who had found it difficult to adapt to a world without work. Mia was oblivious.

"I know, but you could investigate as a member of the public. Remember the documentary we watched, where the police didn't have enough officers to investigate a man's death? The family did it themselves, got lots of evidence, and they caught a serial killer. You'd get to the truth."

"You watch way too many true crime programmes," said Mick. "Anyway, I'm not sure I'd be much good now." He watched her face fall. Confused? Saddened? Both? He needed, finally, to be honest with her. "There's something I haven't told you about me and the police, love."

"What?"

"One of the last cases I worked on nearly went badly wrong - and it was my fault."

"You mean the one where you were fighting the burglar on

the asbestos roof of the garage and you fell through and broke your leg."

"No, that was the very last job I was on. And that wasn't my fault, although to be fair, I was carrying a few extra pounds at the time. No, this one was a thief, he stole things from a lady, then did a bunk. Disappeared out of town, could not be traced. I always had an eye out for him though, never gave up hope that we might get him. Years later, I was patrolling Stanford and there he was, sitting on the square with one of his old cronies. I arrested him, and as we drove to the station, he asked me to stop. When I did, he confessed everything. I asked him questions and noted it all down. Then we got to the formal interview when he had his solicitor present and we were going to write the confession up in a statement. Only his solicitor asked if I had read him his rights. My world fell apart. I couldn't lie, I knew I hadn't. Everything I had was inadmissible, could not be used in court. By then the solicitor had got into his head, we could only get two words out of him. No Comment. I was gutted, it was a disaster."

"What happened?"

"We were lucky. A guy he'd sold some of the stolen goods to was able to identify him, and off he went to prison. My boss and my colleagues were good about it, but the top brass were after me from then on. I could understand that some of them were annoyed because I'd forgotten to do it, but some of the others… I'm sure they were annoyed because I admitted what I'd done. It ruined my last year."

"That's wrong. It wasn't your fault," said Mia. "He would never have been caught at all if it wasn't for you. You were the only one who was still looking for him. And you were the one smart enough to recognise him after all that time."

"I didn't need to be too smart," Mick replied, meeting her

stare. "I've been waiting till you were old enough to tell you. I couldn't mistake him. He was your dad, Mia, the lady he had robbed was your mum. He did it when she was in hospital and you were tiny." He studied her reaction. There was no hint of upset; instead she looked stunned. He could not carry on till she responded.

"My dad did that to my mum?" she said. "When she was sick?" Mick nodded.

"When I finally got him, I was so angry that I forgot my training. It was unprofessional. I never told your mum, but I let her down." Jess got up and stepped over to Charlie's grave, leaving the two of them on the bench. They shuffled together, closing off the distance between them, and embraced. When finally Mia let him go, Mick spoke again. "So when I fell through that roof it was a blessing. That injury meant I had to leave the force, brought my thirty years to an end. I think me and policing are finished, love. I'm not up to it." Mia sat up straight.

"Rubbish! I've seen your two commendations. You were a brilliant policeman, my mum always said so."

Isabel had never heard any of this before. How had he let this happen? She was furious with Mick. Not with the Mick who made an understandable mistake that could have seen her thieving ex slip off the hook. She was furious with the Mick who had warned her to stay away from that man in the first place. With the Mick who got his first commendation for risking his life to disarm a man stabbing another outside a pub. With the Mick who got his second for talking a woman intent on killing herself down from a bridge over the M6. With the Mick who took on a small, frightened girl and was skilfully guiding her into becoming a young lady. With the Mick who never understood how good he was.

She didn't plan it at all. It just happened. She was in his head. She had to put him straight. She needed him to know the things that she had never said when she was alive, that whatever problems she had encountered, he was the one who pulled her through. He needed to know that she had come to admire him far above anyone else in her life.

Mick stood up from the bench. "It's strange talking about this after all this time. Do you mind," he said, "I just want to go for a walk, clear my head a bit? Mia, will you stay here with Jess, if that's all right, Jess?"

"Of course," Jess replied. Mick turned, and with as steady and sure a stride as a man with legs of unequal lengths could manage, he headed off up the churchyard, disappearing around the back of the building. When he was out of earshot Mia spoke.

"You don't think Uncle Mick is annoyed at me, do you?"

"No, I don't, love. I think what he's just told us is a bit upsetting for him. It's brought back lots of memories. Of your mum, but also his work. It must be hard when you've dedicated yourself to a job all those years to leave under a cloud. I've known people who made mistakes in the health service. It can be devastating. He probably wants a moment to think it over on his own."

On the far side of the church, hidden from view, Mick paced left then right along the path. He had long dreaded having that conversation with Mia. It had been harder than he thought, and yet it had helped. He felt better. Why on earth was he beating himself up over making a slip on a case that meant so much to him? Who the hell were they to pass judgment, those bloody bosses, who had no idea of what policing on the front line was like these days? Why did he think that Isabel would have held this against him? The more he considered it, the surer he was of what his sister would have said if he had told her. A host of dark thoughts he'd held trapped, eddying and swirling in the darkest corners of his mind for three years, suddenly took off and were gone.

"He's been up there a long time," said Mia. "Should I check he's okay?"

"No need," Jess replied, pointing ahead. Mick was making his way back to the bench. He sat beside them. Jess tried not to stare, but he looked different. Alive.

"Maybe I could look into it a bit more, if that's what you want, Jess. What do you think might have happened?" he asked.

"Honestly? I don't know. But I think somewhere between Charlie setting out on that bike ride and now, somebody has wronged him, and I can't leave it. So yes, I would love you to get involved. You're sure that the gravedigger is up to something, I bet you're right."

"Even if it turns out to be nothing to do with Charlie, Uncle Mick, it will help to put Jess's mind at ease."

"And what about Mia's criminology career? It would be good for her to work with one of the best in the business. And, after what you've told us about the last little bit of your time in the police, I think it'll do you the world of good."

"Okay," he said. "Let's make a few discreet enquiries, nothing more." He stood up and turned towards the bench, towering over them. "If you are to be on my team, you need to know that I can't think when I'm hungry. Angelo's café in town for a briefing. Rendezvous in fifteen minutes."

"Isabel? Isabel?" said Charlie, "are you okay?"

"Yes, just a bit tired."

"That was you, wasn't it? You've done it, haven't you? Mick says he'll make some enquiries. We've got a chance."

"I can't believe what he's just said. I didn't know any of that. He's been carrying that around himself all that time, worrying about what I'd think. I know everything that he's done for Mia. It can't have been easy for him, a single bloke bringing up a teenage girl on his own. And I just got so frustrated I found myself in there without thinking."

"This is a landmark case." It was the steady voice of the resident medical expert. "Until now there have been no proven instances in which someone with Dean's Syndrome has been able to make one of these so-called visitations to a second individual. Remarkable. Necessitates a rewrite of this whole area. Once you have had time to catch your breath Isabel, I would very much like a debrief on the experience and how it compared to the first."

"Never mind that, Doc, do you see what she's done? Isabel has got them all fired up. They're going after him. I tell you I have a good feeling about this."

*   *   *

Very little has changed front of house at Angelo's since it was opened in the late sixties. There are a few cracked floor tiles where cutlery has been dropped, clumsily manoeuvred iron chairs have knocked chips from around the edges of the marble-topped tables, and the sun has flaked off patches of paint on the back of mirrored signs, but nothing of the original décor, no matter what the wear or the tear, has been replaced. It could not look more authentically Italian if it was down a backstreet in Naples, rather than just off the triangular square in Stanford. The smell of filter coffee permeates its warren of small rooms, a layout that makes it an ideal place for a discreet conversation. Or a meeting of an undercover investigative team. Mick led off.

"Okay, let's recap, what do we know so far? We see a grave being dug and refilled in St Jude's graveyard. Nothing unusual there. Mia spots that there are no flowers, so we decide to find out if they have any family. I talk to Mrs Harkness, who keeps all the graveyard records, and she has no knowledge of this having taken place."

"Could it be that Mrs Harkness is mistaken?" asked Mia. Mick laughed.

"No way. You haven't met Mrs Harkness. Mistakes are something other people make. Intentionally, to irritate her. Her records will be accurate. And that wouldn't explain what happens next. I had a word with the gravedigger, Tom Bennett, no more than a few simple questions. He made up a story about it having been a mix-up. He's lying. Now as far as I know nobody digs holes for nothing, not even if you like holes so much that you got yourself a job as a gravedigger. So, what is he up to? Any suggestions?"

"Who pays Tom, I wonder?" said Jess. "Does he get paid to dig each grave? If so, what if he's trying to fiddle more money out of them?"

"Possibly," said Mick. "If the job doesn't pay well, maybe he's found a way to bump the money up by getting paid for work that wasn't needed."

"I thought he might have hidden something in there," said Mia. "Something he never wanted to be found, evidence of a crime, maybe a weapon? Or a body? Who would think to look for a dead body in a graveyard?" Mick shook his head.

"Mrs Harkness said Tom knows these plots will be used soon. It would be a bad place to hide anything. Unless it was just for a short period – he could retrieve whatever it was when it was dug out legitimately. You're right in a way though, if you want to dig a big hole without arousing suspicion, strikes me a graveyard is an ideal place." Mia thought for a moment.

"Suppose he'd already hidden something and was getting it back? Drugs? Stolen goods? Illicit cash?"

"Very devious," said Mick. "In that case, I doubt we'll ever find out." They all hushed as the waitress came into their little room to collect used dishes from a nearby table.

"Okay," said Mick, once she had gone, "here's how I suggest we proceed. I'll get in touch with a few people about Bennett, try to find out if he's known to the police. Mia, can you have a look on social media, see if you can find out anything there. And Jess, can you check through Charlie's things?"

"What am I looking for?"

"Anything out of the ordinary. Remember the ABC rule, everyone – Assume nothing, Believe no one, Challenge everything. When we meet next week we'll have an update." Mick picked up his cup and drained the last of his tea and grimaced. He had inadvertently punctured a bag while agitating the pot. None too discretely, he regurgitated a mouthful of grainy leaves into his napkin. "Let that be a lesson to you," he said, "you might find something when you least expect it."

Chapter 10

On the day of Charlie's funeral, Diane had squeezed a commitment out of her daughter. During the service, she had taken every opportunity to steal a glance along the pew at Jess. In those fleeting glimpses what she saw was a ghost of her girl, pale and drained. She was bound to be, Diane understood that, but nothing could suppress a mother's desperation to get her daughter back to her old self as soon as possible. That evening she at first coaxed, then she badgered, until Jess gave up protesting and agreed to come for tea every Wednesday… at least for a while. Diane was relieved. She was certain that in the coming weeks her daughter would not eat enough, and what little she did eat would be all the wrong things.

This week, the third post-funeral banquet, she had once again prepared a meal that incorporated each of the principal nutritional food groups, in quantities sufficient to ensure that her daughter had ample goodness to sustain her through the coming week and a few more besides.

"God, mum, how much have you made?" said Jess, as she joined Diane at the cooker, whose every ring bore a bubbling pot.

"Whatever we don't eat tonight, I'll package up for you to take home. You can freeze it, but be sure to do it straight away. You're starting to look a bit brighter. The last thing we need is for you to come down with salmonella." They tucked in, Jess judiciously leaving sufficient capacity for some of the brick-sized banana bread she had spotted on the worktop, certain that she would be pressurised into disposing of a generous slice later.

"It's delicious mum, there was maybe a bit too much after the meal," said Jess, having consumed over fifty per cent of her portion, surely a pass mark.

"I'm only looking after you," Diane explained. "I'm glad you're coming here every week. I don't like the idea of you hanging around the cottage on your own."

"There's no hanging around mum. I'm busy. I'm back to seeing all of my patients as normal, then there's The Stables." She stopped. Probably not the best time to disclose the catastrophic funding black hole. "I've got a few things to sort out there. And I'm getting close to the end of Charlie's chaotic paperwork." Definitely not the time for a mention of the pension. An opportunity to prepare the ground though. "Do you know, he sold his record collection to raise the deposit for the cottage? Never told me about it, did it secretly. I've no idea what else I might come across."

"Did he? He loved those records."

"I know. I bet you didn't get any surprises like that when dad died."

"Surprises? Good grief, no. Everything was organised and catalogued to perfection." She poured a little more coffee into each of their cups. "It's a shame really", she added, a wistfulness in her tone.

"What do you mean?" Diane did not answer straight away.

"I know it's a strange word to use about what a dead person leaves behind, but your dad's things were... lifeless. I've thought about it a lot since Charlie died," she said, "I know it's much worse for you... but I'm missing Charlie. A lot. I struggled at first with his impulsive ways, but I grew to love him. He was so - what's the word - devil-may-care," she said, with an exuberant waft of her arm.

"He was certainly all of that," said Jess.

"Whereas your dad…" Jess left the void unfilled, allowing her mum to choose her words. "He was always cautious, but it got more extreme when he moved from being an accountant to become a risk manager. It took over our lives. He'd tell me that we needed to mitigate this risk and manage that one. Looking back on it now, when we'd done that to everything, all of the chances to have fun were gone too. I suppose that's why I sometimes feel I never did much in life."

"What about raising a lovely daughter?" said Jess, with mock outrage.

"No, I don't mean that. I'm proud of you – and everything you're achieving. But Charlie was the best thing that happened to you. We brought you up to be too safe."

"Don't say that, mum, I was lucky, you were fantastic parents." Diane gave her daughter a smile of thanks. "Dad's gone now, mum. Don't dwell too much on the past." Diane nodded.

"I know. Though they never really disappear, the dead," she said. "Not fully. Every now and then they come bobbing back into your head, offering you their opinion, whether you want it or not. You'll get the same I'm sure. I still get my dad popping in now and then."

"Ah, Charlie's favourite, Grandad Joe. Now there is someone I could imagine would leave a few surprises behind when he went."

"He didn't actually," said Diane. "His came earlier, in his last weeks. I didn't know when he might go, so I sat at his bedside for hours on end. I wanted to make sure he had someone with him. At first I read while he dozed, but after a few days he began to open up, telling me stories from the past.

Not the ones about those wild chaps he worked with at the foundry, he talked about his time in the war. Places he'd been to, people he had been with, things he's seen. It was like he wanted to get it all out before he was gone."

"God, that must have been so strange, after all those years of not really saying anything."

"It was. He was feverish, drifting in and out a bit, so it didn't all make perfect sense." Diane paused. "I hope you don't think I'm batty but I started to make little notes. It seemed to matter such a lot to him, and I thought if I don't write it down his story will be lost forever. And now there are hardly any of them left alive to say what it was like. Just wait a minute." Diane left the room, returning shortly afterwards with a notepad.

"I expected these notes would be one of my surprises for you once I'm gone," she said, opening the first page. Jess could see that every ruled line, end to end, was covered in her mum's writing. "Now," she said, "don't be expecting a precise account of his World War Two experiences. For a start, I'm no Anne Frank. And by then he had a bit of dementia. Oh, and he insisted on me getting him a tumbler of navy strength rum every afternoon." They leafed through the early pages, telling of his time in North Africa, then journeyed further north with him and the Eighth Army, on to the invasion of Sicily. The notes were a mixture of memories, the places, the fighting, his comrades, their day-to-day existence, a mad mixture of drudgery and danger.

"I didn't know any of this. I'm glad you've recorded it, mum," said Jess. "It's amazing. You should write it up. Properly." Diane tutted, flicked the page in her notebook and they were on mainland Italy.

"Ah, here's a bit that you'll like," she said. "It's about the old watch that he left for Charlie. 'As we were moving up the west coast of Italy in 1943, that's when I got the watch. I exchanged it for mine with a peasant lad, about my age. Marco Ascenzo. Although he was Italian, Marco was fighting with us." Before she could continue her daughter interrupted.

"Right," said Jess. "He got it from an Italian. No Indians involved."

"Indians?" asked Diane.

"Something Charlie said. Another case of him making up the bits he wasn't sure about. He was good at that."

"Oh, okay. I know it's a bit disordered, but I think what your Grandad said here is right. He did remember a lot of detail. The notes go right through to the end of the war, the excitement of the victory, but then how odd it felt to come back home, how awkward it was." Jess saw reflected in her mum's eyes that she was reliving the conversation she'd had with her dying father. Diane shut the book. "It's a shame he didn't feel able to share it all when he was younger. I'm sure it would have helped him." She had another sip of coffee. "I think he might have had that new STD thing I hear them talking about."

"PTSD," said Jess. "I think he had it too, mum."

At home that evening, Jess pushed herself to finish off the final batch of Charlie's documents. As she threw an instruction manual for a long scrapped printer into a bin bag, she looked around the desks and shelves, home to orderly bundles, where a few weeks ago there had been disarray. She had found no other administrative time bombs, nothing out of the ordinary.

She flicked through the bundle of cards and letters she had decided to keep. It was the first time that she had reread them.

They were tinged with sadness but this time, instead of provoking tears, they made her smile. Some of the listeners had sent letters that were addressed to Charlie as if he was still alive. They were intense too, written as if he was a close personal acquaintance. Her mind flitted off to her conversations with J.J., then Mick and Mia. What if Charlie did have a stalker? But then where does Bennett fit in? A dark thought crossed her mind. Perhaps an obsessed fan had asked Bennett to help gain access to Charlie, to get a lock of his hair or some other souvenir?

Opening her laptop, she accessed the search engine. "Now," she thought, "is it one word or two?" She entered two. She had guessed right.

*   *   *

The following day Charlie had awoken earlier than normal. It was light enough to see the world above. He looked around him. Rita was awake, the others still sleeping.

"Morning," he whispered to her.

"Morning, son." He waited to see if she would strike up a conversation. Nothing.

"You're awake early," he said.

"Couldn't sleep," she replied.

"Are you okay, Rita?" She could tell that this was not an exchange of pleasantries. He sought an answer.

"Yes son, why do you ask?" Charlie thought that it was obvious why. Rita, normally the hub of the place, was dozing during daytime and had stopped initiating dialogue, limiting herself to responding when the others spoke to her. No comment on Jess's reaction to his visit, on Mick exposing Bennett's lying, on Isabel visiting Mick. Or on the corpse to her left, still steadfastly refusing to awaken from her sleep of death.

"You've seemed quiet the last few days."

"I feel a bit tired I suppose."

"Are you upset about the lady beside you?"

"Not really. I mean I can't say I like it. Every time I look to my left I see her stony old face staring up at me. I know it's not her fault but…"

"I know, a bit like if groundhog day had fallen on Halloween," said Charlie. "It's your birthday in a week. We're going to have a party, like The Doc's. Could be the pick-me-up you need?"

"Perhaps," she replied. "And I'll have my grandchildren come to visit. They try to come to St. Jude's twice a year, on my birthday and the anniversary of my death. I'm hoping they'll make it, they've missed a couple of times recently."

"I didn't know you had grandkids," said Charlie.

"Yes, a boy and a girl…. well, a man and a woman, they're not kids now, they're both in their late thirties. Alan runs the farm. His sister, Sarah, lives down south but always comes up too. I'd like to see them again. Who knows, it might be for the last time."

"What do you mean? Are they going somewhere?" Rita lowered her whisper to the faintest of murmurs.

"Not them, me. I know why you're asking about me, Charlie. I'll be honest with you… I'm wondering if it's coming to an end. Finishing. I feel really tired. Maybe the stream doesn't keep you going forever, eventually it wears off. I've been here the longest. Maybe it really is my time." Charlie was horrified.

"Don't say that, Rita. You're the founder member. We need you."

"Thanks, son. Maybe I will buck up."

"I hope so. Can I ask you a question, Rita?"

"Of course."

"If you don't, any chance I could put my name down for that crossword puzzle book of yours?" Rita smiled, then closed her eyes and, as if comforted to have shared her fears, she fell into a deep sleep. Charlie lay alone once more. There was no one in the graveyard, all was still. And the realisation hit him.

"Doc, Isabel," he whispered, not wishing to wake Rita.

"Yes?" Doc replied, whispering too.

"Listen. What can you hear?" He waited a few seconds while The Doc followed the instruction.

"The stream," said The Doc. "I can hear it but it sounds like a trickle, as if it's barely flowing."

"Exactly," said Charlie. "And look, Rita is getting weaker every day. This other lady won't come round. I've started to feel tired."

"I must confess that I too do not feel my normal self," The Doc replied.

"Oh my God... me neither," said Isabel. Charlie gave a grim nod.

"Co-incidence? I don't think so."

*   *   *

On Saturday, when Mick's novice Major Incident Team reconvened at St. Jude's, they began by going through the week's highlights. Mia, despite having competed against girls older than herself, came third in a judo tournament. She laughed as Jess exaggerated her way through the story of how her mum was filling her with food, then listened with sharp interest to Grandad Joe's war accounts. When finally Mick shepherded them to the debrief on what they had found out that week, he asked Mia to lead off. From her bag, she produced a small notebook. She flipped it open along the short upper edge.

"Uncle Mick gave me this," she said to Jess. "It's a spare pocketbook, a real one, from his days in the police."

"A real one? I'm jealous," said Jess. Mia continued.

"As agreed," she said, "I've concentrated on looking online. I've found a few things out. Tom Bennett, attended Stanford High School, left in 2009 when he was sixteen, with no qualifications. Worked in a supermarket warehouse for a couple of years, before taking this job in 2012." Jess interrupted.

"How did you find all of that out?"

"It's surprising what you can come up with when you know your way around the internet. Particularly social media," she said. "But the most interesting thing I discovered was about his name. He's now called Tom Bennett but up until earlier this year, he called himself Tom Hanlon. I told Uncle Mick as soon as I found out in case it helped him with his enquiries."

"Why would he have changed his name?" Jess asked.

"It's common," said Mick. "Any number of reasons. Sometimes it's legitimate, other times it's to confuse people about who you are, to hide your past. Very interesting, thanks Mia." Mick got up and stood in front of them.

"I started by looking through newspaper archives," he said, "to see if he has committed any crimes that had been picked up in the court reports. Nothing. Then, the hard part. I met Harry, my old sergeant, down at The Bell for a couple of pints. He has to be careful what he tells me now I'm no longer on the force, but he has asked a few people who know a few people... all of them drew a blank. No colleagues have had dealings with him, and none of the shifty characters around here seemed to know him by name, either Bennett or Hanlon. So either he's not committed any crimes or, if he has, he's never been caught. What about you, Jess?"

"I've been through all of Charlie's paperwork now, a bigger job than it sounds. There's nothing in there to suggest that he had any enemies or any strange secrets. It seems like Charlie's only crime was to put off doing jobs that he thought were boring for as long as he could." She paused and drew her breath. "Then I had an idea, maybe some crazy fan was trying to get a trophy or something from Charlie. So I went on the internet and did a search. For 'grave robbing'." She paused to allow Mick and Mia to let it sink in. It didn't. It remained visible, a slick of shock floating across both faces.

"That's a bit grim," said Mick.

"I know, but I found something out. Lots of the articles were historic, about body snatchers. People used to get paid to dig up corpses to be used in medical research. They'd dig straight down and take the lid off the coffin to get the person out. Grave robbers, who wanted to take grave contents rather than the body, were different. They'd often come in from the side."

"You're thinking that's what might have happened to Charlie?" said Mia. "He's dug a false grave at the side to get access?"

"Perhaps," said Jess. "only I can't think that there's anything you'd want in there. I can't remember exactly what I put in the little box, my brains were scrambled at the time, but there's nothing of value. I wondered if maybe an obsessed person persuaded Bennett to get something as a souvenir?" Mick walked over to the end of the plot, eying up distances and depths.

"It's possible," he said, "but risky. Then, if like you say, they were obsessed, maybe they would. It would be good to know what else was in that biscuit tin, Jess."

"I could ask Alex at the funeral directors."

"Okay. Mia, can you look into Bennett, see if you can find anything else, I'll push Harry to cast the net a bit wider. Back here, same time next week – but first..." Mia clapped her hands.

"Angelo's!"

Chapter 11

Rita was vanishing. As her birthday approached, hour by hour, she moved further away from them, like a cruise ship so imposing up close in port, fading to the tiniest of dots as it disappeared across the vastness of the ocean. Charlie gave her an out, suggesting that they postpone her party till next week when she might be stronger. Her feeble agreement was met with relief by the others. All three had begun to feel run down, less able to concentrate and participate. Charlie wondered if Rita had been right. Maybe this was the end.

"If I fall asleep," she said, "will one of you please wake me up when my grandkids get here?"

"Definitely," said Charlie.

He did not need to. Rita was conscious, almost alert, when Alan and Sarah arrived at the graveside. She saw that Sarah was carrying a posy of flowers, small but striking, in various shades of purple. She always remembers, my favourite colour. Sarah laid them on the grass before the headstone, and the two stood silently for a moment.

"Gran's bench?" said Sarah, and they took a seat.

"Have you got the scotch eggs?" asked Alan.

"Have you got the pork pies?" she replied. Gran's birthday. The anniversary of her death. Purple flowers. Gran's bench. Her favourite picnic foods; scotch eggs, pork pies. On such curious foundations, family traditions are built. They each placed their contribution to the spread on the bench between them.

"How's Ann? Are her and the baby okay?" Alan nodded.

161

"Yeah, had her second scan last week, all good. Biggest issue we have is which of her great-granny's names she inherits, whether she is a Rita or a Winnie." Sarah winced.

"Winnie?" said Sarah. Alan nodded. "As in 'The Pooh'?" Once more he affirmed.

"I know, tricky conversation coming down the track," he said. "What about you? Anything new?"

"Yes. I'm moving to a different hospital," Sarah replied. "Addenbrookes in Cambridge."

"Wow. Even I've heard of that one" said Alan. "You must be a famous doctor now."

"Famous? Get lost," she said, flicking out a small hand at his huge ham of an upper arm. "I'll never be famous. Though last month I did have an article on bowel cleansing for colonoscopy published in Gastroenterology, the journal for gut doctors everywhere."

"There you are," said Alan. "Told you, you're being modest. It's a shame gran never got to see how far you've gone. First one in our family ever to go off to university, now in your high-flying job in Cambridge. She would have been so proud of what you've done."

"Gran? I'm not so sure. She'd say I was a deserter for leaving Stanford, have me excommunicated from the family. I'd be an embarrassment to the Jackson dynasty."

"Rubbish. She'd have told all of her friends about you, till they were sick of hearing about it." There was a hesitation before Alan spoke again. When it came to changing the gears of a conversation, Alan had the deftness of a day-one learner waggling the stick in hope, with the clutch only partially depressed. "If she was embarrassed by anyone it would be me." Sarah could not miss the crunch of the cogs.

"Don't be daft. Why?"

"Remember how I called off seeing you the last couple of times, saying I was busy?" She nodded. "That was partly true," said Alan, "I was, but the reason is that I've managed to get the farm into a heap of trouble. I thought if I didn't see you I wouldn't have to tell you, and maybe things will have picked up by next time. But they haven't."

"What's going wrong?" Alan filled his ruddy cheeks with air, before blowing it back out through pursed lips.

"Where to start? It's a combination of things, all pulling in the same direction. The weather. Climate change, ask any farmer around here if it's real. Extremes are now normal, it's either drought or mild and wet. The last few years we've had long spells of heavy rain, so the water table is permanently too high. Deluges lasting weeks. All of the west fields are flooded now. It's ruining the crops. We're producing less than half of what we used to. I have to buy in feed and delay putting the livestock out till later and later in the season. Everything is all to cock." Alan scuffed the ground before the bench with the toe of his boot.

"Then there's Agnew's gravel quarry," he continued. "They used to do a lot of good work to help manage water levels but since they went out of business that has all stopped. The water companies are no help, they're all about profit. They don't maintain the infrastructure, so water is leaking out of the mains adding to the problem. But the biggest disaster was when they built two hundred new houses on what used to be Taylor's Farm. Pouring tons of concrete, covering huge areas with tarmac, it completely changed the drainage around here, we get all the runoff. We can't have another year like this one. As a business, we will go under." Sarah could see the sadness in his eyes. Alan saw it reflected back in her own.

"Can't you complain?"

"I've tried. Guess what? Everyone I speak to blames someone else. Nothing to do with them. I get nowhere. Ann and I have discussed it over the last few months. We're thinking about putting the farm up for sale."

"What, really? Oh, Alan, I'm sorry, that's awful," said Sarah, "it's been in the family for such a long time."

"I know. I've got the weight of that history on my shoulders. It'll be snapped up by a housing developer hoping to get planning permission, the same way that Taylor's was. I'm the one who is going to wreck all those years of tradition. Little Rita or Winnie was a surprise, and Ann and I are happy she's coming, but I don't know what we're bringing her into." They both fell silent.

"I've had a few ideas," said Alan, "and written to the Rivers Authority with a potential solution and I'm waiting to hear back from them."

"Come on," said Sarah. "The Bell. You look like a man who needs a pint of beer."

The Doc looked around the others. They seemed muted. Perhaps they are struggling to comprehend the news, he thought. Perhaps they awaited his lead.

"A consultancy role at Addenbrookes, at such a young age," he said, "well done, Sarah, a tremendous achievement." He looked around again, having expected the others to chip in with their layperson congratulations.

"Really, Doctor?" said Isabel. "I think Rita is more concerned about her grandson and the farm." The Doc blustered.

"Oh yes, of course. Yes. Of course," he huffed. Charlie watched Rita as he spoke. Already weak, she did not need this dire news, delivered by Alan with raw candour, unaware that his grandmother would hear every word.

"I'm sorry, Rita," said Charlie. The pain of Alan's message energised her into speech.

"I can't believe it's gone so badly wrong. After all these years. He puts himself down, Charlie, but Alan is every bit as good at farming as his sister is at medicine."

"I'm sure he is," Charlie agreed. "but he's coming up against problems beyond his control. Climate change, building developments in the wrong place, he's up against governments and councils there, and you know how hard that can be." Rita gave a faint nod.

"You're right, son. I do."

*   *   *

Dear Journal,

Good Morning. A quick note before I get out of bed. I would like to report an improvement today. I think I am functioning a little better. My head is clearer. The numbness that was paralysing my brain, preventing it from doing its stuff properly, is beginning to thaw, and as it recedes I'm feeling stronger, feeling I can get more done. Bye for now. x

Over a second slice of toast (another sign of improvement), Jess reviewed her haphazard list. Drawn up over the previous week, there was no order to the entries, and they ranged from the trivial to the daunting, but she had noted each as something that she really should do, in the hope that the day would arrive when she felt ready to spring into action. Today was that day. She picked up a pen and began to shuffle the order a little, then recognising her self-deception, she laid the pen down. There was no point in moving the simple tasks up the priority order to give herself an easy ride today. She needed

165

to tackle one thing only, the one that she had written down first :

SORT CHARITY FUNDING

Jess's reasoning was straightforward. If she did not resolve this, no one would, and if she did not do it soon, the charity would fold. Over the last year, Jess had schmoozed numerous bodies who were enthusiastic about her project. Like her, most of them were cash-strapped but it was worth a try. She drafted and sent an email to all of them, explaining The Stables Institute's predicament and pleading for any assistance that they might be able to offer. It was unmistakably - and unashamedly - a begging letter. You never know she thought, someone, somewhere might have acquired a pot of money they were desperate to spend.

Next, she reread the message from the Secretary of State for Health. 'There is no appeals process. Please do not reply to this email'. You can piss right off, I will reply. She revisited the business case she had submitted initially to gain the funding, extracting the summary section so casually scorned by Colin Stones, and merged it with the most recent update on the project status that she had delivered. She reviewed the new document she had created. Good… but no good. They already had all of this and it had made no difference to their decision. She needed more. She set off to The Stables.

As she stepped out of the car onto the courtyard, Jess's eyes filled. This was going to be more difficult than she envisaged. How eerily soulless it had become, like a mothballed factory or a disused coal mine. Noise replaced by silence, bustle by stillness, hope by emptiness. She turned the key and entered the reception area. She had expected to see evidence of the abrupt end to the work, a Marie Celeste of half-eaten sandwiches, takeaway cups, and newspapers carrying headlines about what had seemed to be important three weeks ago. Instead, Ray's team had left it immaculate. Unfinished, but immaculate. She moved through the building, using her phone to take photographs that captured the advanced state of the works. In each room, a neatly tied cable dangled from a hole in the plaster ceiling, fishing for the light fitting it would power. In her head she could hear instruments and singing and laughter; in reality, the only sound was that of her footsteps echoing against the bare walls. Jess gathered what she needed and left, locking the door behind her.

By Friday she had assembled a comprehensive and compelling case to say that the works should be finished. The next step was trickier, navigating the endless, perplexing jargon-filled maze of the government's website to find an appropriate recipient. She picked the half dozen most likely departments and sent it to them along with a concise covering note. It had been a time-consuming and probably futile exercise, but Jess was satisfied that she had at least tried.

Her first opportunity to call on Alex was on Saturday morning, when she was walking through Stanford to St. Jude's. Entering Knight's Funeral Directors she was relieved to see that Alex was alone in the office. She was going to feel awkward asking this question.

"Hi, Jess, you're looking well." She invited Jess to sit down and took time to find out how she was managing before, curious as to the reason for the visit, she asked straight out.

"Is there something I can help you with?"

"There is," said Jess. "The run-up to Charlie's funeral was a haze for me. I was so upset. I wonder, can you remember what the items were that I buried with him?"

"I can remember some of them," Alex replied, "but not everything." Jess was disappointed, but not surprised. "Don't worry," Alex added, 'I keep a record."

"Do you?"

"Yes – a couple of years ago we had an incident where a lady gave us a pair of earrings to include with the deceased. A few days later another family member came in, said there has been a mistake, and took them away. It all came out when she wore Auntie Violet's diamond earrings to the funeral. A massive screaming match kicked off, it ended up being one of the most uncomfortable ceremonies I've ever done. Apparently, the wake was carnage. From then on we've been wary. Death. For some relatives, it's less about grieving, more about thieving." Jess smiled. Alex typed in Jess's details. "There," she said, "your list. I'll print you a copy. Do you think you've lost something?"

"Yes. No. I don't know. I can't remember what's in there. It'll give me peace of mind to know." Alex handed her the printed sheet.

"Here you are."

"Thanks again, Alex, you've been great."

"No problem."

*　　*　　*

"Come on, Mia," said Mick, "close the laptop. We're late." Mia replied without breaking off.

"One more minute," she said, "just two more to send. I don't know how your generation puts up with email. So old and clunky."

"I might be old, but don't call me clunky," Mick replied. Mia stopped long enough to give him the briefest of pitying looks.

"That's a dad joke". Mick weighed up whether he should be offended that she thought his material needed further work or pleased that he was like a father figure to her. Over the last fortnight he'd been feeling much more positive about himself. He chose the latter, and smiled. "There, done," she said, grabbing her phone, and following him out to the car.

Jess was sitting on the bench, studying the sheet of paper. She looked up as they approached.

"Morning," she said.

"Hi," Mia replied. "What's that?"

"It's a list of the things that I buried with Charlie. I've just picked it up from Knights. I don't think it helps much though. Have a listen and see what you think." Mick and Mia joined her. "Paperback book. Portable mini radio. Earphones. Ticket stub from concert. Wedding band. Watch. Miniature bottle of rum. Music pendant. Puncture repair kit." She folded the page over. "Can't see anyone clamouring for any of that lot."

"Well," said Mick, "I can give you an update. Remember what I said through a mouthful of tea leaves about information turning up in unlikely places? Last week you mentioned that Charlie thought that the watch was Indian, made by Patel, but your grandad got his watch from an Italian guy. I thought I'll try looking up Patel watches on the internet. Nothing, zero returns. I don't know much about the internet, but I've noticed it hates being beaten," he said, "so it tries to help. What does it do? It corrects your spelling and asks if you meant Patek watches. Spelled with a K, not an L. Antoni Patek, Polish not Indian. He set up a watchmaking company with a Swiss guy, Philippe, in 1851. Patek Philippe, it's still going strong."

"Really?" said Jess. "Do you think that's what Grandad Joe might have had?"

"It's possible. They made watches for the Italian market, so that fits. But get this. They are an exceptionally good make."

"I'm surprised," said Jess, "When you say good…?"

"Well, if I told you that amongst watch fans – I now know there is such a thing – they're known as 'The Rich Man's Rolex'…" Jess put her hand to her mouth. "These things can go for thousands, tens of thousands of pounds. Maybe more." Jess raised her hand from her mouth to her forehead.

"No, surely not," she replied. "I can't see that Grandad Joe's could have been worth anything like that. And how would a poor farm lad in Italy have got one of those? Do you think maybe he had stolen it?"

"Maybe," said Mick, who had already asked himself the same questions. "Another possibility, it could be a fake. For every firm that makes decent quality goods, you'll find a hundred chancers making cheap copies." Mia stood up and turned to them both.

"But hang on," she said, "Tom Bennett digs graves. How would he even know that Charlie had a watch on, never mind a good one?" she asked. In a final escalation, Jess moved both hands to the top of her head. She spoke calmly.

"I know how," she said. "He was in the funeral directors, talking to Lee Knight when I took Charlie's clothes in… along with the box of items, including the watch. He came and joined us as we went through them."

"He would assume it was real, with Charlie being a huge celebrity." Jess gave Mia a queer look. "Well, you know, a little bit famous." The three sat in silence, mulling it over.

"Either way, whether it was real or fake," said Mia, "this could easily be his motive."

"Either way, I think that makes me the top cop of the day," said Mick.

"I think it does," Jess agreed.

"So could you go and report this to the police, to your friend Harry?" Mia asked. Mick shook his head.

"It'll go nowhere. Realistically, the police would never do anything about it." Mia looked disappointed. Mick continued "For them to respond you'd need a lot more than a hunch."

"So he'll get away with it?" As she asked the question, the phone in Mia's hand emitted a ting sound.

"I didn't say that," Mick continued. "We're not giving up on it just yet. When I was on the force we used to get situations like this regularly. You think you know what is likely to have happened, but you just can't prove it. You never knew when something would turn up to give you a breakthrough. And if it didn't, we'd try to do something to shake it all up a bit and see what fell out." He saw that Mia had stopped listening. She was staring at her phone. She held her hand up to indicate they should stop talking. Her thumbs skated across the screen at a rate baffling to both adults.

"You know your top cop status, Uncle Mick? The one you've had for two minutes? I think you need to hand it over."

"Who to?" Jess asked.

"To me," she said. She sprang from the bench and stood to face them. "Jess, I think I might have found your Italian peasant boy."

Chapter 12

Mick watched as a flush of excitement spread wide across the face of his niece. The second to last thing he wanted to do was to dampen her enthusiasm. The last was to give Jess false hope that any genuine progress had been made, until he was sure it had.

"Before we all get ahead of ourselves," he cautioned, "ABC. Assume nothing. Believe no one. Challenge everything. Take a breath, then tell us, what do you have?" The breath Mia took was the deep draught of a hand-diving pearl fisher, unsure when she might gasp her next.

"When Jess told us about the watch and the boy in Italy I'd noted down his name," she said, pointing to the page in her knock-off pocketbook. "I wanted to see if I could find anyone who might have known him. I went online. First, I looked at where British soldiers were in Italy in 1943, to narrow down where he was at the time. Then I looked up Italian names. There are millions of Marcos in Italy, but not so many called Ascenzo. It's unusual, especially in those places where your grandad might have been. I took a chance, hoping that some of his relatives might still be living nearby. Over the last few days, I've done hundreds of searches for Marco Ascenzo, picked out any likely ones, and sent each of them an email." She paused, but briefly, adding, "and that's what I was doing earlier, Uncle Mick, when you were hurrying me along." Mick tried gazing skyward to avoid her look of chastisement, but she held firm till he faced her and took his punishment. Point made, Mia went back to her phone and began to read. "Here's what I said."

"Hi, my name is Mia. I hope you don't mind me sending this to you, but I am trying to trace someone on behalf of a friend. Her grandad was called Joe Hargreaves, and he was a soldier in the British army in 1943. He met an Italian called Marco Ascenzo. I wonder if you know anyone with that name who would have been about twenty in 1943? If so, my friend would love to know, if not don't worry, and sorry to have disturbed you. Thank you. Mia Williams."

"That's a very professional message, Mia," said Jess.

"Thanks. Most of them haven't replied – they probably think it's a scam. A few have got back to me and said they couldn't help, but look what has come in now." The three huddled around her phone screen. With a downward flick of her finger, Mia's original message was replaced by a reply.

"Dear Mia, I was surprised - and excited - to receive your email. I had to respond immediately. I think I may be the person that you are looking for. I did meet a soldier called Joe in the war – I never knew his surname, but together we shared some experiences. He worked in a foundry near Liverpool. I also know that he loved music. If you think I might be the right person, please get back in touch. Regards, Marco Ascenzo."

"Not someone who knows him," she said, "someone who says he is him!"

"Oh my God," said Jess. "Grandad did work in a foundry. This could be our Marco."

"Hang on," said Mick "We don't know anything about the person who sent this."

"You don't, Uncle Mick, but I do. I've done a quick check. Look." Her thumbs danced frantically across the bottom of the screen as she pulled up a series of internet pages. She settled on one that displayed the chestnut-brown face of an old man.

"This is him," she said, "only he's not a peasant boy. At least not any more. He owns a massive air conditioning company in Italy. I contacted him via their website." She flicked through another few screens showing the exterior of a huge factory and the production lines within. She let them take it in before going back to the face of the smiling old man. Beneath his photo the caption read 'Marco Ascenzo – C.E.O. Ascenzo Aria Condizionata'. "I've looked at the obvious things - the email address is right, the web page genuine." Mick's personal pride in her work was tempered only by his ex-professional caution. He closed one eye to help him crunch the numbers in his head.

"Wait. Could he really still be alive?" he said "He would be ancient."

"He is old, about ninety-five I think, but he's alive all right. Look at him." She slid her thumb and forefinger apart, zooming in on his craggy but vital visage. "That's the Mediterranean diet for you, Uncle Mick. No pies and pints for Signor Ascenzo."

"This is amazing, Mia. Well done," said Jess. She turned to Mick. "What do we do now?"

"The next step is for someone to make contact with Mr Ascenzo. By someone, I mean you, Jess." Mia nodded.

"It should be you," she agreed. "It's about your Grandad Joe. Even if it doesn't help us understand what's gone on here at St Jude's, it would be amazing if you could speak to someone who knew your grandad all those years ago." She stopped. "But can I please ask, will you will let us know what Signor Ascenzo says?" Jess looked around the churchyard. It was silent and calm, just the three of them in their peaceful little corner. She thought back to breakfast, to her extensive to-do list. She was pretty sure that making contact with an Italian air-conditioning manufacturer hadn't featured, but Charlie always recommended going with what feels right. She opened her handbag and took out her phone.

"There's no need. I'll do it now so that you can hear for yourselves."

Copying from Mia's screen, Jess entered the telephone number. She typed the last digit and hit call. There was a stretched delay, long enough for them to doubt whether a successful connection had been established. Then came an unfamiliar ring tone at the Italian end of the line. Parp-pause-Parp-pause-Parp, more like a dated electronic alarm clock than a telephone. Uncertain glances flitted between the three faces. The next parp was cut short by a woman's voice, delivering a phrase in Italian at the unintelligible pace of the Terms and Conditions at the end of a television advert. This could be over before it has begun, thought Jess.

"Do you speak English?" she asked.

"Yes. Who is this please? Is it Mia? Mia Williams?"

"No, it's Jess. Her friend," she replied, consciously adopting the status Mia had accorded her in the email.

"Ah! Signor Ascenzo has said that if he receives a call from you, I must put it through to him straight away. Wait, please." A hissy intermission led to a buzz-clunk, then a man's voice. The English was slightly stilted, the voice a little creaky, but there was warmth in every word.

"Hello. I am so pleased to speak to you. Are you Joe's grandchild?" Jess confirmed that she was and replayed how

Mia had found him. He replied with some details of his own. Within a few brief sentences, it was irrefutable; improbable as it seemed, Jess was talking to the peasant boy Grandad Joe had encountered seventy-five years ago.

"And of Joe…" he said, "I do not like to ask…" Jess saved him from having to.

"He died several years ago, I'm afraid."

"Ah, I am sorry to hear that." Signor Ascenzo's voice carried the resigned sadness of a man who had seen most of his contemporaries in life come and go. "He was an exceptional man. But none of us can live forever." Jess looked across the breadth of the graveyard, at the ranks of stones before them.

"No, that is true," she agreed. "I am afraid I have some other bad news, the real reason for my call. It's about a watch that I think you may have given to my grandad." Jess related the events of the last few weeks. When she got to Charlie's death, there was a lengthy interruption as Signor Ascenzo offered his condolences. Then Jess described the suspected theft of the watch. For a moment she thought Marco - or the connection - had gone. He spoke once more.

"No. This is too terrible. Can such a thing happen in these times? If it is true then it must be put right. Let me think." He stopped once more. In the undisturbed stillness of the graveyard morning, they could hear his strong, steady breath. "Okay," he said, "I am not certain what I can do to assist, but I feel we must be bold, we must act. I can perhaps start by telling you everything I know from all those years ago. I have a suggestion. I think we should not speak of this over the telephone anymore. If it is possible you must come and visit me here in Abruzzo. I know the start of this story. Maybe that can help. Please. And you must come with your mother, I would like to meet Joe's daughter. Please say yes, and I will arrange everything."

Jess could not tell how she would have responded had this proposition been put to her a few weeks ago. In the immediate aftermath of Charlie's death, much of the resolve she'd had, that he had helped nurture within her, was severely damaged. Then came that incident, here, a couple of weeks ago, when they were so close that he spoke to her, and that strength, the belief, was rekindled within her, strong as ever. She replied immediately and with conviction.

"Thank you, Signor Ascenzo. I would be delighted. And I'll ask my mum, Diane, if she would like to come too."

"Excellent. I will have my people contact you to make arrangements convenient for you. I am so looking forward to our meeting." As Jess ended the call, Mia clapped her hands together in spontaneous excitement.

"You're going to Abruzzo, Jess," she said.

"My geography is a bit rusty," said Mick. "Just remind me…" Mia rolled her eyes.

"Halfway down Italy's boot, about the lower calf area." Mick nodded, as if it was all flooding back to him.

"Your mum is not going to believe this," said Mia. Although she had never met Diane, she had called it absolutely right.

"I don't believe this," said Diane. "Don't you read the papers? This could be anyone. A confidence trickster. Drug smuggler. People trafficker. That's if it even is a person and not just another computer."

"Mum, Mick has had an ex-colleague in the police check him out. And his company. It's all genuine."

"Well, I am certainly not going, and I don't think that you

177

should either." Jess looked at her mum over the rim of her mug. They stood in the kitchen of her mum's house, staring at one another, daring one another to make the next move. Diane folded her arms tight across her chest, and immediately Jess remembered.

"Look where we're both standing mum," she said. "Me here, you there. Remind you of anything?" Diane looked around them.

"No. What about it?"

"We're in the exact places we were in when I first mentioned that I'd met a boy called Charlie. Remember what you thought then? What you said?" Diane turned her gaze downwards. She must have seen something important beside her feet. "Remember what we spoke about last week? About dad, and living life to the full?" She looked back at Jess, crossed the floor, and gave her a hug.

"I know, you're right. But I'll have to find someone reliable to look after the cats."

* * *

Having taken one of her mother's folded arms and twisted it up her back, Jess knew she could not renege. But she got close. Seventeen telephone calls in four days. How will we get there? Do I need any injections? Where will we stay? How will we get there from this airport where we land… what's it called again? As each problem of logistics was surmounted, the line of questioning shifted to details of their stay. Who would they meet? Is it hot there at this time of year? What clothes should she pack? Are you taking your hairdryer? Jess never entirely lost her patience, though she 'lost' her mobile phone signal on three of the more drawn-out calls.

Boarding at Manchester airport was unusually troublesome. Diane had to retrieve each element of her travel documentation from its individually allocated place of safekeeping, somewhere no one would ever think to look - her included. Once she had found her seat, and opened her book, she did relax for a couple of hours, but when the pilot advised that they were about to commence their descent, her calm façade dissolved faster than the jet's vapour trail.

"Would you recognise me? " she asked, holding her grainy passport photo alongside her. "My hair is a different style, and much more grey."

"Yes, I'd recognise you. The bit underneath your hair - you know, your face – it's identical." Diane tutted.

"I know you said we don't need it, but I've still got my boarding card. You're sure we don't need a visa or anything else?" Jess burst out laughing.

"Mum, you spent all of those years married to a man who measured risk as his job, and when he came home at night, he did it as a hobby. Look," she said, pointing at the screen on the seat in front of her, displaying flight statistics and tracking their progress across a map of Europe. "Altitude - ten thousand five hundred feet," she said. "Speed - five hundred and fifteen miles an hour. You're sitting in a metal tube full of… whatever it is… highly flammable plane-petrol. And your main worry? That your paperwork might not be in order." Diane grinned sheepishly.

"Well, it would be embarrassing, in front of the whole queue of strangers."

Mercifully, Abruzzo Airport was not busy, and the formalities were light touch. The Italian authorities accepted Diane and her daughter into the country without a hitch. They passed through the Arrivals hall and had no trouble picking out their driver. A tall man in an ice blue suit stood prominently, holding an electronic tablet bearing their names. Jess waved, although she could tell from the smile he gave that he had already surmised that these were the people he was to meet.

"Hi, my name is Paulo. Welcome to Abruzzo. Let me take those cases," he said, whisking them from their hands. "Come, this way, I am parked right by the door - don't ask how I managed to do so." He smiled once more and led them to the car.

As they travelled further from the airport, their functional urban surroundings gave way to gentle hills clothed in green corduroy stripes, formed by orderly rows of ancient vineyards. Diane's eyes darted left and right, alerting Jess to birds that she did not recognise, buildings whose purpose she could not fathom, and crops that she had never seen growing at home. Making eye contact with them in his rear-view mirror, Paulo did his best to throw light onto her unfolding new world.

"We are here," he said, pulling off the road to climb the driveway leading to the property. As he did so he spotted mother and daughter exchanging questioning looks. The drive was several times the length of the large cul-de-sac serving Diane's house and half a dozen others. They had anticipated that it might be impressive, but were not prepared for the magnificent villa which came into view. As Paulo had observed their reaction, Jess felt obliged to say it out loud.

"It's a very beautiful house."

"It is," he agreed, turning off the engine. "Signor Ascenzo had it built thirty years ago. It has wonderful views all around. Come, let's go inside." At the door, a small, middle-aged lady, dressed all in black apart from a white apron, greeted them with a shy smile and a nod of the head. They moved through the porch into a cavernous marble hallway. Paulo laid down their cases and said something in Italian to the lady, and she scuttled off to do whatever the Italian thing was.

Paulo led them through to a large drawing room with floor-to-ceiling windows, overlooking immaculate gardens and the rolling hills beyond. To their right sat a figure in a high-backed leather chair. He smiled as they entered and, using a wooden walking stick, he raised himself to his feet. The metal tip clicked on the marble tiles as he walked towards them with short, busy steps.

"Welcome, ladies, welcome," he said, "I am Marco. It is lovely to meet you both."

"Hi. I'm Jess, and this is my mum, Diane." Marco nodded, ushering them to take a seat on the couch opposite him. "Can I offer you a coffee? Or do you prefer English tea? Perhaps a glass of something with a little more sparkle?" he suggested, with a wave towards an ice bucket holding a bottle with a caged cork.

"A glass of wine would be lovely," said Jess. "Mum?" Diane peeked at her watch, which she had adjusted to local time aboard the plane, as soon as prompted to do so by the flight attendant.

"Eh, yes, I'll have a small one," she replied. Jess turned at the sound of someone entering the room. By some mystic power that would have been the envy of Psychic Cedric, the lady from the hallway appeared with a tray holding three elegant champagne flutes. She filled them and handed them around from a tray.

"Welcome to Abruzzo," said Marco, raising his glass, "my home region. I am proud to say I have lived here all of my life. The motto of our people is Forte e Gentile. In English, you would say Strong and Gentle. That is how you will find us. I hope that you will enjoy your visit. You must let me know if there is anything we can do to make your stay more enjoyable." He balanced his cane against the chair. Jess noticed the intricate carving on the silver handle, and how the dark turtle shell pattern on the shaft perfectly matched the rims of the small round glasses he wore. She wondered how many other coordinating sets he owned.

"This area and your home are very beautiful," she said. "I'm sure we will have a lovely time." The first bottle was emptied with remarkable ease, to be replaced by a second. They chatted about their journey across (which Diane apparently found to have been straightforward) before Marco described with delight the region, his life, his family, and his business. He then offered them the opportunity to go to their rooms to unpack and settle in, before the evening meal. When she was ready to go down, Jess tapped on her mum's bedroom door.

"My God, your room is even bigger than mine," said Jess, giggling. "Have you ever seen anywhere like this?"

"Only in films or in magazines. It's amazing." As they approached the top of the stairs, she touched her daughter's forearm, causing her to stop.

"Jess, I'm glad I came."

The meal they ate was a deceptively simple pasta dish, subtle, but with a depth of flavour that they continued to enjoy long after the white porcelain bowls had been emptied. The three remained at the table, talking without pause, laughing without reserve. Marco wanted to know more about them. He intervened periodically to ask a shrewd question to help him better understand them and their lives. Jess watched her mother uncoil as the evening passed. She did not want to fracture the mood, but felt she should at least offer to bring them back to the purpose of their visit.

"Signor Ascenzo..."

"Marco," he corrected her.

"Marco. This is lovely, thank you, but should we discuss the reason that we came here?"

"Ah yes, of course. Joe's watch," he said nodding and looking more serious, only momentarily. "We must, we must. However, with your permission, I would like to wait until tomorrow. You have travelled today, you must both be tired. And we have all enjoyed a glass or two of wine. I think that tomorrow would be better?"

"Tomorrow will be fine," said Jess.

"Excellent. I have somewhere special I would like us to visit," he said. "Now, let us share what is left in this bottle. And Diane, you can finish telling me the story of the time that you and your husband almost took a holiday in Rome."

Mid-morning, following a leisurely breakfast, Marco asked Paulo to bring the car to the front of the villa. It was not the same vehicle that he had used to pick them up from the airport the previous day.

"It's a limousine," Diane whispered to Jess, as they walked down the steps. The elongated silver chassis, glinted under the rays of the bright sun.

"My goodness," Diane said to Paulo, "my little car only has one door on each side. This has three." Paulo opened those towards the rear and invited them in. There were two pairs of vast leather seats in the back, facing each other. "Though I'd imagine trying to park it at the supermarket would be awful," Diane observed as she settled in.

"I thought if we travel in this we could chat more easily," said Marco, once he had slowly and carefully eased his elderly frame into the seat opposite them. Paulo set off, the engine noise imperceptible. "There is so much more I want to know. And to tell you."

"I'm looking forward to it," said Diane. "My dad only spoke about his time in the war when he knew that he didn't have long left to live. I was surprised, he remembered such a lot of detail. He told me that he met an Italian... farm-working chap, who had given him the watch that he wore all of his life. He still knew your name, even after all these years, so you must have made an impression on him." Marco nodded.

"I was like Joe." Marco's face grew sombre. "We find it hard to discuss... we find it hard to forget. It was dreadful for everyone who lived through it. But now that Joe is sadly no longer here, I would like to pass on the little bit that I know about your dad, Diane, your grandad, Jess. Do you know much about Italy in the war?"

"Not really," said Jess. He leaned in towards them.

"In 1940 our leader, Mussolini, decided Italy must side with Germany. Many in our country did not agree with this, hated the Nazis and everything that they believed in, but for several years Mussolini had the Italian Army fight in support of them. I met Joe in the winter of 1943, when I was twenty-one years old. It was an important point in the war. The Allies had captured Sicily in summer, and they began to come up north through Italy. Mussolini surrendered, thankfully he was gone," Marco said, with a dismissive wave of his hand. "Italy decided to change sides, so German troops invaded the north of our country, and many of the Italian Army began fighting against them, alongside the Allies."

"So did you and my dad fight beside each other?" Diane asked.

"In a way. You see, it was not only our soldiers who fought. You will have heard of the Resistance in France?" They nodded. "It was the same here. Italian citizens, like me, started to work in small groups, all over our land, carrying out undercover actions against the Germans. We were fighting them here, in this countryside, in these hills. Ordinary men, doing whatever we could to disrupt them. Our brigade got what it could from within our community but we had very limited supplies. The Allied soldiers helped us with support and equipment, and we would pass on local intelligence to them. And that is how I came to know Joe. We did not share the same uniforms, we were not in an army rank, but Joe and I were shoulder to shoulder, linked by our belief that evil must not win."

Paulo pulled the car into an unsurfaced layby at the side of the road. Jess and Diane turned to look through their respective windows. All around them, in every direction, was hilly terrain, remote, with no buildings, just scrubby vegetation. Marco spoke once more.

"In 1943, it was much harder to get to this place, it took many hours. This road that we have driven up was not built. You could only get here on foot, but the countryside, these hills, the bushes, it was as it is now. For us, it was perfect, a safe place where Joe and I could secretly meet." Paulo opened the doors and helped Marco to step out, passing him his cane. Jess and Diane followed him, feeling a blast of heat as they left the comfort of the air-conditioned interior. Standing outside the vehicle, they could now fully take in the surroundings. Diane thought back to the bedside conversations with her father. As a young man, barely more than a boy, he had been here. It must have seemed so far from anything he knew.

"Come, I'll show you," said Marco. With his stick in his left hand, he set off onto a narrow stony footpath, his pace slow but his gait steady. He turn back to them and grinned.

"Now you see why I ask that you wear your most comfortable shoes." The three progressed along the track, with Marco occasionally shouting back a warning when he encountered a particularly rough section. He came to a halt in a small, flat clearing. For a full minute they waited as he looked deliberately around the slopes, before addressing them.

"Joe and I had met on three occasions in these hills. I was sent from our group because I was one of the only local people who could speak any English. My parents had a successful engineering business, so I had received more education than most. Each time we met we talked for hours. At first we would discuss how we could combat the Germans, but then we moved on. We spoke about our lives, our hopes, and what we were looking forward to when this terrible war finally was over. We were in a cave, it was damp, cold, with little light, but there we grew seeds, the seeds of friendship. And then on the fourth and last time we met," he said, clasping his palms together firmly, "a bond was made between us, a bond that no one will ever break." Marco fell silent.

* * *

Joe was glad he had been put in charge of managing contact with Marco's brigade of partisans. Not all of his comrades would have been so keen to take it on. The Eighth Army was a melting pot of squaddies from all around the world - Yanks, Poles, Indians, Greeks, Brazilians, Kiwis, Canadians. And now they had been joined by Italians. A nation that had until recently been the enemy, was now fighting alongside them against the German forces occupying their country. Some of the guys in Joe's platoon weren't keen on the Italians, didn't trust them, but Joe liked Marco, right from the minute they first met.

The Eighth's progress had stalled again in the last few days, as they fought a slow battle against German forces dug in on higher ground. It gave Joe a chance to meet Marco again, to exchange the latest intelligence. He'd already made this journey three times over the past couple of weeks, so he knew the lie of the land, but you could never be blasé. Joe knew a hell of a lot more about how to stay alive than any man just turned twenty should do. Switch off for a second, son, and you are a goner, that's what his sergeant said. Even in this remote, desolate landscape, he was switched on. Senses alive, with steps confident yet cautious, he moved towards their rendezvous, a concealed cave, where lay a cache of arms and provisions.

As he neared the place, he saw a figure picking his way along the goat tracks that criss-crossed the scrubland. It's okay, it's Marco. Joe was never to know it, but the shabby clothes that the young Italian was dressed in bore no resemblance to his peacetime attire, his present lowly outfit chosen to make him blend in with the handful of people who scratched out a living around there. From their previous meetings, Joe knew that Marco, like him, was desperate to succeed in this struggle, but beyond that, although their worlds seemed so different, he was struck by how much they had in common, the boy from the foundry and this boy from the farm. As he watched him winding towards the cave, Joe unconsciously quickened his step, eager to meet again. But Joe's were not the only set of eyes tracking Marco's progress that day.

It happened in the briefest of moments. Joe saw a figure in German uniform appear on the track ten metres ahead of Marco, rifle raised and pointing at him. A second figure stepped out of the undergrowth, barking unknown words at him in German whilst gesturing to say he should lie down. As

Marco complied, the two soldiers moved toward him, and hauled him back onto his feet. Joe, crouching and fixed still, felt a fear rise within him as Marco was spun around by the shoulder and pushed forwards down the track in the direction from which his captors had approached.

Joe was under no illusion as to what would come next. In their previous conversations, Marco had laid bare the risks he and his fellow brigade members were taking. The soldiers were not out here by chance. Someone had tipped them off, probably someone Marco knew. These occupiers treated any Italian civilians who resisted their cause with barbaric cruelty. Marco would be beaten and tortured, in an effort to make him give up the names of his comrades. Then he would be killed, and his body dumped in his village, a warning to others.

Joe surveyed the hillside to his left, looking for a suitable place, eyes flicking occasionally to the little group below. Staying low, but moving quickly, he contoured round to a small outcrop of rock and lay down. The jagged surface beneath him dug uncomfortably into his belly. He shouldered his rifle. The child within him had long since disappeared. This was no fairground stall, three shots for a penny, win a coconut whatever happens. One chance, at stake the life of a man. The foundry where he was an apprentice was over a thousand miles away, but here on this faraway hill, his heart was banging like its steam hammer. And yet, he had a hand as cold, as steady and precise as the cutting blade of a lathe. He pulled the trigger. The sound of the shot echoed around the scorched walls of the valley. The German to the fore crumpled to the ground. His comrade threw himself flat and, using his elbows, he began to crawl towards the undergrowth. Marco too flung himself onto the track but stayed absolutely still, waiting. A second shot rang out. The crawling stopped.

"I was lying here," said Marco, indicating a spot to Diane and Jess, beside where he stood. "I raised my head and saw that neither of the enemies was moving. I had never felt such terror before. Or since. I was not sure what had happened. I stood up and then I saw him. Joe. He was running down the hill like a maniac. Thank God for Joe. Before he had reached me, I had already begun to pull the first German off the track and into these bushes here. Others were sure to come and so we needed to quickly conceal what had happened. As I did so, I saw Joe reach the second and kneel down beside him. My heart was beating twice as fast as normal. It only took one of those short beats for it to happen. The soldier raised his arm, I could see the long bayonet in his hand and he took a swipe. Joe jumped back but the blade slashed deep into his arm. I picked up the first German's gun and shouted to Joe to move. I fired. The soldier's body shook, then it was still once more. Two seconds, that is all it could have taken. I ran to Joe, the blood from the wound was already seeping through his uniform. You must go back to your camp I said, get help for your arm. But he would not go. 'No, Marco, the Germans must know this place, the cave. The guns, the supplies, we must move them.'"

Marco stopped and looked at Diane and Jess. He could see that they had never heard this story and that both were deeply affected. "Perhaps I have said too much, this is too upsetting?"

Diane shook her head. "No, no, please go on, you must tell us about dad. We had no idea, he never told me this part of it."

"If you are sure," Marco said, with a nod.

"Please, yes."

"I took off the rag of a neckerchief I was wearing and tied it as tightly as I could around the top of Joe's arm. We must be quick I said. We set off running towards the cave. I shouted to Joe 'I know a place to put the supplies, not too far. We can leave them there till everything has calmed down.' And when we arrived at the cave – I can see it in my mind now - I turned to him and said 'Today you have saved my life, Joe'." Marco bowed his head, moved by the memory. He raised it once more.

"We worked fast, quickly, quickly, moving rifles, ammunition, tins of food around to a hidden crack in the rocks twenty metres or so above and to the right of the cave. We were so tired. The boxes of ammunition were heavy, it needed both of us to move them. And Joe's arm was hurting him badly. In two hours it was done, the cave was cleared. We pulled off large chunks of a bush like this one and brushed away all of our footprints. Only then did we stop. I pulled up his sleeve. The cut was from here to here, from the wrist up nearly to his elbow," he said, tracing the path on his own arm. "Then I saw his watch." Marco paused once more.

"I said 'You and I. Forever. You and I. For all time'. And I took off my watch, then undid the clasp on his and replaced it with mine. I put on Joe's. It fitted perfectly. I said 'Now we must go and we must not meet again'. 'Good luck Marco', he said to me. He got up, and was gone." Marco looked at both ladies.

"So that is my story. Joe's story. Our story. I was in the deepest trouble. There is no doubt, I would have been killed. And if they would have found Joe, he would have been killed too. It is that simple. It would have been easy for him to hide, to run, to save himself, but he did not. He chose to put himself at such risk to save me, almost a stranger." Though she tried to conceal it, Marco saw that tears had spilled over the lower rim of Diane's eyes and ran down her cheeks. "Ah, I have upset you. I am sorry."

"No, please don't be. It's such a shock. You make it seem so real. It helps me understand dad better," said Diane, "why he was the way he was."

"You should be very proud of him."

"I am. I was anyway, but now I am more than ever."

Then, with an effort, the old man used the bony fingers of his right hand to raise the refined material of his shirt sleeve a few inches higher on his left arm. He pointed at the simple timepiece he had exposed.

"My watch," he said. Jess and her mother looked at each other.

"Is that…. was that… my grandad's?" asked Jess. Marco nodded his head.

"Yes it was," he replied. "It does not contain diamonds, it may not have been built in the finest workshop in Switzerland, but I believe this to be the most precious watch that was ever made. Come, take a closer look at it." Jess allowed Diane to move first, to get the best view of the watch that had belonged to her father as a young man, before the time when he had even met her mother. It had a deep gold coloured case, a white dial, with clear black roman numerals around the edge, marking the hours.

"And let me tell you, it keeps perfect time too," Marco continued. "I know because since I received it there is not a day that has passed where I have not worn it. It is the only watch that I have owned for the last seventy-four years." Jess looked into the old man's eyes. They shone with truth.

"Does no one ever ask you how you have come to be wearing something so… ordinary?" Marco smiled.

"Occasionally someone does," he said. "and when they do I tell them the story of Joe, and I tell them how proud I am every day to wear the watch of the bravest man that I ever met."

Diane did not even attempt to cover her tears. She sobbed without shame. "That is so beautiful. Thank you," she said.

"There are some things in one's life," said Marco, "that it is sufficient to think about only now and then. There are others that you must remind yourself of every day. When I put this watch on in the morning, I remember why I am here. I remember that there would be no Ascenzo family, no business, no fine villa, were it not for Joe's bravery and goodness. Strong and Gentle. He could have been an Abruzzese." Jess looked at the old man. He looked drained.

"Come," he said, "it is time for us to return. My housekeeper is baking today. She makes the finest panettone in all of Italy." They set off back to the car, where Paulo was waiting for them. The journey back was made in complete silence, all three wrapped, rapt, in their thoughts.

Chapter 13

Mick could sense a change in Mia. He'd mulled it over, observed her, noticed the subtle shifts in behaviour. He could describe it now - she was showing more confidence and more maturity in almost everything she did - but he could not say what was bringing it about. He'd heard that kids grow up more quickly now than in his day. Was that it? Then on Saturday, even though Jess was in Italy, Mia said she would still like to visit St Jude's. He wondered why. Of course, it's obvious - it's being in Jess's company. His niece was blossoming by spending time with an adult woman, one that was not a teacher, one that she described as her friend.

On Saturday morning, as soon as he turned the car onto Stanford's Main Street, Mia pointed at a tiny figure, half a mile distant.

"That's Grace," she said. "When you get to her, Uncle Mick, can you pull over? I'd like to speak to her. Just for five minutes." Mick peered at the small dot in the distance.

"How do you know it's her?"

"Her coat. So cool." Perhaps there is still a teenager within her after all.

"It's black," he said, as they got nearer, "plain black." Mia gave him a commiserative look that a mother might bestow upon their misguided offspring. Perhaps not. As they drew level, Mick slowed down, and seeing them, the young girl in the cool black coat waved.

"Five minutes, I'll be in the churchyard," said Mick, as the car door slammed shut.

It was fully half an hour later when Mia sat down beside him on the bench.

"Five minutes?"

"It's further than you'd think from there." Mick shook his head. Mia surveyed the graveyard from the bench. "It's quiet here without Jess." Mick nodded, to her and to himself.

"I wonder what's happening in Italy," he said. "I hope they're okay. Jess says her mum is a worrier, and it'll be strange for her to meet someone that knew her dad during the war, all those years ago. I hope it's not too much of a shock. They'll be back soon though, and I'm sure Jess will tell us all about it."

"I hope she's found out something that might help us," said Mia. "It's a shame we won't have any new information to give to her."

"ABC, Mia. Assume nothing. We do have a little bit," said Mick. He pointed to the top end of the graveyard. "Bennett," he said. "He was here when I arrived so, while you were with your friend, I took the chance to speak to him." Mia's eyes widened and she sat up straight.

"What did he tell you?"

"Nothing," said Mick. He watched her shoulders slump as she folded in on herself.

"That's no good."

"Don't be so sure," he replied. "In an investigation – forget that, in life - it can be as important to notice what a person doesn't say as what they do."

"What do you mean?"

"I started by asking him some general questions, you know, if he'd worked here long, if he liked the job, how he got into it. He answered all of these, a little cautious maybe, probably because of when I spoke to him before. But then I moved on to specifics like who decides which graves are dug, when will the one he dug by mistake be used, he zipped his lips. Made an excuse and headed off to that far corner. Look, he's still up there, pretending to be busy, waiting for us to leave. So he was happy to talk to me, but not about any of those things."

"What do you think that tells us?"

"What it tells us is that the previous conversation I had with him was no one-off. We are on the right lines. He was up to something when he dug that grave. And, as importantly, what it tells him is that this is not just going to go away. We've got under his skin, we're onto him, and he knows it."

"Did you hear that?" Charlie said. "They're getting to Bennett. And Jess has definitely gone to Italy. She's there now, with her mum. I wonder if this Marco will have any useful info for her? When she phoned him, he sounded old, but pretty switched on."

"The outcome of their visit will be intriguing," said The Doc. "I very much hope it will help us understand the reason for that disgraceful act of plunder that you were subjected to. And, having myself been to Italy on three occasions, I would like to hear how your wife found that fascinating country. Is it a place that you have had the opportunity to visit Rita?" Silence. "Rita?" Doc repeated. Nothing. "She's not answering," he said, with more than a hint of concern in his voice.

"Rita, are you okay?" Charlie asked. Isabel joined in "Rita? Rita? Can you hear us?"

*   *   *

Jess could not be sure if Marco's housekeeper did make the finest panettone in all of Italy, but she was certain it was the best that she had ever tasted. That was one of the few things of which she was certain. Thoughts swooped and wheeled around her mind, kites in a windstorm. Since landing in Italy less than twenty-four hours ago the entire narrative had been reframed. Jess had spent the car journey back to the villa going over Marco's story about her grandad, wondering what it might mean for her mum. They had got almost everything wrong about the original owner of the watch. Marco. Not an Indian, an Italian. Not a peasant, a businessman, one possessing wealth beyond anything that she had ever encountered. Many things were not as she thought, and there were implications. They were to fly back to England tomorrow. She needed to talk to Marco now. Face to Face. That evening, as soon as the last morsel of their meal was eaten, she could wait no longer to address it.

"Marco, there is something I'd like to ask." The old man looked at her but did not speak, inviting her to continue. "Your watch, I mean the one you gave Grandad Joe, was it made by a company called Patek Philippe?" Marco nodded. Jess continued. "So do you think it would have been expensive?"

"I owned it for a few months only, so I know little about it. I was given it by my father for my twenty-first birthday. I was always taught never to ask the value of a gift."

"But you must have an idea."

"My father chose it, he liked fine things, so I think he would have bought a good watch for his son." He paused, then continued. "Though you should understand, when I told him the story of Joe and the exchange I made, he did not behave as if I had given away a valuable item. He was not upset." He raised his head to look at the ceiling of the drawing room, casting his mind back to the moment. "The opposite was true. He said that he was proud, that I had done a good thing. He told me that I must now treasure the one that I have, as if it was the one that he had given to me." Why is he being so evasive, she thought. Then she realised. He's not, it's just that his responses are shaped by what's most meaningful to him, not money, but his relationship with her grandad. She changed tack.

"Can I talk to Marco the businessman?" she asked. "Would he say his original watch could be worth thousands of Euros?" Marco did not reply. "Tens of thousands?" Marco nodded.

"Probably," he conceded. "More coffee?"

"No, thank you," she continued. "Can I summarise what we know?" Jess looked on as Marco's steady hand poured himself another cup, waiting to gain his full attention. "One. We are as good as certain that Grandad Joe's watch is the one you gave to him. Two. We don't know for sure but we think that it's been stolen by the gravedigger. Three. We don't know the exact value, but we think it could be considerable."

"A fair summary. And so?"

"And so, if this is all correct, and if we manage to recover the watch, then you must have it back."

"I must? Must I? Why? I have explained to you, I already own the only watch I will ever need." Jess composed herself to make her case.

"Marco, my grandad wore it all of his life with no inkling that it was an expensive make. If he had known I am sure he would never have made the exchange. And your dad gave it to you for your twenty-first birthday, so by rights, it belongs to you, to your family." Marco took a sip and laid down his cup.

"Okay, you asked to speak to Marco the businessman. He is someone who looks ahead, thinks what may happen and plans for it. Ever since you contacted me, I thought that as you learned the story you might suggest something like this. I have considered how we could address this unusual situation so as to make everyone happy. I have a proposal of my own which I hope you will allow me to make." Wrong-footed, Jess eyed him, waiting.

"I met your grandad, Joe, on only four occasions, but those memories are seared into my mind, as if branded by the hottest of irons. We were in the worst times either of us would ever know. Our meetings were to plan the tiny part that we could play in a worldwide effort to bring this evil to an end. Two young men, different countries, different backgrounds. But it was not just the war and the enemy that we had in common. As we told each other of our lives we found that we shared one thing in particular, special to us both, something that we spoke about for hours." Jess waited for him to continue, unsure of where this was heading. It was not Marco, however, who spoke next. It was her mother.

"It was music, wasn't it?" she said.

"It was, exactly! Music," said Marco.

"He mentioned it when he spoke about you. I remember now." Marco became more animated than at any stage in their visit.

"Each time we met, we talked about it, the acts and the songs we liked. We loved jazz – Charlie Parker, Dizzy Gillespie. And singers like Bing Crosby and Frank Sinatra. We spoke of it more than anything else. Music made us realise how similar we were as people. It lifted us, gave us hope that better times would come. When I asked you yesterday, Jess, you told me about the work you do with your patients." Jess nodded. "You understand the power that music can have to do great things."

"I do. It's the whole reason for the career I've chosen. I have seen how it can change people's lives more than you could think possible." Marco bent down and picked up a tired old leather briefcase from beside his feet. From it, he produced a small bundle of printed sheets which, try as she might, Jess could not read upside down. Marco donned his little round glasses once more.

"You see, after your young friend in Britain did her research to find me, I have also looked into the lady who now owns my old watch." He passed the bundle to Jess. The top one was a print of the home page for The Stables website. She began to leaf through them. Next was more detail from the web pages about the Institute's aims and the services it would provide, then there was the business case she had made to get the funding, passages about the charity she had set up, a biography of herself, newspaper articles where she had talked about what she was trying to achieve. All of it she recognised, but she was stunned to see months of her work collated in this way. Marco watched her as she reflected on her journey. Now was his moment.

"The Stables Institute is in danger of failing to ever welcome a single patient," he said. "Am I right?" He watched the exchange of perplexed looks between Jess and Diane. "Please don't be annoyed," he said. "I know all about the charity you have set up, Jess Munro. I am aware of the difficulty you have with completing the repairs to your building. I know that the work has had to stop."

"It has," Jess said, "temporarily. I am determined to get it open, Marco. I'll find a way."

"I am sure you will," said Marco. "I can hear it in your voice. Forte e Gentile. Strong and Gentle. A descendant of Joe, for sure."

"The right opportunity will come along."

"And I hope that I am lucky enough to be the one who brings it," he said. "My proposal for you to consider is this. If the watch is ever found, I would agree to take it back, as you have insisted, as long as you also agree to take back the watch belonging to Joe." His sharp little eyes watched hers, took in her face, her mouth, and as he could see she was about to acquiesce he struck. "And let us assume we are correct and that there is a difference in value, after all of this time, and with everything that bonds our two families, would it not be fair for us to split the total value between us?" Jess looked hard at the old man before her. She could tell that he had thought this through in advance, several moves ahead, like a wily old chess master. She replied with some hesitation.

"I suppose so," she said.

"So that only leaves one more thing I think. Since we are almost certain that, as a result of our fair exchange, I will owe you some money, then I would like, in advance, to donate to The Stables Institute, to enable the work to recommence without delay." Jess stood up from the table with a force that would have knocked the chess board, sending kings and queens and knights and pawns flying in directions forbidden by the laws of the game, ensuring her disqualification from the tournament.

"No. No. Marco, that is a step too far. It's not right. I can't accept your…"

"Charity?" he said. "Forgive me, maybe I do not understand, maybe charities work differently in your country? They do not take donations?"

"Well, no, of course they do. But I am going to find the money. I've written to lots of interested parties and…"

"How many have replied? And of those, has any offered you money? Not best wishes, not kind thoughts. Money." Jess sighed.

"All of them have replied now. Lots of goodwill, good luck. No money. But I've written to the government too. Half a dozen different departments." Marco eyes were fixed on her. There was no point in trying to dress this up. He knew. "No replies from them as yet," she said, resuming her seat. "Marco, are you only doing this because of Grandad Joe?" She held a steady, level stare as he continued.

"You are wise to explore my motivation. I owe everything to Joe, but that is not the only reason for my offer. I have been fortunate in life in so many ways. Already, every year I donate to organisations here in Italy that offer help to people in need. This one will be special, if you allow me to contribute. Joe and I both loved music. The work of your institute will capture the hope it gave us and bring it to life. It will be a permanent memorial to the two of us. It will keep our story alive, and prevent it from fading from the minds of men…"

"Like the lost lyrics of a forgotten song," Jess interrupted. "One that will never be sung again." Marco's eyes watched her intently. "Sorry, something Charlie mentioned to me."

"He was right. Think of that – how regrettable to lose something so precious. It would be an honour for me to help you. Think of it as a loan if you must. But please, say yes." Before Jess could speak, Diane intervened, speaking directly to Marco.

"Jess has always been brought up to be polite, to stand on her own two feet, and not to take advantage of any situation." Jess was surprised at her assertive tone. "Today I saw how painful it was for you to revisit that terrible incident. My dad was the same. In fact, Jess and I think that he probably had…"

"PTSD," Jess intervened quickly, fearful that her mum might repeat her previous misdiagnosis.

"Exactly," said Diane. She turned to her daughter. "Jess, would your music therapy have been able to help Signor Ascenzo and Grandad Joe come to terms with the things that happened to them?" Jess had not anticipated being put on the spot by her mother.

"Yes…" she replied, "… I'm sure it would."

"You have a chance to help people in a similar situation now. Signor Ascenzo is making a genuine and generous offer. This is no time to delay. You should grasp this opportunity with both hands."

"And as an Italian, I was brought up to know that a mother is always right," Marco added. Jess eyed them both.

"I don't suppose I am allowed to give any answer other than yes." Marco smiled.

"Excellent. Then we now both need to make a phone call." He picked up his mobile, stabbed the screen a few times with his twisted forefinger, and raised it to his ear. He spoke no more than three sentences in rapid Italian, then laid it back down. "There," he said, "Everything was already prepared, awaiting your agreement and my authorisation. I have transferred my donation. Now I suggest you phone your builder friend, let him know that you can now pay him for the work he has already done, and ask that he gets back onto your job immediately." Jess took her phone from her handbag.

"Signor Ascenzo, you are a strong and gentle man."

Dear Journal,

It's just after midnight (Italian time). I was lying in bed and thought I could hear something from mum's room. I gently knocked on her door. I was right, she had been crying, but insisted they were happy tears, from hearing about Grandad Joe. I think she is overwhelmed. It was a reminder that this is not all about me. It's a difficult time for everyone, and we all need to look after each other.

*   *   *

At around the same time as Marco and Jess were making their commitment to each other, Charlie made one to himself. Tomorrow morning, that's it. If there is no improvement by then, he would have to act. By daylight, the situation was unchanged.

"Doc, Isabel. Have you ever heard a song called 'Silence is Golden'?" Isabel shook her head.

"I have," The Doc replied. "By a group called The Tremeloes, if I remember correctly."

"That's it," said Charlie. "The thing with silence though is it's not always golden, it can be other things. Like awkward. I've been thinking… I'm wondering if there is something we should do about the Rita situation." It was the first time that any of them had dared to address it directly. Neither The Doc nor Isabel made a sound. Silence. Deafening. The Doc capitulated.

"Could you clarify what you mean, Charles?"

"It's been nearly a week now since Rita last spoke. Obviously I defer to you as the medical expert but…" The medical expert found his voice.

"If I follow your line of thought correctly, Charles, then I think that I must agree. And one of the many things that a career spent in the business of life and death has taught me is that, at all times, you must be both honest and realistic. To do otherwise is a kindness to no one. With that in mind, please brace yourself both, for a message I have delivered many times – not, may I clarify, due to any professional negligence on my part. It is a message I had hoped that I would never have to convey ever again. Painful as it might be, it is my opinion that Rita, sadly, is now fully deceased." Another silence. Respectful.

"I'm shocked," said Isabel. "Poor Rita."

"I know," said Charlie, "I thought she would always be here." Isabel almost stopped herself, but had to say it.

"And, without being rude… she will always be here. I didn't think that Life or Death had any more tricks left to play. Normally when you lose someone, you do properly lose them. I mean they're gone. We've lost Rita, but she's there - and always will be. It's worse in a way."

"I thought the same thing," said Charlie. "But we can't pretend it hasn't happened. I was trying to think of something to help us all to cope. I came back to what we would do in this situation if we were alive to give us some comfort, some closure. Up there, we'd have a funeral. Now I know - ironically given where we are - that's not practical for us, but I thought that a little memorial service might help us to draw a line under what's happened and maybe move on."

"That's a lovely idea, Charlie," said Isabel "you're such a thoughtful person."

"Yes, a noble sentiment," The Doc agreed. "What did you have in mind, Charles?"

"Something simple. I thought that, since you've been here longest, as our elder statesman, you could maybe say a few words. Then each of us could share a few thoughts and memories?" The Doc gave two nods, slow and thoughtful. This was indeed a difficult situation, but adversity calls for leadership and he was gratified that his senior status had been recognised by the young man. "I don't see any benefit in delaying," Charlie added. "I don't mean we should do it now, I thought tomorrow, to give us all a chance to think what we would like to say."

"Yes, a sound idea. That should be sufficient time for me to draft a fitting eulogy." Charlie caught something in his tone, something that reminded him that The Doc was especially enthusiastic about anything that The Doc had to say.

"I don't think it needs to last long," he clarified, "just enough for us to say our goodbyes."

Charlie had not known what to expect from The Doc. It certainly wasn't what he got. The (well-respected) amateur thespian, from whom he had picked up no discernible interest in matters religious to date, clearly stayed up all night writing the part and rehearsing the role of Sanctimonious Parson. At eleven o'clock the following morning proceedings began.

"This is truly a sombre day for us all," he boomed. "I have been studying Dean's Syndrome for eight years and more, and today, my friends, we enter together a new phase of our understanding. For as our friend Rita Jackson was first to contract Dean's, so too is she the first to have succumbed. Rita's passing serves as a reminder to all of us of our own mortality, of the fickle, fragile, transient nature of the human condition. And yet, I am sure all of you who are gathered here today will agree, that Rita, dear Rita, would not wish us to be downcast in this, the darkest of hours. So it is that today is an opportunity for us to celebrate her very special life. First, I would like to invite Isabel to say a few words."

"Thank you," said Isabel, a little baffled by the introduction. "I have known Rita for nearly three years now. I admit that, at times, we had our differences. Sometimes, because of my own history of health problems, I wished that I wasn't here. I think I took that out on Rita, and I regret that. When I look back now I can see that she was a good person who wanted the best for everyone around her and for the place she loved. And she stood up for herself. I like that. I will miss her."

"A sentiment with which, no doubt, we all concur," said The Doc. "Charles, would you like to add anything to those fine words?"

"I'll try," said Charlie. "I only knew Rita for a few short weeks. When I was alive, I was lucky enough, through my job, to meet and interview some remarkable people. From the first time I met her, even though I'd just awoken from death, I knew that Rita too was a remarkable person. She was funny, she was forthright, and she would have been a terrific guest on my show. It is down to her that we are able to be here today, celebrating her life. It was Rita and her healthy disregard for authority and nonsensical rules that gave us this chance for extra days of existence. I am glad to have met her, and I too will miss her."

"Thank you both. Splendid, splendid words. If I may, let me say that we are unanimous in agreeing that her passing is a loss to us all, and leaves a hole that no one can ever fill… in part because she still occupies it." The Doc paused, conscious that the last bit hadn't come out quite as reverentially as he had intended. Undaunted, he carried on.

"I myself found her to be a most amusing companion, such fun to have around. Certainly, she could be opinionated, one might even say cantankerous but…."

"Enough!" The Doc's loquacious flow was staunched by a voice of protest. Not Isabel, not Charlie.

"I was enjoying it up till then, but 'cantankerous'?"

"Rita?" said Charlie.

"Yes."

"You're back? I don't believe it."

"Well I am. Have I missed much?" Charlie struggled to

think.

"No. No, I mean, yes. The big thing is the stream. We noticed when you were poorly that it had gone down to a trickle. Listen." They all fell silent. What they heard was a solid steady flow of water, exactly how it had previously been.

"It doesn't sound like a trickle to me," said Rita.

"My God," said Charlie. "It's back. Something has changed. It's back now - and so are you!"

"Yes, good news indeed," said The Doc, smarting slightly from both the abrupt end to his scheduled performance, and the brevity of his tenure as elder statesman. "We are delighted to have you back" he added magnanimously.

"Never mind that," said Rita, "I need a word with you. And that word is... cantankerous?..."

"Hello? Who is that?" Everyone stopped. The lady buried next to Rita had just spoken.

Chapter 14

Jess's goal had seemed eminently achievable. In three hours when they landed back at home, she would have revisited that old to-do list and added on anything needed to rekindle the smouldering embers beneath The Stables project, turning them into a roaring flame. The constant drone of the aircraft engines made concentration difficult, but they were as nought when set alongside the constant drone of her travel companion. Diane peered across at Jess's list, misreading some items, misinterpreting others, and helpfully suggesting spurious ones of her own. The cabin crew's glacial advance down the aisle with the buffet trolley had reached their row. Jess put down her pen. She bought them a small plastic bottle of warm white wine each and gave up. After all, she'd done the most important job yesterday. When she had phoned Ray, he seemed just as delighted about recommencing as he was about getting paid. He promised to restart as soon as he could. There was no need to badger him, Jess knew that she could rely on Ray.

Three days after landing, she finally found time to catch up with him at The Stables. She reached the top of the cobbled drive, pulled onto the courtyard, and stopped, eyes skimming left and right. After her recent dispiriting, solitary visit, this was thrilling. Everywhere there was noise, men shouting, machinery buzzing and thumping, activity in every corner of the yard and every room of the building. Spotting her car, Ray broke into a trot in his eagerness to greet her. Jess had never seen Ray run before. She now knew why. It was a hell of a lot of ungainly effort for a such marginal uplift in speed.

"Wow," she said, getting out of the car, and accepting his clumsy embrace.

"We've picked up straight from where we left off," he said through wheezy breath. "After we spoke on Saturday I rang round the guys. All of them were here on Sunday morning, and they are working long days. We're tearing through it. They all want to get it over the line for you." He grinned, watching her as she spun around, hardly daring to believe what she was seeing.

"Come on," he said, "you need to take a proper look inside." In the reception room, an electrician on a step ladder was attaching a light fitting to the cable she had seen hanging through the ceiling on her last visit. Ray took her from room to room. In each she could see headway had been made compared to her photos. At every stop-off point, she thanked whichever tradesmen were grafting away, determined that they should understand how grateful she was for their efforts. As they emerged back into the courtyard, Jess turned to Ray.

"Thanks so much. I've promised to give regular updates to the Italian gentleman whose donation made this possible. I can't wait to tell him, I'll phone him tonight. He'll be delighted."

"I've one more thing to show you," said Ray. He took her over to the well. "All of the rubble has been cleared out, and the walls have been shored up right down to the bottom. It's sound, completely restored. And now there's water down there too - we'd blocked the stream off to carry out the work and forgot to open it back up when we left the site. Our mistake, but as far as we know, nobody died of thirst," he said, chuckling. "It's flowing again. Oh, and one of the guys found this at the bottom." He dipped into his pocket and brought out a large silver coin. "It's a half-crown," he said. "You won't remember them. They went out of circulation in the seventies. Must have been there for years." Jess shook her head.

"Not years. Try a fortnight," she replied. "It belonged to my grandad, he gave it to me when I was a little girl. When I came over here a couple of weeks ago to take photos of the work, I brought it with me to throw down the well. I'm really not superstitious… but I thought we needed some luck." With that, she took the metal disc from Ray's open palm and dropped it down the shaft of the well once more. They heard a distant splash as it entered the stream below.

"Best leave it here," she said.

When she got home later that evening Jess picked up her post from the doormat. She read the return address on the back of the first one. Without looking at the others, she laid the little bundle on the counter and switched the kettle on.

Dear Journal,

Another bittersweet day. Went to The Stables where Ray's team is doing an unbelievable job. No numb feeling today, though it felt surreal, it felt like it was mine. We will be able to provide some great services from there when it's finished. Sweet.

Then, when I arrived home the first thing I saw was a letter from the stonemason saying that they'd finished Charlie's headstone and it's ready to be put in place. Bitter.

Charlie's parents won't be able to come for several weeks so have said I should go ahead with the installation. They'll visit St Jude's to see it the next time they're back up here. I feel bad saying this, but I'm relieved in a way. I've not come to terms with the funeral yet, so I'm not up for a rerun. And I would have felt obliged to say a few words to everyone attending. I'm not ready for that.

*   *   *

The instant that he heard Rita's voice The Doc knew he was in trouble. Cantankerous. Of all the words to use to describe someone that can be… cantankerous. He knew he was now a certainty to be on the receiving end of a virtuoso demonstration of the trait, battered and berated by an acclaimed master. And then, by an incredible stroke of luck, a hitherto dead person came back to life, providing the perfect distraction from his graceless commentary on his neighbour. He seized on the 'Hello' from the far side of the plot and took the first hopeful steps on a (doomed) journey towards absolution.

"Rita, can I humbly suggest that I pick up speaking to the new lady on your behalf, whilst you recapture your habitual sturdiness?" Rita's response was the filthiest of looks. The Doc moved on. "Hello," he said to the new lady. "Don't be alarmed. We mean you no harm."

"Are you a ghost?" the lady asked.

"A ghost? Good Heavens, no. I will explain. But first, what is your name?"

"Yvonne."

"Hello, Yvonne, and welcome. My name is Doctor Dennis Dean, I was a senior partner in a very successful GP practice for many years." He stalled briefly to ascertain who had tutted, but gave up. It could have been any of the others. Perhaps even the new lady herself.

"We – and by that I include you – all have a condition named Dean's Syndrome. The most effective way for you to understand what that entails is for me to give you a brief synopsis of its characteristics. I would hate this to take on the tone of a formal tutorial, so if any of my companions wish to chip in with a layperson's perspective, then of course I invite them to do so."

There was little chance of that. For the next hour, The Doc assailed the newcomer with an exhaustive statement of the situation that she now found herself in. No matter how hard he tried to ramp up the rhetoric, to illustrate how unprecedented, how unique, how inexplicable their situation was, Yvonne accepted it with a casual nod. When finally The Doc ran out of superlatives, Charlie stepped in.

"Can I say, Yvonne - and I don't mean this in any way as a criticism - but when I found all of this out I was taken aback. You don't seem at all concerned." Yvonne shrugged.

"Where's the sense in worrying? I don't expect I can change anything about it, so I'll have to work out how to make the best of it."

"I admire your pragmatic approach," said The Doc.

"I'm not sure what that is, but if it means that I don't faff around, then you're right."

"Good for you," said Charlie. "It feels like so far we've been doing all the talking. Would you like to tell us a little bit about yourself, your family, your job?"

"Job? Never had a job in my life. Family, now that's another matter. I've had two hundred and forty kids in my time."

"Two hundred and forty?" said The Doc, reckoning up what that meant (rapid yet accurate mental arithmetic was another of his strengths). "Surely not. Even if one was to generously assume that each confinement produced triplets then it equates to sixty years of non-stop gestation." Not having a clue what he was on about, Yvonne elected not to reply.

"Did you foster?" said Isabel.

"Yes, that's right. Some for just a few weeks, some for a year, even longer. I know it sounds like a lot but I started when I was young and kept going longer than I should have. But that was because of the kids. They were brilliant. Most of them had a rough start in life and were desperate for a home, some love, and a chance. Don't get me wrong, there was the odd bad one amongst them, but if you want to show me two hundred and forty people who are all angels I think you'll need to take me to Heaven." The others watched as she looked around her. "I didn't understand half of what you said earlier, Doctor, but I'm presuming this isn't Heaven. If it is, it's awfully dark, not like any of the pictures of it I've seen."

"We can be pretty certain this isn't Heaven," said Rita. "I can't imagine Saint Peter would let anybody as cantankerous as me through the Gates of Paradise, would he, Doctor?" Charlie stepped in to rescue The Doc.

"It's been an excellent day," he said. "I've no idea how it's come about but it's fantastic. We were sure that we were down to only three of us remaining, within minutes we're up to five."

"Yes, remarkable," agreed the medic, "though I think I may have mentioned to you and Isabel that you shouldn't jump to any conclusions, given Rita's boundless fortitude," he added, re-writing history in a desperate attempt to curry favour.

The following day everyone stirred a little later than normal. The conversations with Yvonne had continued throughout the previous day, on beyond the time that everyone would normally have fallen asleep. They updated her on their former lives, the world of St. Jude's, and of course the robbery, which she agreed was a disgraceful thing to have happened.

Around mid-morning, The Doc made a pronouncement.

"Can I have everyone's attention? I am considering a radical course of action, one on which I would value your opinion. Now that our esteemed leader Rita is restored to her normal vigour, I am liberated from the burden of seniority, of being custodian to you all. I believe that this presents an opportunity for me to undertake one of these Dean's Syndrome visitations. I am proposing that I transport myself into the mind of Bennett, the gravedigger."

"A visit-what? Oh no, what's all this?" said Yvonne incredulous that, despite yesterday's onerous induction, there was yet more to be learned about her new world. Charlie explained briefly about the communication that he and Isabel had managed to have with family members. Yvonne was surprised and interested, asking notably more questions than she had done during The Doc's lengthy discourse. Charlie returned his attention to The Doc's plan.

"Visit the gravedigger?" he said "Why?"

"My reasons are twofold. Firstly, concerning your stolen watch. With all due deference to your brother, Isabel, I fear the trail, whilst not cold, is lukewarm at best. I may be able to unlock a vital piece of evidence to crack the case. My second purpose would be to facilitate the advancement of mankind's understanding of Dean's. Without wishing to be disrespectful, I have wider medical knowledge than anyone who has thus far made such a trip. This includes a comprehensive understanding of the anatomy and workings of the human brain. I believe I could make important discoveries about the visitation process."

"It would be a bold move, Doc," said Charlie, puffing out his cheeks. "Isabel and I were both whacked out afterward, and we're younger than you. And we were visiting our loved ones. You will be going into the twisted mind of a criminal.

Do you think that it's wise for you to tackle it?"

"This is not a time to be faint of heart," The Doc said. "I believe it is my destiny," he added, making sure that all were aware of the exalted place in history that awaited him.

"Well," said Rita "the opportunity may come sooner than you imagined. Listen." The conversation stopped and they watched as Tom Bennett walked towards them through the grounds of St Jude's, accompanied by Lee Knight. The two were discussing the tasks that needed to be carried out in the week ahead.

"Can you mow the grass at the top end?" said Lee, "down as far as the gate."

"Yes, will do."

"And I noticed this gravestone is becoming unstable." Gripping the top of a tall headstone in the adjacent plot, he demonstrated that it could be rocked back and forth. "Can you raise it slightly at the back to make sure it doesn't topple over before we fix it properly?" Tom nodded. "And Mrs Harkness has told you to dig this one before Monday?" he added, pointing at the vacant plot next to Charlie. Tom looked at Lee uneasily. "We've got the funeral on Monday morning, so we need to make sure it's ready for then."

Tom nodded. The two men turned to set off walking back up the graveyard. The Doc knew that this was the moment. Now or Never. It would have been the latter, but abject terror intervened. His planned approach, based on clinical theory, was lost. Bang! He was up.

As is often the case with pioneering medical procedures, it did not go exactly as planned. The Doc realised instantly that he was indeed seeing the world through the eyes of his host as the others had described. However, in his opinion, neither Isabel nor Charles had sufficiently emphasised the disorientating, swirling, stomach-churning effect that this creates. The closest parallel he could draw from experience was the way he had felt on the occasion that he'd had too much brandy at a dinner dance, and ended up sleeping on the living room sofa belonging to his colleague, Doctor Campbell. Drawing on his extensive medical knowledge, in a flash, he developed a clever strategy to counter the effects of being at the mercy of another for all of his visual cues. He closed his eyes. With those signals shut off, he concentrated on gaining fuller command of his bilious innards. Then, for the first time in eight years, he heard the clunk of a car door closing. He felt safe to take a peep, and found that he was looking at what he could only presume to be a dashboard, but it was not like one he had ever seen before. It looked more like the control panel of an Apollo spacecraft. Lurid digital displays everywhere. Ignition of the engine achieved by pressing a button.

"It appears that automobile technology has continued to advance since I last was a passenger in a motor car," he thought, the lamentable eradication of walnut and leather now plainly complete. "But my role on this journey is not that of a passenger. It would be tempting to watch the world through the windscreen, but my purpose is not to look out, but in." He tried to visualise the relevant pages from his Gray's Anatomy textbook. It turns out however that Gray's depiction of grey matter, invaluable when contemplating a brain from the outside, was pretty much useless when you find yourself inside one. It was far more chaotic than he had imagined. He was being assailed with a continuous frantic stream of thoughts, information, and emotions, there and then gone, darting for cover like small fish faced with the gaping mouth of a predator intent on hoovering them up.

And then a breakthrough. At the press of a button on the

steering wheel, one depicting a telephone receiver, there was a beep, and a voice burst into the vehicle. My God, thought The Doc, the car can talk.

"Hi, it's Giles Sanders from Sotheby's here. Just leaving you another message to follow up on the valuation enquiry you made for your watch. If you still wish to sell the item, please contact me as soon as possible. Thanks."

"I knew it," thought The Doc, "we are definitely onto him." He felt the car slow to a halt. They were parked on a short driveway. He surveyed the building before him. "That is a pretty decent house," he thought. "I'll be very surprised if the coffin of Charles Munro is the only one that you have ransacked, sir." They moved inside. The property was decorated exclusively in black and grey and white tones. The curtains were covered in geometric shapes rather than the floral style he had left behind in 2011. This was this altogether more modern, and it was the taste of a single man, bereft of soft furnishing but bristling with gadgets and gizmos. As the eyes scanned the room they passed over a photograph of a young man standing by a banana yellow sports car. It was the briefest of glimpses but enough for The Doc to recognise the face.

"As I live and breathe," he whispered, momentarily forgetting that he no longer did. It was the last thing that he was to see. In shock, Doctor Dennis Dean lost his concentration, and so his connection. His next sensation was that he had collapsed into his spot in St Jude's. He attempted to speak to his neighbours, to pass onto them what he had heard, what he had seen, but instead succumbed to a deep sleep of exhaustion.

* * *

On Friday, when classes had finished, Mia gave her friends the slip at the school gates, saying that she had an errand to carry out. It was kind of true. They were due to meet Jess tomorrow for the first time since she returned from Italy, and Mia was desperately disappointed that they had so little progress to report. She decided to make a slight detour on her walk home, to visit St Jude's, in the hope that maybe she would stumble across some tiny little thing that they had missed.

She entered the churchyard and looked down towards their corner. Even from afar, what she saw was neither tiny nor little. It was hulking and it was huge. Soil, piled high and getting taller, as Bennett dug out the grave next to Charlie. She watched from the gate, trying to decide what to do. She needed to phone her uncle. No, text him, stay as quiet as possible. He would advise her. Assuming that he had his phone with him. And switched on. And that he spotted the message. And bothered to read it. For a few moments, she waited, willing a response to come through. Then it came.

"Why you there? Stay on obbo. On way." A veteran viewer of many crime dramas, Mia knew what obbo meant, though there was a limited amount to observe, only the top half of a scrawny man, waist-high in a hole, the visible length of his torso diminishing ever so slightly as the depth of the hole increased. She heard the sound of her uncle's car approaching, and looked round as he pulled to a halt. He walked over to the gate and stood by her side. He looked down at Bennett, weighing up the scene.

"Now's the time," he said. "I'm going to challenge him. You stay here." She moved to protest. "No arguments, Mia. He's more likely to feel pressured and clam up if we both go." As he set off down the slope he turned back to her.

"By the way, Mia, well done."

The sound of the digging roused The Doc from his protracted slumber. He was drowsy, befuddled, and felt a little queasy. Where am I? Why am I here? The sensation, the questions, both were indistinguishable from those he'd had waking up on Doctor Campbell's sofa the morning after the dinner dance. It trickled back to him. He was in his grave plot. He heard the digging beside Charlie, looked up, and saw Bennett at work. The gravedigger was intent on his labour and did not notice Mick's presence until he was above him at the edge of the pit. Though Bennett tried to look away immediately, there was the briefest flicker of eye contact. He did not want to speak to the man who had previously been showing too much interest in his work, but this time there was no easy way to drift off to a far corner of St. Jude's. He was in a hole.

"I see you're digging this one again."

"Yes, somebody going in on Monday."

"Are you sure?" asked Mick, "only the last time no one went in."

"Monday."

"Really? You see, I'm not convinced you told me the truth when I asked about this the last time. And I've been trying to work out why. I used to be a police officer," he said, watching Bennett's discomfort turn to edginess. "It does make you inquisitive. And suspicious." He was now struggling to concentrate on his work, on keeping the shovel moving.

Mick continued. "First you dig a grave that no one goes into. Why? Then you tell me your name is Tom Bennett, only then I find you've recently changed it from Tom Hanlon. What's that about I wonder?" Now the young man looked pale, haunted. He was in trouble for sure.

Beneath them, the others heard a gasp come from Yvonne. "Hanlon. I knew there was something familiar about him. I know him. It's Tom." And then The Doc blurted it out.

"It's not him," he said, the first words he had spoken since his return. The other looked at him in surprise. "At least not only him. He needs to tell the truth."

The young man stopped what he was doing and looked down at the floor of the grave for what seemed an age. Mick held his nerve, waiting, waiting. Tom looked up, and looked him in the eye.

"Truth is like the sun," he said. "You can shut it out for a time, but it ain't goin' away."

"What?" said Mick, nonplussed. "What made you say that?"

"I didn't, at least not first. It was Elvis. Elvis Presley. He was my favourite foster mum's favourite singer. We used to sing along to him all the time. I know all the words. She taught me everything about him, about his life, the records he made. That's how I know he said that about the truth. Dunno why, but it came into my head just then." Mick had assumed that over his career he must have heard every cockeyed response possible. ABC. Assume nothing. This gravedigging geezer from Stanford had just replied to his question by quoting The King of Rock n' Roll.

Inside Tom's head, Yvonne was willing him on. "Tell him the truth. The truth, no matter what it is, we'll sort it out."

"Look mister," said Tom, "I haven't done anything wrong. I keep the churchyard tidy and I dig graves, that's all. I dug this one before cos I was told to. Then I filled it in cos I was told to. And now I'm digging it again. I just do my job."

"But Mrs Harkness is definite that she did not tell you to dig it."

"She didn't. Knight did."

"Alex Knight?"

"No the other one. Lee. Usually Mrs Harkness tells me, but he said she must have forgotten so I dug it on his say-so."

"And he told you to fill it in?"

"Yes. And he was very particular in saying that I shouldn't say to anyone we'd made a mistake, that if I did I might get into trouble. He told me she's fierce, Harkness, so I should do what I'm told. Less bother that way. I don't want trouble, I like this job. I am polite to the people who have lost a loved one."

"But it wasn't you that made a mistake, it was him."

"I know, but then he gave me an envelope with money in it. For my work, for doing the digging. Two hundred pounds. I didn't want it but I didn't know how to tell him no, what with him being the funeral director. I've still got it, I haven't touched it. It doesn't seem right somehow. But by then I've got the money, I'm involved in whatever it is. It means I'm to blame too." Mick was transported back to his days on the force when he just knew that what someone was telling him was true. He needed to keep him talking.

"No, it doesn't. Not if you haven't done anything wrong."

"Well I'll tell you something else," said Tom, "I dug it on that Tuesday and filled it back in on Wednesday morning but in between times someone had been in it. Interfering. I'm always very careful about how I shore up the sides but this one was wrong," he said, pointing to the one adjacent to Charlie. He then pulled his slender frame up with the ease of a gymnast to join Mick on the surface.

"And they'd used my tools to do it. I always put them away

in my shed clean but they were covered in soil. I don't know who's done what but I want no part of it."

"Is this the truth?"

"The God's honest truth. Oh, and you were asking about my name. The only reason I changed it is because Hanlon was my dad's and now I'm older I realise he was no good at all to me and my mum. So I'm using my mum's name now."

"Don't worry about this, Tom," said Mick. "If you have done nothing wrong, then I will make sure that everybody knows that."

The Doc had come round sufficiently that Charlie felt he might be up to answering a question or two.

"Knight? Did you know that, Doc?"

"I did. I made an unfortunate error as I set off on my journey and visited Knight instead of Bennett. It only came to light when I saw boastful photographs of him around his home."

"But it's worked to our advantage, Doc," said Charlie. "Yvonne knows Tom. Look at her," he said pointing at Yvonne's casket. "She's spark out, in the same deep sleep as you've just woken from. She's been, she's got to him and persuaded him to say something he would never have dared to without her. It's brought the truth out." Instantly The Doc puffed himself up.

"Yes, when I said error that was perhaps the wrong expression. It was more an adroit change of plan. I always intended to visit the thief and that is what I have achieved."

"Whatever you did, however it happened, it's worked out," said Charlie. "Though I think we all need to own up to an error. Jess said that Bennett and Knight were both there when she took the watch to the funeral directors. We decided

Bennett must be the culprit. Was it because he was the guy that owned the shovel? I don't think so. Truth is we chose to blame the quiet misfit in the dirty overalls, not the slick guy in the smart suit. Not our finest hour."

"And, Charles, I have some further news," The Doc added. "The sands of time may be running out. Knight has been in contact with Sotheby's of London, with the intention of selling your watch."

Chapter 15

Charlie could hear his mum's voice in his head. He knew exactly how she pronounced each syllable. Small wonder, because of all the guidance she had offered him, Mrs Munro had given her impatient youngster one suggestion more than any other :

"Don't wish your life away."

Given his recent catastrophic loss of that commodity, Charlie decided that in all likelihood it was a directive from which he was now exempt, so on Saturday morning he granted himself free rein to will the clock forward. Jess was back from Italy and would be meeting Mick and Mia, and the intervening hours were going to drag. Until there was a welcome distraction.

"Uuuugggh. What day is it?" Yvonne had woken up.

"It's Saturday," he said. "How are you? You've been asleep for hours, ever since you visited Tom. What you did, it worked by the way."

"I know, I could hear him speaking. I'm so pleased. Not for me, for him." They gave her a few more minutes to come round more fully.

"I presume you'd fostered him in the past?" asked Isabel.

"Yes," she said. "I knew him as Tom Hanlon, I looked after him for about a year. He came to me in crisis, a terrified ten-year-old. Dad in prison, mum a drug addict, they couldn't look after him any more. No one else in the family wanted him, so he'd been passed around between childrens' homes." Isabel's thoughts flew straight to her own situation, and to Mia. Things could have turned out so differently for her little girl. Thank God for Mick.

"Was he in a bad way?" she asked.

"Yes. Lots of the kids I took in were damaged, but Tom was worse than most. He refused to speak when he first came. I persisted for weeks and weeks. He'd been bullied at various homes, and his way of coping was not to say or do anything that could get him into trouble. All he wanted was to get through each day without being noticed."

"That's an awful way for any child to feel," said Isabel.

"I know. Eventually, I managed to get him out of his shell... well not on my own, I had help from Elvis. Tom might seem strange to all of you, but the change from the boy I knew to how he is today is nothing short of a miracle." The Doc looked at Charlie.

"Charles, am I correct in thinking this Elvis Presley business is a version, albeit an amateur version, of the music therapy which your wife practices?" Charlie had always suspected The Doc would be a sceptic.

"It is," he replied. "You've done a great job, Yvonne. "We thought it was Tom who stole my watch. We were completely wrong. We owe him an apology. He said you were his favourite mum. Since we can't apologise to him, will you accept it on his behalf?"

"We all make mistakes, Charlie," she replied, "I'm sure he would accept your apology."

"Thank you. And by the way," said Charlie "you've timed your wake-up perfectly. We're expecting our visitors soon."

*　　*　　*

After Tom's revelation, Mia had wanted to go straight to the police station. Mick eased her back without dampening her spirit.

"We're not at that point yet," he said, "we need to build a solid case. Before we make a move, let's tell Jess what we know, see if she learned anything in Italy, then we can plan the next steps."

As Jess joined them, Mia and Mick exchanged a wordless look, knowing that they were thinking the same thought. They had only known Jess in the period since Charlie died, and so had no idea that the tired, careworn air they had observed was foreign to her. A few days in the Italian sunshine, meeting Marco, even spending all those hours with her exasperating mum, had lifted everything about her. Her complexion shone, her eyes were brighter, her posture had straightened.

"Wow, you look lovely," said Mia.

"Thank you. I don't know if I'd go as far as lovely, but I think I'm starting to feel better."

"I'm dying to hear about Italy, but first can we tell you what has happened here? You won't believe it."

"Yes, of course," said Jess. Those three tiny words breached a pent-up dam. Mia let rip, a cascade of words, Tom and Knight and grave tampering and hush money, all thundered down onto Jess with unstoppable force. She took a pounding, battered by the pace, the weight, the content. Jess waited for the torrent to turn into a trickle before she spoke. She was incredulous.

"Lee Knight? Are you sure? You don't think Tom Bennett has concocted this whole story to cover for himself?" Mick shook his head.

"No," he replied. "Copper's nose. The first time I spoke to him he was all hesitation and fidgeting. This time his story came straight out. Knight was there when you handed the watch in, so got a good look at it. What he told me fits with everything we already know."

"Except the Lee Knight we know. I'm stunned. He was so good to me. Charlie was going to be buried up there," she said, pointing to the far side of the cemetery, "squeezed in tightly between two others. He stepped in at the last minute and arranged for me to get this quiet plot in the corner." Mick clicked his fingers.

"You've never mentioned that. There you go, another piece slots into place. He wasn't being kind. He got you this because it gave him a route in from the side, a way to access Charlie's coffin after the funeral. He's planned this ahead all right."

"I'm shocked. Flabbergasted. Never judge a book by the cover. He had such a tidy beard." She looked at Mia and Mick. All three burst out laughing. "You know what I mean. He doesn't look like someone who could do something wicked."

"I know, we were dumbfounded," said Mick. "But what about you, what about Italy? And your new Italian friend?" Jess gave them a sketch of her weekend, telling them about Marco and his lifestyle. She told them about how he had researched her and her charity, and had given her funding to restart the work.

"That's fantastic news, Jess," said Mick.

"I know, it's an incredible turnaround." Then, sparing no detail, she went on to describe the incident where Grandad Joe had saved Marco's life and they had exchanged watches as tokens of friendship.

"That's amazing," said Mia. "Your grandad was a hero, a real war hero. I wish I could have met him."

"He didn't seem like a war hero to us. He was a lovely, gentle, mischievous grandad."

"And he'll never know it, but by saving that man, he also saved your charity," said Mia.

"He did, but it wouldn't have been possible without you," Jess replied, giving Mia a squeeze. Mia tried to suppress a blush.

"Grandad Joe's story proves what you say, Uncle Mick, that you should always do the right thing, you never know what other good will come from it."

"Did Marco have any evidence of having owned the watch?" asked Mick. "Maybe a photo of him wearing it?"

"No, he only had it for a few months before they made the exchange. When we got home, mum and I looked to see if we had any pictures of Grandad with it. Nothing. Thing was, even in hot weather, he always wore long-sleeved shirts. I know why now, that bad scar he got on his arm. What do we do next, Mick? Should we go to the police?"

"I suggested that," said Mia.

"We could try," Mick replied "but I won't lie to you. Even with what we've got, the force is so overworked that there's no chance they'll drop everything to look into a crime that might not even have happened. There are so many cases that they know about and don't have the resource to investigate. We've very little real evidence. He could simply deny everything that Tom has told us." Although Jess and Mia looked deflated, there was something else he needed to point out.

"We have another problem. Time is against us. This new grave is due to be occupied on Monday. After that, Charlie will be boxed in."

"Uncle Mick!"

"Oh, sorry Jess, unfortunate choice of words. He'll be surrounded. The chances of what's happened ever coming to light will be even more remote. This burial is good news for

Knight, bad news for us." Mia's eyes went to the pile of soil and the boards covering the empty plot next to Charlie.

"Or maybe it's exactly what we need, Uncle Mick," she said.

"What do you mean?"

"Something just occurred to me, something you told me a while ago. About burglars." Mick had no idea where she was headed.

"Go on," he said.

"When you were in the police you told people who had been burgled to change their security, they should get an alarm, fit new locks. You said burglars like to come back to places they robbed before, because they know the layout and are confident if they've done it once they could do it again."

"Yes, we used to get lots of repeats," Mick agreed.

"Look. Now the grave has been dug, it's exactly like when he robbed it."

"True," said Mick "but Knight's got the watch, why would he come back?"

"Since all of this happened I've read loads of articles about vintage watches. I know what makes them valuable - a top-quality maker, good condition, and rarity. But none of those matter unless they are real. The very best ones all come with a unique serial number, a box, and paperwork that prove that they're authentic. If you've got any of that it can add loads to the value."

"But we don't," said Jess.

"No, but Lee Knight doesn't know that. We know the grave beside Charlie's is open for the next two days. Suppose we got a message to Knight that amongst all the things that are in there with Charlie, you've put the certificate for the watch, say, in his jacket pocket."

"I think I can see where you're going with this," said Mick.

"Like those burglars, he might be tempted to come back. And we could catch him in the act." Mick looked at his young charge, unsure of whether he should feel proud or ashamed.

"You, young lady," he said "are too devious by far. But we'd have to show him the bait in a way so it isn't obviously a trap."

"I'm due to pay the outstanding balance for Charlie's funeral," said Jess. "I was going to drop into the office after I left you. Alex said that was fine, that they'd both be there." She looked at Mick and could tell he was taking this seriously. "I could do it when I go in." Mick mulled it over, looking for flaws.

"Right," he said "If this is to work we need to think it through properly. We will get one chance at this. The funeral is on Monday, so he'd have to do it either tonight or tomorrow night. There's a time pressure on him too, so I think he'll at least try tonight, to give himself a second bite if there's a hitch. We have to act quickly. Jess, you go and pay the Knights. Mia, let's get off to your judo. I'll need to have a chat with Harry, my old pal from the police. Then we meet up in Angelo's at four o'clock. But before we leave, let's go through what Jess needs to say."

"Okay," said Jess, "but I need to warn you, I'm not much good at telling even little white lies. Full-blown fibbing is well outside my comfort zone."

"We'll help you plan what to say," said Mia. "It'll just be like being an actress delivering lines."

"That's not a strength of mine either. My only previous experience was when I was five. I was Donkey Number Two in the school nativity. It wasn't a speaking part."

When she turned the corner into the main street, Jess could see only one thing. Knight's office. Everything else, cars, pedestrians, street signs, lamp posts, shops, all a blur. She exhaled sharply, slowed her breathing, then slowed her footsteps as she neared. She looked inside, ensuring that sister and brother were both there. Her throat was so tight as she opened the door. Would there be enough space in her windpipe for the words to squeeze out? Alex was at the reception desk, while Lee tapped away at a laptop at a desk to the rear. She had to force herself not to look at him, instead doing her best to chat naturally with Alex as they went through the process of paying.

"I can't thank you enough," Jess said. "I don't know how I would have managed without all your help with the arrangements, the cars, order of service, it made an awful time just that bit more bearable."

"It's no problem," Alex replied. "I'm glad we were able to help make the day work out the way Charlie planned." Jess had already decided the longer she delayed, the greater the chance that she would forget or fluff her lines.

"And all of the advice and support you gave me. All of the little personal touches, like putting all of those bits and pieces in for Charlie to take with him." As soon as she uttered these words Jess noticed that Lee Knight's fingers began to tap the keys more softly and less frequently. She had her audience. Her confidence grew.

"I know it might seem daft but I just wanted to send him off with everything he might need. I don't suppose he'll ever finish that book he was reading. Or drink the rum." She made a conscious effort to shut out all sounds other than the tapping on the keyboard. "And I doubt he'll need the guarantee for grandad's watch that I stuck in the pocket inside his jacket."

There, her key line was delivered. The tapping stopped. She flicked her eyes left for the tiniest fraction of a moment. Lee Knight was looking over at her intently.

"It's not daft at all," said Alex. "God, we buried someone with a Chinese takeaway. Banquet For Two and a bag of prawn crackers. In church, even through the incense, you could catch a whiff of chow mein." Lee Knight shut his laptop as if having completed the task at hand, freeing him up to join in.

"I think a watch guarantee is a first for us," he said, smiling. "Was it a sort of certificate?"

"Yes, I think so," she said, readying herself to parrot the information that Mia had given her. "I didn't look at it too closely. It was quite old-fashioned and had some reference numbers on it, and a lot of writing, I think it was in French. Anyhow, it was no use to me, it belonged with his watch, so Charlie's got it if he needs it." She gathered her belongings. "Thanks... and don't take this the wrong way, but I hope it's a long time till I visit you here again." And with that, Jess turned and left the office, took the six steady strides required to take her beyond their window and out of their sight. Then she set off for home, practically running, anxious to put physical distance between herself and her falsehood. She closed the door, and before she did anything else, she sent a text to Mick and Mia.

"Back home now. God knows how, but I did it. He took the bait I think. He even asked me about it."

Although their phones pinged almost simultaneously Mia was first to read. She had replied before her uncle had even opened it.

"Stanford Oscars 2018. Best female actor - Jessica Munro."

"I'd be amazed if he doesn't come back looking for that certificate," she said to her uncle.

"Well if he does, we will be ready for him," said Mick.

As soon as he received the text from Jess, Mick contacted his old colleague, saying he needed to talk to him urgently. He rejected Harry's suggestion that they meet at the police station, proposing instead a bench in Stanford's public park.

"That's a bit MI5," said Harry. "How will I recognise you? Will you be wearing a red carnation in your lapel and carrying a copy of The Times?"

"Look, just meet me in the park, eh? There are too many prying eyes and flapping ears at the station."

Harry sat down on the bench next to Mick at the appointed time. Then, staring into the middle distance, he greeted his friend in what was an effort at an Eastern European accent.

"Good afternoon, Mikhail. I see that the swallows have returned to our shores rather earlier than usual this summer." The words came out like someone having a bash at ventriloquism for the first time. Mick smiled. The better Harry's mood the more likely his plan was to succeed. He began by giving his old boss a summary of what they knew and what he believed had happened.

"So what do you think?" he asked, "is it something your guys could look into?" Of course Mick already knew the answer.

"Not a chance," Harry confirmed. "There is no way that I'm going to divert any precious manpower into investigating a crime that you don't even know for sure has taken place."

"Okay, I get that," said Mick, who would have fallen off the dilapidated bench at any other response. "But we've had an idea about how we might trap the bloke who we're sure has done it." He described their ploy to flush out Knight by

233

tempting him to stage a rerun of his initial crime. Harry's reaction was more forthright.

"Whoa. There is no way that we will take part in any kind of stakeout."

"I'm not asking you to take part," Mick said.

"Can you imagine if I went to the boss with this?"

"There's no need to go to the boss," Mick reassured him. "All I'm asking is that you have a patrol somewhere around that can respond quickly if I gave you the nod that it's going off, that a crime is being committed. What's wrong with that?"

"Mick, I've always trusted your judgement, but I don't think I want to get dragged into any of this bollocks." Again, this was pretty much what Mick had anticipated, even down to the testicular reference. Harry would be worried he'd get skinned alive if any of the top brass got wind of his involvement in something like this, with him of all people. But Mick knew Harry. Harry wasn't top brass, and he never would be. Harry was an old-fashioned cop, a thief-catcher, loved a challenge and hated to see some smart-arse getting away with it. The good guys had to win and the bad guys had to go down. Mick began to push those buttons.

"It's not bollocks, Harry. It's important. Okay, on the face of it, someone has been robbed, had their watch stolen. We've seen hundreds of these down the years, we'd have loved to solve them all, but couldn't. But this one is different, so sneaky. A professional, trusted by the family, has robbed a dead man, a man who couldn't defend himself. But the watch is a tiny part of what he's taken. He's robbed a young widow of her right to lay her husband to rest. It doesn't get much worse than that." Mick watched as Harry took in his words. He wasn't smiling any more.

"Okay," he said. "But if you cause me to show my backside

over this, I swear you will be buying every pint that I drink for the rest of this year. And I will be thirsty."

Mick and Mia joined Jess in Angelo's at four. Although the cafe was almost empty, she was sitting in the small back room, far from anyone who might overhear. They listened as she described in exact detail who said what and how Knight had reacted.

"Perfect, Jess," said Mick, "You've done a great job." The ex-policeman's words made her feel less bad about her fib. Disconcertingly good in fact. Mick then explained how he had secured constabulary back up, albeit pretty unwilling, pretty limited, and with the potential for an astronomical bar bill if it went wrong.

"Is there anything else to do?" asked Mia.

"There is," Mick replied. "I need to plan the stakeout in much more detail. I think that it would be best if I attended alone and…" He got no further. Mick genuinely believed that, because he had won around his crusty old police colleague earlier that afternoon, persuading Jess and Mia would be simple. How very, very naïve.

"No! Why just you?" said Mia, "it was my idea. And Jess is the one who has set it up."

"Shhh!" said Mick. "Calm down. Think of the possible outcomes. Firstly, nothing at all might happen. Maybe Knight won't show after all. He could decide to stick with what he's got, not want to risk losing it by going back to the scene. A waste of all our time. Or, on the other hand, if he does appear, who knows how it will play out? It could get frightening for you, Mia, or dangerous, or maybe upsetting for Jess, to see him interfering with Charlie's grave."

"You're only saying this because we're women," said Mia,

cunningly sliding herself into adulthood in case age became a factor in a future phase of the discussion. "And that," she added with emphasis, "is sexist."

"I had assumed that I would be there too," said Jess. "After all, it's my husband who is the victim. He can't be here so I want to go in his place. I've shifted my diary around at work so that I'm clear for the next two days." Mick had not anticipated this strength of reaction. Not for the first time in the last few weeks, he thought back to his time on the force. No one involved in a job like this ever wanted to miss the climactic moments. He had to acknowledge that Mia and Jess were instrumental in getting them to this point. If Knight did kick off he felt sure that he would be able to keep them safe. They needed to stay in line though. He laid it on thick.

"I'm reluctant," he said, "extremely reluctant. If you do come you must stick to the plan, and we must stick together at all times. And at no point should you engage with Knight directly. I'm looking at the Karate Kid here in particular," he said, flicking a thumb in Mia's direction. "No Enter The Dragon heroics." They both nodded in agreement.

"Very well. The practicalities. The best observation point is The Tomb of the Posh Gentleman." Mia saw that Jess looked non-plussed.

"That's what I call the huge fancy one that has metal railings all the way around it." Jess nodded, as Mick continued.

"We'll be high enough up to see down to the grave, and far enough away to be discreet."

"What will we need to bring with us?" asked Jess.

"Your mobile phones, on silent before you arrive. And warm clothes, I know it's July, but I've checked the forecast, clear skies, so it will get cold. And dark colours only, which will be easy enough for Mia. I don't think she owns anything that's not black."

"Uncle Mick, I'm a teenager. We only wear black. It reflects the depressing phase of life that we're going through in a world that refuses to understand us."

"Course it does. Jess, you could bring some food if you like. No crunchy content, no packaging that rustles."

"Will do."

"I'll bring along a torch. It doesn't get dark till about a quarter to ten, so let's meet in the car park at nine sharp. St Jude's should be deserted, the sun will be low, but there will still be enough light for us to settle in. Jess, I guess you'll be on foot. I'll park up on the street round the corner, out of sight. Remember, nine sharp."

* * *

Dear Journal,

It's 7 pm, and I'm ready for a Saturday night out, the first time since Charlie died. The venue - St. Jude's churchyard. The event — to catch a graverobber. Last week, my Italian trip threw up lots of surprises, but today I got a shock. It is Lee Knight who has stolen Grandad's watch. I feel betrayed and disgusted.

To steal personal possessions from a dead man's grave. It's beyond dishonest. And he had the nerve to sit there today, chatting to me without any shame, staring me in the face, all the while scheming about how he could do it again. What sort of a person would even consider doing that? How callous, how lacking in any empathy.

Jess laid her pen down and looked at the last phrase of the short paragraph she had written. She recognised those words. They were not hers. They had appeared in a list that was part of her nursing training. Not the Stages of Grief list, the one whose failings she had exposed several weeks ago. This was from a different list, one from her psychiatric training. She reassessed her encounters with Lee Knight. She cast her mind back to how he had appeared when she first met him, to his polite, borderline insincere, behaviour towards her. Now it seemed like Glib Superficial Charm. She thought of those stories he told her on hearing of Charlie's job, the unlikely tales he recounted of his famous acquaintances and a lavish lifestyle, and she saw that they were Egocentricity, perhaps even A Grandiose Sense Of Self-Worth.

On her laptop, she typed in 'Professor Robert Hare's Checklist' into the search engine. There they were. Callous and Lacking in Empathy. Glib Superficial Charm. Egocentricity. A Grandiose Sense Of Self-Worth.

"God," she thought. "I nearly missed it, and I've been trained. How easy is it for him to go unnoticed by people with no knowledge of this?"

Alex Knight had no psychiatric training. Maybe if she had, she would have interpreted the excuses and half-truths her brother habitually told customers as Pathological Lying and Deception. She may have seen his willingness to fob work off onto others as evidence of a Parasitic Lifestyle.

Tom Bennett had no psychiatric training. Maybe if he had, he would have viewed the whole episode where he'd been coerced into digging and refilling the grave, then sworn to silence about it, as Conning And Manipulative behaviour.

Mick Williams had no psychiatric training. Maybe if he had, he may have thought that this peculiar crime, robbing a grave at dead of night, was indicative of a Need For Stimulation. He might have seen the ease with which Knight had taken the bait to return to the grave as a sign of his Impulsivity.

The more she considered it, the surer Jess became. That afternoon, the man who had carried out this unspeakable act against her deceased husband, had brazenly faced her and demonstrated a Lack Of Remorse Or Guilt. She knew Lee Knight for what he was, and it disturbed her.

*　　*　　*

Jess arrived early at the car park of St. Jude's. Only five minutes, but they were five long, creepy minutes. This was exactly the sort of setting that, growing up, she had been taught to fear. Isolated, and with the light failing, in the eyes of her father there was no mitigation that could make this a tolerable risk. For him, this would have been reckless folly. Though it was not yet cold, she shuddered. From a nearby tree, an owl emitted a string of mournful, ghostly hoots. Suppose Knight arrived first? She moved to the darkest corner and waited. Only when Mick and Mia appeared did she dare to emerge, relieved, from the shadows. Mick put his finger to his lips, not that either of the others had any intention of speaking. He indicated with a hand gesture that they were to wait there. Pushing open the gate he surveyed the churchyard in every direction. When he was satisfied that it was deserted, he ushered them in. The three crept over to the posh gentleman's resting place.

Mick laid a thick tartan blanket on the grass, ostensibly for their comfort, actually to provide the boundary markers for everyone. He invite Mia and Jess to sit down and held his finger to his lips once more.

"No noise from now on," he said, the words riding faintly on his breath. "None of us stands up or moves off the blanket. We assume he could arrive at any moment." Both nodded, and all three shuffled position to ensure a clear view of the plot in the lower corner. They sat deathly still, solid as the stones around them.

Mia's head was buzzing. She was grappling with a dilemma, and decided it was an unsolvable riddle. The only way she could think to clarify the stakeout rules might potentially break the stakeout rules. Go for it.

"Are we allowed to whisper?" she whispered. Fortunately, Mick's response left her in the clear.

"Yes, only don't get too excited and allow the volume to rise."

"Okay," she said, barely audibly. "If he does turn up, when do you think it will be?"

"Well, he's got to wait until it's properly dark, to minimise the chance that there will be anyone around, but he won't want to go in the middle of the night because then it is so quiet that you really will stick out if someone sees you coming and going. I would guess around midnight." Mia checked the time on her phone. 9.48 pm. Still a couple of hours to go.

A hushed half-hour passed without event. Their eyes, focussing alternately on the gate and on their little corner of the graveyard, adjusted to the creeping darkness.

"Does anyone want anything to eat?" Jess asked. "Sandwiches - cheese and ham." They all dipped into the little bundle she laid before them, ensuring that they kept a careful eye on their target. There was a rustling and movement to their left. Mick swivelled his head around. A sleek rat was eying their food, but thinking better of it, he scuttled off into the safety of the hedgerow. The others looked round just as it disappeared.

"Hedgehog," said Mick.

"Aw, wish I'd seen it," said Mia.

"Did you do this a lot when you were in the police, Mick?" asked Jess.

"A fair bit," he replied, "but never in a graveyard. Mostly it would be from empty premises, opposite a drug dealing den or a house where we thought that someone on the run might turn up"

"Was it exciting?" asked Mia.

"Not really. Often you'd be there for days and nothing would happen."

"Were you scared?"

"Not scared, more alert I'd say," Mick replied. "Some of the people we dealt with could be unpredictable. Volatile. But we'd been briefed beforehand with any intel, so we were ready for them." Jess considered the words. Briefed beforehand. Any intel. She should share her thoughts.

"We need to be careful," she said, "I've got a theory about Knight. I think that he might be a psychopath." Although their features were indistinct in the limited light, Jess picked up doubt on both faces. "Let me explain. I know what you're thinking," she whispered, "the same thing that most people believe. Psychopath. He's the one holding up the meat cleaver, the one with the bulging eyes and gritted teeth, isn't he? If only. It's true, some of them are violent, but there's much more to it than that. In the eighties, a professor called Robert Hare listed all of the traits in what he called his Psychopathy Checklist. It's been revised since then but it's still in use. You won't find meat cleavers on his list, no bulging eyes. It's personality characteristics, things like being callous and unfeeling, breaking rules, being full of yourself, blaming others and never feeling guilty." Mick was listening intently.

"I recognise those things in a good few of the people I've locked up," he said.

"I bet you do - they reckon about a quarter of people in prison are psychopaths. But there are other traits too. They can come across as charming, they're manipulative, and telling lies is second nature to them. It's estimated that one percent of the whole population are psychopaths, so there are plenty of them roaming around. Lots of them rise to the top, in business, politics, all walks of life. They're hard to spot, but they cause chaos and misery in the lives of the people they come into contact with. Every chance the government bigwig who axed my charity funding was one. Now I haven't formally assessed Lee Knight, but I know a bit about him, and I see red flags. Lots of them."

"That's interesting, Jess," said Mick. "I don't think it changes what we do here but… shhhh." Mick was interrupted by footsteps on the gravel car park. The gate swung open and a figure entered. A second immediately followed, weighed down by a carrier bag in his right hand. Mick peered at the two of them through the dark. He could pick out their outlines. Neither of them was Knight, too short, too slender. They wandered towards a bench in the centre of the graveyard and the first sat down with a clumsy thump. The other joined him, before rummaging in his carrier bag. They heard the unmistakable hiss of a can being opened. Then a second.

"Uncle Mick," said Mia, almost forgetting the whispering directive, "that's Kieran and Oliver. They're in my class at school. I can't believe they're out here drinking alcohol at eleven o'clock at night. I've met Oliver's mum. She's really hoity-toity. She would kill him if she knew he was here."

"She'd best be quick if she wants to beat me to it," Mick muttered. "There's no way Knight is going to come in with them sitting there." Oliver emitted a boisterous, gassy belch, which Kieran thought was the funniest thing ever. Their voices grew louder, as the cider numbed their inhibitions. They were chanting puerile phrases at each other from some comedy programme that Mick had never heard of.

"Should I go over and tell them that they need to go home?" asked Mia.

"No. They'd want to know why you were here. We're going to have to sit it out." Mick heard another can open. And another. Then, there was a flash of light as one of the boy's phones pinged.

"It's Stevo," Kieran said to Oliver. "Him and Monster are in the park and they've got a bottle of voddy. C'mon, let's go and see them." With some difficulty, they managed to haul each other up and set off in a meandering fashion broadly in the direction of the gate.

"Monster?" said Mick.

"A.K.A. Jason Barclay," said Mia. "He's the same age as me, but you should see the size of him. And his face." Mia gurned. "He's scary." Once more, St. Jude's fell silent.

12.15 am. The gravel in the car park crunched into life once more. Mick glanced at Jess and Mia. Their faces were taut, their eyes big and bright, shining like train headlights in a tunnel. At the gate, they could pick out a silhouette. Taller, stockier this time, not the figure of a schoolboy. Not even Monster. The torch in his hand burst into life. The three froze, motionless, as the beam swept across the graveyard, first right, then left, like a wartime searchlight, seeking out the enemy. He began to walk down the graveyard, keeping to the grass verges to avoid the crunch of the gravel path. He did not make straight for Charlie's grave, instead heading towards Tom's shed. He disappeared inside, then re-emerged, carrying a spade. They watched as he strode towards Charlie's plot. None of them spoke but gave a nod to each other that said 'this is it'.

Beneath the ground, Charlie, Rita, The Doc, Isabel and Yvonne had all managed to remain awake. Unable to see anything in the darkness, they tried to interpret the sounds above. Footsteps approaching.

"This is it," said Charlie.

Lee Knight propped his torch on the top of the urn-vase that Jess kept on Charlie's grave, crushing the blooms it contained.

"Hold this for me would you, Charlie-boy?" he whispered, "only I think you've got some paperwork that you forgot to pass on." With both hands now free, he moved the boards covering the new grave to the side, laying them down with care to avoid any disruption to the ground surrounding the plot.

He retrieved his torch. "Much obliged," he said. He shone the torch into the hole, lowered the spade in, then jumped down after it. He scanned the beam along the earth face adjoining Charlie's plot, estimating where he had previously breached the wicker wall. "About here I reckon," he said. Knight plunged the blade into the soil of the side wall.

Charlie grimaced.

Mick held his hands flat, palms facing down, urging silence, as Knight jumped down and disappeared from their sight. Sound echoed up the graveyard. Tchick. Tchick. The tunnelling had commenced. Mick set the plan in motion.

Sitting in the station, Harry heard his phone ping. He opened the message.

"He's here. It's started."

Harry got straight onto Ian and Stella in patrol car P17. No response. He tried again and got a garbled reply from Stella.

"We're busy boss, massive ruck in the town centre. All day drinking in the sunshine. We'll get there as soon as we can. Keep you posted."

Harry sent a text to Mick.

"Sit tight. They're tied up."

"What's happening, Uncle Mick? Are the police coming?"

"Shortly," he replied, "they're all busy at the moment", trying to remain calm, but knowing there was not a lot of time. He flicked his eyes between the grave and the gate, the grave and the gate. A minute past. Then another. And a third. The tchick sound had stopped. He's through. Mick could not risk waiting any longer.

"Stay here," he said to the others, "do not move." And he was off, crouching as he moved down toward the corner.

Lee Knight shone his torch into the channel he had created. He could see the hole he had smashed through the coffin wall on his previous visit.

"Perfect. Bang in the middle," he said, congratulating himself on the accuracy of his efforts. He twisted sideways and stretched, squeezing his body forward, pushing himself through the cramped space. He altered the angle of the torch until he could see the lapel of Charlie's jacket. He nudged forward a little more, and plunged his arm in, feeling under the lapel for the inside pocket. He dipped his hand in. Nothing. He rooted around some more.

"Shit. Must be his other pocket," he said. "Excuse me, Charlie, you don't mind if I stretch across, do you?" When he had stolen the watch, Knight made only minimal contact with the corpse. Now he would have to extend across Charlie's torso to reach the far side. He inched his hand across Charlie's chest, not in the slightest phased by this near embrace of a cadaver. But then, if you don't care much for the living, why worry about the dead? Before he reached the other side of Charlie's jacket, his hand came into contact with something unexpected. It was the edge of a piece of paper. He managed to catch it between his forefinger and thumb.

"Gotcha." He began to ease his arm out, holding his prize tight. "Almost there."

And then, from above, he heard an almighty metallic clatter.

Out of the dark stillness of the night, Mia and Jess heard a curse. Though Mick hadn't named any names in his expletive laden outburst, they knew who was in the firing line. Oliver had added littering to his previous offences of underage drinking and being a complete dick. As Mick had sped down the graveyard, he had taken an upright half-empty can of cider perfectly in his imperfect stride, volleying it forward with force. It clattered off a gravestone, then rattled down the gravel path, before coming to a standstill. Its remaining sickly contents glugged out onto the stones. Mick stopped moving and crouched down. He hated Oliver.

"Bloody hell," he thought, "he's bound to have heard that." In his pomp, Mick could have down there in no time, but with legs of diverse lengths and a paunch to the fore, he was no longer built for the chase. He was still a distance from the grave. Knight would be up and off before he got anywhere near. He set off again, moving as quickly as his compromised physique would allow.

On hearing the clatter, Knight stopped, but only briefly. Someone is up there. Could just be a harmless drunk, but the stakes were too high to take the chance. Go, get out.

"Sorry, I need to be off, Charlie," he whispered, as he

resumed withdrawing his hand, quickly but carefully. Still clutching the paper, he reversed his arm, his elbow now out of the hole. Charlie heard the voice and felt the movement. He felt a rage surge within him. As Knight's limb was about to disappear out of sight, Charlie felt a peculiar sensation. It started in his left shoulder, then moved down to his arm. Then he felt a flinch in his fingers. Jesus. He could grip. His hand grasped the intruder's wrist, fastening tight, with the strength of the jaws of a pit bull. Knight wriggled and pulled on his arm, trying to free it.

As he hirpled down toward the grave, heart going one hundred and twenty, Mick could not understand why Knight had not emerged. Why hadn't he made a break for it? Maybe he's quickly trying to cover his tracks down there? Closer and closer, still no sign of him. Now he was near to the edge. He arrived and looked down. Knight was looking up at him. Unaware that the thief was held firm, and with no regard for his problematic anatomy, Mick threw himself off the edge. The full weight of the former officer, every pound of his non-Mediterranean diet, crashed down onto Knight. Charlie watched as the intruder's hand lost hold of its prize, and was then ripped from his deathly grip, as it disappeared out through the coffin wall. Mick wrestled Knight into an armlock, then became aware of dancing flashlights above him.

"Stop. Police. Stay where you are." Mick looked up from the darkened hole and saw four sets of eyes looking down at him, those of two police officers and the more familiar faces of Mia and Jess. He clambered off Knight and onto his feet.

"Before you do anything else," he said, "read him his rights."

"I am arresting you on suspicion of tampering with a grave. You do not have to say anything, but it may harm your defence if you do not mention when questioned something which you later rely on in court. Anything you do say may be given in evidence."

Knight stood up and as he did so, by the light of the policeman's torch, he caught sight of a shimmer at his feet.

Part Three : LIFE

"Life is what happens when you're making other plans."

John Lennon

Chapter 16

Jess studied the cracked glass sign above the door. 'Police Station'. She felt a flurry of nerves. Her only previous visit to the hub of law enforcement in Stanford was as a twelve-year-old. She had found a ten-pound note blowing along Main Street and her dad had advised her that she should hand it in immediately, or she risked being locked up for Stealing By Finding.

"Bound to have changed a bit in twenty-odd years," she thought. She pushed open the heavy door and entered. It was much as she remembered, the work of an interior designer targeting the 'shabby-intimidating' mood. She looked at the public information notices pinned to the cork board. They had been updated but still covered the same topics - best to look both ways before crossing a road, be constantly vigilant to the threat posed by long-fingered, silhouetted pickpockets, and call this number if you have an acquaintance or neighbour who, ideally, you would like to spend some time in prison.

In the sparse interview room, Mick's old colleague Harry, along with a young P.C., stepped Jess through the events of the past weeks. It was painful to go back over the circumstances of Charlie's death and then his funeral, but she saw that they felt as awkward asking these questions as she was in providing the answers.

"I'm sorry but I need to show you a few photographs as we go along," said Harry, tapping on the keyboard of his laptop. "Some of them might be a bit upsetting."

"That's okay." Harry turned the screen to face her. Jess saw an image of Charlie's grave.

"Can you just confirm that this is where your husband was buried?"

"Yes, that's it." She listened closely and responded as they moved through what had happened leading up to the night in the graveyard, her suspicion that something was wrong, Mick and Mia's assistance, how they had tracked Grandad Joe's watch to a man in Italy, and their plan to ensnare Lee Knight.

"And here, I'm sorry, this is a photo taken by the Scenes Of Crime Officer," he said, flicking to the next image, "this one shows the plot next to your husband. A channel has been dug through to his coffin." Jess hadn't been able to see it clearly on the night, and the reality hit her hard. She took a deep breath.

"Yes, that's what happened."

"Thanks. I'm sorry, but we have to check. Now if we go back to the watch, could you describe it to me?"

"Yes, it's a man's watch, with a white face, tiny black numbers all around the edges, and three other little dials in the middle. The case and strap has silver and gold bits on them." As she spoke Harry flicked his eyes between her and the small polythene bag before him, comparing each of the details to the item it contained. He slid it across the table. Before he had the chance to ask, Jess was nodding.

"Yes, that's it," she said.

"Sure?" he asked.

"Definite. Charlie had only worn it a few times, but I remember it clearly."

"When we arranged for you to come in today, we asked if you could bring in any photographs of it that you have," said Harry. "Did you manage to find any?"

"No, sorry, I couldn't. Charlie had only started to wear it

recently, and mum and I looked at every photo we could find of grandad. We know he wore it every day, but you can't see it in any of them. He always wore long-sleeved shirts, so it was covered up. Even in the summer."

"Really? That's a bit odd."

"Yes, I found out why when I was in Italy." She looked at them, weighing up whether this was detail they wanted. "Signor Ascenzo told me how grandad was badly injured during the war, stabbed in his lower arm. He had a huge wound he said, but couldn't get it treated immediately. My mum said she had seen it occasionally, it had left an ugly scar. I suppose it was fixed up as best as they could in a field hospital. I think grandad must have been ashamed of it, which is ridiculous. I would have told him that if I had known about it."

"We have spoken to Lee Knight and we also searched his home address," said Harry. "We found this watch there, but he is adamant that it belongs to him."

"No. It's Grandad's. Or Charlie's. You don't believe him, do you?"

"We're trying to establish the facts at the stage. I don't want to say too much but it was stored in an unusual place. One of the first things we did when we seized it was to have it valued. I don't know what you were expecting, but it has come back as being worth about four hundred pounds." He looked at Jess, trying to gauge her reaction. A flicker of disappointment ghosted across her face.

"I'm slightly surprised," she said. "Now that I've met the original owner, Signor Ascenzo, I thought it might have been worth more. I'm sure he did too." She looked at the watch on the table before her once more. "Still, that shouldn't matter, should it? It's still a crime, stealing is stealing, no matter what the item is."

"That is true," said Harry, "but I'll level with you, Mrs Munro. If a four hundred pound watch had been stolen from your house, it's unlikely it would get much of our attention. This is different. Maybe it shouldn't be, but it is. I can assure you that we will investigate, establish if a crime has been committed, and make sure that the property ends up with its rightful owner."

"Thank you."

"I think we've got everything we need, so we'll get this typed up for you to review. Just a couple more things. Can you give us contact details for Signor Ascenzo, if you have them? We need to talk to him to corroborate your story."

"No problem, I've got them here," said Jess, taking her phone from her bag.

"And we've already got your details – I presume you're okay with us getting in touch with you with any updates on the case, or if we need any more information from you?"

"Of course. I've got a busy week ahead, but I'll always get back to you as soon as I can."

*   *   *

Isabel was first to spot the two heavily laden figures lumbering towards their corner of the graveyard, their stagger haphazard under the weight of the burden the bore. They stopped nearby and checked their paperwork, as if confirming a delivery address.

"Are you expecting a parcel today, Doc?" asked Charlie. The Doc looked up.

"Not I, Charles. Observe the livery manifest upon their overalls. I think that this consignment is intended for you." Charlie read the silver embroidered letters. *Prestige Memorials.*

"Oh no. It's my headstone, isn't it?"

"I'd imagine so. You don't sound too pleased to receive it. Why so? We all have one. They are quite the fashion in this neighbourhood."

"Makes it a bit permanent," said Charlie, "literally set in stone. I might be apprehensive because… I don't want to seem ungrateful… but some of them I've seen, the designs are a bit schmaltzy. I hope Jess hasn't got me a picture of a bundle of LPs and a turntable with an angel floating above... or worse, one with a photo of me on it. They give me the creeps. I don't think anyone needs to know so precisely who is down there."

"Usually there will be some sort of commemorative ceremony," said Rita.

"Wow, exciting," said Charlie. "I'd imagine Jess will invite a few friends and family along then." Above them, the two men had unpacked and grunted into position the hefty signage informing the world as to Charlie Munro's whereabouts. He scanned the front of the shiny black stone, then read it out.

Charlie Munro
Born 12th March 1983
Died 22nd April 2018
Aged 35

He wrote his life's song
The words, the tune, the tempo
A song that will never be forgotten

The last words caught in his throat.

"Oh, Charlie, isn't that lovely," said Rita.

As one of the men completed the fixing in place, the other was tidying around, gathering together the packaging debris and placing it in the empty crate. They moved off, back towards the gate, with considerably greater ease than their journey down. As soon as they had disappeared from view Jess, who had been watching the whole operation from the opposite side of the cemetery, made her way across. She stood before the stone, immovable, staring. Then she leaned forwards and touched it. She felt that the dark material was beginning to warm as it absorbed the rays from the July sun.

"Hi Charlie. Your mum and dad couldn't make it today. I hope you don't mind, but I decided not to invite anyone else. I would have felt I should make a speech." She laughed. "You'll be thinking it's my dread of public speaking that stopped me. It's not. The words would have ended up being for other people, and I wanted to say words for you, for us." She took a piece of paper from her pocket. "Here goes."

"Dear Charlie." She looked around, checking that there was no one there to overhear. "These dating websites spend millions on computer programs to match people with their perfect partner. All it took for us was a faulty hospital name badge and your clumsy foot." She surveyed the text on the stone. "Thirty-five. You crammed a lot into too few years. You would have been the best presenter Radio Two ever had. Then who knows what you would have gone onto? You would have become famous, but it would never have changed the person you were." Her eyes carried on down the lettering before her, blurred by tears.

"I hope you like the stone," she said. "I promise you Charlie, as long as I live, your words will not be forgotten, your song will stay on our lips and in our hearts. At your funeral, when I first stood in this spot, I was utterly bereft. I did not think I could cope with life any more. But, in some way that I cannot work out, when I was in the darkest place, you got to me the way you always did, and pushed me to stay strong. I'm trying to write the next verse of my song, Charlie, it's hard, but I'm trying. I miss you. Every day."

Jess touched the stone once more. She lifted her hand from the black granite, placed it gently to her lips, then laid it back on the stone. She sighed. "Right, Mick and Mia will be here shortly, so I'm going to sit over here and compose myself."

Beneath her, everyone heard Jess's words, but not one of them spoke.

As soon as she entered the graveyard, Mia saw Jess and began to walk at a brisk pace, leaving Mick trailing behind, trying his ungainly best to keep up.

"Oh my goodness," she said, admiring the headstone, "you never told us that this was coming."

"I didn't want a big fuss. It was put in place earlier this morning."

"It looks great," said Mick. "I like the words, very fitting." He sat down beside Jess. "Good week?"

"Busy, but good. There's such a lot to do to get back on top of the charity and The Stables work. I've been bombarded with phone calls and emails about it, on top of my normal patient caseload. Oh, and I've been interviewed by the police." She told them about making her statement, mentioning at several points how much she appreciated the way they had treated her, knowing that Mick was sure to feed it back. "They showed me a watch, one they recovered from Knight's house. It is definitely the one grandad left to Charlie."

"That's great news," said Mick.

"There is a downside. They've had it valued. It's come in at four hundred pounds." Mick did not reply. He sat quietly. "Is everything okay?" she asked.

"Yes, fine," he replied, his tone low, flat, and failing to match the words. "Only my hunch was that it would have been worth more. I know you're really busy and I feel like I've wasted your time on this." Jess observed the ex-policeman as he spoke. He seemed deflated, as if he personally had in some way let her down.

"Mick, no. Think of this. I sat in a police station where they showed me Grandad Joe's watch, the same one I had buried with Charlie weeks ago. They found it in Knight's house. If they can prove he stole it then we'll get it back, and he'll be held to account for what he's done. That's not a waste of time. Forget the value. Harry has promised that they will investigate it thoroughly. He's committed to getting to the truth." What she didn't mention to Mick was the nagging thought she'd had ever since her interview. She was sure Marco believed it was worth more than this. If there is no money in the watch, is there no money for The Stables?

Below them, the quiet, uplifting serenity of Jess's ceremony had been ripped into tatters.

"Four hundred quid," said Charlie. "Jeez. That's me, always getting ahead of myself. I cherry-picked my way through the facts, desperate to write the story I needed to hear. I wanted to believe that Jess's problems were solved."

"It wasn't just you," said Isabel. "We were all upset by what had happened to you. We wanted to believe it and got carried away." The Doc countered immediately.

"True, Isabel, but I fear it was I who was the main offender. I set the hare-brained hares running and Charlie's hopes soaring with my flawed diagnosis of his timepiece."

"Stop, all of you," said Rita. "You have absolutely nothing to apologise for. Charlie was robbed, and no one would ever have known until he made Jess aware something was wrong. Isabel, you convinced your brother to help look into it. Doctor Dean, you found out we were wrong about who had done it, leading Yvonne to fill that young man with enough courage so he felt able to tell the truth. And now the real culprit been arrested. All in all, a good effort if you ask me. You should be proud of what you've done... for God's sake, you're all dead."

"You're right. Thank you everyone" said Charlie. Rita continued.

"And listen to what your wife has just said. The police are going to do everything they can. I don't think that grave robbery will ever be taken lightly. Leastwise I hope not. Or none of us can sleep safely in our coffins."

*   *   *

Harry picked up the scrap of paper from his desk. In Jess's neat writing were the contact details for the Italian. Time was he would have tried to convince the boss it was essential he went over there to interview the guy in person. A bit of sunshine, pizza for breakfast, a couple of glasses of cold birra of an evening. There was no way he would try it on now, definitely not for a four hundred quid watch, not even one that had been robbed from a dead man's grave. God, last month he'd struggled to get a return train ticket to Chorley signed off. He made arrangements to set up a video call.

When the video link was established and pleasantries were exchanged, Harry's keen eye roamed over the room in which the bespectacled elderly gentleman was sitting. He was sure that the old guy had said he would be at home. Harry was no computer whizz but he knew that there was some clever dick way that you could put a fake backdrop on your screen to impress. This one was bloody convincing. He began by walking Marco through the history of his watch, meeting Jess's grandad, then the unexpected contact from Mia. Every question he asked, every response he received, all of it tied in with Mrs Munro's version. Finally, he was left with just one query.

"If you don't mind me asking sir, can you give me a little bit about your personal background?"

"Of course."

"Are you at home at the moment?"

"I am."

"It looks like a grand house. Does it belongs to your family?"

"Yes, to me. My father established a very successful business, which I have expanded. I had this villa built about thirty years ago." Harry steadied himself.

"Sir, we've had the watch valued and it came back at four hundred pounds. Does that seem reasonable to you?" He winced as the old man's shoulders shook with laughter. When he managed to stop, he spoke.

"That would be around five hundred Euros? No, I don't think so," he said. "If you were my doctor I would demand a second opinion." He began laughing again. Harry waited until Marco regained his composure.

"Mrs Munro was surprised when we mentioned it to her," he said.

"You have told her this?"

"Yes. I'm now wondering if something has gone wrong," said Harry, "at our end, I expect. I think we have all we need for the moment, so thank you for your time. We will be back in touch soon."

"Thank you, Sergeant, for the work you are doing to try to resolve this. I am sorry for laughing, I did not intend to make light of a most serious matter. I made an exchange with Joe and although he is gone, it is very important to me that the spirit of our arrangement lives on through his family. I have great faith in your UK justice system" he said.

"I wish I had," thought Harry as they exchanged their final goodbyes. He made his way back through the open plan office. "Burgess, put that bloody puzzle book away and come in here. I could do with a chat."

Harry would admit to sometimes being a little brusque with his colleagues. No more than that though. In the past he'd worked for a few table-thumping, coffee cup launching bawlers, who thought their histrionics made them strong, got them respect. To Harry, they looked like knobs. His style with the team was firm – you had to be sometimes – but it was always respectful. Today Burgess had pushed him close to his limits.

"Please tell me you're taking the piss," he pleaded, staring at the big witless moon-face before him.

"I'm not taking the piss," said P.C. Burgess. "And I don't get what your problem is. You gave me two jobs to do. See if I could locate any of the jewellery from the Grafton Road burglary. Get a value on that undertaker's watch." Harry nodded. "And you're always moaning about how long I take to do anything," Burgess continued, "so I combined the two. Multi-tasking. I went to Spence's. The jewellery wasn't there but he gave me a price on the watch. Four hundred quid."

"You asked Spence… he was your jewellery expert."

"Yep. He's got years in the business. He's a licenced pawnbroker."

"Oh yeah, he's licenced all right. Double-O Seven. James Spence, Licenced To Fence. Why do you think it's the first place we go looking for stolen gear?" Burgess stared back at him, a face barren of thought, looking for all the world like a bear who had been challenged to solve a quadratic equation. "Let me tell you why. He's a crook. You didn't think to get it confirmed by someone qualified? And honest?"

"Didn't see the need," he said with a sniff. "Fencey's all right."

"Burgess, don't say anything else... just get me contact details for Sotheby's."

*   *   *

Dear Journal,

This morning was hard. Charlie's gravestone arrived. I chose it, I decided what would be written on it, they have made it and installed it exactly as I asked, and yet somewhere deep inside, I resent it. I wish it was not there. Tonight I had better news. I received a text that I want to copy into here, so that if I ever lose it from my phone I will still have it forever –

Jess, the police have told me they believe the watch is worth only a small amount. I know I am old and I may have only a short while yet to live, but my commitment to your project is timeless. You must not worry about the watch value, you must not worry about anything. Marco x'

*   *   *

Sitting at the keyboard, Giles Sanders fingers struggled to dance at the furious tempo being set by his whirling brain. He reread his short message, hit the red exclamation mark with confidence and aplomb, before pressing the Send key. Ralph would be intrigued to see this. No dramatic tutting this time, Ralph Chapman simply opened it and read.

"*Ralph, just when it appeared we'd lost track of the 1518, see below and attached, Giles.*" He replied straight away.

"*Thank you Giles. I shall contact the gentleman now.*" By the time Giles had read the reply, Ralph was already on the phone.

"Sergeant Turnbull? Ralph Chapman from Sotheby's here. It's about the request that you sent through this morning."

"That was quick," said Harry, "I only just sent it. That's the internet for you I suppose."

"Indeed, that is the internet for you. About the photographs of the watch that you have sent us..."

"I'll give you a little bit of background," said Harry. "I didn't want to say too much in the email. We have recovered this watch in the course of an ongoing investigation, but we don't know much about it. We're hoping you might be able to provide us with some information, how old it is, where it's from, rough idea of value, that sort of thing."

"I am sure we will be able to help," Ralph replied, "but first let me give you some background of our own. Remarkably, someone contacted us several weeks ago about what I believe to be the very same item."

"Really? Can you tell me who?"

"A Mr Keith Glen. Mr Glen is not a regular client of ours, but submitted an initial valuation inquiry, to which we replied, but have received no response. We have tried to follow up several times, as we were potentially very interested in the article, but with no success."

"Did you think it might be worth a bob or two then... in your professional opinion."

"I'm sure you will understand that Sotheby's would never offer a firm valuation without examining the item itself.

However, if you would like an indication as to our thoughts, without prejudice if you like, I immediately alerted our international expert on watches to the potential opportunity. He is on standby to come over from Geneva to give Sotheby's definitive view, should Mr Glen resume our dialogue. I think he would be able to come over in the next few days, if that would be useful to you?"

"It certainly would be," said Harry, before adding "we wouldn't be able to pay his expenses, mind. Not from Geneva. Not his taxi from the airport, to be honest."

"No, of course not. Sotheby's would be delighted to assist the police, as they have us on numerous occasions."

*   *   *

Harry had never welcomed anyone to the station as sharply dressed as Sebastian Weiss. The closest was that lawyer from Manchester who was trying to wangle a professional football player off a drink driving charge, and to be honest, he wasn't classy like this bloke, he looked like a spiv. Weiss was accompanied by Ralph Chapman who, Harry observed, treated his international colleague with a level of respect that bordered on cult-like reverence. Harry ushered them through the main room and into his small side office. He caught sight of the gleaming cufflinks, peeping out from under the cuff of Sebastian's suit jacket. "This guy has not come here to look at a four hundred quid watch," he thought. "Bet those cufflinks would fetch more than that. Each." He slid yesterday's polystyrene burger box off his desk into the bin.

"Can I offer you gentlemen a drink?" he asked, knocking the roughest corners off his normal accent. He was doing his best to channel the waiter at the overpriced restaurant he and his wife had gone to for their twenty-fifth wedding anniversary, a challenging role given his current setting.

"A coffee would be lovely," said Sebastian.

"Doubt it," thought Harry, exiting the room and looking for young Peter. Thank God, he's in.

"Pete, can you make a pot of coffee in that fancy jug thing of yours?" Pete looked at him dead-pan.

"Thought you said I wasn't to use it cos it stinks the place out?" Harry shook his head.

"Don't get smart. Can you just make it… please?" and headed back to the office. Pete got up and drifted towards the kitchen.

"Drinks are on their way," said Harry. "Now, about this watch." He jerked open the top drawer of his desk, took out a clear plastic evidence bag, and crossed the room. He laid it on the table where his guests were sitting. He picked up a box of disposable plastic gloves, took a pair for himself, before offering the box to Sebastian. "Sorry, it's already been swabbed for DNA and prints but we just need to be careful." Sebastian nodded.

"Of course," he said, "but I have a pair of my own if that is okay?" He reached into his leather satchel. Harry looked at the cotton gloves he'd brought forth. They were made from the whitest fabric he had ever seen.

"Yes, they should be fine," he said.

"Excellent," said Sebastian, pulling them on and straightening the cloth around each finger. Pete arrived, carrying a tray. He laid down his battered cafetiere, a plastic bottle of milk, and three heavily stained mugs, each promoting a different local business. Finally, he plopped an opened bag of sugar onto the table. The white granular surface was festooned with crusty brown deposits, left behind by previous creators of hot beverages.

"Thanks, Pete," said Harry. He poured each of them a cup, thinking it was unlikely Sebastian was going to touch any of these wretched items, at least not whilst he was sporting those gloves. Sebastian dipped into his satchel once more, this time pulling out a black velvet cloth which he unrolled on the table like an oversized placemat. Harry opened the evidence bag, and removed the watch. Then, picking up on Sebastian's meticulous approach, he laid it ceremoniously on the soft cloth. Sebastian stared at it for several moments, as if he was dining at a fine restaurant and had been served an exquisite starter, too beautiful to spoil by eating. He picked it up and looked at the dial. His nimble fingers then set to work, moving it around at speed, this way then that. He dipped into his pocket and brought out a small brown leather case, from which he produced an expensive-looking jeweller's eyeglass. Now he set about studying the timepiece more thoroughly, starting with the white face. His small audience waited patiently until finally, he paused, then laid the watch carefully back on the velvet surface.

"Where does the person you are investigating say that he obtained this item?" Sebastian asked.

"At a car boot sale," Harry replied.

"Sorry? A car boot… I do not know of this thing." Ralph Chapman stepped in.

"It's an event, typically held in a muddy field, where people sell items they no longer require from the boots of their cars." Sebastian raised an eyebrow.

"Ah, interesting. I think I would like to attend such a sale."

"I very much doubt it, " Ralph replied. "They are tawdry affairs. Riff-raff selling rubble to rabble."

"Perhaps that is generally true, Ralph," he said, "but it is not the case here." He swivelled round in his bucket chair to address Chapman directly. "I believe it may be one of the Three." Harry looked from one to the other, hoping for some clue. Bloody experts. Sebastian had picked the watch up once more, so he asked Chapman.

"You've both gone a bit Lord of The Rings. What does that mean, one of the three?" Chapman correctly read the policeman's wishes.

"Sebastian, I think the sergeant is keen to have your expert opinion of the item."

"Yes, of course. Where do I start?"

"With the basics," said Harry, "I don't know anything about it except that we found it hidden in an undertaker's house, and the dodgiest jeweller in North West England reckons its worth about four hundred quid." Sebastian gave the short, haughty snort of a thoroughbred racehorse holding prime spot in the Winners' Enclosure.

"Okay. Let us begin with the maker. Patek Philippe. They have been making watches of the very highest calibre for nearly two centuries. In 1941 they introduced their Perpetual Calendar Chronograph 1518 - known to us simply as the fifteen-eighteen. Many experts, myself included, judge it to be the most beautiful, most iconic wristwatch in the world. It is believed that only 281 were ever made. So already you can see that, if genuine, this watch would be a very interesting piece. However my friend," he continued, holding an index finger aloft, "this watch is not all that it seems. Look at the casing. What do you see?" Harry leaned forward and peered at the item on the desk.

"It looks like it's made out of two different metals," he said. "Gold and something else. Silver?" Sebastian shook his head.

Harry tried the next most obvious candidate. "Platinum maybe?"

"No. It is steel!" Harry saw the flash of light in the expert's keen eyes.

"So is my kitchen sink," he said. "Am I right in thinking that it's been cobbled together in some forger's garden shed?"

"Sergeant, let me tell you about Patek Phillippe and steel. Almost all fifteen-eighteens were made entirely of gold, one of two colours, rose or yellow. But during World War Two, gold became scarce, and the company manufactured four entirely of steel. The first of these was discovered around the mid-nineties, and their rarity has made them very desirable. All four are now in private collections. It has been rumoured for some time that three fifteen-eighteens were made from a combination of gold and steel, but none has ever been found. That is, until maybe today." Harry glanced at Ralph Chapman. The Sotheby's man looked like he might be about to faint or lose continence, or both. Sebastian was in full flow of another sort.

"Now, if you consider that there are four steel examples in existence, all documented, and that we are now looking at only one of three… and that no one knows where the other two are, or if they even still exist…"

"This one is rarer," said Harry.

"Exactly. So rare, you could say that currently, it is unique. A truly historic piece, and a very precious thing. Assuming, of course, it is real."

"Right," said Harry "and is it?"

"Over the years, sergeant, I have been asked to appraise numerous examples of this model, some genuine, many counterfeit." He paused. "This is, without doubt, the finest example of the fifteen-eighteen I have seen." Chapman emptied his lungs, shaking his jowls. Weiss continued.

"You have asked if I can estimate the value of this item. The last of the four steel watches was sold at auction in Geneva a few years ago. The price? Eleven million Swiss Francs. The market is hard to predict. However, before coming today, I have already consulted with colleagues and I have contacted a few notable collectors. Based on their opinions and what I see before me, the estimate that I have arrived at for this piece is twenty million Swiss Francs.

"Bloody hell," said Harry. He then realised he'd never been to Switzerland, in fact, he couldn't even have told you which currency they used. The bitter disappointment of a childhood family holiday to Italy flooded back. With his special new wallet brim full of colourful notes, all with numbers in the thousands, he'd felt like a king. Until he went to pay for that first ice cream and found out how little change he got from his one thousand lira. Better to check. He sniffed.

"How much is a Swiss franc worth then?"

*　*　*

As they sat on the bench, having finished telling the story of her interview and the low valuation, Jess could tell that both Mick and Mia were deflated by the news. They needed something positive.

"Hey," she said "with all of the excitement around Knight and our trap, I don't think I showed you my photos from Italy. Wait till you see Signor Ascenzo's villa," she said, taking her phone from her handbag.

"Was he very rich?" Mia asked.

"Oh yes, film star wealthy," she said opening up the screen. They looked on as she flicked back through the photos. "There," she said, "that's Marco and my mum. And here they are in the gardens of the villa with a glass of wine. Mum got tiddly, she's not used to it. And here, this is them in front of the house." Mick craned his neck to see the screen.

"Wow. That is impressive. He must be worth a fortune."

"Talking to him you would never know it. He was a humble man, very down to earth. He looked after us so well. Here, let me find the one I took of the marble staircase." As they looked on, the image on the screen flipped. Incoming call.

"Excuse me," she said, "I'd better get this. It'll be something to do with The Stables."

"I don't think so," said Mick. "I know that number. It's Harry."

"Hello," said Jess."

"Hi, it's Sergeant Turnbull."

"I know, I'm with someone who recognised your number." Harry did not reply. "Your friend, Mick," she said.

"Ah, right," he said. "Mrs Munro there's something I need to update you on, but I can ring back if it's not convenient."

"No," said Jess, "now is fine. There's nothing I'd be concerned about discussing in front of Mick and Mia. I'll end up telling them anyway, so I might as well put you on loudspeaker," she said, tapping the button.

"Okay. You'd better sit down."

"We all are."

"It's about the value of the watch. There was a hitch at our end, so we went out for a second opinion. It turns out it's a very rare thing, so it's worth more than what we thought."

"That's good news," said Jess. "Is it much different?"

"It's not four hundred pounds. It's more like seventeen million pounds." Mia was the swiftest to react, darting out a hand to Jess's phone in case it dropped from her grasp.

"Oh my goodness," said Jess. "Oh my goodness." Mick

stepped in.

"That's a helluva difference, Harry," he said, "how do you know which figure is correct?"

"If I say the first estimate came from Fencey, courtesy of Burgess, and the second was from the senior watch guy at Sotheby's."

"Seventeen million pounds?" said Jess. "For a watch? Grandad Joe's watch? Honestly, it's mind-boggling... almost frightening."

"That's how I felt when they told me. The day they came to look at it, I'd picked it up from the evidence store in the morning, left it sitting in my top drawer when I went out at lunchtime. Don't worry, I've had it put into safe storage now."

"Oh my goodness," said Jess, "I think we're all a bit stunned."

"I know it's a lot to take in. So far the only people that know the value are you, the two guys from Sotheby's, and a couple of people on my team. If it's okay with you, Mrs Munro, I'd prefer that we keep it that way in the meantime... otherwise, I can see this turning into a media circus."

"No, that's absolutely fine, I don't want any publicity or questions."

"Great, I'll make sure that we keep it confidential at our end for now. If you need anything else from us please get in touch. Bye."

"Bye." Jess hit the red dot to end the call.

"Did you hear that Charles?" said The Doc. "How extraordinary. Seventeen million pounds."

"Doc, I know you arrived here from a different time zone, where a pint of milk was sixpence, but believe me seventeen million pounds is still a fortune. Harry's worried about leaving it in his drawer in a police station? I wore it for my leaving do, out on the lash in some of the dodgiest watering holes in Liverpool. My watch was worth more than every single pub we went into. No, scratch that, more than the total of all of them together."

Chapter 17

Dear Journal,

Maybe writing it down will help me to grasp this.

£17,000,000

No, it doesn't - if anything, having to keep track of all of those zeros and commas made it worse. My head is spinning. This changes everything. I need to speak to Marco, but before I do, I'll wait an hour or so, try to get my head around it.

Three hours on from Harry's phone call Jess abandoned that plan. The time needed to get her head around this would be measured on a calendar rather than a clock. When Marco answered the video call and she saw his craggy features, her smile was spontaneous.

"Jess? I was not expecting another update on The Stables so soon."

"Hi, Marco. It's another update, but not about The Stable this time. It's about the watch."

"Ah, some progress on the case I hope? The sergeant showed it to me on the video call. Good news, I was able to confirm to him that it is my watch, or, should I say, was my watch. It was strange to see it again after all these years."

"Yes, your watch. After they had spoken to you, the police decided to have it revalued and found that it was worth more than they originally said. I thought that it was perhaps going to be a few thousand pounds."

"And it is not?"

"Marco, please don't be shocked. The expert has estimated seventeen million pounds."

"Che bello!" he said, clapping his hands together. "Let me see, that's about twenty million Euros I think." Jess studied him. His eyes gleamed.

"You don't seem too surprised by this ridiculous number."

"No, I had no idea what my father paid in the first place. Of course, I knew that some models can become worth much more over time, but then I have not thought about it too much. As you know, I already have a watch that is priceless."

"This one is really rare, the only one of its type they've ever seen. That's why it is worth a fortune. The silvery metal beside the gold, it's not silver at all… it's steel."

"Steel!" Marco exclaimed. "Steel and gold, of course. When he gave it to me my father joked, saying it was perfect for an Abruzzese. He would not say why. That explains it. Steel and gold. Forte e Gentile. Strong and Gentle. How typical of my father!" He clapped his wizened old hands together once more. "I have some news for you too, Jess," he said. "I hope that you do not mind, but when the sergeant told me that this watch had been found I decided to have my watch valued too. I knew we would need that figure to complete our transaction. It is worth one hundred and twenty pounds."

He placed both hands on the table, palms down, in a manner that said there was serious business to discuss. "Now," he continued, "the arrangement we have is to divide the total value of both watches between us. "Let me calculate what that means. I believe that I will owe you eight and a half million pounds. Less of course the sixty pounds that is half the value of Joe's watch. That then is eight million, four hundred and ninety-nine thousand…" Jess stopped him before he could finish rhyming off his figures.

"Marco, no. It's ludicrous. Of course we can no longer make the exchange you proposed," she said, "it's crazy." Marco fixed his eyes on her.

"Are you saying that you have changed your mind? I thought we had an agreement?"

"Yes we did, but that was before any of us knew how much was involved. Or at least before I knew. I want to give it back to you. It's yours, your twenty-first birthday present from your father."

"Jess, I am old and…" She did not want to hear the rest.

"What about your family, what about their inheritance?"

"My two sons' futures are completely secure, they have more than enough for many lifetimes. They no longer ask anything from me, other than my time."

"But it is too much, far more than I need for The Stables," Jess protested. "I wouldn't know what to do with the rest. I'm not used to lots of money. Marco, I'm a nurse, an ordinary person." Marco picked up a bundle of papers from the desk. It was the dossier he had created with the history of her charity.

"This is not the work of an ordinary person," he said. "I was fortunate to meet you, Jess. It was Fate, il Destino. And since that day I have spent many hours contemplating the work that you do. I had an idea, something we might do if a situation such as this arose. You say this is a lot of money for one charity. But what about two?"

"Two?"

"What if you were to set up a similar one here, for the people of Abruzzo? Not now, of course, you must establish your own first, but in a few years, once I am gone. I wondered, with a little reconfiguration, could it be that this villa would make an excellent centre? Do you think that would be possible?" He stopped and they sat in silence for a moment. Then another. And another. "So, what do you think?" Two of them, no one else. No dad to point out the risks. No Charlie to consult. Just her, her own opinion, her judgment. Jess looked at Marco's face, creased with age, alive with passion. This is no fool making a rash proposal on a whim. This is a shrewd businessman, a man of the soundest judgement. "I believe in you, Jess. Do you?"

"Are you certain that this is what you want to do?" she asked.

"Jess, I am an old man now, how much longer for this world? We have a saying in Italy - 'L'ultimo vestito ce lo fanno senza tasche'. It means 'the last suit is made without pockets'. In English, I think you would say 'you cannot take it with you'." Jess smiled.

"Signor Ascenzo, if we get the watch back, I will accept." His smile beamed back at her, then she watched his eyes moisten.

"Thank you. You have no idea what this means to me."

Jess was worried that her phone would shatter. Whilst she had been at one end of the kitchen speaking to Marco via her laptop, it was at the other, going crazy on the counter. Although on silent, it vibrated as someone repeatedly called, quivering its way to the edge and a suicidal leap onto the quarry tiles of the floor. As Marco vanished from the screen, it went again. She leapt up, determined to catch it before an expensive, screen-cracking plunge - and determined to tell whoever it was to stop repeatedly calling when it was bloody obvious she was unavailable.

"Mrs Munro. Sergeant Turnbull here, so glad I've caught

you. I've got some news."

"Oh hi," said Jess, instantly mollified.

"When I rang the other day, I didn't mention to you that we'd had submitted the case file to the Crown Prosecution Service. Not because I was hiding anything from you, it's because straight away everybody asks me two questions that I can't answer - when will we hear back, and what will their decision be? Questions, questions, how do I know? CPS, I'll never make sense of them. Anyhow, I can answer both now. They rang yesterday. They said it was a tight call but they think there's enough evidence to justify taking this one to court. They gave us the go-ahead to charge."

"That's great news," said Jess.

"It is. We had Lee Knight attend the station this morning." Jess felt her stomach flip. This made it feel real. It made her feel responsible for bringing the force of the law down onto this man.

"How did he take it?" she asked.

"Not at all bothered," said Harry, "took it in his stride."

Another one to tick off on Professor Hare's psychopathy checklist; Failure To Accept Responsibility For His Actions. The wave of guilt that had surged through her crashed, turned and ebbed away, disappearing down the shore, far from sight.

"Look, I can't make you any promises," said Harry. "It was a marginal decision, but the CPS could see that each of the statements the witnesses made independently were consistent, so they think that it should go before a jury. We'll do everything we can to build a strong case in the run-up to the trial. I hope we can get the right result for you. And your husband, and grandad. And Marco."

"Thank you. Given what you've said, I'm almost scared to… but can I ask a question?"

"You just have," said Harry, guffawing. "Go on."

"I haven't a clue… what happens next?"

"I'll run through it with you," said Harry, "and, to be fair, I've got a question for you."

*   *   *

10:15 p.m. Maybe a bit late to ring. Suppose he's in bed? Ah, sod it. Harry sifted through the contacts list on his phone. There he is. He hit dial.

"Robert? You okay?" he asked. "You sound knackered… did I wake you?"

"No, still up, but I am tired. I've travelled down to London today, just arrived back up here."

"Right. Reason I'm ringing is I was wondering if you're still writing that book of yours?"

"Don't mention that bloody book."

"Eh?"

"Sorry mate, didn't mean to sound off. Bad timing. That's what took me down to London. I went down there to finalise it with the publishers. I've written up twelve cases, real crackers, unusual, unique. Anybody reading through them would get a good idea of how the court machine works. Or doesn't work. I tell them about the people that turn the handles, the judges, the cops, the barristers, but mainly it's about the public, the poor sods that get sucked in, chewed up, and spat out the other end."

"Sounds good. So what's up?"

"I've called it Baker's Dozen. I've got twelve, they want another one to make it up to thirteen, and I've got nothing good enough to go in."

"Well, not for the first time, Robert my old friend," said Harry, "you might be owing me a pint. First though, the person involved does not want any publicity right now. I've had to ask for her permission to let you know obviously. So not a word. To anyone."

"Course not, Harry, you know me well enough."

"Okay. Ever heard of a DJ called Charlie Munro?"

"Yeah, the guy on Radio City?"

"That's right. Wait till I tell you about this case."

*   *   *

Lee Knight was not to blame for the way things had turned out. He was about the last person you could blame. If you feel like pointing fingers, start with the widow Munro. She cocked it up from the off when she'd contacted the office. If the stupid cow had told him properly who the deceased was, he would have jumped at the job. The chance to bury someone famous, he'd have gotten some great kudos out of that. But no she didn't, so instead he'd slung the work over to his sister. Not the end of the world, he could easily tell people he'd done the job anyway, invent a celebrity guest list, maximise his part in the whole affair. No big deal.

Then he'd seen the watch in the office. If that watch was right - and it definitely looked right - it could be worth money. Serious money. But Munro is dealing with his sister now.

Alex, there's another one. She's as much to blame as anyone. If he had been doing the job there's no way that watch was going underground. He'd tried to intervene, offered to do the final aesthetics, and seal the casket. There would have been none of this hassle if she'd listened. He'd have filched it the same way he filched that set of cufflinks he took a fancy to a couple of years ago. Nobody would have been any the wiser. But Alex ploughed on and did it herself on one of his days off. When he got annoyed with her, she said she didn't think his offer to help was serious, he'd never offered before. Really? After all that he had done for the business? Ungrateful witch.

There was no way that he was going to pass up the chance to have that watch. He was the one that had spotted it, none of these other dummies had. It was his by rights. As usual, it was up to him to come up with an answer. Get at it from the side. A bit of smooth talk and Munro agrees to a change in plot. She thinks it's a favour. Game on.

What a buzz it had been, down in the cemetery at dead of night, down in that hole, down amongst the stiffs, smacking his way through the DJ's goody-goody, planet-saving wicker coffin. What a buzz. Whispering, chanting to himself, one word with each crashing blow of his hammer. Dead! Men! Tell! No! Tales!… Dead! Men! Tell! No! Tales! And then, seeing the prize, shining under the bright lights of his kitchen when he got home, knowing it was his, knowing he had outwitted them all.

He'd got onto Sotheby's, sent them a few photos, used a false name, untraceable phone number and email address. He'd know he was onto something if they showed any interest. And did they. Phone calls, emails, every day. But he wasn't ready to break cover, not yet.

So it's all going to plan, then up steps the gimpy old copper. If you want to blame anyone for this unnecessary hassle, blame him. What was he on anyway? It wasn't his funeral, it had jack shit to do with him. Nosing around and asking questions. And you can blame Bennett while you're at it, too chicken to tell the cop, who isn't even a cop anymore, to piss off and mind his own. Too weak to stick to the story. Couldn't hold his own water, that Bennett.

Then there's her again, the bloody nurse with the tambourine. If she would have mentioned the certificate from the start he would have got it at the same time as the watch. One visit, all done. Instead, the fat copper somehow shows up that night, launches himself into the grave, and starts flailing around on top of him. In the melee, ping, off comes the neck chain. Clumsy fat jerk.

Because of all this, he has to go down to the police station where the custody sergeant has the nerve to ask him if he has any mental health issues. No, fine thanks. Retard. Then Turnbull, the copper who interviewed him, question after question after question, all for a watch that was going to rust and rot away in the ground.

As the interviews drag on something occurs to him. Why don't they just confront him with the certificate from the coffin? Then it dawns on him. It doesn't exist. They can't prove this bloody watch isn't his, they had no evidence at all. He'd told them he bought it months ago at a car boot sale. Made sure that the date was long before the DJ had died. That meant there was no chance they could claim that maybe it had been pinched by someone else, and ended up there… you've purchased stolen goods that must be returned to their rightful owner. And the time gap would help, make it harder for them to prove otherwise, especially from a boot sale, all cash, no receipts, no questions asked. Why was he in the grave at night they asked? He was down there looking for his chain which he'd lost earlier that day. He was so worried, it is of great sentimental value, officer. Thanks, Gimpy.

Then, just when it looks like they've all finally come to their senses, off we go again. He's back in the cop shop, this time to be charged. More bull from the retard, reading the charging sheet out, all pleased with himself. He'd soon wipe that look off their smug faces. If they think they'll make this stick then they've got another think coming. Don't be counting your chickens boys, you don't know it, but there's a fox in the henhouse.

He needed to understand their system. The price of legal textbooks confirmed everything he'd always known about the law. A closed shop, money-making swindle. Anyhow, there was no way he's got either the time or inclination to plough his way through these dreary tomes. He changed his internet search criteria and found what he was after. There were plenty of other books on crime and the law, ones that weren't bogged down with all that bloody theory, ones written by anonymous whistle-blowers, that told you about real-life stuff. For his first batch, he went for one by an ex-judge, a barrister, and a policeman. "Judge For Yourself", "The Call Of The Bar", "Cop This." Reasonable coverage, enough to get him going. Then he read a couple more by lawyers, they seemed to be most useful, full of tips about what to do and, maybe more important, what not to do if you want to win at this game.

He hadn't rated the barrister provided by the state. If the government could afford her wages, she wasn't going to be smart enough to represent him. For now though, as he wasn't paying, he let her stick around, right up until the point of Disclosure. This, he now knew, is the point where the Prosecution must give to the Defence all of the material that has been gathered on the case. Now that she'd done all of the donkey work, she was passed her sell-by date. He fired her off.

The next day he flicked through the information in the disclosure files. There was nothing new, nothing to fear. Then he got to the statement of Sebastian Weiss. Interesting. There might be three of these things. And then he reached the valuation of the watch. He counted the zeroes out loud. One Two. Three. Four. Five. Six.

He smiled. Oh. My. God. He had hit the jackpot. Showtime.

Chapter 18

Robert Baker could recall every detail of the first case that he had covered thirty years ago as a fresh-faced cub reporter. It was a convoluted web of fraud and deceit that started out as a love triangle but, as the evidence unfolded, sides were added to the shape one by one, until it had morphed into a love hexagon. It provides a spirited start to *Bakers Dozen*.

Chapter 1: The Thief, The Nurse, The Poisoner, His Wife, The Other Thief, and Her Lover.

Many of Robert's colleagues hated doing the courts, particularly Magistrates Court, typically more Old Bollocks than Old Bailey. And it's true, there are only so many ways that even a seasoned wordsmith can describe an instance of urinating in a public place, but for Robert it was worth a thousand tawdry tales of brawling, shoplifting, and drunk and disorderly to delight in the theatre of a gripping Crown Court case. Like this one, the one that his old friend Harry had given him an early heads up on.

* * *

Extract from Chapter 13 of "Baker's Dozen: The Life and Crimes of a Crown Court Reporter."

Here we are, my last chapter. Thirteen, the full Baker's Dozen. Well, you never believed for a minute I would sell you short, did you?

Day One : Self Defence

I have never witnessed a scene quite like that outside Preston Crown Court - nor any other court for that matter. It's the journalistic equivalent of the Gold Rush. Prospectors have travelled from all corners of the U.K., from Switzerland, Italy, America, and across the world, descending on the tight area around the building, desperate to stake their claim on the most prosperous-looking square yards of pavement. What has driven the world's news agencies to pitch up en masse? Is it the value of the item in the evidence bag, or the macabre way in which it was obtained? Both. In the twenty-first century, any robbery from a grave was always going to arouse some interest, at least locally. When the purloined article is a wristwatch worth seventeen million quid, well there's your front page splash, right there.

I'd predicted these out-of-towners would encroach onto my patch, so I was prepared. I called in a few favours and guaranteed myself daily access for the duration of the trial via a small, undistinguished wooden door at the rear of the building, where security is controlled by a long-standing contact. Three sharp raps and I'm in. He's got good news. Judge Rawlings is to preside. The Enforcer. She'll make sure this case clips along at a decent lick. Even better, he confirms the venue is Number One Court in the old building. The new Court across the road might have more modern facilities and fittings, but it's anonymous. You could be witnessing justice being dispensed in an airport departure lounge. A slight concern, Number One has been closed for two months for a facelift. I get there and look around. It must have been a light touch. Two flat screens, each the size of a single bed, have been hung on the wall on either side of the bench, but otherwise it looks like the same dark wooden Victorian bearpit I'd sat in so often. I'm relieved. I like it how it is.

It's late afternoon by the time we get underway. Rawlings enters and takes her place, high above us mortals. Under the grey wig, she wears the same alert expression that she always does. The only time I've ever seen her change it for another is in rare moments when some fool dares to challenge her authority, and she switches to a look of fearsome sharpness that could wipe the smirk from the Mona Lisa's face. The man whose job it is to lead the Prosecution and avoid incurring her wrath is Carson Bryce, a promising young QC. His opposite number for the Defence? Our first twist. Rawlings explains it to the jury, using language as close to layman's terms as a Judge can achieve.

"Members of the jury, I must explain to you that the Defendant has decided to dispense with the council allocated to him, and is to represent himself. This circumstance is called Defendant In Person. It has been explained to him that he will be subject to the same rules of evidence and procedure as counsel would be. It has also been explained to him that my role in this case is to ensure that the trial is fair, so there may be some occasions when I need to give him guidance, to ensure that he complies with those rules. He has been provided with all the materials and will continue to be provided with them throughout the trial."

I survey the jury, seven men and five women, as they listen to Rawlings. Next, she gives them her standard opening speech, explaining what is going to happen and the part that they have to play in it. It's clear, concise, and unambiguous. The usual response, their expressions range from studied interest to bafflement.

Defendant In Person. The accused representing themselves

without a specialist law advisor. I've seen it before. It's usually a terrible idea. Take this case. What makes a bloke who spends his day fitting up stiffs for their wooden overcoats think he's going outmanoeuvre the guy with a law degree and a load of courtroom experience? Based on the attempts I've observed, it typically does not end well.

*   *   *

Day Two : The Ferret and The Funeral

First witness for the prosecution, P.C. Cheg. Smaller, more wiry than your average policeman, he twitches like a kid that's eaten a snack made with far too much sugar and laced with additives that ought to be banned. Giving evidence, he has a tendency to depart off down cul-de-sacs of irrelevant detail, so that Bryce has to repeatedly shepherd him back from dead end to main street. Bryce has him describe how he had attended the home of the accused, conducted a search, and seized several items relating to the alleged offence. These included a laptop computer, several paper notepads, and a gentleman's wristwatch.

"And for the jury, can you describe where exactly within the house you found the wristwatch?"

"Yes. I can. It was in a kitchen cupboard, buried inside a large - five hundred grammes - bag of dried pasta tubes. Penne, not rigatoni. The one with the ends cut at an angle, smooth surface." Bryce moves him on.

"And did that strike you as at all an unusual place to have stored a wristwatch?"

"It did, sir. As a result, I felt duty-bound to go through all of the contents of his pantry to see if there were any other items of jewellery secreted in foodstuffs. Effective searching is about thoroughness. It was time-consuming – there were multiple plastic, three litre cereal and dried food containers - but I didn't find anything else." Bryce concludes and it's our first opportunity to observe Knight. No sign of nerves. The way he stands up, the way he speaks, everything is measured.

"PC Cheg... or would you prefer that I call you Weasel?" Cheg is puzzled. "Is that not the nickname I overheard your colleagues use when you searched my house?"

"No. That would be Ferret." He feels like he should explain. "It's because I'm good at finding things."

"Ah yes, my apologies. Ferret. So you've described how you attended my house and spent hours weaseling through…. sorry, ferreting through all of my personal belongings for what you could find, and came up with a watch." What comes next was a surprise, even for an old stager like me. Knight holds up what looks like a tin of beans. "P.C. Cheg, what is this?" Cheg stares at the object.

"It's a tin of baked beans. Heinz." He squints closer. "No Added Sugar."

"Wrong, officer, it is not." Knight prises off the lid. "It looks like one but it is a cleverly disguised container. Have you seen one of these before?"

"I have," Cheg replies. "They're used as a place to conceal valuables, so that in the event of a burglary they are less likely to be found."

"Precisely. The kitchen cupboard is such a good place to conceal valuables that these products are made commercially. Soft drinks bottles, mayonnaise jars, soup tins, all available. You said earlier that you found my watch in a bag of dried pasta, the inference being that I was hiding goods for some illicit reason. In fact, as I did not have one of these containers, I placed it in the bag of pasta to reduce the chance of it being stolen. All of a sudden, it no longer seems like such a clandestine action, does it?"

"I suppose not," Cheg replies. Leaving it at that, Knight sits down. My eyes flick around the courtroom. Judge Rawlings. Q.C. Bryce. Jury. Then Knight again. All of us saw it. It was an assured, even confident performance, and Knight knows it. The scales of justice, so finely balanced at the outset, have already tilted marginally.

The afternoon session begins with Jess Munro, wife of the deceased. Bryce sensitively steers her through the shock of her husband's death, the arranging of his funeral, and her request that the funeral director should place several items into the coffin, including the watch. Nobody involved in this trial wants the security headache of transporting something of this value in and out of court, so she identifies it from an image displayed on those colossal new screens. It's the first time any of us have seen it. Handsome thing. It's got three small dials on the face, one showing little moon and stars symbols... but seventeen million? If some evening I'm desperate to know what phase the moon is in, I'll draw back the curtains and take a look at the sky.

Throughout Jess Munro's evidence, I'm watching Knight, the Defendant in Person. He's listening to her, looking at her every so often, but he spends as much time with his eyes on Bryce. When it's his turn I can see what's going on here. He's copying Bryce, watching what he's doing, picking up what's expected, and mirroring it. And he's a quick learner. He sets off using the same sympathetic tone.

"Mrs Munro, let me begin by saying how sorry I am for your loss. I know this whole case must be adding to your trauma, I'll do everything I can to minimise any upset to you."

She doesn't reply. He points to the watch on the screen. She confirms it's the one that she arranged to have placed in the coffin.

"Mrs Munro, it is clear from the police photographs that someone has tampered with your husband's grave, and a watch was stolen. But I submit that it is not this one. Do you have the original box? A receipt? A photograph? Anything?" In each case, she replies in the negative. "So you have no evidence at all of ever having owned this watch?"

"No." Knight continues in a mood of sincerity and compassion.

"Mrs Munro, would I be right in thinking that it has been a difficult time since your husband's death?"

"Of course it has."

"Indeed. Through my profession, I understand the terrible effect that grief can have on those closest to the deceased. Do you remember visiting our office on the twenty-sixth of April this year?"

"I remember visiting the office, I don't remember the date."

"No, of course. Hard to remember details from such a traumatic period. Let me help. During a visit that day did you not tell myself and my sister that recently you had walked out of a supermarket without paying, only to be apprehended by a store detective?"

"Eh, yes."

"Are you dishonest Mrs Munro? A thief?"

"No. Definitely not."

"No. So am I right in saying that the reason you gave for this incident was that you were so overwhelmed with grief that you weren't thinking properly and made a mistake?"

"Yes."

"And you mentioned other similar mistakes, due to your 'brain-fog' I think you called it?"

"Yes."

"But you want us to believe that you were not mistaken about this watch?"

"No, I am not."

"Can we now move on to your late husband's funeral. Do you remember that I fulfilled your request to have two life-sized photos of Mr Munro printed off to be displayed on the day?"

"You did."

"They were prominently displayed at the church door and, although indistinct, you can just see the edge of a watch on his wrist as he points at the Radio City tower. On the day of the funeral itself, there were many people there were there not?"

"Yes, Charlie was very popular."

"Indeed. So much so that the church was full and the service had to be relayed via a loudspeaker to the substantial crowd that had gathered outside. Did you know all of those present, were they all close friends and family?"

"No. Some were people Charlie knew but I'd never met, some were just well-wishers whom neither of us knew."

"And during one of the readings was the assembled crowd told that Mr Munro was buried wearing exactly what he had on in the photographs?"

"Yes, something like that."

"So anyone in this huge crowd of unknown fans, remote acquaintances, random well-wishers, general hangers-on, Uncle Tom Cobley and all, would have learned that your husband had been buried wearing his watch?"

"Well, yes."

"Thank you, Mrs Munro." Knight takes his seat once more and Judge Rawlings announces that they will break for the day.

Beyond Reasonable Doubt. That's the yardstick Rawlings has given the jury. The Prosecution must convince you there is no other possible explanation. You must be sure, she has told them, else you must acquit. This guy, Knight, he gets it, and he is doing everything he can to create reasonable doubt. He is already giving Carson Bryce a headache.

* * *

Day Three : The Swiss Ticker and The Pit Digger

Day Three. Rawlings has put another shilling in the meter and fired up those drive-in movie screens again. They are earning their keep already. This time they're displaying a witness. He introduces himself as Sebastian Weiss of Sotheby's, and tells us that he's sitting in their Rome office. I cast an eye over his surroundings. They are sumptuous. Weiss says he's their Head of Horology and explains what that entails. For most of us, where clocks and watches are concerned, our learning ends when we've worked out what the long and the short hands are up to. Not this guy. He writes whole books about what makes them tick. He describes how he examined this watch at the request of the police. He's seen a few timepieces in his time, but this one excites him. It's a genuine Patek Phillipe 1518, exceedingly rare, made from gold and steel. Bryce asks how rare is rare. Hitherto unknown says Weiss. There may be another two in the world, maybe not. Its rarity makes it valuable. How valuable? Twenty million Swiss Francs, or seventeen million of your Great British Pounds. There is a gasp around the court from those who were not already privy to this detail. Judge Rawlings commands everyone to settle down.

Knight keeps it short, to the point of being dismissive. Never mind the value, what matters here is who owns it. Can Weiss shed any light on that? Weiss talks at length about provenance and Certificates of Authenticity and... Knight cuts him short.

"Herr Weiss, to be clear, are you able to say anything about who this watch currently belongs to, or who has previously owned it, or indeed anything at all about its ownership history?" Weiss pulls himself more upright in his chair, affronted at having his expertise junked in this manner.

"No, I cannot," he said.

"Thank you, Herr Weiss," said Knight, as he sits down once more. Rawlings checks the time and sends us out for lunch.

There is no canteen in the old court building, so I head out to the supermarket on the main street to pick up a sandwich - and a bunch of other stuff that I shouldn't be eating and drinking, but that have been bundled into The Big Deal at an irresistible price. As I exit court I see Lee Knight walking a few yards ahead of me. He's after something to eat too, but turns off before I do, entering one of the flashiest restaurants in town, Number 70, which coincidentally is the number of quid he'll be paying to dine there. On my way back to court, I glance through the window. He's still in there, tucking into the carcass of a small gamebird with seasonal vegetables and fondant potatoes. I look at the gluey little cake that I'm eating. Is this shortbread really what the world's millionaires splash out on when they feel like treating themselves?

The afternoon's only witness is a gravedigger. He's the one who dug the hole that was used to access the coffin. The guy is nervy. Bryce gets him to state that he did the work because Knight told him to. I watch Knight rise, chest puffed out like that pigeon he just dined on, cheeks ruddy as the wine he used to wash it down.

"So your story is that you always take instructions from Edith Harkness on which graves you need to dig."

"Yes."

"But for the first time ever, out of the blue, you decided to dig this one without her say-so."

"Yes. But only because you told me to," Bennett replies.

"Me? That is not true. I don't know what you think I said, but I would never have given you such an instruction." Knight jots something down, then continues. "Were you academically talented Mr Bennett?" He doesn't answer. "Did you leave school with lots of qualifications?"

"None."

"None? So it's possible, perhaps even likely, that you misunderstood something I said. Let me ask you another question. You and I were in our office on the twenty-sixth of April this year, when Mrs Munro was there, discussing the details of her husband's funeral. Do you remember?"

"Yes, I do."

"And she mentioned that she would like him to be buried wearing a watch?"

"Yes."

"And then you were you present throughout the funeral when it was broadcast across the churchyard."

"Yes."

"You heard that her husband had indeed been buried wearing a watch?"

"Yes, I did."

"So we can add your name to the long list of people who could have decided to steal it." Bennett's creased brow, his parted lips, and widening eyes tell their own story. He is upset.

"No, I would never do that," he insists.

* * *

Day Four : World Wars and Family Feuds

Word is getting around. As I arrive on the fourth day the crowds are larger than ever. These high-profile trials are always the same – all the hoopla, it's catnip for cranks. I'm early, so rather than go straight in I decide to take a wander through the jamboree. Vans with enormous satellite dishes on their roofs line the streets surrounding the court, rival news agencies butted up tight against each other. It's only eight-thirty and already the pavement bins are overflowing with takeaway coffee cups and food wrappers. I pause beside a Swiss crew doing a piece to camera. They are interviewing a sleazy-looking local, claims he's a pawnbroker who was asked by the police to give an opinion on the watch. He explains that, as he is bona fide expert, he was able to confirm to the police that the Sotheby's guy got it almost right. Really?

When proceedings start for the day, we are back onto video link. This time we cross the threshold of the home of an elderly Italian gentleman, claiming to be the original owner of the watch. His face is brown, cracked like weathered leather, yet soft at the same time. Bryce talks him through his statement. In a steady voice, Signor Ascenzo describes how he had been contacted by the UK police, asking about a Patek Phillipe watch. He told them it was a twenty-first birthday present that he exchanged with a soldier called Joe during the war.

Knight accepts the opportunity to cross-examine. Straight away I notice he does something that he hasn't done with any previous witness. He has written his questions down and reads them out from his notes. I soon find out why. They're peppered with obscure, archaic language, words that few native speakers of English would know, far less an Italian.

"Would you say you were a philosophunculist, Signor Ascenzo? Do you have a cacoethes for inventing stories? Could you perhaps be more pauciloquent in your responses?"

Signor Ascenzo's grasp of English knocks my restaurant menu Italian out of the park, but he has no hope of navigating this verbal labyrinth. Each question has to be rephrased, with Knight then switching to childishly basic language. The net effect is to make Ascenzo appear to be a bumbling simpleton. Rawling spots what's going on and tells Knight to make his questions more understandable. Having already inflicted some damage, Knight concludes by addressing the story of the watch.

"Assuming you did meet a British soldier in the war, can you be certain that it was this watch you gave him?" he continues. "Is it possible that it was a different one? Did you have others?"

"Yes."

"Well, could it perhaps have been one of those? If you have remembered the incident from your war story correctly then you must have been under extreme pressure at the time and - I don't want to be rude - but it is over seventy years ago Signor Ascenzo."

"My memory is good. I know this is watch I gave," he replies, fixing a stare on his inquisitor. Knight stares back, then resumes his seat.

The sixth witness takes the stand in the afternoon. Knight's own sister, Alex. She's immaculately turned out and you can tell she's caught the jury's attention. Bryce questions her once more about the watch, asking several times if she, as the person who had prepared Mr Munro for his funeral, could confirm that the watch in question was the one she had put around his wrist. Alex assures him this was the case. Bryce sits down, like all of us, unsure how this familial exchange might go.

"Perhaps it's best that we explain to the jury what your relationship to me is. You are my sister?"

"Yes. We work together in the family funeral business." Lee Knight's eyes widen. He is straight in.

"That's not strictly true, is it, Alex? Not any more. We did work together, until I was suspended from the business. By you and my father."

"Not suspended as such. We had a family meeting and decided it was better if you stepped away until this matter was sorted out."

"Whose idea was that, Alex, was it my elderly father's or yours?"

"Mine I suppose, but we all agreed it was for the best. Best for the business, best for you."

"And by a happy co-incidence, best for you too. I am not allowed to get close to the financial side of things, Alex. Is the business profitable?" Alex Knight could see what her brother was doing.

"You have never once showed any interest in the administrative or financial side of things. You mocked me for the time I spent 'faffing around with pieces of paper' instead of doing the real work."

"That was not my question."

"Yes, it is profitable," she replies. I can see she is trying to remain calm.

"So with me out of the way, say if I was to be found guilty of a crime and had to go to jail, it would leave you to inherit the entire family business from our elderly father?"

"I don't know."

"Well I don't think it would do you any harm in your campaign if you could distance me from the business, discredit and marginalise me, would it? All I am saying is that perhaps you are not unbiased in this and that perhaps it might influence your memory of what happened?" His sister is shocked. She barely responds. I can see her eyes well up.

"No. I'm telling the truth," was all she could muster. Knight sits down. It's going to be cold as frost around the Knight family Christmas dinner table this year.

*   *   *

Day Five : A Couple of Coppers

Friday, Day Five, the last two Prosecution witnesses take the stand. One an ex-copper, the other still serving, old sweats, who know their way round the courtroom. Their experience does not intimidate Knight in the slightest.

"Do you prefer Michael or Mick?

"Mick."

"Mick. You used to be in the police force did you not?

"Yes. I served as a police officer for thirty years."

"And would you say that the things that you experienced have made you acutely sensitive to criminality?"

"I know there are some dishonest people out there if that's what you mean."

"Might all of that exposure to wrongdoing have made you something of a vigilante, a bit gung-ho, ready to do whatever it takes to get your man?"

"I don't think so."

"Was there a case, widely reported in the papers, where you arrested a man but failed to read him his rights as you should have done?"

"That was one mistake and…"

"If we move on to the night of my arrest, you had encouraged Mrs Munro to set up a trap, and you were in the graveyard at dead of night, hoping to catch a criminal?"

"If there was one, yes."

"If there was one," he repeats, looking at the jury. "However, there wasn't. When the police, your ex-colleagues, approached me, did I offer an explanation of why I was there?

"Yes."

"I said that I had lost a gold chain, didn't I?"

"Yes."

"This chain here?" he said holding a small polythene bag aloft. Mick craned forward to see it.

"Yes, that looks like it."

"Did I explain to the officers that I had lost it the previous day, and was so consumed with worry that I was unable to sleep, then it occurred to me it may have fallen into the open grave when I had been in the churchyard?"

"Yes."

"And at the moment the officers arrived, I spotted it beside my feet."

"Yes."

"But you chose not to believe what you saw with your own eyes. Your suspicious personality was so intent on catching a criminal you immediately jumped to that conclusion."

"No."

"Thank you, Mr Williams."

"So, Sergeant Turnbull, your role was to pull together the evidence in this case. Have you done a thorough job?"

"The Crown Prosecution Service gave us authorisation to charge, based on the evidence we had gathered."

"All of it circumstantial. Do you think that any one of the witnesses has presented a damning piece of evidence that I have committed any crime?"

"Not one in particular, but when you put it together it's obvious what you've done. It makes a strong case."

"I think that is for these twelve upstanding citizens to decide, Sergeant, not you," he says, with another flourish towards the jury. "And to help them with that we can perhaps point out some aspects of the investigation that Mr Bryce has chosen not to dwell on, but the police were obliged to disclose to me." Knight shuffles his papers.

"Sergeant, did you seek to verify my account of having purchased the watch at a car boot sale"?

"Yes."

"And what were the results?"

"We couldn't find any evidence that you had."

"No, and nor could you prove that I had not. Did you speak to all of the stall holders there that day?"

"No, with time having passed we couldn't find some of them."

"How convenient. Or remiss. Or both. What percentage would you say you did speak to?"

"I don't know exactly."

"Let me help you. On a typical day there will be one hundred and twenty stalls there. So did you speak to, let's say, as many as sixty?"

"No."

"So less than sixty out of one hundred and twenty. Sergeant, if my maths is correct, that is less than half, is it not?"

"Yes."

"Less than half. So there is not even a fifty-fifty chance you could ever have verified my story. Worse than the flip of a coin. Thank you, sergeant."

Rawlings checks the clock and calls an end to proceedings for the day. We're going into a second week. We'll start with Knight taking the stand in his own defence, assuming all goes to plan. Plan? Court of Law? Did I really say that?

Chapter 19

At lunchtime on Friday, after Mick's evidence, Robert Baker perched on the stone steps of the museum in the market square, all of the purpose-made seating having been snaffled by media interlopers. Today he'd forgone the associated trimmings that make up The Big Deal, but now that his flimsy sandwich was finished, he wished he'd indulged. His phone pinged. It was Harry.

'Could do to catch up with you after I give evidence this afternoon. You around?'

Robert replied.

'Was going to go up to the graveyard at St Jude's after court, see the scene for myself. Meet me up there.'

Harry pulled onto the church car park and saw Robert getting out of the only other car there.

"Okay?" he asked.

"Fine," said Robert.

"C'mon, I'll show you where the action took place." He led Robert through the gate and down the path to the bench beside Charlie's plot.

"That's the policeman - Harry," said Charlie to Isabel. "Mick's friend. He was here a few times after it happened. Do you know the other guy?"

"Never seen him before," Isabel replied.

"Nor me," said Rita. They stopped talking to tune in on the conversation above.

"That's where he's buried, there," said Harry, pointing at Charlie's grave. "We're saying Knight got this plot here dug out," he said, "then came in from the side. Smashed through the wall of the coffin to gain access, then had the phoney grave refilled. The church has left it vacant since, till all of this is cleared up."

"Clever. Could easily have gone undetected."

"Too right. If the guy's wife and Mick hadn't got the sense that something wasn't right, snooped around, then tempted Knight back we would never have caught him. Assuming we have caught him." He paused. "I know Carson Bryce is desperate to win this one. He's been a guest on Charlie Munro's show. He really liked the guy, and said he'll do everything he can to get it over the line. You reporters spend way more time in the courtroom than us cops. Honest opinion, no bull, what do you think?" Robert looked at Harry. There was no point in trying to sugarcoat it.

"Honest opinion? As it stands, I think you're sunk. There is no way they'll convict on what we've seen so far." He watched Harry's face. The policeman looked disconsolate rather than shocked. "Bryce has done the best with what he's got, but therein lies your problem. These days juries love things that you can show them, things you can point to, stuff they can touch. CCTV images, printouts of mobile phone records, a car captured on ANPR cameras, forensics, some DNA that can't be explained. Actual hard physical evidence. You've got none of that. Knight's doing well. It's his word against your witnesses - I know there are a few of them, but he's played a canny game, chipping away at them all, undermining their testimony. I've seen qualified barristers do worse. And he knows how to put on a bit of a show. I think he's taking some of the jurors with him."

"Yes, but if they use their common sense, then…"

"Trouble with common sense is, Harry, it's not as common as they'd have you believe."

"What do you reckon to this lot, the jury?" Robert scoffed.

"You know my views, they are nigh on impossible to read. A jury of your peers they call it. My peers? God, I hope not. Twelve random punters who happen to have lived in this country for five years plus, have never committed a crime - or at least not been caught. Oh, and if they're mad, which there's every chance some of them will be, it is as yet undiagnosed. These look like a fairly typical bunch."

*   *   *

Typical? Robert Baker was right; jurors are nigh on impossible to read. There was nothing typical about Juror Ten. At first glance, there was nothing remarkable about him either, but he was exactly the sort that made Robert unwilling to speculate. Everything about his appearance said moderate. Mid-twenties, mid-brown hair, mid-height, clothes all a mid-beige. He blended in remarkably well with the new colour scheme of the courtroom walls, but this anonymous guise camouflaged a man that was by no means typical. Those brown-rimmed spectacles were windows into the mind of a man of remarkable knowledge.

He knew for a fact that no man had ever landed on the moon. He knew that the government put fluoride in water as a way to get rid of industrial waste. He knew who was really behind the deaths of John F. Kennedy and Princess Diana. He knew that the vapour trails from jet aircraft are used by scientists to seed the atmosphere with mind-controlling chemicals. And that global warming was invented to make big money for big business. He knew all of this and many, many other things. Most certainly, he knew that a shadowy elite existed, a Deep State, controlling the everyday lives of the populace for their own nefarious ends, employing the mechanisms they had invented for the purpose. Like the justice system. He knew - before he had heard one single piece of evidence - that Lee Knight was innocent.

As Mick and Harry were meeting in the churchyard, Juror Ten was waiting for the bus home to his cluttered digs. He was joined at the stop by a girl of about twenty. He recognised her. It was Juror Eight. She returned his smile of recognition. He sidled over to her.

"So what do you reckon so far?" he asked. Eight did not reply. "You know, about the case?" Still Eight offered no response, then, seeing that he would stare at her forever to get one, she ventured "I think the judge said we should only discuss it when all twelve of us were in the room together."

"Yeah, but you must have an opinion. I have. I think the whole thing is a put-up job. That undertaker, he's a normal guy, but through his work I bet he's found something out about some suspicious deaths, with top people involved. They need to shut him up, get him out of the way. All of a sudden this fancy watch appears, everybody is scrabbling to claim it's theirs and he's accused of stealing it. He gets carted off to Wormwood Scrubs, two months later he's dead, shanked by some psycho, who's done it in exchange for an early release. Meanwhile that Munro and her old pal in Italy make off with the money. I happen to know she was trying to set up a business and got into financial difficulties. There's her motive."

"How do you know that? You haven't been looking on the

internet have you? The Judge says we mustn't do that." Ten backtracked.

"Oh no, course not. It's something I've heard that's all. I've got solid connections in business around here," he said, somewhat surprisingly for a man who could not accurately be described as being 'between jobs', as he'd never had one in the first place. "Not much goes on around here that gets by me. Anyway, say it was true, it would kind of explain why she is so keen to claim it, don't you think?"

"I'm not sure," said Eight.

* * *

Jess did not know what was up, but something was. From the moment Mick and Mia sat down, she knew there was an issue. She did not press to find out, banking on Mia airing it soon enough.

"Jess," said Mia, "have you ever heard of Blackstone's Ratio?" Oh, oh. Blackstone's Ratio? Sounds like it could be the name of the type of band that Charlie couldn't play on the radio on account of them sounding like a cursing competition set to questionable music. Mia must be a fan, Mick doesn't think they're suitable. Approach with caution.

"No I haven't," she replied. "Is it a group?" she asked. For the first time since they'd arrived Mia's face lit up.

"No," she laughed, "I thought you were an expert on music? Uncle Mick has been telling me about it, so if it's a group, they'd have to be ancient." Mick feigned offence, pleased to see Mia's mood improve.

"On the way here," he said, "Mia and I have been chatting about how the trial is going, and the chances of getting a conviction. That's why I was telling her about Blackstone's Ratio."

"So if it's not a group…" Mick carried on.

"A long while ago, in seventeen-something-something to be more exact, an Englishman called Blackstone wrote papers about laws and trials. He said that it was better that ten guilty men walk free than one innocent man is punished – Blackstone's Ratio. The idea stuck, it's what gives the world the 'beyond reasonable doubt' thing."

"And I'm fine with that," said Mia. "In theory. But look what it means for this trial," she said. "Lee Knight should not be allowed to get away with what he did. It was wrong. It makes me raging mad to think that instead of being punished, he will walk away with all that money as a reward. It's so obvious to me he's guilty."

"But it's not what we think, or the police or the CPS or even the judge that matters in the end," said Mick. "It's all down to the jury. The law says that to find him guilty they need to know he's done it, they've got to be sure." He looked at Jess. "I thought it was important that we're prepared for whatever might happen. If Knight can convince enough of them that they can't be sure, then they have to find him not guilty," he added. Jess took the cue.

"And we have to be realistic, he has some useful equipment at his disposal," said Jess, "right there, in his psychopath's toolbox. That superficial charm. The way he manipulates people, how he lies without any nervousness. Uncle Mick and I have been in court with him. The setup suits him. He's turning it into a big show with him in the starring role. He's stringing the jury along without them realising. Once you know what to look for in people like him, you can see it. But for anyone who doesn't know him, he does a good job of covering it up." Mia had been angry with Uncle Mick on the way there. Now Jess had confirmed everything that he had

307

said, her anger turned to disillusionment. Above them, the Stanford sky darkened, mirroring her mood.

"You're right," she said, "and it's a disaster." She blew the heavy, resigned air from her lungs. "Jess, can I ask, do you wish you had never found out about any of this?"

"No, of course not, even if it doesn't work out as it should. At least I will always know that we tried, we did our best. If it wasn't for what's happened I would never have got to know you and Uncle Mick. Now that would have been a disaster. And it's only because of you that I found out about Grandad Joe from Marco, and got his help for my charity."

"That's true," Mia agreed. A few large spots of rain spattered onto the flat gravestones in St Jude's.

"We'd better go," said Mick. "We're at a judo competition in Manchester today, so no Angelo's for us. Sorry about that, Jess."

"Don't have any worries on my account. It's Mia's opponents on the mat this afternoon that you should be feeling sorry for."

Jess remained on the bench long enough to allow the others to leave. Beneath her, no words were exchanged between the graves. Only once she too had gone, taking the long way back to the gate, did anyone speak.

"Reasonable doubt," said Charlie. "The courtroom is full of it, but there's none here. They've confirmed exactly what Harry and the reporter said yesterday. Knight is defending himself, and he's winning."

"Look, Charles," said The Doc, "it's Saturday, the end of the week, not the end of the trial. Dispatches could have been more positive but, as policemen in pursuit of justice, Harry and Mick are bound to be apprehensive. And the other chap, a newspaper reporter, well they are sometimes not the most reliable of information sources."

"You've missed off Jess, Doc," said Charlie. "You heard her. She believes Knight is a psychopath. I'm sure you know all about them, but I know a bit too. A couple of years ago, Jess mentioned to me that they were all around us. I thought it would make an interesting item on the show. I managed to get an expert in, Professor Gough. One of the scariest discussions we've ever had. What Jess described is exactly what Prof. Gough said. Very dangerous, devious, soulless people. Knight, defending himself in court, charming, lying without a care. We've lost."

As she walked through Stanford towards home Jess was not thinking about the trial. She wasn't thinking about anything in particular. The tempo of raindrops had sped up from a clip-clop to a gentle canter, her feet were beginning to get wet but she wasn't bothered about that either. For the first time in weeks, she had managed to switch off, get her mind into neutral. The conversation with Mick had helped. The trial would be over next week, for better or worse, and she would move on. Her sloshing steps would take her past the office of Knight's Funeral Directors and she would not even turn her head to the window. She would carry straight on. With only three short shopfronts before she was there, that plan was demolished. Alex emerged onto the pavement and turned around to lock the door. As she fumbled with the key she looked round and saw Jess approaching. They were almost face to face. Alex had to say something.

"Hi," she ventured, making herself busy by replacing the keys in her handbag.

"Hi," Jess replied. There was an awkward silence as they

both tried to weigh if this two-way, two-word, four-letter exchange had boxed everything off. Jess saw the drawn, pained expression on Alex's face. It had not. She stopped.

"I've been stood up by my usual Saturday afternoon café crew," she said, "and my feet are soaking. Fancy a coffee?" Alex looked like she might cry.

"Yes. I'd love one." They walked the short distance round to Angelo's, exchanging small talk, whilst each drafting a script for what they might say when, inevitably, the talk grew larger. Once seated, Jess took the opening lines.

"Alex, I'm really sorry about what has happened, how this has turned out. I want you to know that I'm still grateful for everything that you did for Charlie's funeral. I wish I hadn't dragged you and your family into this mess, but I genuinely believe that Lee has done this thing."

"I'm the one who's sorry," Alex replied. "It's not you who has made this mess, it's a member of my family, my own brother. He's the one dragging everyone through it. I know the court case isn't finished and we don't have a verdict yet, but I just want to let you know I am ashamed of him. I know that watch is yours. I put it onto your husband's wrist myself."

"I know. It belongs to us be we can't prove it and he knows it. I've had my mum turn her house upside down to see if there is anything that could help. Nothing."

"I'm furious with him. In a way, it does not surprise me that he has done this. Even growing up Lee was a strange boy. I remember we went to a pantomime, and he was the only kid that didn't shout 'he's behind you'. I asked him why not, and he told me he would rather see what happened if the bad guy caught the good guy."

"That is weird," said Jess. They both took another sip of coffee.

"He thinks he is somehow entitled to the best of everything and does what the hell he wants to get it," Alex continued. "He doesn't seem to think that rules apply to him… no… I don't even think he knows why we have rules. I've always known that he could be cocky, selfish, uncaring, but this week he has taken it to another level. The way he treated me when I gave evidence, he was so cruel. The things he insinuated about me and the business were totally false. But he told all these lies about me in a public place, without any shame, knowing they would hurt, knowing they would appear in the papers and on TV." As she spoke Jess nodded. Alex could have been reading out Professor Hare's checklist. Jess looked at her face, a study of betrayal and pain.

"Don't take it personally, Alex. He was very unkind to me in court too," she said. "Remember when I was in your office shortly after Charlie died and I mentioned that I had left the supermarket without paying?" Alex nodded. "He asked me about it, made me go over what had happened. It was so embarrassing. He was trying to make it look as if Charlie dying had made me go out of my right mind."

"God, did he? Jess, I'm sorry."

"I mean I did go a bit strange for the first few weeks, but not crazy. I'd mentioned it in your office, in confidence I thought. I never expected him to make me tell the world." Jess stopped talking. She could see that Alex was staring at her, but looking within herself for the confidence to utter the next sentence.

"Jess, that story about you and the supermarket… it's made me think… can I ask you about the things you put in the coffin?"

"Of course."

"Do you remember you gave me two photos to put in

311

there?" Jess looked mystified.

"Did I?"

"Yes. Look, don't feel foolish for forgetting, it's absolutely normal. For lots of people, that period is a bit of a blur. In one of the photos, Charlie was in what looked like a recording studio or something with an older man. The second one was more of a close-up, They had their arms draped round each other's shoulders. I'm wondering if it was your grandad." She saw Jess's face light up, a flash of recognition.

"God, yes, of course. Charlie took grandad into Radio City in Liverpool to see the show being made. Grandad was thrilled, went on about it for ages. While they were there, Charlie arranged for the station's photographer to take a couple of snaps. I have no memory of giving them to you… but I definitely didn't come across them when I was scouring the house."

"They were in the pile of stuff you gave me. They made me smile. The two of them looked so happy. It was comical because your grandad was so much shorter than Charlie, he had to really stretch up like this to get his arm around him." Jess looked as Alex held her left arm up, curled and aloft. Her sleeve fell down from her wrist exposing her watch. They both looked at each other, synchronised on the same thought. Alex spoke again.

"Have you got copies?"

"No, I only had those prints. And J.J. tried to get in touch with the photographer to tell him about Charlie's funeral but couldn't find him. He's emigrated, they think he's somewhere in Canada." Alex sighed. "But," said Jess, "what's to stop me going to get them back?"

"You mean out of Charlie's…"

"Why not? If your brother can do it to steal something that's not his, why can't I to get something that belongs to me?" Alex was already taking her phone from her handbag.

"I want to help you, Jess. Please. Let me make a quick call."

By the time they entered through the cemetery gate the downpour was a deluge. Through the murky grey air they could see a slender figure, waiting by Charlie's plot.

"He wasn't meant to be working today," Alex said, as they hurried down the path, "but when I told him what we were going to do, he said he would meet us." When they reached him, Tom began to rub his chin.

"Thanks for coming," said Alex.

"I'm not going to get into trouble for this, am I?" he asked, before resuming the stubble-rubbing with greater vigour.

"Of course not, I promise you," she said. "If there is any trouble, it's me who is to blame. I'm authorising you to do this."

"I got in trouble when your brother authorised me."

"Tom, this is different," said Jess. "We need to get to the truth." Tom looked at his shovel. Faced with the reality of what they were about to do, he was not yet convinced.

"Is this the honest thing, the truthful thing?" he asked. Jess nodded.

"It is." Without another word being exchanged Tom raised the spade and thumped it into the ground at the side of Charlie's plot. He did not stop. Jess and Alex were soon alongside a mound of soil as high as their waists.

"You're very quick," said Jess.

"Soil is soft," Tom replied without breaking his rhythm. "This is the third time I've dug this out." After another twenty minutes of energetic digging he stopped. He looked up at them.

"What is it?" asked Alex.

"We're down far enough now but… I don't want to start going across, towards your husband. It's not what I do. It doesn't seem right." Jess replied with a nod.

"Okay," she said, "I understand. It would be wrong to ask you to do that. Can you help me down? If anyone does this it should be me."

"Are you sure?" asked Alex.

"I'm certain. Grab my hand, Tom." Using his outstretched arm for support, she splashed down, landing among the puddles on the rough base of the hole. Tom handed her the shovel.

"You need to go in about there," he said, pointing out an area on the earth wall before her. Jess hesitated momentarily before, taking a firm grip on the handle of the shovel with both hands, she smashed it into the soil with all of her strength, dislodging a huge clump. And again. And again. The harder the rain fell, the harder she pounded into the earth. Tom moved back as far as he could so as to avoid being struck by a flying elbow or handle. He watched in disbelief as this slight woman heaved and thrust the blade time after time.

"Slow down," he said. "You're close to being through." The words jolted Jess out of her rhythmic onslaught. She stopped, then recommenced with shorter more measured strokes. She heard a dull thud and felt a shudder travel up her arms as the spade struck something more solid.

"Is that it?" she asked. Silent, Tom nodded.

She got down onto her knees and took a closer look at her work. "I think I just need to widen it a bit." Tom handed her a trowel and Jess began to hack away at the edges of the channel. She pushed her shoulders round and found that she could feel the wall of the coffin. The thunderous skies made the visibility fuzzy and murky.

"Miss Knight, there's a torch in that tool bag, could you pass it down to me?" said Tom. Alex rummaged in the bag, found the black rubberised torch, and gave it to the young man. He switched it on and directed the beam down the gap, past Jess's shoulders.

"That's better, thanks," she said. "I can see the big hole in the side of the coffin," she shouted back. As she squeezed closer, Jess pulled her jacket up over her nose and mouth, braced for the nauseous stench. There was nothing.

"Be careful, Jess," said Alex. Jess inched her shoulders forwards once more and then, with a tentative stretch of her arm, she pushed her hand through the ragged wooden gap into the body of the coffin. She stalled, recognising the familiar feel of the woollen fabric of Charlie's jacket. Gathering herself once more, she moved her hand left but encountered nothing. She retraced her movement back to the right. Her nails made contact with the metal of the biscuit box.

"I can feel the box," she shouted. "I'll try to prise the lid off."

"No, Jess! They're not in there," Alex shouted. "They were too big to fit and… I know it's stupid but I didn't want to spoil the pictures by folding them over. They're loose in the casket, but they should be nearby." Jess moved her arm around, up and down, blindly groping for something that felt like paper, but whatever way she tried, she encountered only Charlie's clothing or the tin box. Her movements became more hurried, and what had started as a systematic search, turned into frantic floundering.

"They're not here," she shouted. "Maybe Lee took them

too. Or maybe they've fallen apart." As she uttered the last of these words, she stopped. She was sure she had tried here before… how had she missed them? They were there, she could feel them, two pieces of paper, lodged between her forefinger and thumb. She pressed her digits together, gripping firmly.

"I've got them. I think I've got them." Carefully she began to remove her arm, maintaining her grip. Tom's torchlight hit her hand. She pulled them through, doing her best to cause no damage to the images. Jess placed them inside her jacket, shielding them from the raindrops. She sprung back to her feet. Beside her, Tom was smiling.

"You're very brave," he said, "you've done great." She looked up and saw that Alex was standing over the hole, arm outstretched to pull her up. Jess grabbed her hand and felt Alex tug. She got half way out but with her feet slipping on the sodden muddy wall, it seemed more likely that she would pull Alex in. Seeing their struggle, Tom hauled his lanky frame up and took Jess's other arm. He pulled and she flew towards the thumping rain and the sky from which it poured, her feet landing at the edge of the hole.

"Thanks," she said, moving to stand at one side of Alex. Tom took a position at the other, ducking low to join them under the protection of the umbrella. Jess lowered the zip and removed the photos from her jacket. She dropped the paper forwards so that first image became visible. It showed the two men sitting at the big mixing desk in the Radio City studio.

Jess couldn't help herself. She stared at her husband's face, as he smiled back up at her. Her gaze shifted, this time fixing on her Grandad Joe's warm, wrinkled smile. For a moment she could believe they had never left her.

"It's the other one we need to see," said Alex. Jess was snapped back to the task. She flicked the first photo to the back exposing the one beneath, a close-up of the two men, just as Alex had remembered.

"Look!" shouted Alex. There! You can see it. Clear as day." Although this particular day was not very clear, as Jess looked at the old man's wrist she could see that Alex was right. Even in this muted light, it was visible. The numerals, the hands, you could even read the maker's name, now familiar to her, on its face.

"Fuck you, Lee Knight," said Jess. She then looked at Alex. "Sorry."

"Sorry? I'm not. Fuck you, Lee Knight."

He had not dared to articulate it, but before either woman had unleashed, Tom had taken one look at the photograph and thought the same thing.

"Look," he said, pointing to a huge stretch of blue sky moving in their direction, "it's going to dry up. If you two want to go, I'll make sure that this all gets filled back in."

*   *   *

Lee Knight could have told that little voice in his head to piss off. He had no reason to go back. He'd been there thousands of times. Why go now? Yet something was intriguing him, more than that, compelling him to return, just once more. He swept onto the car park. There were no other vehicles there, he could pick his spot. He pulled into his old favourite, got out of the car and locked it. The air, moist and clear following the earlier downpour, was refreshing. He smelled it, breathed it, then walked through the gate. He was the only one here. Then a sound. It's Bennett, down in the bottom corner. He held his ground, watching the gravedigger as he toiled. Was this what his sixth sense had been telling him? "I do not believe it," he thought. "I knew I was right to come back for a final look. First the trial, now this."

The previous day Robert Baker had opined that the Defendant in Person was doing well. Had he heard this, Lee Knight would have been outraged. Doing well? Is that it, you clapped-out old hack? His had been a stellar performance. Bloody legal eagles, overpaid rip-off artists, he had clipped their wings good and proper. He had put on a spectacle, held his own in every argument. They could not stop him. He had succeeded in doing what he needed to do. He had filled the jury's heads with doubts.

He looked down the graveyard and laughed, not to himself, out loud. Now dumb Tom Bennett was there in St. Jude's, filling in the grave next to the DJ, replacing the sods over some poor sod, making it all but impossible for anyone to trouble the site ever again. Deep joy. Six foot deep. The perfect end to a perfect week. He strode down to meet him, chest expanded with righteous self-regard.

"Hello, Tom. Looks like working on this plot has become your full-time job." He chuckled. Tom offered no reply. "Has there been a burial here today then?" he asked. Tom looked up and fixed his eyes on Knight's.

"What does it have to do with you?" Knight's expression remained unchanged. "Perhaps," he thought, "I will reconsider my decision to walk away from the funeral game when this trial finishes. Maybe I should come back for a few months so that I can contrive a way to get your scrawny arse fired." He said none of this.

"Only asking, mate. Just wondered what was going on. Why are you so touchy? Is it the court thing? I'm only trying to prove my case. No hard feelings, mate." Bennett ignored him, continuing to bed the last few turfs into place. "It's those two women, eh? The DJ's wife, she's gone screwy. And it's rubbed off on Alex. The police have been thick enough to believe them. Honestly, I've done nothing wrong."

"Yeah well," said Tom, "you'll find out soon enough what's going on. Mate." Knight sat down on the bench. He lit a cigarette, drew in and exhaled with force. Tom put the last of his tools into the barrow, then dipped his hand into the grubby cloth bag he carried everywhere. Knight watched as he pulled out a small picture frame, walked over and placed it carefully on Yvonne's grave. He pushed his barrow back to his shed, and put it inside. Knight allowed himself another smile as Tom took a new padlock from the pocket of his overcoat and secured the door, before heading out of the graveyard. He craned forward to see what he had left. He shook his head.

"Weirdo." It was a photograph of Elvis Presley. Then he took in Charlie's headstone for the first time.

"Black granite. Nice. Not sure about the words though. Let's see… I'd have gone for 'Charlie Munro, DJ. Performed his last time-check on 22nd April 2018. No further use for his watch'." He put the cigarette to his lips and took another draw, and levelled with himself. This is why he'd had to come here today. He had unfinished business with Munro, a loose end in his head that he wanted to tie off. He blew out the smoke.

"Are you going to come and get me, Charlie? Eh? Are you going to rise up from your grave, grab me round the throat? Strangle the life out of me? C'mon."

"I can't believe he's had the audacity to come here and to speak like that," said Rita.

"Quite," said The Doc. "The chutzpah of the man. But this may be his big mistake. Charles, by coming here today he has presented you with a golden opportunity. Why don't you go, get inside his head and scare the wits out of this villain, perhaps change the course of the trial?" Charlie neither moved nor spoke. The Doc looked up and saw that Knight's cigarette was all but spent. "Charles," hissed The Doc, "Carpe Diem! Seize the day!"

"No, Doc," said Charlie.

Knight took a last draught, then flicked the butt onto Charlie's grave. "Didn't think so," he said. He walked off, leaving the stub smouldering in the damp turf.

"Charlie, I'm not criticising," said Isabel, "but why did you not try what the doctor said?" Charlie shook his head.

"No. What sort of person would that make me? When I was alive I did my best to help people fix their heads. I don't want to scare anyone, go haunting their mind. Not even him. And anyway, I am certain I wouldn't have had any effect."

"Certain?" asked The Doc. "How so, Charles?" Charlie gave himself a brief moment to frame his answer.

"Isabel connected with Mia and Mick, I have with Jess, Yvonne with Tom. They're all good people, and we managed to speak to them, to influence them in a positive way, to remind them of a strong person deep inside themselves. Then there was your visit to Knight." He could see that The Doc had joined the dots and looked dejected.

"You did a fantastic job, Doc. The information you brought back was vital, set in chain Yvonne giving Tom the courage to tell the truth. But it didn't change him at all. You heard what Jess said. Knight is a psychopath. One of the things Prof. Gough told me is that they don't feel fear like the rest of us. Knight just carried on as if nothing had happened. You couldn't make any impact on him the way we did with our loved ones… and it wasn't just you."

"What do you mean, Charles?"

"I've been in touch with him too… but I mean literally. When he came looking for that certificate, I found I could move. I grabbed his wrist. I mean physically grabbed him, held him tight with my left hand. That's what he was on about just then. He was seized by a dead man but still feels no fear." The Doc did not speak. He did not ask for more detail. He made no request for a fuller debrief. He was stunned. Charlie continued.

"We've done what we can for the living. Now we need to leave them to get on with life and whatever it throws up. They've got some more evidence now, maybe the corner is turned. And Prof. Gough told me about one more trait of psychopaths that might work in our favour… reckless self-confidence."

Chapter 20

On Monday morning, when Lee Knight left his photo-filled mancave, the shrine to himself that he called home, he was pumped up, ready to dominate the witness box. He would address the jury first, then would bat off any questions from Bryce. When he arrived at court the clerk informed him that the Judge needed to see him and Bryce. Here we go, he thought, more legal mumbo jumbo, drawing it out, milking the system for every last chargeable hour. Rawlings was in her usual position at the bench when they entered the courtroom.

"Mr Knight, I need to inform you that I have received a request from the prosecution regarding some new material that has only recently emerged, which they wish to present in court. I am minded to grant this request. There are two pieces of evidence to consider," she said, passing a thin manilla envelope to him. Knight laid it down, unopened.

"It's too late surely. They had their shot last week," he said, cocking a thumb towards Bryce. "We agreed it was my turn now. Starting first thing today." Bryce could not contain a subtle smile, so lowered his head to hide it. Cocky little arse, of all of the judges to misjudge.

"Mr Knight, I should not need to remind you who is in charge of court proceedings. We agreed nothing. Do not begin to attempt to tell me what will and what will not be heard in my court. I and I alone will make those decisions based on the law and on precedent, subjects on which I am significantly better versed than yourself." Shit. Over the weekend Knight had forgotten what an egomaniac this old hellcat was.

"Of course, your honour. Absolutely," he said, with all the deference he could muster. Rawlings continued.

"In making my judgement I have had to balance whether the inclusion of this evidence is more or less likely to lead to a just outcome. I have concluded that it will assist in that regard and it is therefore admissible. This is my final decision. Please do not waste my time and your own in seeking to debate this. I suggest instead that you concentrate on how you wish to test this evidence in court."

Knight opened his envelope and looked at the top sheet of paper. It showed a reproduction of a photo of the DJ sitting with an old geezer. He tried to assess if it could be used to identify the watch, the one that was now his. Well, maybe it could, maybe not. It was arguable and he would happily make the argument. He flicked over and looked at the page beneath, another photo, the same two people, this time in close-up. Try as he might, he could not prevent himself from staring at the watch on the old man's wrist. The image was professional. Clean. Sharp. He had a problem. To dwell on it give it would be to give it credence, so he flicked over to the next sheet. This one was full of text, a statement from the DJ's wife. He stared at it, giving the appearance of studying the content, but his mind was elsewhere, whirring, plotting. This could get messy. He needed a plan, quick. Then he remembered something the Swiss guy had said. And he remembered Keith Glen. Only then did he actually begin to read Jess's statement. Definitely her watch. Woe is me. Blah, blah, blah. Two pieces of evidence. These two photos. Problem solved.

"I am happy to grant you some time to consider the pack," said Judge Rawlings. Knight tossed it onto the desk.

"No need," he said, "there's nothing new here."

"It is not my role to coach you. Are you certain?"

"Yes. The sooner we dispense with this, the sooner I can get on with giving my evidence."

"In that case, I will recommence proceedings forthwith."

* * *

Extract from Chapter 13 of "Baker's Dozen: The Life and Crimes of a Crown Court Reporter."

Day Six : The Detail and the Devil

There are few scheduled events in our world that are as unpredictable as a criminal trial. The preparation is thorough. Judges, police, barristers and court officials ensure that evidence is gathered, paperwork is collated, exhibits are assembled and the courtroom is put in order. Then into that venue, you introduce ordinary citizens - defendants, witnesses, jurors, the public gallery - and before you know it, your carefully crafted script for the play is shredded, and what unfolds is an erratic high school drama group improv session. The judge must have an iron fist.

Monday morning got off to a delayed start, nothing out of the ordinary there, but when we did begin, it was from a point that none of us expected. Two new pieces of evidence – as late as this? The Prosecution case is supposed to be wrapped up. Whatever it is, The Enforcer must have thought it was significant, to allow a deviation from her schedule. Rawlings explains to the jury that although these pieces of evidence had arrived late, they should not read anything into that, the new material was to be weighed up objectively with everything else.

Mrs Munro returns to the stand for the second time. She looks self-assured as Bryce has her testify that these are two snaps that she located at the weekend show her grandad wearing the watch, and then a gasp whips round the courtroom as she describes how she retrieved them… from her dead husband's coffin. The photos were taken at the radio station where he worked, and Bryce gets her to confirm they show the multi-million pound timepiece. It looks to me like they do. Unfazed, Knight cross-examines.

"Mrs Munro, why the delay in bringing these photographs before the court?" he asks.

"I had forgotten that I'd asked for them to be placed in the coffin."

"Ah yes, we return to the mental stress and extreme amnesia of grief. I am looking at these photographs, and they are good quality. It's clear to see that they show a watch which is the same model as mine." He drops his eyes to some papers before him, then looks back to her. "Have you heard the name Keith Glen?"

"Yes. In my interview the police asked me if I knew him."

"And do you?"

"No. It was the first time I had heard the name."

"Unless, of course, you have forgotten about him too. The police asked you because the aforementioned Mr Glen had sent photos of a watch very like this to Sotheby's, with a view to selling it. He did this only shortly after your husband died." Knight casts a glance over to the jury, making sure that they're keeping up. "Mrs Munro, can you remember how many of these watches the police said were in existence?"

"The experts had told them they didn't know for sure, they thought there might be three."

"That's right. Three. Not one. Three. Let me put a scenario to you. I bought my watch, perfectly legitimately, many months before your husband's death. After his passing, Mr Glen, a person you may or may not know depending on the reliability of your memory, stole your husband's watch, the same model but a different watch, and embarked upon the process of selling it. Could that be the case?"

"It would mean two of these rare watches turning up out of the blue, which seems unlikely."

"No, two did not turn up. Yours was always there, in your grandfather's possession, it's simply that no one knew what it was. Only one turned up out of the blue as you put it – mine. Is that impossible?"

"Not impossible, I suppose."

"Thank you, Mrs Munro", resuming his seat. I'm expecting Bryce to take the opportunity to ask his witness a few follow-up questions, to try to weaken Knight's argument. He doesn't. I soon find out why.

"We now come to exhibit E317, Your Honour." Everyone, Knight included it appears, is wondering what's on the piece of paper he's holding. The screen to the left of Rawlings fires up, showing a document the colour of nicotine fingernails. It looks a bit like my old college diploma. I read the heading.

"PATEK PHILIPPE. GENEVE. CERTIFICAT D'ORIGIN." It's definitely not my diploma. It's followed by more French text, handily translated into English beneath. "We certify that the watch", then there are three typed Reference Numbers "was manufactured and adjusted at various temperatures and positions in our Geneva workshops." Knight jerks to his feet.

"Your honour," he says, with an extravagant point of the finger at Bryce, "he had two new pieces of evidence to bring, the two photos. He can't bring anything else now." I've seen Rawling pull that annoyed expression many times. This time it's different. I'm sure I can detect a flicker of satisfaction peeking through it.

"Mr Knight, sit," she says, as if the Defendant In Person was a disobedient mutt. He does, but he's not about to receive a bone-shaped biscuit to reward his obedience. Rawlings continues in scolding fashion. "I advised you to study the late evidence pack closely, advice you chose to ignore. The photographs and associated statement represent the first piece of evidence. This second exhibit is also contained in your evidence pack. I suggest that you now examine it and prepare your response." Knight picks up the envelope, dips his hand in and finds there are some more sheets in there. He tries desperately not to look surprised. "Mr Bryce, you may continue," says Rawlings.

An image appears on the video screen to Rawling's right, We are back in Italy with Marco Ascenzo. As before, there is a pleasant softness to his face, but this time there is also steel in his gaze. Bryce orchestrates his testimony with precision, has him describe his indignation at how the evidence he gave on his previous visit had been distorted and dismissed.

"Can you describe your response?" Marco nods slowly.

"I set out to verify my story. I knew that if I could find the Certificate of Authenticity for my watch it would prove that I once owned it. I believed we would have it, somewhere, but we have a large family business and this generates much paperwork. We looked in every file in the company offices, in my home office, even in our attic."

"And so you found it?"

"No." Bryce pulls a surprised expression. Of course, he knows what's coming. "Anna, my housemaid did. In the kitchen. It was in a bundle of old papers that had belonged to my mother."

"I must ask you Signor Ascenzo, as I am sure the defence council would, how do we know that this certificate itself is genuine?"

"Yes, of course. Herr Weiss of Sotheby's, as you know, was already in Italy. He drove across from Rome, and has studied it." Bryce is alive, delighting in every word. He can't resist.

"Finally, can I ask, you say your housekeeper found it in some papers in the kitchen. Can you be more specific?"

"Yes. It was in amongst my mother's old pasta recipes… much as the watch was found by the police in a bag of pasta. I may not understand all of the English words that Mr Knight tried to humiliate me with last week, but here is one I do know. Ironic."

As before, Knight is asked if he wishes to cross-examine. For the first time, he forgoes the opportunity, sitting closemouthed.

The final Prosecution witness is called, another familiar face. Sebastian Weiss appears via video link, dressed in that continental way, suit, white shirt, but no tie. The creases on that suit are so keen they could slice through diamond. Bryce has Weiss confirm how he was asked to assess the document. He revels in every question he puts, savouring the anticipation of arriving at the crux of the matter.

"Can you explain how this Certificate of Authenticity helps us with this watch and this trial?" he asks.

"I can. All items made by the company are assigned a reference number, which you can see on the certificate. This number is also inscribed onto the inside of the case of the watch. In my initial examination of the watch, I recorded this. I compared my notes with the certificate, and confirmed that the two matched. I should add Signor Ascenzo has of course not seen the inside of the watch, or my notes, so I was already certain that, as the number was correct, the certificate must be genuine. The following day, in conjunction with the experts at Patek Philippe, I was able to confirm that this is the case."

"So what does that tell us about the history of this watch?" Bryce asks.

"Mr Knight questioned me about ownership of the watch on my previous appearance. I can now give him the information he so desperately desires. This certificate is the horological equivalent of DNA evidence. It proves beyond any doubt the hands through which this watch has passed, from Signor Ascenzo to Joe Hargreaves, who bequeathed it to his grandson-in-law Mr Munro… before it ended up by some means in the pasta of Lee Knight." The court falls silent.

"Do you wish to re-examine this witness, Mr Knight?" asks Rawlings. Knight waves a hand to decline. "In that case, I think this concludes the Prosecution case. We will resume in the afternoon with The Defence."

*   *   *

Charlie had watched as these dates rumbled slowly towards him. He had given them much thought, yet he still had not devised an appropriate approach. Rita's would be soon, she'd be the first to reach this particular milestone since he'd arrived. The anniversary of her death. From the time when he was alive, Charlie was familiar with the drill for landmark days – Christmas, wedding anniversaries, birthdays - but this, what do you say? Happy Deathday! Really? He had held off as long as he could. It was tomorrow. With sensitivity, he eased her into a conversation on the subject, then asked some more direct questions.

"Do you celebrate it, Rita?"

"Not celebrate, that would be a bit strange," she said, before stopping to consider. "I suppose other people mark it for me. Alan and Sarah always come to St Jude's."

"Ah yes, you mentioned it before," he said. "Well, that's definitely something to look forward to."

The following day Alan arrived first. He'd received a message from Sarah that the traffic was bad so she was running a little late. Charlie watched him as he sat on the bench, awaiting her arrival. He was there, yet absent at the same time. Charlie decided he looked more woebegone than on his last visit, but then visiting a grave on someone's birthday is presumably a bit more cheery than on the anniversary of their death. Perhaps there is no celebrating to be done up there either. When Sarah arrived thirty minutes later, Alan forced his face into a smile.

"Sorry," she said, leaning forward and giving him a peck on the cheek, "I hate being late. And when I finally got here I struggled to park." She looked around the graveyard. Small clusters of people were wandering around, not the usual types you see around St Jude's. "It's so busy today. What is going on? Who are all these?"

"You're kidding?" said Alan, "they're all journalists and media people. Don't you ever listen to the news?"

"Actually, no. Can't stand it, all those politicians dodging questions."

"There's been a trial going on here for the last week. The guy who's buried here, one down from gran, had his grave robbed."

"No! Really? Who would do that?"

"Wait till you hear this - the accused is the undertaker. The police story is the dead guy was buried wearing a watch that the undertaker took a fancy to, so he broke into the coffin and took it."

"Oh my God. That's terrible. Is he guilty?"

"Don't know yet, we'll find out soon. He says he got it at a car boot sale. But get this... the watch is worth seventeen million quid." Sarah put her hand over her mouth, stopping words that were not coming to her anyway.

"Yep, you heard right. Seventeen million," said Alan. "Family say they never knew, thought it was just some old thing passed down the generations. Then they did some rooting around and say it was a gift from a rich Italian bloke. So, depending on the outcome, either the wife or the undertaker is in for a massive payday."

"Wow. Fancy sitting on treasure like that without knowing it. When I get home I'll check to see if there's a Rembrandt in the loft."

"If you find one, you can send a few quid my way if you like." Sarah removed the posy she had left on Rita's birthday, now tired and bedraggled, and replaced it with some vibrant purple begonias, before sitting down beside her brother.

"The farm?" He nodded. "Not getting any better?" Alan replied with a doleful shake of his head. "I thought you'd written to… was it the Rivers Authority?"

"I did. That was a waste of time. They've agreed to look at it, but have told me it could be at least a year till I hear back. We'll have gone bust by then." She touched his arm.

"Alan, no one understands this place better than you. There has to be some ingenious way for you to put it right." Once again Alan shook his head.

"There isn't. Short of waiting till it's dark one night and diverting Blind Beck by blocking it off up at Top Moor." Sarah's baffled look reminded him of how sketchy her understanding of the farm's topography was. "Then it'll all flow down via The Fold" he explained, "completely missing all of the west fields."

"There you go," she said, "that's your answer. Do that then." Alan shrugged.

"Unfortunately it's not that easy. It's not our land technically. Never mind technically, more like not at all. When the council bought the Stanford estate they took ownership. And you can't just change a watercourse like that…"

"But if it would fix the problem…"

"I don't think I would be comfortable doing it without proper permission from the authorities," he said. "I'll mull it over." Though neither of them said it, both of them knew that meant no. "Anyway, enough of my troubles," he said, eager to shove these woes far from his mind and that of his sister. " Have you got the scotch eggs?" Sarah smiled.

"Have you got the pork pies?"

"Rita, are you okay? He sounds really upset, your grandson" said Yvonne. "At the end of his tether. You must be worried about him."

"I am. It's been getting steadily worse for a while, but god, I never thought it would end up here. He's a lovely lad, Alan, but he's a farmer, he's practical, that's how he tackles things. He'll never get anywhere writing letters. The only pens he knows anything about are the ones he keeps livestock in."

"If he's more of a practical guy then that's the way he should go about it," said Charlie. "Stick to what he's good at. What was that about diverting Blind Beck? You know everything about round here. Would it work?"

"It would definitely divert a huge amount of water away from the west fields. And it wouldn't affect any of the neighbouring farms, I doubt anyone would even notice. But, you're right, I do know everything round here, and Alan is right, it's not our land, and it would be illegal."

"Says the woman who redrew the boundary of the churchyard," Charlie replied. "How come you've gone compliant all of a sudden? Why don't you go up and see if you could influence him, get him to see sense?" Rita did not reply. Charlie continued. "If you don't feel able to do it I could try for you," he said. "No guarantees, but I would do my best."

"I know you would, son, but there's more to it than that. Charlie, it's called Blind Beck because it flows along the surface then disappears underground. You know where it runs then? Right underneath us. If Alan was to divert it, the flow through our stretch will stop completely." The others listened. You did not need the medical expertise of Doctor Denis Dean to figure out the implications. Just in case, Rita spelled it out. "So it might not affect any other farms… but it would affect us. If you remember when the flow dropped off for whatever reason in the summer, it nearly did for me. I only recovered when it returned. If he does this, it will be the end for us all." No one dared to speak. No one tried to counter her assertion because she was correct. No one tried to offer an alternative because there was none. No one tried to express any view at all. Charlie looked up at the two figures on the bench. Regardless of how this was going to go down with the others, he had to be honest with them.

"Obviously it's not just up to me," he said, "but I think he should do it anyway. Your family has built the farm up over generations. And you worked all your life to try to preserve the countryside around Stanford, to preserve its history."

"But it will end this, Charlie, end us, kill us all off," she said.

"Rita, one of the first things you all did after you had welcomed me here was to tell me not to get my hopes up, that I was very definitely dead. I'm suggesting he does this because it benefits people who are definitely still alive. And others who have still to come. Like your Alan's little Rita… or Winnie The Pooh, if that's what she ends up as. Life has to be for them, the living," he said. He could tell she was listening attentively. "Suppose your hero - the 12th Earl of Stanford, the kind one - suppose he still owned it, not the council. What would he do? We don't have much time. Once Alan finishes off that extra scotch egg he is eating, they will leave. When he comes back here next time for your birthday, Jackson's Farm will be sold." Before she could reply Yvonne stepped in.

"I agree with Charlie. I don't know how we came to be here," she said. "I don't know about becks or the watery table or any of it, but to my way of thinking if you can do something to help your grandkids then that's what you should do. If he sold his farm and lost his livelihood, you would feel terrible lying down here every time he comes to visit, knowing you could have advised him." There was no response from Rita. Hush, hush. Then Isabel spoke.

"They're both right," she said. "Because of you Rita, we were given a chance that no one normally gets. We were allowed to support our loved ones after we died. It's your turn now. You need to help your grandson, whatever the consequences. Our time has come. And another thing, I spent most of my final years up there halfway between life and death. In the end, I was in so much pain I just wanted to go peacefully, but the doctors were prevented from doing that. It was cruel. But this… this is a way for us to control how this extra little bit of our existence finally ends."

Unusually, The Doc had listened to these statements, without comment or interruption. Isabel's last remark prompted him to take to the stage.

"I am a physician. As a medical graduate I took the Hippocratic Oath, and remain bound by its terms. Let me quote a short passage." Charlie winced. Time was tight… but everyone needed to say their piece. The Doc was lost in thought, trying to recall the exact form of words. When finally he did began to speak, it was without ostentation. He did not hide behind his legendary powers of projection, but spoke the words softly.

'If it is given me to save a life, all thanks. But it may also be within my power to take a life; this awesome responsibility must be faced with great humbleness and awareness of my own frailty. Above all, I must not play at God'.

"I do not believe that I or any of us seeks to play God," he said. "In my opinion, Charles is correct. We are not alive."

"So that's all four of us now," said Charlie. "What do you think, Rita, will you give it a shot? Rita?" There was no answer. "She's gone," he said, "before Alan left… or we had a chance to change our minds."

"I would have been disappointed with anything less," said The Doc.

*   *   *

Of all the pre-trial reading that Knight had done 'The Call of The Bar' had turned out to be the most useful. The rebel Q.C. turned author had passed on an array of advice pertinent to any Defendant In Person. That morning in court, when Knight's world had plunged precipitously, from everything falling into place to everything falling apart, he fixed on one such tip. If you have nothing to say that will help your case, do not get up. Sit on your arse and say nothing. It was this that persuaded him not to cross-examine either of those two foreigners. This certificate was bad news. The less air time it got, the better. Rawlings would call a break, and a break was exactly what he needed.

Knight looked around the tiny little office he had been allocated for the duration of the trial. It gave off bad vibes. One tiny window, a small desk, a single chair… god, if there had been a set of bunk beds and a bucket to shit in, it could be a prison cell. He desperately needed to think. Think, think. They had managed to pin the watch to the DJ beyond dispute. This meant he had a stolen watch in his penne pasta, never a good look. Why had that old Italian git gone digging around and found that certificate? And why had the Judge allowed them to include it? Whatever. The watch was gone, he knew it. The objective now was for him to come out of this trial looking the way he should. To be found innocent was not nearly enough. He needed to emerge from the burning wreckage of this pileup looking like the hero; if he managed it correctly, he might sell his story for fame and fortune. Since the facts did not naturally lend themselves to this outcome, it left Lee Knight with one preferred course of action. It was not one that featured in any of those texts he had read, it was straight out of his own book. He would have to lie through his teeth.

Extract from Chapter 13 of "Baker's Dozen: The Life and Crimes of a Crown Court Reporter."

Knight decides to take the stand. He doesn't have to. He could have left the jury with the evidence to date and hoped for the best. One part of me is not surprised at his choice. He's on the back foot, but he's the type that always fancies himself. From what I saw last week, he's the kind of guy that would back himself against last year's Derby winner in a race over one mile, four furlongs, and six yards. Another part of me thinks he has not thought this right through. It means he will now be cross-examined.

Knight gets to kick off by making a statement to the jury, addressing them directly.

"Ladies, gentlemen, can I begin by saying that at no stage have I lied to you. But I regret to tell you that I have not told you the full story. This is not because I sought to deceive you. It is because I needed to protect people that I love. Protect them from a ruthless Merseyside gang leader, whose name you have already heard in this trial, a man called Keith Glen. And now, no matter the danger I am putting myself in, I must tell you the part of the story that you have not yet heard."

"Mr Munro wore his watch when he went with Radio City colleagues on a leaving celebration around Liverpool city centre. That night it was spotted by Mr Glen who was determined to steal it. Mr Munro's tragic death meant that Glen's plan to rob his house became a plan to rob his grave. And I, simply because of the honest profession I pursue, became an unwilling participant in his wicked scheme. I was approached by one of Glen's henchmen, who threatened the lives of me, my father and my sister if I did not comply. I was forced into creating a false grave to give them an access route to Mr Munro. I presume that one of Glen's associates carried out the robbery. I was then pressured into hiding the stolen goods until the thieves were sure that their crime had gone undetected. And that is how it came to be found in my kitchen cupboard." He bows his head, then looks upwards as if seeking forgiveness from his forefathers.

"This has been a terrible experience for me. First I was fearful for my life. Then I have been vilified through this process, by the police and in this court, when all along it has been me who has been the victim. I wish for nothing more than to put it all behind me and get on with my life." All of this is told with the same confidence and swagger that he's displayed throughout. This is the case that keeps on giving.

Rawlings calls a halt to the morning session. The afternoon will start with the cross-examination by Bryce. I bump into Harry on the way out. He's going to the canteen at the new court, meeting a colleague who is here to give evidence on another case. He invites me to join them. It turns out to be the most important sandwich of Harry's career. His colleague is already there. He's a multi-tasker, relocating a mound of chips from plate to mouth with one hand, whilst writing answers in a puzzle book with the other. We get our food and join him. He has worked on the Munro case so we describe what we've just heard.

"Well that's a crock," he says, "There is no such person as Keith Glen."

"What do you mean?" Harry asks. P.C. Burgess, flicks over the pages in his book and finds a blank space, beside a word search grid. He starts writing.

"Look," he says. We both focus as he explains.

"How long have you known this?" asks Harry. Burgess shrugs.

"Since I first heard you talking about Glen. Gangland kingpin my fat arse."

"And you didn't think to mention it?"

"Thought it was obvious," he replies, returning to his book and his chips. Harry hurries down the last of his lunch and heads off to see if he can catch Carson Bryce.

When Bryce conducts the cross-examination, he mercilessly attacks Knight's statement. Why did you not mention any of this at the outset? Why is it that no one, either the police or their network of informers, has ever heard of Merseyside gangster Keith Glen? Why do you have no evidence of any contact with this man? Why would a villain like Glen put a man he barely knew in charge of seventeen million pounds worth of booty? Why, if you care for your sister so much, did you systematically destroy her reputation here in this very court? Why, so soon after the funeral, were you searching the internet for Spanish villas and luxury sports cars?

Knight does his best to keep his composure but his answer to each question is flimsier than the last. He is rattled, I'm sure most of those present can see it. Bryce certainly can. He asks another. Knight does not attempt to answer it directly.

"Listen to yourself," he says. "Why? Why? You're like a child who had just learned the word." Bryce does not flinch or try to intervene. I bet he hopes Rawlings won't either. "Here's a question for you, Mr Bryce. Keith Glen is the criminal here. He has threatened me and stolen that watch. Why have the police not found him? Why is it me that is in the witness box and not him?" This is what Bryce has been working towards.

"Mr Knight, I think you'll find that I am here to pose the questions, not to answer them. However, since you ask, the explanation is simple. Keith Glen does not exist." I start to think that Harry did manage to speak to Bryce at lunchtime. With his next play I know he did. "Why is it," he asks, "that when I rearrange the letters of Keith Glen, that I can make the name Lee Knight?" Knight is dumbstruck. "Is it because you invented the pseudonym, Keith Glen, to use with Sotheby's in an attempt to demonstrate to yourself how much smarter you are than everyone else? Is this whole story you have told us today a stream of hogwash, picking up flotsam and jetsam as it meanders this way then that, in an effort to navigate the immoveable facts of this case that stand in its path? In short,

Mr Knight, have you lied from start to finish?"

Knight looks at Bryce, eyes cold as stone. The court is packed but deathly still. If anyone heard a pin drop, it was the one from the hand grenade that Knight was about to launch at Bryce.

"I have buried a few people in my time, usually six feet under, in St. Jude's. You will be next, my learned friend, but it will be six inches down, on some remote moor." Amidst the ensuing uproar, Bryce sits down. The chaos does not last long, not in Judge Rawling's court. She silences the packed room and delivers a withering rebuke to Knight before handing back to Bryce.

"No further questions, Your Honour."

*   *   *

They all mattered to Harry, every single case. It's probably why he had never come to terms with this phase of the justice process. Months of planning, gathering evidence, making representations to the CPS, ensuring that due process is followed, the trial overseen by an experienced judge, then whoosh. Out comes the rug from under his feet, and twelve rank amateurs are locked away in a room to reach the critical conclusion. To surrender all control, when he and his team had invested so much into an investigation, was always going to be stressful. Stick dozens of vehicles outside the court holding hundreds of pressmen, all ready to beam the results of his work around the globe, and those stress levels are higher, way higher, up where the oxygen is thin and you can start to get sick and dizzy.

Harry was not alarmed when they hadn't reached a verdict on the first afternoon. They'd had only a couple of hours before Rawlings sent them home. They couldn't have done much more than select their foreman. By mid-morning the following day he was starting to get a bad feeling. All twelve of them had front-row seats when the defendant had threatened to murder the prosecuting QC and stick him in a shallow grave. What the hell was going on?

Wrong question. Not what was going on… who was going on. Juror Ten. The previous afternoon had been entirely lost. Juror Ten had a captive audience of the sort he rarely could access, an overly polite group of strangers in an unfamiliar situation, too courteous to interrupt his flow. It was an opportunity he would exploit, explaining how governments of all persuasions contrived to suppress ordinary citizens, how the police service and justice system were integral parts of their sinister, secret connivance. This trial, an extension of their corrupt regime, was a state-sponsored charade aimed at fooling the masses into believing the authorities were controlling crime, when all the time they were the ones committing it. By the end of the afternoon when they were allowed to go home, they hadn't even managed to nominate a foreman, and Juror Five had had it up to the gills. He was One Angry Man.

Juror Five was a self-employed tiler, a busy, in demand, masterly tiler, who was not impressed by the sixty quid per day loss of earnings on offer for his time in court. He'd make that in less than two hours, never mind a day. He was not disposed to stand back and watch his income slitter away down the grid so that he could listen to this windbag, guffing on about dark forces. The following morning he was ready for Ten. He took the seat nearest the laminated instruction sheet on the table, and took charge, much as if his daytime role was CEO of a large corporation. They would do this once and do it right.

"We have to elect a foreman it says here. I'm happy to do it. Okay with all of you?" All except one of the others nodded in agreement, and relief. "Good. It also says I have to make sure you've all get an equal chance to give your opinions." Ten semi-raised his hand, seeing his control slip and ready to challenge the process. "You're last," said Five, "you spoke enough yesterday, and to be honest mate, it sounded to me like you'd been huffing paint thinners. Right," he said, turning to the lady on his left, "would you like to tell us what you think." Continuing with this blunt but inclusive style, he went round the table, asking each person to articulate the key points as they saw them. When he got to Eight, Ten piped up.

"I've already spoken to Emma. We got the bus home together. She thinks the same as me," he said.

"Have you banged your head or something?" said Five. "You heard the judge. If it wasn't said in here, it doesn't count, mate. Emma?"

"Thank you. I'm perfectly able to speak for myself. Here is what I think."

Extract from Chapter 13 of "Baker's Dozen: The Life and Crimes of a Crown Court Reporter."

We reach lunchtime on the second day. Still no verdict. Rawlings gives the jury a majority direction. Within minutes they are back in the courtroom. The Clerk stands.

"Have you reached a verdict upon which at least ten of you agree?"

"Yes."

"How do you find the defendant?" We're all waiting. The verdict. One word or two?

"Guilty. Eleven to one." I look first at Knight. He is unmoved. Then I turn my attention to the jury, trying to figure out which one of these meatballs thinks he didn't do it. I have my suspicions but, as I told you earlier in this book, the jury room is like a randy teenage holiday or a freemasons' meeting; what goes on there, stays there.

As she stands up, Mrs Munro unfolds a piece of paper, then takes a small sip of water. She looks confident and determined. The whole court can hear the deep breath she takes before she speaks.

"You might think that I would be pleased to be reading out my Victim Impact Statement. It means that it has been proved that a crime has been committed and that someone has been found guilty of it. Surely it means that I have won. Won what? It means that I am officially classed as a Victim. That's not something I have ever aspired to be, nor is it something that I will ever allow to define me. But I cannot deny that these events have had a profound impact on me. I am not the only victim that has been created by what has happened, and what I say, I want to say on behalf of all of us."

"Firstly, there are those who have had to give evidence in this court. They have each been put through an unnecessary, upsetting experience, where their good character and integrity have been called into question. Every one of them, even a member of Mr Knight's own family."

"Next, my Grandad Joe and Marco Ascenzo, two people who met as young men all of those years ago, as they bravely fought for the freedoms we enjoy today. Two men who between them made a pledge and have kept it faithfully ever since, until Mr Knight tried to destroy it for his own selfish ends. Two men, both courageous, robbed by a coward."

"Then there is me. In writing this statement I have been careful to tease apart what I feel about losing my husband and what I feel about this crime. I love Charlie, I ache for him and there is not a moment of a day when I do not wish that I could have him back. These events have just layered further misery onto my sad situation. More uncertainty, more anger, worry about the outcome, and concern for all of those being dragged into this, through no fault of their own. The upset and stress of this crime may diminish in time, but it will never leave me."

"Finally, there is my husband, Charlie Munro. Who of us can say with any certainty what happens to us when we die? Heaven? Hell? Paradise? We do not know what we will feel, but we have a hope, summed up in three words. Rest In Peace. Charlie most certainly did not get to do that. His peace was wickedly shattered by Mr Knight and his greed. And as we conclude here, I hope that he now can. Rest In Peace, Charlie."

All eyes in the courtroom look on in hushed silence as Mrs Munro refolds her paper and sits down with a calm dignity. Rawlings looks moved. She orders a fifteen minute recess. When she comes back, nothing about her demeanour augurs well for the convicted man.

"Lee Knight. It is difficult to imagine a more intrusive, distressing, and repulsive robbery than the one that you have committed. In a pre-planned enterprise, you preyed upon the most vulnerable of victims, one who had no opportunity to defend himself or report your nefarious actions, by virtue of the fact that he was deceased. Subsequently, you have shown no remorse whatsoever and have put the witnesses in this case through untold distress as you sought to discredit them in a despicable effort to foist the blame onto anyone other than yourself. Mrs Munro has described eloquently on their behalf the unnecessary suffering you have caused. You will be brought back before me in this court in three weeks' time for sentencing. I must warn you that because of the nature of your crime you must expect a custodial sentence. Take him down."

Chapter 21

It had not been easy to get Mia to agree to the pact. First Mick and Jess needed to explain to her what a pact was. Then they had to justify why they should have one. The deal they'd struck the previous Saturday was that, whenever the trial finished, they would hold off from any discussion until they were all together at St Jude's. No phone calls, no texts, nothing. They would face the outcome the way they had faced everything else to date. Face to Face. The unspoken reasoning of the two adults was that they knew the trial was going badly, and this would give them all some breathing space to soak up the implications of the result. If he had known that the trial would be over by Tuesday afternoon, Mick might not have been so enthusiastic. From Mia's perspective, Saturday was a distant dot on her horizon. She held out, barely.

"How do you feel?" she asked Jess, as soon as she joined them on Rita's bench.

"A few different emotions," Jess replied. "There's a lot for me to come to terms with. I didn't celebrate. I think I was relieved it was over. In a way, I felt bad about him going to prison. I mean I'd never have known how valuable the watch was if he hadn't done what he did."

"Can I stop you there, Jess?" said Mick. "I locked up a lot of people over the years. Some of them made bad choices, regretted it, and I couldn't help but feel sorry for them. Knight is not one of those. When he saw that watch he could have told you it was valuable, got the money to you, or your charity. He didn't. He planned to steal it. He was thinking about himself, and Italian sports cars with personalised number

346

plates, and he was happy to do things that most of us would be terrified to do so he could get it." Jess thought back to the wild afternoon when they had retrieved the photos from Charlie's coffin. She nodded.

"As I sit here looking at Charlie's grave, I know you're right. I don't know much about prison, I don't know if someone like him will learn anything from it, or from anything else. I hope he does."

"That's not for you to worry about," said Mick, "it's entirely up to him."

Jess may not have celebrated but, unheard by her, a boisterous roar went up below her feet. Foremost amongst the chorus was Doctor Dennis Dean, his legendary projection technique allowing him to all but drown out the combined efforts of the others.

"He's guilty then," said Charlie, "and he's going to prison."

"Justice is served, Charles. Justice is served," boomed The Doc.

"I'm happy for you Charlie," said Isabel. "And for Mick."

Above them, Jess continued, unaware.

"You will definitely both come tomorrow, won't you? It's only a little get-together, but after all of the ups and downs it will be nice to mark the occasion."

"We will definitively be there," said Mia. "Uncle Mick has bought a new shirt from that fancy clothes shop for old men in the village. It cost…"

"That's enough, Mia," Mick interrupted. "Jess isn't interested in my shirt."

"Is she not?" said Jess. "I can't wait to see it."

When Charlie awoke the following morning, for a few brief seconds he enjoyed that delightful feeling of a newly-born head, no conscious recollection of the days before. No history, just boundless future possibilities. He lay at peace, enjoying the stillness. And then the first reminder of his reality flitted in and settled. Stillness. No sound of running water. It's happened.

"Good morning," said The Doc.

"Morning," Charlie replied. "Have you noticed?"

"I have."

"Noticed what?" asked Yvonne.

"The beck," Rita answered. "Listen. It's stopped. Looks like Alan's done it today. First light, Sunday morning, least chance of being spotted, not that there's ever anyone around Top Moor."

"I really hope it works," said Yvonne.

"It will," Rita replied, before adding, "for him and for the farm. God knows what it means for us though. What's your prognosis, Doctor Dean?" This was the first occasion where Charlie had ever heard Rita canvas The Doc's medical opinion in earnest. She must be concerned. The Doc's response was uncharacteristically circumspect.

"I can't be sure," he replied. "The only real precedent was the reduced flow a few months ago. All of us were unwell to some extent and you became very ill indeed."

"Rita seems like a tough old stick to me," said Yvonne, "was she really that bad?" Charlie laughed.

"Put it this way, Yvonne, when you woke for the first time we'd just held a memorial service for her. It was fairly serious."

"Indeed," The Doc continued. "On the basis of that experience I think - and it is my fervent hope - that we will all painlessly slip away. I must add however that I cannot say how long it may take and in which order we shall… depart. My instinct is that, now that the flow of water has fully ceased, our decline may be precipitous."

"I wonder if that was the last time I'll see Jess," said Charlie.

"Maybe, maybe not," said Isabel. "Try not to worry about it, Charlie. You and I arrived at this place by different roads. You lost your life suddenly, it was there one day, gone the next. I bet you'd never spent much time thinking about dying. Whereas me, I was ill for all those years, and I thought about it constantly. I carried those worries around with me. I wished I hadn't. My advice is don't waste time fretting about what might happen, grab hold of the here and now, enjoy what you've got."

The Doc's professional skills were rusty. Even he might admit that. But then anyone who had been retired for seven years, then dead for a further eight, was bound to be a little out of the way of things. The next day, like most Mondays at St Jude's, was quiet. There were no visitors to their gravesides and little activity elsewhere within the churchyard. No distractions to divert them from the painful truth; despite his enforced career gap, The Doc had called this right. Yvonne's condition was the first to deteriorate. First, she became unable to perform the flip around to view the others. Then it worsened, and her ability to speak faltered, before failing her entirely. The others did not know what to say, but knew that to be timid was to be cold-hearted. They did the only thing that they could think to do, speaking comforting words to her, even though they did not know if they were being heard. As the day drained away, so too did their strength to maintain these failed attempts at dialogue, until they stopped trying altogether. Yvonne Carter, mother to two hundred and forty children, was no longer with them.

By this time, Isabel had let the others know that she too had now lost the ability to make any sort of gesture. Even in the absence of accompanying body-language, they recognised the passion in her voice as she spoke, mostly about how Mick would look after Mia, and that under his guidance she was sure that she would turn out to be an exceptional young lady. They all agreed, not because it was the kindest thing to do, but because it was true. Despite their own worsening conditions, they stayed awake to speak to her into the small hours of the night, when Isabel too fell silent and slipped away.

* * *

"All of you who know me – and that is all of you - will know I've always dreaded standing up and talking to groups of people. Thank goodness J.J. stepped in and read my words at my husband's funeral. But since then, I did stand up in court and told the world how I'd been affected by a crime. Mind you, I don't know how - I was even nervous standing in front of Charlie's newly installed gravestone on my own and saying a few words when there was no one but me to hear them."

"Today I feel different. I couldn't be happier to be standing up and speaking. Thank you all for coming to the official opening of The Stables Institute. This idea, setting up a specialist facility to provide music therapy to patients, was a dream of mine, a dream that has now come true. I want to thank everyone who has supported me in this, family and friends, fellow health professionals, builders, you all know who you are - most of you are here." Jess looked around the foyer of The Stables, lit bright by the faces of those within.

"Unfortunately, two important people could not make it. The first is a gentleman called Marco Ascenzo. It is true to say that if it was not for the unbelievable generosity of this extraordinary man this place could not have been completed. He stepped in and supported us when our government let us all down without a care. Grazie, Signor Ascenzo." A ripple of applause echoed rhythmically off the walls. When it had subsided, Jess spoke again.

"The second person is Charlie. When he was alive he drove me on. Sometimes he drove me mad, but always he drove me on. He believed in me at times when I didn't believe in myself. And suddenly he was gone, and then this project fell apart. Somehow, even though he was no longer here, I felt Charlie with me. He convinced me that I need to keep going, to never give up. Because of Charlie, because of Marco, because of all of you, that is why we are able to provide this service to our community. Thank you." Jess lowered her head to indicate she was done and applause rang around the foyer once more. She raised her head and smiled.

"Okay, help yourselves to the food and drinks, anyone who'd like to know a bit more, I'll be happy to show you around." As she picked up her glass, Jess caught sight of a movement to her left. She turned to see that J.J. had joined her and was shaping up as if he was ready to address those gathered.

"I'd like, if I may, to offer you a bit of a tour, Jess," he said to her, but also to the audience. "There is one room in your new building that you have never been in." Jess looked quizzical.

"Is there?" she said, wondering if, not for the first time, J.J. had tackled the free fizz with too much early enthusiasm. "I don't think so. Oh, other than the Plant Room, the one where

Ray told me all the boilers and machinery used to run the place is installed. I didn't dare go in, he put a sign on the door that says 'Service Personnel Only'."

"Well," said J.J., "Ray may not have been exactly truthful." Jess searched the room for Ray. He bowed his head slightly to avoid her gaze. She felt J.J. nudge her arm.

"C'mon then, Jess, shall we take a look at your boiler?" He extended his arm, inviting her to step into the corridor leading to the room in question. She could hear music playing faintly, getting slightly louder as they neared the door. Once there, she turned and looked back at J.J. and the others who had all followed her.

"Aren't you going in?" J.J. asked. Jess turned the handle, the music becoming clearer and crisper as she pushed open the door. She scanned the room. To her right the entire wall was occupied by a line of expensive looking storage cabinets, and in the centre of the room there were numerous comfortable chairs in vivid calypso-coloured fabrics, arranged around small tables to make a cheerful, relaxed space. She looked for the source of the sound. At the far end of the room was a state-of-the-art hi-fi, with two large and two smaller speakers mounted on the wall. Then she noticed that one of the chairs housed a figure, facing away from her. Although she could see only a small portion of the head through a wisp of grey hair, she recognised it instantly. No native of Stanford had a scalp so tanned. She strode across to him.

"Marco! You told me that you couldn't come?" She sat down beside him and felt his strong bony fingers clasp around her hands.

"I had to come over and complete some paperwork to release the watch from police security. We finished early and as I had nothing better to do… I'm joking. Did you really believe I would miss this occasion?"

"I'm so glad you're here," she said, "though I'm not really sure where here is," she said.

"Do you like the music?" he asked. "Joe told me it was one of his favourites. Now's The Time by the great Charlie Parker."

"I do like it." She smiled.

"This copy once belonged to another great man called Charlie. Charlie Munro. He had quite a collection you know. Look." Jess turned to see that, whilst her attention had been on Marco, J.J. and some of the others had opened the doors on the line of storage cabinets. Inside, there were shelves from top to bottom, each one packed solid with vinyl records.

"Are these…" Marco nodded.

"Charlie's record collection." As she gaped at the shelves Ray approached, with a screwdriver in one hand and a small sign in the other. He held it up and she read it aloud.

"The Charlie Munro Suite."

"If it's okay with you, boss," said Ray, "can I change the sign on the door?" Jess managed a nod, only just, before bursting into tears and throwing her arms around the Italian. Minutes passed before she surfaced once more to thank him, over and over again.

"Now that you have come to visit me, Signor Ascenzo," she said, "there is somewhere that I would like to take you."

"What a charming little church," said Marco. He stopped and leant on his cane, admiring Saint Jude's from the gateway to the cemetery.

"It is," Jess agreed. She gave him a moment to look around him before leading him down the gravel path to Rita's bench.

Marco surveyed Charlie's plot.

"It's a beautiful stone, Jess," he said.

"I'm glad you like it. It's growing on me… slowly."

"No photograph of Charlie on it though? We often put a photo on gravestones in Italy."

"No. I tried to think what Charlie would want and I wasn't sure that he would be too keen. In hindsight, however, it would have been easier than putting photos of him inside the coffin." Marco smiled. "Charlie would be thrilled that his record collection is back, complete. How on earth did you do it? In fact, how did you even know that he had sold it?"

"Your mother mentioned it to me when you visited Italy. I made contact with J.J. immediately. He did all of the hard work, locating the dealer in London who had bought them from Charlie. Fortunately, we got to him quickly. He had not had a chance to sell them and so the collection was still intact. And when the dealer heard Charlie's story and our plan, he agreed to allow us to buy them back without hesitation. He refused to accept a penny more than he had paid for them. I thought that the room would be a good place for your clients to relax, listening to a great record collection."

"Thank you, it's amazing." She slipped her hand into his. "You know, the day that Charlie's headstone was installed, I made a promise to him. I said that the lyrics of his life would not be forgotten, that his song would always be sung. You have made that promise come true. It will be a lasting memorial to Charlie." Though she tried to hide it, Marco caught a chill in her eye. He allowed her to settle before pursuing it.

"Why were you sad just then?" Her eyes filled.

"It was as soon as I said a lasting memorial… I thought about the charity in Italy. A lasting memorial to you. I never want to start it, because it means that you will no longer be here."

"Jess. We do not live forever. None of us can. And that is a good thing too. The old must always be replaced by the new. All we can aim for is to make sure that when we leave, the things we have done in life will have made this world a little better." Jess nodded, wiping her eyes. "Good," he said. "Now I have one other small thing that I have been working on, something I will only commence with your approval." Jess already had Marco down as the shrewdest, most inventive man she had ever met, but as he talked her through his idea, she gained yet more respect for this remarkable individual.

"Do you approve?" he asked, "because if not…"

"Of course I do. You're a genius. Come on." As Marco set off to retrace their steps, Jess pointed left. "When I leave here I always take the long way round," she said, taking his free arm. They set off to complete their circuit in a clockwise direction, with Marco asking questions about St. Jude's along the way. They had reached the furthest corner, diagonally opposite to Charlie's plot when Jess stopped. She walked towards the wall between a set of gravestones, before halting again.

"I've one more thing to show you," she said. Marco took the few steps needed to stand beside her, then followed her eyes.

"In loving memory of Joseph Hargreaves
2nd May 1923 – 7th July 2015
Life is for the living,
Death is for the dead,
Let life be like music,
And death a note unsaid"

"I always come and say hello to Grandad Joe before I leave," said Jess. Marco said nothing. She watched as, using his stick for support, he bent down onto one knee. He stretched out and touched the top of the stone, moving his hand side to side, tracing the contours of its surface. Jess heard him begin to speak softly in Italian. She did not recognise any of the words but understood them all. His voice stilled. He made no effort to move, but read then reread the inscription. He patted the stone twice.

"I am overjoyed to have met you one more time, Joe. My English Abruzzese." Marco pulled himself back to his feet. Jess linked arms with him.

"Let's go," she said, "I know a place that does the best fish and chips you will ever taste."

"Did everyone hear that?" said Charlie, momentarily forgetting that everyone was rather a grand appellation for their diminished group. "Marco. He was here. The man who first owned the watch, the one who gave it to Grandad Joe."

"The one who made the big donation to The Stables," Rita added.

"And he's managed to get my record collection back, intact, and installed it at The Stables. I cannot describe how much that means to me. It's unbelievable, don't you think, Doc?" There was no answer. "Doc?" The response, when it came, was laboured.

"It is. The music therapy, Charles… there was no such thing in my day. I must be honest, when I first heard of Jess's work I was most dubious." He paused, each breath slow and heavy. "But I have thought about it since. In my flower-power days, music convinced my generation that we could change the world… and we did… at least for a while." There was another hesitation, then his lips moved again. This time no sound came out. Charlie and Rita waited, knowing that he wanted to speak. Finally, they heard his voice, fainter than ever. "I am sure her institute will be a great success."

"Doc," said Charlie "are you okay?"

"No, not really." Charlie tried not to sound concerned.

"You're maybe tired," he said, "try to get some rest." There was a gap once more, then the reply.

"I have often spoken of my belief... that one should be honest with the patient." There was another pause before he continued. "That principle... should extend to myself. I fear that my vital signs are fading. Fast."

"Come on, Doc," Charlie replied, "I don't think the world is ready to lose its expert on Dean's Syndrome." Each silence grew longer.

"No amount of expertise can forestall the inevitable. Charles, Rita, my good friends, it would seem that my last observation is that... Dean's is not a permanent condition."

These were the last words that The Doc spoke.

Time crawled. At least Charlie felt it did. Just as when he had first awoken here, he was finding it difficult to track the moments. He could not say with accuracy how long it was until he and Rita spoke again.

"Rita, how are you feeling?"

"I don't know, son. I'm frightened." Charlie had never put fear and Rita within a ten mile radius of one another.

"Of what?" he asked. "Frightened of dying?"

"God no," Rita replied, "I've done that once before. No, I'm frightened that I've done the wrong thing. I'm not sure if I was right to have persuaded Alan to re-route the water."

"You were right. We all agreed, every one of us. What would have happened if he had sold the farm? More houses?

More problems? You've stopped that, in the same way that you used your initiative to prevent a bloody great road cutting through above where we are lying now."

"I suppose so."

"You know so. A wise man once said - We do not live forever. None of us can. And that is a good thing too. The old must always be replaced by the new."

"That's familiar. Who was it? No, don't tell me. Confucius? About five hundred years B.C.?"

"No. Marco, about twenty minutes since... at my best guess." Rita smiled weakly. Time stalled. Neither spoke. Rita's strained voice broke the silence.

"I'm tired son."

"Me too."

"You will stay with me, won't you?"

"Of course I will. Cross my heart and hope to die." Charlie looked up. Above, outside, it was becoming dark, the afternoon coming to an early end, as it does in winter. He listened hard for any sounds coming from the direction where Rita lay. There were none. The movement of time had ceased. With all the effort he could draw, he managed to close the fingers of his left hand. With his thumb, he felt the metal band of his wedding ring. Charlie relaxed, and then he too was gone.

*   *   *

Dear Journal,

This evening I realised that I hadn't written anything in here for a while, the thought hadn't crossed my mind. I wondered if perhaps I didn't need you now. I've reread you from the start. It took longer - and many more tissues - than I'd thought. It reminded me of where I was at the start of this, in the deepest darkest dungeon of hell. I'm not out of it by any means but I have climbed, I've peeked over the edge and I can see some light and feel some warmth.

Looking through you tonight has taught me one thing. Even if I never write in you again, I will always need you.

*   *   *

Jess watched as her mum scanned the list of flights on the departure board. It was time to explain.

"There's no use looking for Abruzzo, or Rome, mum. Or anywhere else in Italy. We're meeting Marco in Geneva."

"Geneva? Geneva in Switzerland?"

"Yes, unless you know of another one." Jess smiled. She would never have dared to spring a surprise like this on her mum six months ago. She would have gone into meltdown. Diane's fear of the unknown, the known, and everything in between was not gone but, day by day, it lessened.

"Are you sure?"

"I'm certain. He's an international businessman, he gets around all over Europe."

"I'm sure he does," said Diane, "it's just a bit of a shock to someone like me who doesn't. I've brought Euros. I think you can spend them in Switzerland. If not, don't panic, I expect I'll be able to exchange them for Swiss Francs."

On landing, a familiar face helped her to settle. Paulo was waiting for them, welcoming them, relieving them of their luggage, and easing them into another luxurious vehicle. As he took them to their hotel, he chatted to them with a familiar warmth. Standing at the reception desk, Diane counted the huge flower displays around the foyer. Fourteen.

"Ladies, we will take your luggage to your rooms," said the receptionist. "In the meantime, Signor Ascenzo has arranged for a bottle of something special to be chilled for you in our lounge. If you would care to follow me?" Diane, now relaxed, confirmed that she would care to very much.

The following morning, Jess watched as her mum stood in front of the mirror in the room, fussing with the bow on the neck of her blouse, trying to make it look even.

"Now the bit on the left is longer than the right. Or is it?" she asked. "I've messed around with it so much I can't tell any more."

"It's fine," Jess replied.

"Mind you, since you won't say where we're going, the whole outfit could be wrong for all I know."

"Mum, it's perfect. Come on, or we'll be late. Paulo is waiting with Marco in the car to take us."

As Paulo pulled up at their destination, Diane's eager eyes were drawn to the gold lettering, standing out proudly on the black background above the arch of the doorway.

"PATEK PHILLIPE MUSEUM," she read. Marco nodded.

"I think you should explain, Jess," he said.

"Mum, Marco has been in discussion with the company who originally made the watch, and has come to an arrangement for them to buy it. This is their museum, where they display their best items. Including his."

"Ours," Marco corrected. Jess eyed her mum, as she took this in.

"Ah, I see," said Diane. "When did you find out about this, Jess?"

"The day of The Stables opening," she replied. "Marco asked me if I thought it was a good idea."

"Our families are partners in all things, Diane," said Marco. "Let's go in." Paulo opened the car door and offered Jess's mum his hand, supporting her as she stepped onto the pavement. The doorman heaved open the oversized steel and glass door to the building, inviting them to enter.

"The museum does not open to the public until two p.m.," said Marco, "so they have invited a small number of notable people to come this morning to look at their newest acquisition for the first time."

"Am I a V.I.P. today?" asked Diane.

"Not only today," he replied.

They were led to an immaculate wood-panelled room, filled with spotless glass cases. Within each, the watches and other pieces shone under intense bright lighting. Diane surveyed the room. There were perhaps two dozen people there, standing in small groups, chatting in low tones.

"Who are these people, Marco?" Diane whispered.

"Some of the top people at the company. There are a few distinguished experts in horology and a couple of the foremost collectors in the world. And this gentleman here," he said, nodding towards a man who was making ready to speak, "he is the director and curator of the museum." The conversation in the room fell away, awaiting his words.

"Good morning, everyone. Welcome. I know you are all anxious to see the latest addition to our collection so I will not delay that moment for long. I will only say that, as you know, we do not add any new items to our exhibition lightly. Quality and historical importance are at the forefront of our minds as we make our decisions. The display you will see today is perhaps more special than any other in our museum. Why? Because of the story associated with it, of two men who met at a time that demonstrated the worst Man can do. Amidst these terrible events, these two strangers looked upon one another in a way that gives us all hope. Visitors to our museum will be able to enjoy our display, and take with them in their hearts some of that hope." Applause, understated and polite, went around the room.

"We are fortunate to have one of those men here today, and the daughter of the other. It is my honour to ask them to please step forward and be the first to view our newest display." The applause began once more, and Diane did her best to control a blush as she and Marco made their way forward. The curator removed a burgundy velvet cloth that covered the square case beside him. Diane stared through the glass. Her eye was immediately taken to the gleaming watch positioned in a central position in the bottom half of the case, the twin colours of gold and steel clearly visible. It looked stunning.

Her eyes explored the remainder of the display. There were three other items. Centrally and at the top of the case, directly above the first, was another watch, which she immediately recognised. It was the one that Signor Ascenzo had been wearing the first time she had met him, the modest timepiece that had sat on the wrist of her father when he has set off to war. On the left hand side of the two watches was a photograph of a young man. Despite the passing of time, she could tell that, without doubt, it was Marco. The final item to the right was another photograph, a man of similar age, in military uniform, her dad, Grandad Joe. All four items had been connected by placing them on a raised circular gold band.

"I hope you approve of our display," said the curator. "I have positioned the pieces so as to make no statement about monetary values, and no indication of ownership."

"It's beautiful," said Diane. "Thank you." Jess had joined her now and the two of them did not speak but just stared into the case. Jess took her mum's hand and gave it a gentle squeeze.

"Since you are here," said the curator "if you would like, I will show you some other items that I think you will find interesting?"

"If it's not too much trouble," said Jess, "we would love to see them." She followed the curator to a nearby case, but Diane lingered with Marco. Jess glanced back and watched as they were joined by a tall gentleman, perhaps thirty years Marco's junior. Seeing they had struck up a conversation, she returned her attention to her guide.

"It's a remarkable piece, Signor Ascenzo," said the tall man. "I would very much have liked to have it as part of my collection."

"Which?" said Marco. "The Timex or the Patek Philippe?" The man grinned.

"You know I would have paid considerably more than you received from this private sale if you would have put it up for auction?" Marco nodded once more.

"Yes, but then few would have seen it, and the story that comes with it may have been gone forever. To me, keeping that story alive is beyond price." The man nodded, and moved off to a nearby group.

Once her tour had finished, Jess rejoined her mum and Marco, in the midst of an animated exchange.

"What are you two finding to talk about?" she asked.

"Not much," said Diane. "I was just explaining to Marco how I'm going to write up those notes that I took talking to my dad". Jess smiled.

"And I will help where I can," said Marco. "Why don't we discuss it over lunch? I know a place that serves the best raclette in all of Geneva."

Epilogue

There we have it. The story of how I completed "Baker's Dozen : The Life and Crimes of a Crown Court Reporter." Immediately after the trial I took two weeks off work and threw all of my energy into writing it up. Almost daily, the publishers contacted me for a progress report, keen to get it out there quickly to capitalise on interest surrounding the case. They even suggested a redesign of the front cover to add a subtitle 'Including The Gravest Crime of All Time', as it had become known in the tabloid papers. I told them in no uncertain terms that the suggestion was tacky and that there was no way I was going to allow it. You see, by this point, I was in the driving seat.

When he first told me about this case, my good friend Harry suggested that I would owe him a pint, some sort of finder's fee. We meet once a month, and he claims that pint every time. Not that I mind; without him, I might never have finished the book. Besides, Harry has a connection, one way or another, to all of the key players in the case, and those meetings allow me to catch up on how they are moving on with their lives. Let me fill you in.

First, my mate Harry, the copper who led the investigation. He has retired from the force now, and says he can scarcely believe that his biggest case by far came in the last few months of his thirty years of service.

The man he caught, Lee Knight, was sentenced to five years in prison. He came to learn that I had written the book and contacted me to say if I did not rewrite it so that it told 'his truth' then he would sue me. I of course told him he could stick his truth where it belongs. After his experience so far, God knows why he wants to go back to court. Some people never learn.

His sister, Alex Knight, still runs the family firm. It has fully recovered from the setback caused by the scandal surrounding the case. In fact, now that the part she played has come to light, the business is going from strength to strength. As my old dad used to say, unless they figure out how to make people live forever, you'll never be out of work as an undertaker.

Mick often joins Harry and me for a pint in The Bell at Stanford. He has got his hands full looking after Mia, who is now at an age where she has a boyfriend. Not sure if it is related, but Mick is glad that she continues to progress upward through the judo grades. She is also studying hard at school, hoping to get the results that she needs to go to university to study Criminology.

Now well into his nineties, Marco Ascenzo is still going strong. He devotes his time to carrying out the legal and organisational paperwork required to establish a music therapy charity in Italy. He still has a penchant for good food, fine wine, and Charlie Parker.

Jess Munro. Her institute is already winning awards for its work. She and Marco are in constant contact. Whilst she awaits the dreaded go-ahead to start in Italy, she is looking into how she can renovate further buildings at the Hall to expand her service. She is also working closely with the owner of Jackson's farm, adjacent to the Hall, to explore how the therapeutic use of animals might help some of her patients.

And her mum Diane? She has almost finished writing up her dad's war memoirs, the story he found so hard to tell. One day she hopes to have them published. She still worries about Jess, but doesn't say so quite as much.

* * *

And Rita, Charlie, The Doc, Isabel, and Yvonne? That group of five are indeed a hopeless cause, and will remain that way…

unless the course of Blind Beck was to change so that once more it runs beneath that corner of St. Jude's.

THE END

About The Author

Willie Sharp was born in Falkirk in 1961. After graduating with a degree in Zoology from Edinburgh University, he moved to North West England, the setting for his debut novel "Lost Lyrics Of A Forgotten Song". He wanted to write something that was unusual and memorable, so if you're after a retread of a well-worn formula this is probably not for you. If you'd like an ingenious, uplifting story with a twisty plot, told with a lot of heart and bit of humour, then you will enjoy this book.

Willie still lives in Lancashire with his wife Fiona and two cats, Stanley and Gigi. He occupies an unshakable fourth place in the family's hierarchy, a position that guarantees all of the lowliest tasks and affords him no voting rights at house meetings. He says that, without doubt, the most satisfying aspect of writing is hearing the feedback of his readers. If you have any thoughts on the book he'd love to hear them. You can leave a review on Amazon, or contact him directly at willie.sharp@talktalk.net.

By The Same Author.

Willie's only other work dates back to his university days. "Size and Natural Selection in the Fruit-fly, *Drosophila Melanogaster*" is not currently available to purchase. Frankly, it's somewhat niche.

However, if enough people enjoy this book, he may write another. In truth, he's already jotted down a few ideas…

Book Club Questions

1. What did you think were the predominant themes of the book?

2. Which character developed the most, why, and how? Who was your favourite character?

3. What did you think about the idea of the dead living on?

4. The book involved multiple storylines and a cast of characters coming together. How well connected do you feel the stories were? Were you happy with the conclusion of the storylines?

5. There are no known cultures in the world that do not feature music. Why do you think it is so widespread? To what extent do you think it can be used to help those with conditions such as Asperger's Syndrome and Alzheimer's Disease?

6. Everyone was quick to conclude that the culprit must have been Tom Bennett rather than Lee Knight. Is society making much progress in tackling such unconscious bias?

7. Mia began to come of age during the book, with Jess acting as a role model. How do the twin influences of real people and on-line influencers affect how young people go through this today?

8. When the others convinced Rita to divert the beck, do you think it was the right thing to do?

9. Joe and Marco both find it hard to discuss their war experiences, and Charlie talked about mental health being a taboo subject early in his career. To what extent do you think that this situation has improved?

10. How would you describe the book to a friend?

Printed in Great Britain
by Amazon